The Mystique Lakinshires
&
Gala's Conflicts

Connie Koehler

Mystique Realms

Kelvor Elves

Timestill Forest

The Singing Lake

Stream

Mermary's Lake

Tuberous Tribe

Tiaff's Castle

To Muddy Crud

Path

The Ridge

Path

Dwidling Mountain

Boggy Swamp

Gurgling Mudlump

Big

Copyright © 2023 by C. F. Koehler
All rights reserved. Printed in the United States of America. No part of this book may be used or reproduced in any manner whatsoever without the prior written permission of the publisher, Connie Koehler, except as permitted by U.S. copyright law. For permission requests, contact Constance Faith Koehler, the publisher—author—book cover artist—and illustrator, 2660 14th Street S.W., Vero Beach, Florida 32962
cfkartbyfaith@gmail.com
Registered With The Library of Congress on May 31, 2023
Connie Koehler
The Mystique Lakinshires and Gala's Conflicts.
ISBN-979-8-9885036-0-6
The story, all names, characters, and incidents portrayed in this production are fictitious. No identification with actual persons (living or deceased), places, buildings, and products is intended or should be inferred.
Publisher © 2023 Connie Koehler
Book Cover © 2023 by Connie Koehler
Illustrations © 2023 by Connie Koehler
First edition 2023

If my demise comes before my children, Chad Koehler and Todd Jenkins, my children receive my royalties and the royalties to anything else I publish, all rights reserved to them.

For

With all my love and many thanks, this story is for my family, friends, and wonderful readers.

This adventure would not have been possible without you. I thank you from the bottom of my heart.

ACKNOWLEDGMENTS

First and foremost, I thank my creator for all my gifts. I am forever grateful to my children, Chad Koehler and Todd Jenkins and Todd's wife, Ashley, and my grandson, Christain Koehler and his girlfriend, Sami Mortillaro, my granddaughter, Kloey Jenkins. They always listened as I read to them (Troopers). I am thankful for my parents, siblings, cousins, aunts and uncles, nieces and nephews, and friends. Thank you for your critiques, advice, belief in me, and encouragement throughout my writing journey.

My dear friends, Ellen Spielman, Rex Clarke, and Mr. and Mrs. Stuckey, all my workmates including Chief Don Thomas, Officer Patti Able, and Officer Richard Steele, gave me their patience as I read to them. I am grateful to my editor, Chelsey Clammer, for teaching me how to edit (I'm still learning). I thank Abbie Emmons for teaching me a great deal in the many aspects of writing, from plot and theme to character building and more. I am grateful for Stephen King's book *On Writing* (Brilliant) and for my English professors at the Indian River State College Mueller campus. I greatly appreciate Billie Atamer, a lovely woman with extensive writing experience. Billie helped me with my About Author page and prologue. I enjoyed reading her book, *The River Rat Kids*. It, along with her young adult novel, *Banjo Billy*, was nominated for the Moonbeam Book award. She has written many books. I admire her.

And for my readers, thank you, thank you, thank you!

Thank you, EVERYONE!

Punctuation

Gala — Gālə
Lakinshire — Lāke-in-shire
Conkay — Con-kāy
Faithin — Faith-in
Ddot — Dot
Dahc — Dāke
Acub — Ā-cub
Ashlin — Ash-lynn
Appara Comforte — Ə-pair-ə Com-for-tā
Braid-e-tida — Brāēd-ē-tīdə

ā as in lāte – dāte or māte
ə as in əbout - əbove or əlone

Chapters & Chapter Scenes

Conflicts 1
Daily Plans 8
    Doubt 16
    Crystal Ball 29
    Wrong Spell 32
    Dark Mysterious **Shadow** 49
Confession 61
    Good to Know 68
Unfriendly Guest 83
Coronation 92
Show Some Courage 97
Taken 106
Getting Ready 126
Redtalon 144
Mystique Blueblood 173
Interment 214
Transcendence 221
Good Morning 233
Stinger 250
Timestill Forest & Gnome Bloom 262
The Whispering Tree 291
Mental Trance-The Curse 330
One Year and Two Days Ago
Love-Horror-Curses 346
Present Day
A New Task for Helsin 377

- Farewell 394
- Helsin Intercepts 399
- Vek's Horn 404
- Tracks 411
- Fay-Folk 412

Wands 424
Water Bbeings 434
- Helsin's Discovery 451

Earlier That Evening
Before Gala and the Newlads Met Serenity 470
- Idanab Wakes 476

Present Moment in Time
Wizard Tiaff's Castle 484
Clues 489
- Helsin's Spy Ring 496
- Spyraven Through Different Eyes And
  New Clues 497
- Wicked Must Die 508
- Dragon 511

Reunite 516
- Time to Rid Evil 519

Truth 525
- Promises Will Be Kept 531

One Year & Three Days Later 543
Announcements 545

Conflicts

Blood ran down the dark warlock's head and dripped off the tip of his nose. He fell to the swamp's muddy bank. Dark-red blood filled the ground beneath his head. Eight blood-splattered wings glided through the air. They swirled, twirled, and fell upon his back. An ebony wand danced in mid-air as red, black, and golden spells shot from its tip. Witches danced in triumph; their screechy cackles echoed in the darkest of days. Hideous Gob-Diggers with large mangy feet crushed bloody bones with their sharp-blackened teeth. A young wizard ran and ran and ran in place never to escape.

Beads of sweat rolled down Gala's face as he tossed and turned. His breath was heavy. "Nooo!" he shouted as he sprang from his pillow.

Faithin ran into his room, sat on his bed, and embraced her son, "Shhh, my sweet fella, I'm here."

"Mother..." Gala hugged her neck.

Faithin held him close, kissed his forehead, and wished she could do more than comfort him. While wiping the sweat off his face, she assured, "One day they'll stop. The High Council's spell didn't work. Were you able to remember anything, anything at all?"

Gala pulled away, grit his teeth, balled up his fists, and began hitting his head. "No! I remember other dreams, but I can't remember the miserable nightmares! What's wrong with me?"

Faithin grabbed his hands. She opened his fists and stroked his palms to calm him. She took a deep breath and let it out. "I'm not sure why," she answered. "But every time your father and I try to see your nightmares, a frightened lock refuses to let us in. It's been an entire year since they began; we've tried everything; none of our spells, none of our charms, nothing works. We're not giving up. We'll keep trying. Something must have scared you. Most likely it'll be you who unlocks and opens that door. It'll be you who faces your fears and conquers them."

"The only things I'm scared of are Gob-Diggers and what lurks in the Boggy Swamps. I've never seen a real Gob or gone down to the swamps, so I don't know why I have these blasted nightmares."

"Well, something happened. You need to find out what it is you're afraid of. When you do, your nightmares will go away. I'm sure they will, or my name isn't Faithindale Cosset Lakinshire. But you can just call me Mom for short." Faithin winked and clicked her tongue on the roof of her mouth.

Gala managed a small smile and said, "I wish they'd just go away."

"Me too, sweetheart, me too," she sighed, gave him another kiss, and scratched his back. After sitting in silence for a moment or two, Faithin rubbed Gala's earlobe. She brushed the back of her fingers across his soft cheek. In a quiet voice, she persuaded, "Your father's serving breakfast this morning. Why don't you get dressed and come help me set the table." Faithin stood up. She ruffled her fingers through his thick black hair and coached, "While you're at it, brush this handsome head of hair. Oh, look! You've acquired another curl overnight."

Gala furrowed his dark brows. He pulled away, leaned back against his headboard, crossed his arms, and complained, "But Mother, I want to sleep in my bed back in Whittlewood Forest. This room is nice; it reminds me of home, and the Bluewing Fairies are great friends, but I miss all my old friends. Don't you realize that I wouldn't have these nightmares if we just stayed where we belonged."

Faithin took in a bucket of air. Her eyes widened. "Gala Chief Lakinshire!" she snapped.

"Well! It's true. Why'd we have to come here anyway? It's not that I don't like it here. I like homeschooling, but I liked Whittlewood Academy too. I learned a few spells you and Father didn't even know. I had a lot of good friends, Helsin and the rest of the fellas. Back then, no one was mad at me either, not even Helsin. Lately, everything I do, I do wrong, always messing up my spells. I wanna go home. I wish I wasn't a wizard. I can get by with just being a Transfigure."

Faithin's brows creased tight. She began her first stern words in a slow deep tone. Hardly coming up for air, her reprimand accelerated. "Hold—your—tongue—before I get a hold of it and make you sit with boredom the rest of the day doing nothing; you'll be thankful! How fortunate you are to have qualities, magic powers, and the ability to transfigure. Do you realize how many would kill for both? Stop!" She jerked up her hand. "Don't answer that. I'm just saying. Believe me when I tell you that you'll be happy to have both!" She put her hand down and paced the floor.

"Okay, Mother. I'm sorry. I just miss our old home. Maybe I have nightmares because we live close to the Boggy Swamps." Gala uncrossed his arms. He leaned forward, stretched his arms out across the blanket that covered his legs, and hung his head. He knew he had better curb his tone.

Faithin stretched her arms towards Gala, then drew them back to cup her heart, and said, "Sweetheart, I understand your feelings. Rest your mind because the Gobs and other things that live in the swamp stay in the swamp. And for our old home, we'll visit again. Since we moved into this grand castle..." Faithin spread her arms wide. "...and became protectors of this land, your friends from Whittlewood came to gatherings. They even stayed overnight. When we first moved here, you could hardly contain your excitement. You, Helsin, and your other friends were proud. It's a great honor that The Wizard's High Council chose us to protect these lands and their inhabitants. I know it's trying at times, but it's our duty as Mystique Transfigures. You'll get used to it and be glad for it. You'll thank the giver of life and love for all your gifts. Everything will work out. You'll see. Especially when you find your confidence and solve the nightmare problem." Faithin paused then changed the subject, "The day is slipping." She clapped her hands. "Zippety-zip-zap to it. Meet me in the kitchen. Your father is cooking one of your favorites." She winked, then walked out.

Gala sat on the edge of his bed. He admired the painted mountain scene on his walls. He sighed and thought, "I suppose she's right, but it still doesn't change how I feel about magic. I'm just not any good at it. I'm just a flub-of-a-wizard. Even Helsin agrees with me on that one. The last few times he came to visit, he acted like he was better than me. He was cocky, arrogant, and downright mean. I thought he was my friend. Oh well." Gala shrugged. "If he treats me like that, I don't want his friendship. I have other friends, great friends. Ddot is one of the best friends I've ever had. I'm glad we're neighbors. Helsin didn't even like my room, but Ddot likes it just as much as I do."

Gala gazed up at his magical dome ceiling. It changed to the current conditions outside. Most mornings, when the sun's rays peeked over the eastern mountains, the sky on his ceiling became an orange sunrise color. It shone throughout his room. The mountain scene on his walls would shroud in misty dew. It was what he saw at that moment. When mid-day emerged, the sky on his ceiling turned blue. Puffy white clouds would shadow mountains with scattered showers. When dusk approached to wish him good night, an orange sunset illuminated his entire room. On clear evenings, twinkling stars blanketed his ceiling. On occasion, a shooting star streaked across. Severe weather was minimum so as not to frighten him or his friends who stayed overnight. Gala remembered a time when he and his friends were telling spooky stories. Thunderbolts boomed and crackled overheads. The tiny hairs on the back of their necks stood at attention. Their souls flew out of his bedroom and waited for their bodies to catch up.

Gala shook his head and chuckled as he turned to examine an unfinished painting.

    The painting hung above his fireplace. It's a gift for his parents. He painted their old home in Whittlewood Forest. He thought, "I'll add Mom's favorite velvet red roses next to the wildflowers dancing in a soft spring breeze. I'll paint Dad's favorite Whittlewood tree with a swing hanging from a strong bough. It'll look exactly like the one we had in Whittlewood Forest. But for now, my dear masterpiece, you'll have to wait because Dad's good cookin' is calling my name." Growling pangs jabbed at Gala's stomach. He thought out loud, "Father's pancakes are one of my favorite foods, but I didn't realize I was this hungry." He patted his belly.

    After Gala washed up and brushed his hair, he summoned his wand, "*Appara Comforte*" POOF! It appeared in his hand out of thin air. His wand, a magic tool, was crafted from a Whittlewood tree which crafted his parent's magic tools. Cradled by the winding wood at the top of his wand was a pointy-tipped teardrop diamond. A spherical white diamond, imbued with specks of blue diamonds, was nestled tight in its base. As he pointed his wand at his armoire, he took a hard deep breath, let it out quickly, and said, "Here goes nothing. *Ouv-es-tiaire*!" Lickity-split, before an eye-blinked-quick, his wand turned a gold color. Then a gold sparkling light shot out from its tip straight towards his armoire. "Sizzle—Hiss—POW!" His spell hit his wardrobe and burst in all directions like an exploding star; its doors flung open. BANG! They smacked against the stone wall almost cracking off their hinges. Gala scrunched his face and shoulders. He waited for his parents to say something or come running. After a few seconds, the only sound he heard was his father whistling from within the kitchen. Gala relaxed then rolled his eyes, dissing himself, "Sheesh! I'm just an ole flub-of-a-wizard. Maybe I'll practice that some other time, maybe NOT. *Conceal!*" POOF! His wand vanished into thin air.

    Gala decided to put his magic clothes on by using hand magic which he had down pat. After he swiped his palms over his body, a set of magic clothes vanished off a shelf from within his wardrobe. They suddenly materialized over the bath towel he had wrapped around his waist. Then, his towel emerged onto a pile of dirty clothes in one corner of his untidy room. At least his room didn't look half bad for a boy his age, fifteen going on sixteen. Before Gala walked out of his room, he snapped his fingers toward his clothes rack. A violet cloak shimmered. It rose off its peg, glided through the air, wrapped around Gala's shoulders, then fastened its dragon-shaped clips onto his shirt.

Daily Plans

While Gala helped his mother set the table, he saw his father in the kitchen. "Good morning, Father."

"Good morning, Son. How about some pancakes smothered in sweet Fairy Honey?" Conkay walked past Gala's nose. He held a platter with steaming pancakes stacked high in one hand and a jug of honey in his other.

Gala's mood brightened. He closed his eyes, sniffed the air, licked his chops, then answered, "Yes sir! Lay 'em on me! I knew that's what you were cooking."

"I was going to whip up some Appledees but decided on pancakes. I must have been reading your thoughts." He winked.

Conkay was an excellent chef and a brilliant alchemist. These two passions were his favorite accomplishments. His innate abilities as a Mystique Transfigure set him apart from any other wizard. The same was for Faithin. Her powerful abilities set her apart from any witch—good or bad. Transfigure flowed in their blood; it was in their genes. Gala loved to transfigure. He was exceptional at it. Anyone without the gene would risk remaining in the form they practiced never to return to their natural state. Mystique Transfigures can transform at will. But only if they practiced before their twenty-first birthday. As far as anyone knew, this ability began between the ages of ten and twelve. A Transfigure can transform into approximately ten forms before they turn twenty-one. It takes months to perfect a form and that depends on persistence and discipline. Gala started at the age of ten. Five and half years later, he completed and mastered eight forms that he named. No matter what form he changes into, only his parents and friends know who he is, so they just call him Gala. Nevertheless, he still likes to give each form a unique name. For instance, he calls his dolphin form, Phin. Gala hoped to perfect many forms before he turned twenty-one. But, he also needed to perfect his magic powers.

    Although Gala didn't realize it, his parents knew of his potential. They knew he had the power to create immeasurable magic. His innate genes would enable him to become a powerful Mystique Transfigure, more powerful than themselves. But, a dreadful fear somehow robbed their son's confidence and hung on to him with gripping force. This fear could create havoc if not resolved. They hoped he would conquer it before it conquered him or before he destroyed everyone and everything he held dear.

    Gala asked, "So, Father, am I going on rounds with you this morning?" He was hoping he didn't have to because his father would make him practice his magic spells.

    Conkay smiled a satisfying, secretive kind of smile. He replied, "Your mother and I have other plans for you today."

    Gala turned his head to hide his expression of relief. He lifted his brows. Under his breath, he muttered, "Phew." Then he asked, "So, what are your plans?"

"You know that tonight is Acub and Ashlin's soul mate joining and their coronation. It'll be a grand celebration followed by interesting stories, including the ones we share."

"I'm excited and happy for them," added Faithin. "They've loved each other for as long as I can remember, approximately fifty nights of three full moons ago. You know that's a long time because three full moons in one night don't happen often."

Gala poked at their age. "Wow! That was l-o-o-o-o-n-g ago." Faithin's head jerked up. She wore squinting eyes and pinched lips. Gala looked away. He continued with a series of explanations and questions seldom letting up for air. "Acub told me that when he and Ashlin first met, eye-to-eye, they knew they were soul mates. He said that all Bluewing fairies have that knack. After they become of age, and as soon as their eyes meet, if they're soul mates, they know it, instantly. Ddot and Dahc aren't old enough, and, although Lucky's older and from a different clan, he has the same knack, he's not ready either. When they do meet their soul mates, they'll remain together for the rest of their lives. How charmed is that? I think it's magical! Wonder if that'll happen to me and Floreena? Did it happen to you guys? Did you know you were soul mates when you looked into each other's eyes? How did you guys meet?"

Conkay lifted his brows. "Phew wee! Talk about needing some air. Let's sit down and eat before you pass out. We'll answer most of your questions in the story your mother and I reveal tonight during the clan's story time. Our story will be one of the most magical presentations ever performed. We've had it worked out for months and have been eager to share it." Conkay and Faithin smiled at each other.

"I can't wait to hear it! Tonight's going to be fun!" Gala began eating. He savored each bite, closed his eyes, and released approval sounds, "Mm-mm-mm."

"We have a big day ahead of us. After breakfast, I'll look in on the land, the Bluewings, and the Treeagers, and make sure everyone's doing well. You and your mother go down to Crystal Lake, so you can practice your Phin. Your mother will give you a hand if you need it. When we're done, we'll meet back here and get ready for tonight. I want you to practice Phin for about an hour, then make another choice. Choose something big and strong. Let me think—what should you transform into?" Conkay sat back in his chair, crossed one arm across his chest, and cupped the elbow of his other arm. He began tapping his chin with his fingers. As he glanced around the dining room, he twisted and pressed his lips. He acted as though he was thinking yet knowing exactly what he had planned. "Let's see now—Umm—oh!" He snapped his fingers. "I know! I got it—I got just the thing for you!" He placed his hands on the hardwood table, leaned forward, looked straight into Gala's violet eyes, and said, "It's perfect! You can choose something like mine or your mother's or just a dragon of your makings."

Gala's eyes popped wide, and for the first time, he was speechless. A gigantic grin took over his face. His parents chuckled. They winked at each other, then looked back at their wide-eyed, grinning son with a bit of surprise. It was like magic! His plate was empty; his cheeks were swollen with pancakes.

Conkay sat back and said, "Practice your dragon for a couple of hours and give him a name." Then he sat forward and looked back into Gala's eyes. Gala stopped chewing; he knew that stern look. His father reminded—more like warned, "Remember the danger. You must stay alert, always—know your surroundings. Understand?"

Gala raised his brows and nodded. After his father sat back in his chair, Gala started chewing again.

"When I'm done with my rounds, I have got to perfect that confounded crystal ball, or else it'll end up in shards. That should take a few hours; we'll meet in the lab, then concentrate on our gift for Acub and Ashlin. Afterward, we'll go help the clan finish their decorations." Gala's eyes became vacant like he was staring into space. Conkay tried to get his attention. "Gala—hello. Planet Mageus to Gala." There was no response. As Conkay passed his hand in front of Gala's eyes, he whistled. He finally snapped his fingers and said, "Come in Gala—you who—can you hear me?"

Gala nodded like a bobble-head doll. Despite all his chewing, his mouth was still stuffed when he answered, "Yea wer. Wank oo, Wawer." Without a mouthful of food that would have sounded like: Yes sir. Thank you, Father.

"Slow down. Don't speak with Chipmunkin cheeks full of nuts. You won't want to choke or spit up and waste that delicious food, would you?" Faithin scolded with a bit of fun.

Gala chewed as well as he could, then he swallowed and apologized. "I'm sorry, Mother. Thank you, Father. Thank you for the best-tasting pancakes ever! I'm ready to get started. I'll wash my dishes." He rose, picked up his breakfast dishes, then hurried from the table.

"Never mind that." His father shook his head and chuckled. "Just go on ahead and leave the cleanup to me. I plan to use a bit of magic. Wait outside; your mother will be right behind you."

"You're the best father ever!" Gala put his dishes back on the table and rushed out towards the front doors. Like having two left feet, he tripped over each piece of furniture.

"Watch your step! Don't want to break your neck before you get to practice your dragon!"

"No sir! Thank you, Father!" Gala yelled back as he opened the front doors.

Conkay turned and kissed Faithin on her cheek and whispered in her ear. "Will you please see if you can get him to practice a simple magic spell before he practices his dragon?"

She pulled back slowly, cocked her head, and gave her husband a look he knew very well. Then she whispered, "Yeah, sure thing Master Lakinshire, make me the wicked witch."

He lifted his handsome black brows. "No, no, my sweet gem. It's because you're better at it than I am. You know how frustrated I get. I usually end up being the meanest mage Gala's ever known; he stays mad at me for hours, sometimes days. Please?" Conkay's crystal blue eyes, brightened by his thick black lashes, gazed into Faithin's. He saw her eyes as the rarest of precious gems, and she never failed to melt into his.

"Okay, okay. Resisting you is like resisting my Truth Serum, which is impossible to do. Besides, I know you're right." She kissed his soft, tender lips. He wore a dashing black mustache trimmed thin for tender moments. After she kissed him short and sweet, she stepped back. In a flirtatious manner, she tilted her head, puckered her lips, blew him a kiss, and turned. Her body swayed out of the dining room, leaving her husband dazed and smiling as he watched her every move.

Before walking out, she turned to face him. Conkay kissed the palm of his hand and blew. His magic kiss floated through the air and landed right on her rosy, tender lips. Faithin reached up, touched his magic kiss, and said, "We'll see you in a few hours, my love."

"I await your return, love of my life." After Faithin shut the door behind her, Conkay turned towards the table. He snapped his fingers. The dishes levitated up from the table as if standing at attention waiting for orders. Conkay used his hands and fingers to instruct the cleanup. He looked like an orchestra conductor dancing around. Whatever he pointed at moved when he moved. He moved his fingers from the dutiful dishes toward the sink. A plug floated down into the sink's drainage cavity while water pumped from the sink's spigot. He pointed one hand towards a container of liquid soap and his other at a sponge. When he lifted his arms, the soap and sponge rose into the air. The container tipped; soap poured into the sink, and then the container sat back down on the counter. Conkay nodded at the obedient dishes. They glided their way through the air and lowered down into the soapy water along with the sponge. A plate rose out of the sink. The sponge swished both sides, washing the plate clean. Then the plate floated under the flowing water. While suds were being rinsed from that plate, another plate rose so the sponge could wash it. A wind wafted in from the kitchen window blowing the dishes dry. Every clean dish found its way to where they were stored waiting to be used again. Conkay nodded, satisfied his dishwashing was under control. He pointed at a cloth and instructed it to wipe clean the dining table, countertops, and the cookery stove. As the cloth carried out orders, Conkay pointed at the broom and mop. "Clean," he commanded. His magic spell prepared a mop and bucket to follow behind the broom. Conkay's body turned in circles to wring out the mop. The whole kitchen was alive with rhythmic cleaning. Meanwhile, Gala and Faithin were outside getting ready to transfigure.

Doubt

Faithin didn't disturb Gala when she walked outside. His blank stare indicated to her that he was absorbed. Gala thought, "I get to practice transforming into my very own dragon! No more waiting; finally, Father knows I'm ready. I passed all the tests given to me concerning dragons. I know the danger posed on their existence by Stealth Dragon Slayers. We don't have a language book for dragons, but I know they use hums, buzzes, clicks, roars, and growls to communicate. I saw the dragon's flight mechanics by watching Mother and Father in their dragon forms. I sat studying for hours. I read every book and examined every illustration until I couldn't keep my eyes open or my head up. One of my parents had to help me to bed. My very own dragon—I get to transform into my very own dragon!" Gala pulled his bent elbow with a balled fist downwards to greet his lifting knee and blurted, "YES!"

Faithin almost jumped out of her skin and was not the only one startled by Gala's sudden burst. Thousands of fluttering wings took flight into the morning's orange sky. Faithin and Gala looked up. The alarmed Wispling birds moved together in murmuration, in harmony. They looked like one dark cloud forming different shapes as they flew off into the sunrise. One would have thought they had the art of transfiguring mastered to perfection.

Faithin and Gala looked at each other with widened eyes and smiles. They laughed. After a few more chortles, they closed their eyes and listened to the music that most mornings bring. Birds were singing while leaves rustled in the breeze. Playful Furhoppers, Chipmunkins, Squrlies, and other animals ran through the bushes and trees. The morning's sun peeked over the eastern mountains. Glittering light danced through the forest and touched the dew-covered ground. Misty water drops rode in on a cool eastern wind dampening Gala's and Faithin's faces.

Magnificent waterfalls spilled downwards and out from around their mountain. During the day, when the sun's rays touch the falls, sparkling rainbows will appear. Bluewing Fairies dwell in large grottos secluded behind falls. On the northeast side of their castle, a pool spills over about eight hundred feet to Crystal Lake. Crystal Lake surrounded their entire mountain and created a wide moat. Its water was crystal clear, hence its name.

Their mountain's summit was large. Behind their castle, a forest and lush grasslands expanded over a wide range. It's where they grew their gardens and raised their livestock.

After Gala and his mother wiped the water from their faces, Faithin held out her arms. Her entire body and magical clothes twirled into golden dust particles. She sparkled for a fraction of a second before transforming into a sizable golden eagle with white head and tail feathers. Her eagle form was her height, five and a half feet tall. She winked at her son. Then, she flew up and perched on the wall of their castle's bridge, which they call Bridge.

Gala transformed into what looked like a mixture of an eagle and a large fiery Phoenix he called Nix. He was also quick—a blink-of-an-eye quick. He had Nix down pat. But lately, every time he transformed into Nix, wicked faces flashed across his mind. They were like a fleeting thought. The faces only flashed when he transformed into Nix, so he never gave it much regard. He hadn't found the need to mention it to his parents or his best friend, Ddot, and he usually told Ddot everything.

Nix perched on the creamy stone wall of Bridge alongside his mother. Faithin spread her enormous wings and took flight. She soared over their castle and scanned the layout of the land. On the south side, a rapid stream fell from Crystal Lake downwards through a steep gorge. It flowed throughout the valleys of green rolling hills as far as her eagle eyes could see. She turned her gaze to the northern mountains located in front of their castle. Next, she scanned the northwest forest and the mountains on the west side of the castle. Another rapid stream fell from Crystal Lake into a gorge between two mountain ranges. One range, The Ridge, seemed to have no end. The other range dwindled to a flat wide area of swampland—the land of Gob-Diggers, also known as Swamp Gobs. This was where no decent creature wanted to venture. It was where evil found refuge from its foe and where Gala never wanted to set foot.

Nix watched as his mother soared over the mountain that Bridge joined to theirs. Its summit was an open range, long and wide. An assortment of yellow and purple wildflowers danced in the breeze. Groups of trees scattered throughout, while thick green forests ran along its borders. On its south border, was a steep drop to Crystal Lake. Also, a four-foot stone wall extended about twenty feet on both the east and west sides of Bridge's entrance.

Faithin's sharp eagle eyes saw a tiny bug on her beautiful fig tree that grew on the east side of Bridge's entrance. The large shading tree stood in splendor, always producing sweet fruit. It was a gift from Conkay. Anyone who traveled by could eat a fig or pick a few to take along their journey. Faithin had a kind heart, but you wouldn't want to bring the worst out of her by being greedy. The force of her wrath had scared the shit out of many. Everyone living in the protected land knew this aspect of Faithin. Thus, remained non-greedy. The Lakinshires took excellent care of their domain and everyone who lived in it. No one starved or did without. There was no need or room for greediness.

Faithin flew down and picked a fig with her eagle talons. She flew up and over Crystal Lake. After soaring two complete circles, she flew downwards, parallel to a waterfall. When she laid her wings to her sides, she picked up speed; her squinted eyes began to water. Gala's heart pounded! He held his breath as he watched his mother get closer and closer to the lake. Swoosh! Before her beak touched the water, she swooped upwards. Gala took a breath. The force of her momentum caused the water to ripple. Faithin glided across the lake to the sandy white bank on the same side of their castle. She flapped her wings to hover. Right before she landed, she transformed back into herself. "*Appara Comforte.*" POOF! She summoned her wand. It appeared out of thin air. She pointed her wand at rocks further up the mountain and beneath the mossy ground. After she whispered a spell, her wand turned azure. A sparkling golden glow of dust particles shot out from its tip, hitting each rock. The rocks rose upwards. They twisted and turned and changed into a forest-green, sponge-like texture. They piled together, creating a cushioned armed seat. Faithin sat, rested her arms, and looked up at Nix. He looked like a reddish-orange speck on the wall of Bridge. She waved her wand. Its tip shot out a fountain of gold, red, blue, purple, green, and orange light particles. They danced around like the grand finale of fireworks. It signaled Nix that she was ready to watch him.

 Nix spread his wings and began his descent. He put his wings to his side, which caused him to drop through the air like an anchor. Before he dove into the ice-cold water, sparkling gold light encompassed him. Lickity-split before an eye-blinked quick, Gala transformed into Phin. Like a shooting arrow, Phin entered the deep water without creating much of a splash. He spiraled out of the lake, lifting a funnel trail of water behind him. While doing a flip, he transfigured into himself, then back into Phin.

When he dove back into the water, he purposely splashed his mother with his tail fin. Faithin pointed her wand at the water, waiting. As himself, Gala came back up to the surface, snickering. With one word and a flip of her wrist, her spell splashed water into Gala's face.

"Ha-ha-ha! Got you back, you little showoff! Okay, my wiz-stinker, no more splashing, burr! That's cold!" Faithin crossed her arms, rubbed her shoulders, and took a bite of her fig. After a few more giggles, Gala attended to his practice.

Faithin pointed her wand towards a patch of assorted wildflowers. Under her breath she said, "*Braid-e-tida*" which meant braid into my hair. The wildflowers broke off their stems. Fresh flowers grew in their place. The flowers floated over and began to braid into Faithin's long blonde hair. It relaxed her as she watched Gala transfigure back and forth from himself into Phin, then from Phin into himself. He did this for about fifteen minutes until an unbearable boredom set in. He spiraled up and out, high above the water for one final spin as Phin. Water sprayed from his body, drying him. He transformed into Nix. Then, right before he landed on the bank next to his mother, he transformed into himself.

"Mother, I'm bored. I can transform into Phin without thinking. Can't I start on my dragon? Father will understand." Gala picked up a stick and rapped it several times on a rock. His mother was bored too, but she wasn't about to let Gala know it.

Faithin tilted her head. She turned her shapely blonde brows inwards and upwards as she squinted.

While she pressed her lips, she took a deep breath through her nose and let it back out with a contemplating sigh. As she blinked her thick blonde lashes, fast, Gala could see she was considering his request. But, what he didn't know, is that his mother also had something else in mind. Gala tapped his chin waiting for her answer. She finally spoke her first word with several E's, "Weeeell, okay. But on one condition."

"Anything Mother, anything you say!" he agreed without thinking.

"Okay. I'm holding you to it." She squinted her eyes, pointing and shaking her finger at him. "You have to practice a hand spell you've been neglecting for the past year and practice a spell with your wand."

Gala's enthusiasm flew out the castle's window. He hung his head, rebelling as he grumbled, "Oh Mother, you know I'm not any good at casting spells. I told you I can't do 'em." While he was complaining about how rotten he was, he picked up a stone and threw it skipping across the lake. When it reached the other side, it skipped back across and landed in his hand. He threw the stone again, and again it skipped back to him. "Every time I try, I get confused and I don't remember the words, and I haven't—"

"Wait a minute! Do you see that?"

"See what?" Gala looked around to see what she was referring to.

"The stone coming back to you," Her eyes glanced at the stone in his hand.

"Yes. But Mother, this is different. I've been doing this for as long as I can remember. It just comes naturally to me. I don't even have to think about it." He made it sound as though it was the simplest spell to do.

"Exactly. It's second nature to you because you learned to do it before you lost your confidence. What's true for your transfiguring abilities is also true for your spells."

"What do you mean?"

"Son, before your nightmares, before your lost confidence, you were doing great. You were sure of yourself. You learned a few hand spells like your *Skipping Stone* spell. Although you love to transfigure, and whether you know it or not, I'm telling you now, it's not the only reason you excel in it. It's because it flows in your blood. It's an innate Mystique Transfigure gene. It's not a mere act of harnessing your energies to perform magic as other sorcerers can do without the gene. Gala, magic flows in your blood just as—"

Does it? How do you know this, Mother? I doubt it does. I can't see or think in which—"

Faithin clapped her hands. "Don't interrupt! As I was saying, magic flows in your blood. It's part of you, in you, your genes; Just because you can't see something, doesn't mean it isn't there or isn't so. You can't escape it. It's there. It's your lack of sureness that has robbed you. The *Skipping Stone* spell is natural because you perfected it with confidence. You transform with ease because you trust in transfiguring, besides the fact that you love to do it. The nightmares must have something to do with your uncertainty. Overcoming fear can be hard, but you must try. Believe in yourself. Don't let nightmares keep you from your mystique potential."

"But Mother, remember the racing contest at the last gathering when I tried to help Lucky, I mean Eric? If Helsin wasn't there, we'd be calling Eric Unlucky instead of Lucky. You and Father saw what Helsin did; it was remarkable how he saved Lucky's wings and his life. That spider would have sucked Lucky dry if I had been left to protect him. Heck! Lucky and the clan may never trust me to protect them with my so-called spell casting, and no telling what—"

"That's enough! That happened after the nightmares began and after you lost your self-confidence."

"That's what I mean. I have tried just as you said. I-I've tried, a-a-and tried, a-a-and I'm still not any good at it. A-and, I don't think it has—"

"I don't want to hear another fumbling excuse. You give up too easily. You haven't been practicing or studying as you should. If you were, you might see things differently. Because of what happened to Lucky is the more reason you're going to study and practice. You are going to study and practice, and then study and practice some more! By all the realms of magic, you will perfect your spells! You will be the protector of this land and all its inhabitants. That includes your best friend, Ddot. You know what, he happens to have faith in your abilities whether you know it or not. The whole

Bluewing clan has faith in your abilities just as your father and I do."

Gala paced the bank. He shrugged his shoulders and waved his hands as he rattled on without coming up for much air. "Ddot might, but I think you're wrong about most of the clan, especially Acub. Acub's nice to me all right, but not like he once was. Sometimes it seems he's mad at me. I'm pretty sure Acub thinks my messed-up spell-casting had something to do with his parents. I don't understand why. I don't know what happened to his parents any more than he or anyone else does. Do you think Acub's also mad at me because of what happened the day Helsin saved Lucky's life? I only make things worse. Helsin is good with his magic. He could become the most powerful wizard of all time. He ought to be the next protector after you and Father. Acub seems to have more faith in Helsin than he does in me. I even think Acub likes Helsin more than he likes me. And don't say it."

"Say what?"

"Say that I'm only feeling sorry for myself." Gala stopped pacing and hung his head.

Faithin sighed. "Well. You do seem to be wallowing in self-pity." She sighed again then stood up. The rocks to her seat returned to their natural state. Faithin put her hand under Gala's chin then lovingly turned his face up towards hers. Her tone was soft, "Listen, Son, about Acub, his parents are missing. This is a great loss, extremely painful. Not knowing what happened can lead to all sorts of ideas. And most of those ideas are nowhere near the truth of what happened. Not knowing can be worse than knowing. Not knowing can cause mixed feelings of hope and anguish. When knowing loved ones have transcended, the loss may be easier to deal with by way of a healthy grievance. You're not the only one he's been treating this way. Everyone deals with his or her loss differently. They become angry, isolated, and all kinds of different things. Just give Acub some time. He loves you."

"Mother, I'm scared I'll keep messing up. I'm scared I can't do magic the way you think I can. I don't think I have the gene in me as you say I do. Helsin's right. I'll never amount to a great wizard. What he said makes sense." Gala changed his voice trying to sound like Helsin. "Gala! Why don't you give it up before you cause irreversible damage? You're never going to amount to a great wizard by causing disaster."

"Don't listen to him! Considering his background, I suppose he's a bully in his own right. I suppose he's hurting and can't lash out at what or who hurt him. I think Helsin needs to feel better, so he says negative things to you in hopes this will fulfill his need. But in reality, if this is what he's doing, being mean only makes him feel worse about himself. He just doesn't realize it. I happened to notice that he isn't like that with anyone else. You two used to get along before his parents transcended. You even got along for some time after he moved in with his uncle and his estranged aunt, who he says is seldom around. We've never met them. I get the impression he's angry at them and jealous of you or both. You could help him get past that. Trust me. Don't let him bother you. You cannot worry about what he thinks. Gala, sweetheart, I know you can do this and I'm not saying this because I'm your mother. I tell you what. Let's forget about the simple hand spell for today. Let's work a little with your wand. I want you to cast the Congeal spell on a spider using Sorcermizic language. It's simple enough. I tell you what. If you put your heart into practicing this spell, then you can work on your dragon. Have you given your dragon a name?" She changed the subject.

"Yes 'am. His name is Redtalon. I have him planned out. I've had him planned out for a long time. He's a lot like your dragon and a lot like Father's. I added my touches, of course. Here, I sketched him out." Gala reached into his pocket and pulled out a folded piece of parchment, a bit wrinkled and worn. With humbled pride, he held it up.

"Redtalon is a great name! Excellent drawing; he's perfect! I can't wait to see you in his form. The sooner we get started, the sooner you can practice him."

Gala folded his drawing and stuck it back in his pocket. He summoned his wand, "*Appara Comforte*" POOF! It appeared out of thin air, out of pure will. He followed his mother along the grassy part of the bank. "Here's one!" His voice shook. He wasn't scared of tiny spiders, but he did fear he'd flub up the spell. He pointed at a little black, hairy spider in the center of her dew-covered web.

"Good eye, Son. She's perfect. This spider eats her prey whole instead of liquefying and sucking their insides out."

Gala wrinkled up his face. "Gross, Mom! That's just downright disgusting."

"Ha-ha-ha! I'm only teasing. Come on, let's get started. After I steer that yellow beetle over her web, I'll touch the web right beneath the beetle. The spider will dart towards the beetle. Before she reaches it, you cast the spell."

"But Mom! What if I don't stop the spider? How on wizard's magic am I going to live with myself knowing I was the culprit to the beetle's demise, and what if—"

"For hunger's sake, a spider's gotta eat," Faithin sounded serious but was only making light of things. As if to shoo off negative vibes, she wiggled her fingers toward Gala and said, "You'll do much better without all that negativity. Lighten up and relax."

While Faithin and Gala were getting ready to cast their spells, Conkay finished his rounds and was ready to tackle his crystal ball.

Crystal Ball

After entering and scanning his spacious untidy laboratory, Conkay sat at his workbench. He had left everything he needed to perfect his crystal within his grasp. There were instructional books, tools, herbs, potions, alchemist supplies, and his crystal ball, which sat cradled on its pedestal. He crafted the pedestal from gold imbued with precious gems to give it added sparkle and power. Conkay thumbed through the pages of his alchemy book. He read instructions to prepare a substance that would enhance the use of his crystal ball. He poured an alchemy solution and a magical potion into a crystal bowl, and stirred. The thick substance changed from an orange color to purple. Conkay wiped, wiped, and wiped his clammy hands off on his cloak. With vigor, he shook the nerves off his hands before he picked up his crystal ball and its pedestal. With a hint of hope attached to his sigh, he submerged them into his concoction. The mixture bubbled as it conformed to both the ball and its pedestal.

    Conkay watched his ancestral clock for the one-minute mark. His nerves jumped when time was up. After he removed his crystal and its pedestal, he closed his eyes while pausing for a deep breath. He spoke his spell in a soft voice, *"Downsize."* Unsure it had worked, he peeked through squinted eyes. Conkay's heart thumped. His eyes popped wide.

"Gee wizards, it worked!" After he returned them to their original size, he set the pedestal on the table. He held the crystal ball cupped in both hands. Conkay closed his eyes. A rainbow-colored light encompassed him and sparkled for a nanosecond. He transfigured into his Bluewing form. The crystal shrank down into his hands. Hardly containing himself, he blurted out, "ALL RIGHT!" Once again, he closed his eyes. Within a blink of an eye, he transformed into himself.

After Conkay returned the crystal to its original size, he placed it on its pedestal. He faced his palms over the ball, moving them in a circular motion. Mixed with hope and fear, he asked, "*Show me Acub's parents, Trill and Quo.*" The crystal did nothing. Conkay gave a slight shrug of his shoulders. He thought out loud, "My crystal is blocking them for some reason. I'll ask it to show me Faithin and Gala. *Show me the loves of my life.*" A golden antique glow encompassed the crystal while it filled with purple fog. The fog dissipated. Although he couldn't hear or see their surroundings, he could see his wife and son down on the bank of Crystal Lake. He saw Gala holding his wand and thought, "Good. She persuaded Gala to practice his spells."

Conkay's ancestral clock made a clickety-clack clank, clickety-click clunk noise which diverted his attention. His ancestors carved detailed sculptures of themselves within the clock's mahogany wood. The wood came from a tree within the magical Whittlewood Forest. Precious gems and diamonds adorned the massive clock. It also contained mystical properties Conkay had yet to figure out. It reminded him of when his grandfather first introduced him to time travel. Conkay lifted one brow and thought, "As long as I get it right, I have time to travel to the realm I like to visit, Earth. I have to be extra careful."

He told his crystal ball to sleep. After Faithin and Gala faded from the crystal ball, it resumed its natural state. As Conkay prepared for time and realm travel, Gala and Faithin were ready to cast their spells.

Wrong Spell

Faithin explained, "I'll make sure the beetle is out of harm's way." She pointed her wand at the beetle and spoke two words under her breath; her wand turned azure. A steady stream of golden dust particles shot out from its tip surrounding the beetle. The beetle could move its body but couldn't go anywhere. Faithin used her hand to steer the beetle towards the spider's web. She reminded, "Gala, wait until the spider starts after the beetle."

"Okay." Gala choked; his hand shook as he readied his wand. Imaginations of flubbing up flooded his thoughts. As he pictured an enormous spider, his mother tapped the web. The spider was quick, but Gala was lightning speed quicker. While pointing his wand at the spider, he chanted two words under his breath. His wand turned a gold color. A sparkling golden light shot out from its tip and surrounded the spider. The spider came to a complete halt. Not one single hair on any of her eight legs moved. Gala yelled, "I can't believe it! I did it!"

"Yes, you did! Let's do it again! Are you ready?"

"Yes, I'm ready! Wait! No! What's happening!?" SPUTTER-POP-POOF! The spider grew, large! "Oh no, run Mother! Run! Change into your eagle, your dragon, something! Take flight Mother!" As Gala had envisioned, the five-ounce spider grew three and a half feet in height. It weighed fifty pounds. And it continued to sputter and pop because the spell was still processing. Faithin feared for the safety of her son, everyone. When she saw the spider's eight black eyes fixed on her, she feared for herself.

She released the beetle, and yelled, "Gala! What were the words you chanted? I have to reverse the spell! I can't break your spell without knowing what you said! I've got to use the reverse spell NOW!"

"I said, Growsce Magna!"

"That means to grow large!" Faithin lifted her wand to perform the reverse spell. The spider jumped up to bite her and knocked her wand out of her hand. Its tip flung straight into the ground. Faithin was going to use a hand spell to retrieve her wand. But, when she backed up from the spider, she fell. Gala sucked in a bucket of air. Faithin hurried to her feet. The ever-growing spider, now four and a half feet tall, weighed seventy pounds. It stomped Faithin's wand further into the ground. Faithin yelled, "Throw me your wand!" Gala threw his wand, and although it seemed like slow motion, it wasn't. The wand shot straight into Faithin's hand. Under her breath, she spoke the reverse spell; it didn't work! She looked at her wide-eyed son and yelled, "Here, Gala, catch!" She threw him his wand.

Gala reached out and caught it. His thoughts raced, "What can I do!?! I've got to stop the spider! He guessed at the reverse spell and spat. A golden bolt of light shot out from his wand and zapped the spider's abdomen with an electric shock. The spider jolted, tucked her body, and turned her gaze on Gala.

"No!" Faithin felt the way Gala looked—death gray. He took off running. The spider chased as fast as it could while the spell continued to process. Faithin's stomach sank to the center of their planet. She transformed into her eagle and flew after the enormous beast. It sputtered and popped again, and now was half the size of Faithin's eagle. Faithin flapped above the spider's head trying to divert its attention. All she managed to do was slow it down.

Gala concealed his wand on the run, dodging death. He felt overwhelmed with fear, shame, confusion, and his lack of confidence sunk deeper. If he thought clearly, he could have used the same advice he gave his mother. He could have transformed into his little bird, Bunt, or his fiery bird, Nix. Gala saw a shallow crevice and ran inside with no way out! He pressed his back tight against the wall. Eight ghastly black eyes peered in at him. His heart pounded through his chest; his eyes popped out of their sockets. The spider reached in with her spiny legs and tried to grab him. She pierced his arm and caused a deep gash. Blood shot out and splatter against the crevice walls. Gala closed his eyes trying to focus, blocking out thoughts of pending doom.

Faithin grabbed the spider's abdomen but couldn't hold on for long because the spider grew even bigger. It blocked Faithin's view of Gala. Faithin grabbed and grabbed at the spider. Her talons scratched its abdomen. The creature screeched and turned away from the crevice. It crept and crawled up the mountainside. Faithin flew down to the crevice and looked inside. "GALA!" She saw nothing but blood-splattered walls. Overwhelmed with emptiness, a massive hole carved its way through her heart. Her heart fell into her stomach and drowned. She screamed, "MY BABY—MY SWEET PRECIOUS CHILD! NOOOOO! WHAT HAVE I DONE?! GALA! My sweet child is gone! I should have killed that BEAST!"

    Faithin flew after the spider, grabbed it around its head, and with both talons she squeezed tight. The spider's legs and body squirmed about. Faithin squeezed tighter, tighter still, until its head almost popped. But then, she released her death grip and held on with a secure grip. Oh, how she wanted to kill that monstrous beast; she knew it wasn't the spider's fault. She knew it was her fault, all her fault. She was the reason for her son's demise. The spider wiggled, sputtered, and popped. It grew even larger until Faithin's talons could no longer keep a strong grasp on its head. She dropped the spider. It turned and jumped up trying to bite Faithin with its gigantic fangs. Faithin dodged, flew upwards, and transformed into her magnificent dragon. She grabbed the spider from behind. It wiggled and squirmed as Faithin flew it up to the snowcapped mountains so it would freeze and be still—not die. On the mountaintop, Faithin lay down on her side, and the spider had finally stopped growing. From the depth of her gut, Faithin wept; she screamed out, "WHAT HAVE I DONE?! MY BABY! — MY SWEET PRECIOUS BABY IS GONE!"

Faithin heard a loud whump and what sounded like a ton of sand racing behind her. As the noise grew closer, she could feel the ledge beneath her belly rumble and shake. She turned. Her eyes popped wide. A tremendous snow slide headed straight toward her. Still gripping tight to the spider, Faithin flew upwards. She made a near escape above the swift-drifting cloud of snow. It tumbled downwards covering and crashing down trees while animals scarcely eluded destruction. It came to a halt after splashing into the pool of melted ice. Faithin sighed as she used her tail to push the fallen snow off the ledge. She lay back down on her side and continued to wail—a much quieter grief-stricken moan.

Inside, on the crevice floor where Gala had entered, a red ruby lay among other gems. The ruby started to vibrate and shake. It flickered with red and gold light. Finally, a steady, bright, golden light shone, followed by a loud ZAP! SNAP! POOF! Gala! He transformed back into himself. He listened for any sign of the spider. He heard nothing, so he ran out of the crevice. Gala saw his mother's dragon form lying on an outcrop of the high mountain on the northeast side of their castle. As his ruby form, he couldn't hear anything. He had no idea his mother thought he was dead. Gala felt ashamed, frightened, and sorry for himself. He could tell that the spider had stopped growing and his mother had a secure hold of it. He didn't know how long the spell would last. His thoughts raced. "I have to do something, but the only thing I'm good at is transfiguring. I'll have to tell Father. He'll know what to do. Goodness giver of life, he's gonna kill me!"

Gala felt something running down his arm. When he reached to wipe it, he saw blood coming from a deep gash the spider's leg had caused. He hurried down to Crystal Lake and washed off the blood. He summoned his wand and waved it over the palm of his hand. A multi-color healing charm materialized. But then it turned black and melted into a sticky, oozing substance. It spread across his palm and dripped between his fingers. "Yuck! Sheesh! Can't I do anything right!?" Gala washed his hand and concealed his wand. This time, without using magic, he reached into his pocket for another healing charm and ate it. The bleeding stopped. But it would take fifteen minutes for the charm to completely heal his injury.

Gala transformed into his small, fast-flying, colorful bird, Bunt. Bunt had red, blue, green, and yellow feathers throughout his little body with a solid red tail. Bunt flew to the castle then straight into his father's laboratory and called out, "Father!" His father was not in the castle, so he searched outside. He found no trace so flew to the waterfall cave of the Bluewing Fairy clan. After he transformed into his Bluewing form he yelled, "Acub! Acub! Where are you?" Gala bent over, hands on his knees, panting like a wild animal after a hard run.

"Here I am." Acub flew over and stood in front of Gala.

"Have you or any clan member seen my father?"

"Yes. We saw your father about twenty-five minutes ago. Do you need our help? Is everything all right? We heard rumbling and wailing. We were on our way to investigate when you arrived. What's wrong? You're out of breath."

"Oh no, nothing's wrong. I'm out of breath because of my rigorous transfigure practice. I need to get going; keep everyone inside until I come back. Use your protective charms for the entrances of your cave. There's really nothing to worry about but use the charms just the same. I'll explain later." Gala rushed, knowing that harmless lies were sometimes necessary.

"Okay. Talk to you when you come back."

Gala transformed into Bunt and flew back to the castle, straight into the library. After transforming into himself, he got out the Spells-Charms book and thumbed through the pages until he found the reverse spell. "Norma Magna, Norma Magna, Norma Magna," he repeated the words out loud. He did his best to imagine the spider shrinking to its original size, but all he could see was an enormous beast. He flew up to his mother as Bunt and transformed into his Bluewing form to retrieve his wand. It was freezing! Gala saw his mother weeping while she held the massive spider that was less active but still a threat.

Faithin's dragon form was beautiful. She was white and blue with wisps of her garment colors, purple and pink, throughout her scales. She and Conkay created their dragons with expansive wings.

They have retractable claws for tender moments. Their thick skin and scales withstand fire and ice. Conkay's dragon breathes fire. Faithin's does not. She created her dragon with gills to live in water—webbed claws to swim. She didn't think she would need to breathe fire or ice until now.

Gala hovered and called out, "Mother!"

Faithin jerked her head up and squealed, "GALA, MY SWEET, SWEET CHILD!" She sat up, and with joyful tears she almost released the spider to embrace her son. "Thank the giver of goodness, life, and love you're not, I mean, YOU'RE HERE! But sweetheart, you're going to freeze up here. You have to transform into Bunt or Nix." She sniffed, trying to stop the wetness from dripping out her nose.

"Mother, I have to be able to hold on to my wand to cast the reverse spell. I can't do that as my bird forms."

"You know the reverse spell?"

"Yes 'am."

"Well then, we can do that down on the ground."

"I'd rather do it here. That way no one can see what we're doing. Let me cast it now."

"Tell me the words before you point that wand."

"Norma Magna."

"That's it! Cast it now!" She sniffed again and wiped her nose against her arm.

Gala looked at the enormous spider; his body shook with nerves more than it did from the freezing air. Without conviction, he stuttered the words, "*N-nor-ma, ma-mag-n-na!*" The spell didn't work!

"Gala, sweetheart, close your eyes. Imagine you're standing in front of The Wizard's High Council. You're in front of the most powerful wizards in all the realms. You see them bowing to you, showing reverence. They know you're the most influential wizard they've ever seen. You're filled with love and compassion. Do you see yourself?"

"Yes 'am."

Before Gala's wings froze, Faithin hurried with her hypnotic instructions, "Okay, son. While you're standing in front of the wizards, you're showing them the reverse spell to *Growsce Magna*. You're confident. You see your mother guarding the enormous spider locked in the holding crate. Keep your eyes closed and hold on to that image. Now point your wand towards the spider."

Gala did as his mother suggested. With his vivid imagination, without stutter or hesitation, he said, "*Norma Magna!*" Faithin heard conviction in his voice and saw that his wand glowed gold, not azure. Gold sparkling light shot from the tip of his wand surrounding the spider, and then SPUTTER—POP—POOF! The spider became tiny within Faithin's dragon paw. Gala's eyes were still closed, imagining the wizards were showing him respect. As frost began to cover his blue wings, he started to fall.

Faithin reached out with her free dragon paw and caught her precious son. She drew him near, blew her breath to warm him, and said, "Gala. Wake up. Transfigure into Nix." Gala didn't hear her. She got louder. "GALA, Sweetheart, Wake up."

He snapped back into reality and transformed into Nix. "Whoa! Glad my wings didn't freeze, and wizard wonders, look at that! The spider's small, normal, I mean, back to her natural state."

"Yes, the reverse spell worked! You did it! Let's go, Son. Let's take little miss spider back down by the lake." Faithin smiled her beautiful dragon smile, thankful and relieved.

Gala thought, "None of this would have happened if I studied and practiced like I was supposed to." Gala wanted to crawl inside a hole somewhere far away and hide forever.

After returning the spider home, Faithin and Gala transformed into themselves. Faithin turned and pulled Gala to her bosom. She pulled him to the ground and held on tight. Her eyes turned beet red. Uncontrollable tears rolled down her face. Her throat choked up as she cried from her belly, "O-oh my swee-eet child, I-I thought I lost you. I-I thought the spider a-ate you, sta-a-aining the cre-evice walls with y-your bl-ood a-a-as a reminder of my gr-grave mistake." Faithin calmed her stomach. She sniffed a few more times while she wiped her face. She got up and pulled Gala up into her bosom, hugging him a little longer.

After a long minute, she put her hands on his shoulders, slightly pushed him away to look into his eyes. His eyes were watery red. "Gala, my sweet child, I'm relieved you weren't spider breakfast. I'm angry with myself. But do you see the importance of studying and practicing?" Gala nodded as his mother continue, "If wickedness caused this, we would have to try and stop it with another spell. I dropped my wand, and my hand spells wouldn't have been helpful with this type of spell." Faithin paused. She cocked her head to one side as her eyebrows turned inwards and her forehead wrinkled. She wondered. "When I looked inside the crevice, I saw blood. I didn't see you. What happened? Where were you?"

Gala sniffed. He lifted his shirt to wipe his eyes and face. He hardly came up for air as he answered, "I was so scared. I didn't know what to do. I couldn't think. I just couldn't think, Mother! I was scared upon scared. That's why I ran instead of transforming into Bunt or Nix. I thought about that after I entered the crevice and after the spider stuck my arm with one of her spiny legs. It was too late to transfigure into any of my forms because they're too big, need water, or they're eatable. So, when I saw my blood against the gems, I knew I had to do something, or that spider would eat me. I decided to transform into a ruby. I closed my eyes and focused the best I could, putting the spider out of my mind. I did it, Mother! I did it without any help! I became a ruby! After some time had passed, I switched back into myself. I didn't know you thought I was dead. I didn't hear anything. Now that I think about it, being a ruby felt different. I can't explain it, but anyway, after I saw you up on the ledge, I went looking for Father and couldn't find him. Oh, yes! I forgot! I gotta tell Acub everything's okay. I'll be right back. And Mother, don't worry. I didn't tell him what happened. I just told him to use the protection charms and be sure everyone stayed inside." After Faithin nodded, Gala transformed into his Bluewing form and flew to the clan's cave.

"Did you find your father?" Acub asked while the whole clan listened. Some fairies fluttered in place or were sitting down. Others were standing, including Ddot, who was standing next to Acub.

"No. But I'm sure he's around somewhere. I'll talk to him soon enough. I can't wait until tonight. Your ceremony's gonna be a lot of fun," Gala changed the subject.

"I hope so. We've been anticipating this night for quite some time. Just think. In a few more hours, Ashlin and I will be what you call hitched." Acub winked.

"Hitched?" Gala wrinkled his nose and his top lip. "What in all the realms of magic does that mean?"

"According to your father, Ashlin and I will have joined as soul mates. I think it was your father who told me that." Acub smiled. He patted Gala on the shoulder and said, "Well, Gala, guess we'll see you and your parents when you come to help us decorate."

"Okay, see y'all later." Before Gala left, he turned towards Ddot. They reached their bent elbows with clenched fists towards each other. They tapped their forearms, making an X. Then they tapped the front of their fists. Next, they opened their hands and clasped their wrist. Before letting go, they shook once.

"See you later, Chum," Ddot said.

"Okay, Bud, see ya later." Gala nodded then hurried back to his mother.

After Gala transformed into himself and stood in front of his mother, she reached for his arm. "Let me see that."

"It's nothing, Mother. It's almost gone. I ate a healing charm." Gala turned his arm so she could get a better look.

While inspecting his wound, she fought the tears of humbled gratitude. She swallowed and asked, "Did you remember the reverse spell?"

"No ma'am. After I couldn't find Father, I went into the library and opened the Spells-Charms book. I rehearsed the spell while trying to visualize the spider shrinking, and then I flew up to you. Mother, I'm so sorry. I'm...I'm so ashamed. I promise I'll study and practice my spells and learn my charms." Gala hung his head. Although he wished he didn't have to learn spells, he would make an honest effort.

Faithin put her hand under Gala's chin and lifted his face towards her gaze. She smiled and said, "I believe you will. You'll get by just studying and practicing, but you're going to need your confidence as well. Precise visualizing is good but best when you manage it quickly with self-assurance. You need to believe in yourself. You need self-control, feel the feeling just as you do with your *Rock Skipping* and other spells. Let's not think about that right now. You can start practicing tomorrow. I'm glad you, WE, learned something from this experience. Sometimes the lessons we learn come with a great loss. Thank the giver of goodness, life, and love, no severe harm came from this lesson. And sweetheart, there's nothing to be ashamed of. As your father and I've explained, we all make mistakes. If we don't learn from our mistakes, or at least make an honest effort, it's not a good thing. But I tell you what, I surely learned from this one. I'm sure you did too, right?"

"Yes 'am. I'll never forget it either."

"Good. This makes me prouder. I might become frustrated if you didn't learn. I wouldn't like it the least bit, especially if there wasn't an honest effort. I'll love you, forever, no matter what." She reached out and gave him a tender kiss on his cheek then, again, she confessed, "Son, it's not entirely your fault. It's my fault. I'm your mother. I'm your teacher. A better choice to practice the *Congeal* spell would have been on a butterfly instead of a spider. On top of that, your wand turned gold, not azure. We forgot to give ourselves permission to use each other's magic tools. I could have used your wand to reverse the spell. By all the powers on Mageus, I certainly hope I learned my lesson. I could have lost the most precious thing to my heart. From now on, until you get it down pat, we're practicing on harmless butterflies, but no more today. I've had enough heart failure for one day, CORRECTION, for a lifetime!"

"Mother, what on Mageus is a butterfly or butterflies?"

"Oh." Faithin chuckled. "That's what your father likes to call flutteries. If it's one fluttery, he'll call it a butterfly. If it's more than one fluttery, he'll call them butterflies."

"I learned another word from Acub. He said that after he and Ashlin join their love with a ceremony, they become what he called, 'hitched.' Acub thinks he may have heard the word from Father. I wonder why Father does that, have two different words that mean the same thing? Does it have something to do with our Sorcermizic language?"

"It might. Our Sorcermizic language is a mixture of our native language and words your father made up. Our language protects our incantations. But that's not the only reason your father makes words up. He does it for fun. You know your father is different like that." Faithin didn't want Gala to know his father picked words up from traveling to different realms. She didn't want him to know Mageons speak English which originated from Earth. She doesn't want Gala to learn the art of time and realm travel because it's dangerous. In the past, hundreds of their ancestors traveled to Earth, never to return. Gnomes, elves, dragons, and fairies never came back, either. Faithin feared that the art could be harmful to their existence. It could cause other changes besides unfamiliar words. She hurried and changed the subject back onto the focus of the day's events. "But anyway, just know that when your father asks about today, and you know he will, I'll tell him it's my fault. I shouldn't have picked a dangerous creature in the first place. Also, I'll tell him it won't be long when you have your *Grow* spell and its reverse spell down pat."

"So, you don't think Father will get angry at me?"

"If he does, its only because you should have known the *Congeal* Spell by now. I'm sure he'll be angrier with me for putting us and everyone else in danger, but he won't be mad if he knows we learned our lesson. Your father has made serious mistakes, too. He'll understand and get over it. He'll be grateful we're alive. After that, you can bet your lucky-charms he'll chalk it up for another remarkable story." Faithin winked and clicked her tongue on the roof of her mouth.

"I hope so."

"Don't fret my wiz-binker. It'll be all right. Oh yes, I found my wand on the ground all in one piece. I thought for sure the spider broke it. If she did, your father would fix it, make it as new as when the Whittlewood tree first gave it to me."

"How would he fix it?"

"He would use his alchemy skills."

"Oh yeah, okay."

"After you get your spells down pat, your father can teach you alchemy. Would you like to learn more about it?"

"Sure. I think it's interesting, a bit confusing, but still interesting."

"Good. I'm glad you like it."

"So Mother, not to change the subject, what are we gonna do now—go home and prepare our gift for Acub and Ashlin?"

"Are you kidding? We have plenty of time for that. I hope you're ready because I want to see your Redtalon!" Her eyes twinkled.

"ALL RIGHT!" Gala punched the air with his fists. He was more than ready.

Faithin clapped her hands. "Okay, fella. The day is slipping. Zippety-zip-zap to it. Let's practice your Redtalon."

Faithin thinks that her husband had stopped time and realm travel. Conkay has been careful in keeping her from knowing that he hasn't. However, secrets have a way of revealing themselves. While Faithin is working with Gala, Conkay is in his laboratory contemplating the art.

Dark Mysterious Shadow

Conkay looked around his laboratory to ensure no one was there. Although he knew Faithin and Gala were down by Crystal Lake, he had a strange feeling someone was watching him. Over the past year, in various parts of the castle, he felt the same, but brushed it off. He knew Faithin thought he had stopped practicing the art of realm and time travel. But, if Gala regained self-assurance, Conkay would teach him without her knowing. He justified, "It's educational where I'm traveling. If Faithin knew this, she'd allow me to travel. She'd let me to teach Gala. Then my wizard nerves would calm down, and I wouldn't be paranoid." Conkay looked over at his ancestral clock to note the time. He told himself, "If I get my timing right, I'll be back at this exact time, before Faithin and Gala returned to the castle."

Conkay held his staff up with both hands. He calls it Force. He made two complete circles round his head of wavy, black, shoulder-length hair. On top of Force, cradled within an intricate carved design of dragon claws, nestled a ruby-red amulet. The ruby emitted a rainbow-colored light. The light expanded above Conkay's head then swirled around his entire body. Using the bottom of Force, Conkay tapped the floor twice. With each tap, he said one word, the same word with each tap. The light warped like a water ripple. It was a time and realm portal. In an instant, Conkay disappeared. With the same warped light, like a flash, he reappeared in a library on Earth. An eerie feeling took over. It felt like someone was standing behind him. He commanded, "Creepy crawling chills get off my neck!" Like lightning, he turned and saw nothing but an empty library. Conkay turned back around. He thought, "I've got to get over this paranoia."

"Clink-clank." The deadbolt to the front doors unlocked. Conkay ran and hid behind an enormous indoor elm tree. The elm stood about twenty feet from a counter and ten feet diagonal from the front entrance. Its top branches reached towards the sunroof of the five-story building. Its lower ones grew towards large windows that hid behind long burgundy drapes. The spacious library was dark except for the sunroof and a soft ember of light coming from a lamp on the counter.

A librarian entered the front double doors then flipped a switch. Golden chandeliers adorned with crystal and flame-shaped light bulbs lit the entire library. Every chandelier hung on a golden chain intertwined with gold wire resembling rope. They were at different lengths so all the floors were lit.

Walls were tall and wide with shelves upon shelves of books. Bookshelves had brass ladders on tracks and brass lifts able to reach each book. Staircases had gold railings. Elaborate glass elevators had golden gates. Every floor had shellacked cedar tables and burgundy cushioned seats. The floor's pathway mapped out with rugs embellished in a gold and burgundy design. It was a majestic view Conkay always enjoyed and fashioned the inside of his home to resemble.

Conkay usually arrived before the library opened, so he had time to ride up and down the elevators. He sometimes read books that sparked his interest. Folklore was a favorite. When he finished having fun, he used magic to unlock the back doors and slip into the empty halls. Then he would lock the doors behind him. But this time, his time travel was off by about four hours.

As Conkay watched the librarian walk towards the back double doors, he tiptoed to the front entrance. He wanted to appear as though he had just arrived. A chime alarmed the librarian that someone had entered.

Without turning around, the zealous librarian greeted, "Top of the morning to you. Feel free to look around. I'll be with you shortly."

"Thank you, sir." Conkay gasped. He had forgotten to change his attire and conceal Force. He snapped his fingers. Lickity-split before an eye-blinked quick, he was wearing different clothes. He dressed the way most men dressed in that realm. After he spoke a word under his breath, Force vanished. It looked like it disappeared into thin air. As soon as the librarian unlocked the back double doors, Conkay huffed, "A **Shadow!**"

"Pardon me?" the librarian asked without turning around.

"Oh. Nothing, I'm talking to myself." As Conkay ran up to the back doors, the **Shadow** slipped out. The librarian jerked around. Smack-dab, he and Conkay were face to face.

Almost jumping out of his skin, the librarian stepped back. He took another step back and presumed, "Didn't you just come in?"

Conkay stuck his head through the double doors. He saw the **Shadow** enter an opened door leading into the room where he was going. "Yes. I'm so sorry. Forgive me, sir. But I need to get to the gene lecture down the hall."

"You have about two minutes before it begins. You may not be aware, but there are three other entrances and exits to the halls. You do not have to wait for the library to open to get to them."

"Oh? I was unaware," He fibbed. "If there is ever a time that I need to get to a room before the library opens, I will use one of the other entrances. Thank you, sir. Good day." Conkay gave the librarian a bow.

"Good day to you." The librarian returned a bow.

Conkay knew about the other entrances but loved the library and always traveled to the same spot. Although he was improving, Conkay has yet to perfect his timing. He hurried into the lecture room. The room resembled a large movie theater equipped with rows of cushioned seats. The seats faced a stage hidden behind long burgundy curtains. It was crammed packed with students, medical doctors, and research scientists. They held paper, pens, pencils, recording devices, or notebook computers.

The lecture was imminent. Conkay spotted an empty seat through drapes decorating a small balcony. On his way up, he noticed a man sitting where Conkay often sat. As usual, the man dropped his notebook. But this time, it fell at Conkay's feet. And, instead of saying what Conkay always heard him say, 'Damn it,' the man said, "Forgive my clumsiness."

"At least I didn't step on it. Here let me get that for you." Conkay picked up the notebook and handed it to the man.

"Thank you, sir."

"You're welcome." Conkay nodded. He hurried to the balcony, tied the drapes out of his way, then sat down. He scanned the auditorium for the **Shadow** and thought, "I'll never see the **Shadow** in this crowd." Conkay understood the risk of altering the future even from his mere interactions. But he thought no harm would come from his run-in with the librarian or the man.

The stage curtains opened. A scientist, wearing a white lab coat, stood in front of a microphone. Beside him stood doctors and assistants dressed in white and wearing gloves. Next to them was a bed covered by thick glass, airtight for decontamination purposes. Lying on the bed was a patient in suspended animation wearing a breathing mask. There were rubber tubes, machines, and monitors on both sides of the bed. Video cameras projected everything on large screens. This would allow the entire audience a clear view of what happens on stage. The doctors will perform a procedure called gene extraction and replacement.

The scientist explained what genes were, how they worked, and how they interacted with the body. He also explained how they extract them from blood and replace them with other genes. Conkay heard the speech one hundred times or more before, but still, he listened with passion. It was a successful innovation of medical science the realm had perfected. They implemented the procedure for those who could afford it. It saved millions from diseased genes. It was like magic, but a different kind of magic.

Conkay had noted many differences between Earth and Mageus. Although sickness didn't happen often on Mageus, when it did, whatever riches you had didn't matter. Mageons would use their innate energies, magic healing powers, charms, spells, and herbs to heal their wounded and sick. Billions of humans were unaware of the healing potentials herbs provided. They seemed to have forgotten their magic energies. This knowledge might have been hidden from them, intentionally. Conkay hadn't studied Earth's ancient history or visited enough to know. He had witnessed a small fraction of humans who used their energies for healing. But for many injuries, doctors used machines, titanium plates, rods, screws, and such. They used synthetic creams for other wounds. And, humans swallowed what they called pills for an unbelievable amount of ailments. There were countless shapes, colors, and sizes of these pills.

Conkay remembered Earth in her infancy, filled with beauty. She had trees everywhere, as far as his eyes could see. He heard animals in the distant forests, birds singing, and people laughing or talking. It felt natural. Like Mageus, the Earth's atmosphere was clear, fresh. Earth's abundant waters and fruits tasted clean. There weren't any pollutants. Earth was in balance. Everything worked together in harmony. Conkay thought that although Gob-Diggers on Mageus were filthy, they were natural beings. They unknowingly kept balance in the swamps.

Over the years, Mother Earth had suffered. She seemed sick with sadness from lack of love or no love at all, same as her waters, sick and unloved. Conkay tasted her drinking water and ate her assorted fruits and vegetables. Although they didn't taste too bad, they had a strange aftertaste, as if caught with an illness. Conkay figured this could be the reason humans had diseased genes and Mageons didn't.

Conkay liked to refer to Mageus, Earth, and other planets as 'She' or 'Mother' because they were beautiful like his mother. All the mothers he had ever known had taken care of their young. They made sure they had everything they needed to survive and live happily. He thought, "Now that's pure love."

Conkay thought about the similarities between Mageons and Humans. They had similar anatomies, inside as well as out. However, a human with a Transfigure gene was unheard of. Conkay thought about their life spans. Mageons lived longer than humans. One year to Mageons was equivalent to five Earth years to humans. Being a bit overconfident, he chuckled and muttered under his breath. "Ha-ha! We look younger, live longer, and we're wiser."

A woman sitting below the balcony in front of him heard what he said. She jerked her head around, looked up with furrowed brows, and said, "Shush!" Then she curtly turned back around. Conkay didn't say a word. He only lifted his brows and then focused on the rest of the lecture.

When the lecture was over, Conkay was eager to travel home. He wanted to learn what Gala named his dragon and was excited to know what type he had created. He remained seated until everyone left the lecture room. He stood behind the balcony's curtains and scanned the room for the **Shadow**. It was nowhere in sight. Conkay changed back into his clothes then held his hand open and muttered a word under his breath. Out of thin air, Force appeared in his hand. Twice he tapped the bottom of Force on the floor. He said the same word with each tap then choked on his breath! The **Shadow** jumped out from the curtain's folds into the warp! No sooner than they returned to Conkay's laboratory, the **Shadow** whisked out the lab's opened window. It seemed spectral. Conkay chased after it but was too late. His mind rattled, "Wicked sorcery! Where is it? Too many trees, too many shadows—I can't see—what was it up to? How often did it tag along? How much does it know—who is it—*what* is it? My traveling days are over! Damn it!" He was mad at himself for not trusting his gut feelings in the first place.

Conkay glanced over at his great ancestral clock. Its hands pointed at a different set of symbols, numbers, moons, and stars. He had been gone longer than he expected. "Damn it! Damn it! Damn it! I'll never get my timing right! I've got to tell Faithin and Gala. We'll have to secure the castle with a protective spell. The Wizard's High Council put a spell on Bridge. Besides our Bluewing friends, Bridge doesn't allow anyone to cross without clearance. Unless, of course, it's not working." Conkay paced the floor, racking his brain, wondering how the **Shadow** found its way into the castle.

 Right about that time, Wiley, a Treeager, tied his Gentalsteed to a post at the right entrance of Bridge. Treeagers have green eyes with chestnut brown freckled spots throughout. They have veins that bulge through their skin like grapevine stems and leaves. Their veins are in assorted deep greens which were unique to each Treeager. They also have soft, strong hair the same color as their veins. Most Treeagers have copper tan skin whereas others have burnt sienna or a mixture of both. Their thick skin allows them to spend the entire day outside. Treeagers tend to health-essential crops. These crops assist in keeping Mageus a healthy living planet. Treeagers do not have any known predators. They live throughout the planet and seldom venture from their homes. This was the first time Wiley had ever visited the Lakinshires and was unaware of the spell on Bridge.

 Wiley stepped onto Bridge. Bridge vibrated beneath his feet and moved like a conveyer belt. Wiley spread his arms to keep his balance while Bridge moved him back to the entrance. In a deep tonal voice, Bridge asked, "What is your name?"

Wiley jumped. He didn't see anyone. He looked left, right, and down at Bridge. He lifted his green brow, then answered, "My name is Wiley."

Bridge bellowed, "Wiley." Wiley's name, vibrated across the air, through the castle to Conkay's ears.

Conkay said, "Welcome, Wiley." His words vibrated back across Bridge.

Bridge bellowed, "Welcome Wiley."

Wiley's eyebrows turned inwards and upwards. His chin lifted to his pressed lips. He thought, "Hum. Okay. I think I can cross now." He shrugged his shoulders. He stepped forward like before. Bridge didn't move, so Wiley kept walking. It wasn't long when Conkay greeted Wiley on Bridge.

"Good morning, Wiley. Is everything okay?"

"I wasn't expecting your bridge to move, let alone speak."

"I'm sorry. I didn't think to tell you. The only time Bridge doesn't ask for names is during our celebrations or gatherings."

"No harm."

"Would you like to come inside?"

"No thank you. I haven't time. Urgent matters arose. I have to make haste and travel to the east. I'll be back when our closest moon is full. My neighbors will keep an eye on my place while I'm away, so there's no need for you to check in on me."

"Thanks for letting us know. Is there anything I can do?"

"Oh no, thank you though. You're a great wizard and much appreciated, but the urgency isn't something a wizard can fix. My cousin, Vine, her newborn died. She hasn't been herself since. The midwife had to pry the child from Vine's arms."

"I'm so sorry. At least I can do something for you on your journey. Although you have no known predators, Gentalsteed's do, so I want you to take these." Using Sorcermizic language, Conkay summoned his wand, "*Appara Comforte*" POOF! It appeared out of thin air. He pointed the tip of his wand in the palm of his other hand and said, "*Char pro ect*," which meant protection charm. After four charms appeared in his hand, Conkay concealed his wand. POOF! It vanished from his hand. Then he handed the charms to Wiley. "If you feel threatened, eat a charm, and give one to your Gentalsteed. The charms will keep you hidden long enough for you to find safety. The effects last for an hour."

"Thank you."

"Let us know when you return."

"I will. Thanks again for the charms. Please send my blessings to Acub and Ashlin. See you soon." Wiley bowed.

"I'll be sure to tell them. Farewell, Wiley." Conkay bowed and watched Wiley ride away before returning to his laboratory. Then it dawned on him. "Bridge worked for Wiley but didn't or couldn't detect the **Shadow**. Maybe the **Shadow** never stepped onto Bridge. It had to have glided across, or it entered through another entrance like the window it had glided out of."

The castle's back door worked in the same manner as Bridge. As soon as anyone touched it, the door asked them their name. No one could enter unless one of the Lakinshires gave their permission. Conkay decided to include Bridge in the protective spell. He thought, "I wonder if this castle has hidden passages that I'm unaware of. I'll have to explore, but later, not today, no time." Then he shook his head, squinched up his face, and concluded, "On second thought, there can't be any. I'm sure The High Council would have told us. Damn it!" He raised his brows. At that moment, Conkay realized something. He knew he was overconfident while comparing his wits to humans. Although he acquired useful knowledge, he also picked up cuss words. Conkay knew he made, at least minor, alterations not only to his realm but to others as well. He could no longer time travel, not the way he had been at any rate. While waiting on Faithin and Gala to return, he tidied his laboratory.

Confession

After Conkay heard his loves enter the castle, he called them to join him. Gala gulped hard and followed behind his mother. A worried attack chilled his bones. His nerve-racking thoughts questioned how his father would react. Would he be unrelenting? Will he understand his and his mother's near-death experience with the monstrous spider? Would he blame the incident on Gala's carelessness and lack of study? On entering the lab, Gala saw his father immersed in concern. "Have a seat. I have something important to confess." Conkay pointed his wand with a stiff arm at the floor. He moved his wand up, down, and sideways drawing them a chair. It's called, wand drawing, but Conkay wasn't particularly good at it and didn't do much of it. Gala was the artist. Wand drawings were those drawn on atoms in the air. They only lasted for about an hour before they began to fade back into their natural existence.

Faithin and Gala looked at each other. They sat on their wand-drawn seats then looked up at Conkay. While pacing the floor, Conkay blurted out his confession. It came out in one breath like Gala usually does when excited, anxious, or nervous. "I didn't want to tell you when I first felt it because I thought I was imagining things. But I wasn't. I did feel something, and I saw it today. It's been happening off and on for about a year. I've felt a strange presence, as if something or someone has been watching me. I felt it in the library and the den. But I usually felt it here in the lab. I brushed the feeling off because I thought I was only paranoid for practicing the art. And—" Conkay stopped pacing, stopped speaking. Sweat drenched his clothing. He took off his burgundy cloak and handed it to his rack. His rack held out its arm. It grabbed Conkay's cloak and hung it on an empty peg. Conkay turned around. He took a deep breath then let it out slowly. He looked over at his wife. She was wearing consternation from her face to her crossed arms down to her tapping foot. Conkay gulped hard. Although reluctant, he continued, "I know you don't like it Faithin, but I've been time and realm traveling."

Gala's eyes popped wide, and his mother's foot stopped tapping.

Faithin uncrossed her arms. She clenched her fists. Her voice had a mixture of concern and disappointment, "Conkay Chiefler Lakinshire! In the name of the giver of goodness, life, and love, how could you—"

"I know. I know," Conkay interrupted Faithin. "I'm sorry, but there's no time for that now. We must focus on guarding the castle and Bridge. You can scold me later." His bottom lip curved upwards. His head tilted; his shoulders drooped. He pleaded, "Please?"

Gala was more curious than scared; he thought, "Magic wonders! I can't believe it. Time and realm travel?" He asked, "What did you see, Father?"

Conkay sought approval from Faithin before he answered Gala. He puckered and smacked her a kiss through the air. She rolled her eyes and gave a head gesture for Conkay to go ahead and answer their son. Conkay regained his posture, turned towards Gala, and said, "I saw a **Shadow**. I'm not sure how long or how often it has been lingering around. Have either one of you felt a presence, a strange feeling that eyes were watching you?"

"No sir. I haven't."

"Neither have I." Faithin gave her head one shake from side to side. She pressed her lips together, hard, and held her brows in an angry V-shape.

"Then it has only been me. It must want something from me. Until I, or we, can figure out what, or who it is, we'll be extra careful, and I will NOT do any more time and realm traveling."

"When will you stop, now, forever, is this it for you?"

"Yes, my sweet, precious gem."

"Don't you 'sweet, precious gem,' me. Are you being truthful?" She squinted her darting eyes, crossed her arms, and tapped her foot.

"Yes. This is it for me." Conkay looked into her eyes. Then he looked into Gala's. He switched back and forth while he made his pledge, "I promise both of you that I will no longer time and realm travel. Okay?" He reached out, took Faithin's hand in his, and pulled her up from her seat. Their eyes locked. She could see he was sincere and worried, so she accepted his apology. Conkay pulled her to him. When they embraced, they could feel Gala watching, so they reached their hands out to him. Gala came into his parents and gave a group hug.

Conkay kissed Faithin on her tender lips then patted Gala on his shoulder and said, "Let's get started. We'll bring the celebration inside the castle.

Our *Protection* spell will allow anyone attending tonight's celebration to enter. If someone tries to enter who is not on our guest list, Bridge and the back door will ask for names." Conkay started to hand his crystal ball and pedestal to Faithin. He cupped her shoulder with his free hand. He was tentative with his instructions, "Please lock these in the chamber next to the holding crate. Oh yes, to shrink the crystal ball or its pedestal, say or think of the word *Downsize*. And do not to use the *Shink* spell on anyone. Animate beings are far different than solid objects. Gala, if you prefer, you can say *Swink* in place of *Downsize*." Everyone smiled because when Gala was four years old, he had cast that spell on his toy dragons. He didn't even know he was casting a spell. Conkay continued, "To return them to their natural state, think or say, *Natural State*."

Gala grinned and asked, "And I can say, *No Mo Swink*?" Gala's parents laughed.

"Yes, you can say *No Mo Swink*." Conkay reached over and rubbed Gala's head. "Now, if you want to see someone, face your palms down over the ball. Move your hands in a circular motion, and at the same time, ask the crystal to show you who it is you want to see. It will only show those you know, those you have met. And, it will never show anyone doing private things.

"You mean like personal hygiene, intimacy, or anything of that nature."

"Yes, my gem. And currently, you cannot hear anything or anyone. And, although you can see them, you cannot see much of their surroundings.

It's a work in progress. When you're done, just tell it to *Sleep,* Understand?"

Faithin gave a yes nod.

Gala answered, "Yes sir."

"Faithin, my gem, I also need you to bring me the guest list and the Spells-Charms book. Oh yes, we'll scratch Wiley from the list. He had to travel east and won't be here for the celebration. I gave him our last four protection charms. We'll need to make more when we have the time."

"Okay, will do," Faithin said as she tried to take the crystal and its pedestal from Conkay. He wouldn't let go. She looked up and saw his sorrowful eyes. She put her hand on his cheek, gave him a reassuring kiss, and said, "I love you always, no matter what."

"I love you too, always, no matter what." He released his hold of the crystal and pedestal. He cupped Faithin's shoulders with both hands then leaned close to her face until their lips touched. Their eyes closed. Conkay caressed Faithin's lips with his tongue, tasting her sweetness. Faithin reciprocated. Their lips and tongues mingled in tender ecstasy. Before getting carried away, Faithin gave Conkay a few quick pecks. She slowly pulled back to gaze into his eyes. He winked; after she returned the wink, she carried out her tasks. Conkay turned towards Gala and coached, "Son, help me gather all the items we need for the *Protection* spell. I want you to place them here on the table." Conkay wrote down everything he needed Gala to collect. After he handed him the list, he put his hand on his shoulder and said, "Son,

I haven't forgotten your accomplishments. I want to hear about your dragon."

Faithin stopped at the threshold of the lab's doorway and turned to look at Gala. She winked at him and interjected, "Let's just keep our focus on the *Protection* spell for now. We'll talk about our experience after we're done." Gala and Conkay nodded in agreement. Faithin turned and walked across the hall. She passed the den and walked into the library where they kept their Spells-Charms book. It was hidden behind shelves of books in a confined compartment under lock and key.

Faithin reached for the key, but it wasn't hanging on its hook and the door was open. Her pounding heart fell into her stomach. She remembered Gala had used the book when he was looking for the reverse spell to *Growsce Magna*. She immediately  turned. When she saw them on the table, she put her hand on her chest. She looked up, shook her head, and thought, "Thank the giver of goodness, life, and love! My sorcery! We cannot leave this unattended!" Faithin used both hands to pick up the cumbersome book then rested it on her hip to help her left arm hold it in place. She snatched the key, hung it up, and after slamming the hidden door shut, she marched into the den.

She grabbed the guest list off the end table next to her chair and placed it inside the book. While she muttered, she would either shrug her shoulders, bend her arm, or twist her hand in all directions.

Like Conkay and Gala, Faithin almost didn't come up for air as she ranted. "We'll have to rehearse, do some drills, simulations that seem real, so Gala can get into the habit of keeping the book locked up, at least concealed on him. We need to cast a *Lock* spell on the book. I'm sure he'll get the hang of it. He has to get his confidence back. Now, we're worrying about a mysterious **Shadow** lurking about and why was it following Conkay? He'd better not time travel if he knows what's good for him, for everyone! We have the celebration tonight." Faithin looked up, lifted her arm into the air, and chided, "Oh, my sorcery! I can't worry! I have to remain focused on the task in front of me—one thing at a time." She took in three deep breaths trying to regain her composure before returning to the lab.

Good to Know

After Gala set the items his father wanted on the table, Conkay showed Gala a magical frame. The frame held a picture Conkay got from Earth.

"Son, this frame belonged to our ancestors and has magical properties. The frame allows me to enter any picture or painting it holds."

Gala raised his brows. "What? Magical frame? Enter?"

"Yes. I'll show you in a minute. After I enter, everything in the picture becomes real. It'll do the same for anyone who enters. This picture is of a laboratory on Earth. It's filled with tables, beds, and machines where human scientists study genes. To be precise, it's where they extracted genes from someone's blood and replaced blood with other genes."

"Gene extraction—picture—human scientists? I thought that was a painting of weird-looking beds and other weird-looking stuff. What's a picture? What's gene extraction? What are human scientists?"

"I'll explain everything when our time is more convenient. For now, I want to show you how to use this frame. After that, put it on one of your paintings. Okay?"

"Okay."

"Don't be alarmed when I'm no longer standing here. Instead, look for me inside the picture."

"Okay."

Conkay touched the corner of the frame. POOF! He disappeared. Gala squinted, scanning the picture. "Wizard wonders, there you are, Father! I see you! You shrank! Can you hear me?" Gala slapped his hands down on his knees and laughed.

"Yes. I can hear you. How do I sound?"

"Your voice sounds squeakier and not so loud! What about me? What do I sound like?"

"Your voice sounds deeper and like you're talking slower." Conkay touched the back side of the frame from within the picture. Before Gala knew it, his father was standing next to him.

"Goodness giver of life and magic to boot, that's total mystics! I can't get over it! You looked like you were part of the picture, same size, texture, everything!"

"Oh yeah, it's a lot of fun, all right. But, it can be dangerous too." He removed the picture and handed the frame to Gala. Conkay put his picture in a similar frame without magic properties. As he hung it on the wall, he told Gala, "After you put the frame on your painting, touch the corner of the fame and wish to enter. When you do, you're inside your painting."

Gala brushed his fingers across the intricate carvings of the frame. He asked, "Do you have to touch a corner when you wish to go in? Will any corner allow entrance or what?"

"Yes, touch any corner. And yes, doesn't matter, wishing or saying aloud will let you in."

"What's it like inside? Does it feel strange or awkward?"

"It feels just as real as it feels right here."

"Do you get out the same way you get in?"

"No. To get out, touch anywhere on the back side of the frame and think of the word 'Return.' You must think about it, not say it. Also, after you enter, whatever your frame faces that's what you'll see. In other words, if you're in the painting the frame holds, and the painting is facing your bed, then you'll see your bed."

"Mystique wonders! Thanks, Father! Can you bring things that are part of the painting out with you?"

"You're welcome, and no. Only that which is not part of the picture or painting can come out through the frame. You can bring something or someone in with you. All you need to do is touch whatever you want to enter before you touch the corner of the frame. That also goes for coming back out. Understand?"

"Yes sir."

"Don't tell anyone about this frame. Not even Ddot. Your mother and I, now you, are the only ones who know. As I mentioned, it can be dangerous, especially if someone goes in and doesn't know how to get back out. Do we have a deal?"

"Yes sir, we do. Don't worry. This will definitely remain our secret."

"Listen carefully Son. If you're inside your painting and the frame gets damaged, you're stuck until I can create another frame. If you're in the painting and the frame is removed, you're also stuck until the painting is put back in the frame. Do you understand?"

"Yes sir. If two people went inside your picture and they had that gene extraction thing done, would they be okay?"

"That's a good question. I believe it would be safe because the genes are part of the two individuals. However, if they got genes from someone who was part of the picture, they might return without those genes. One day we'll see all the things the frame can do. Okay?"

"Yes sir. I can't wait. It's gonna be fun."

"I agree. Go on ahead and put it up. Bring a couple of stools for you and your mother on your way back. Okay now. Off with you. No lollygagging or daydreaming about. We have a *Protection* spell to create."

"Yes sir." Gala hurried to his room. He took his painting from above his fireplace and placed it inside the frame. After he hung his frame and painting, he hurried to the kitchen and grabbed two stools. He returned to the lab seconds before his mother returned.

Faithin set the Spells-Charms book on its podium. She removed the guest list and opened the book to the *Protection* spell. "This spell requires a potion along with a verbal incantation. It says here that if penetrated by extreme heat or cold, the spell will weaken and break. Let's hope that doesn't happen." Faithin thumbed through the book, cover to cover. "There's nothing here about a **Shadow**. It could be a dark spell from Magic of Menace, better known as Dark Magic. We haven't heard anything about Dark Magic since the Great Battle of Dragon Slayers."

"I'm guessing Magic of Menace is wicked. Right Father, Mother?"

Faithin answered, "Yes. Although we know about it, it's something we DO NOT practice."

"Your mother and I DO NOT have any of the Dark Magic incantations. It's said that owning anything dark or that contains Dark Magic can affect the owner's mind, body, and spirit. It can make them unruly, irritable, wicked, and downright spiteful."

"Do we have anything to worry about? Can our Magic of Light defeat Magic of Menace?"

"Yes!" both his parents answered, and then looked at each other.

"You explain my Love, while I complete the potion part of our *Protection* spell."

"Dark Magic mixed with the Magic of Light can be a great tool in defeating wickedness. However, it can be quite precarious to dabble in. It's best never to own anything that contains Dark Magic. Your mother and I have seen good turn evil just from owning a tiny piece of cloth used for Dark Magic. Only good sorcerers strong in confidence, heart, and spirit experiment and learn it. They need to be compassionate, understanding, and love must be their ruler. They must be stern. They must have wisdom, intelligence, and have the right motives— good intentions."

Faithin added, "Moreover, they cannot have children that have not reached maturity. If it got into a child's hands, no telling what could happen."

"Your mother's right. This is one reason we stay clear of it. Do you understand?"

"Yes sir. I'll always remember it. Why is there Dark Magic?"

"There are Mageons who can perform magic without having the mystique gene. There are those, like us, who can perform magic because it's innate. The mystique gene flows in our blood, which makes our magic stronger than those without the gene. We are true mystics. Whether it flows in your blood doesn't matter, it's how you use magic that matters. Everyone has motives, good or bad. Using magic to get what you want is okay, if your motives are pure. You also know the rules. We do not cast spells on others unless we have consent or it's for a darn good reason. When used for good, it is the Magic of Light. If you tell a trivial lie to protect others from panic, or any type of harm, you mixed good with bad but for good reasons. Therefore, it isn't Dark Magic. However, to answer your question, Dark Magic occurs when magic is used for ill intent."

"Tell Gala what happened to one of the wizards on The High Council."

"That's a good example, my gem. Many years ago, a mage, Grock Faraway, sat with the wizards of The High Council. He met a beautiful sorceress named Tamian. Grock became obsessed with her. He wanted her to love him. However, she loved someone else and they soon wed. Faraway became angry. Riddled with jealous rage and lust, he couldn't contain himself. He practiced magic to control others. Every successful incantation he performed made him more ruthless. He created his book of magic spells. He tried to steal Tamian's love. But his spells did not win him her heart. Faraway became a desperate necromancer. He raised his father from beyond the grave seeking his help. It worked. Faraway won Tamian's love, but only through magic. Tamian left her husband to be with Grock. She changed. Because Faraway used his magic with wrong intentions, it became dark. His spells cursed. The High Council found his book of spells, learned of his contempt, and his forbidden act of raising the dead. They offered Faraway a chance to redeem himself. He had to destroy his book, surrender his lust for power, and take the spell off Tamian. But he refused the offer. He accused The High Council of being jealous. Crock and Tamian plotted to take over The Wizard's High Council. But, The High Council anticipated the attack. Therefore, their wands were ready. They used Magic of Light and a spell from Faraway's book to counteract the attack. The High Council was able to banish the Faraways into the Boggy Swamps. All their possessions, including Grock's book, went with them. And any child born of Grock's blood was also banished. The last time anyone saw the Faraways was during the Great Battle of Dragon Slayers. The battle extended over the swamp's boundaries enabling the Faraways to join. They helped the Dragon Slayers kill dragons, their keepers, and their riders. No one has heard from or seen the Faraways since that battle."

"Did you guys fight in the battle?"

"No," Faithin said.

Conkay explained, "No. Your mother was with child, you, so we stayed safe at home in Whittlewood Forest."

Gala rattled on with more questions almost in one breath. He used his hands to talk, occasionally he shrugged his shoulders and furrowed his brows. Sometimes he tilted his head and gave a few little nods. "So, what you're saying is that Dark Magic is just magic used for wrong motives, ill intentions, and yet you can use Dark Magic with the Magic of Light for good, and it was good to banish the Faraways into the Boggy Swamps —where all foul, evil, creatures like creepy Gob-Diggers, nasty Nixies, Harpies, or those blood-sucking Gurgling Mudlumps, Sharp Teeth Gullies, or those other flesh gobblers lurking and flying about dwell— although the sorceress was under the necromancer's and Faraway's spell, and Faraway himself could have gotten better if only he converted himself back to being a good wizard?"

Gala's parents chuckled at how fast and longwinded Gala spoke. His forgiving spirit pleased them. Yet, his father advised, "Son, it's good to forgive, but remember, trust is something earned. So yes, yes, yes, and yes it was good to banish them there. Our realm would not be a pleasant place to live if Faraway got the chance to rule."

"That's for sure! I don't even want to imagine the chaos that would befall those under the rule of a contemptible mage."

"I agree with your mother. So, Son, we encourage you to always have good motives before or during, or anytime you perform magic. Do not, I repeat, do not use Dark Magic until you completely understand it. If you were to find a book of Dark Magic, it would be best to destroy it if you can."

"What do you mean by, 'if you can?'"

"Some books have *Protection* spells. No one can cast those spells except under certain conditions. And, you can only destroy them in specific ways. The best thing to do is to stay away from Dark Magic. Agreed?"

"Yes sir."

After Conkay rubbed Gala's head, he walked over to a counter and began polishing Force. Faithin smiled as she went back to mixing ingredients. Gala sat down at the bench, summoned his magic pen, Inkle, short for Inklewrite, and began to doodle.

Faithin thought about Gala leaving their Spells-Charms book unattended. Without bringing this fact to Conkay's attention, she suggested, "Talking about *Protection* spells. It's a good idea we put one on our Spells-Charms book. We know anything is possible and we don't want to take anything for granted. We could put the *Protection* spell on our book and the key to the hidden door. One of us might accidentally leave the door open and forget to lock up the book."

Gala's head popped up. He held his breath, but when he saw his mother put her finger to her pursed lips and give her head a quick shake, he relaxed.

"So, Love. Don't you think that's a good idea?"

"That's a wise decision, precious gem of mine. I know the exact ingredients for that spell." Conkay blew Faithin a sweet kiss. She blew one back then Conkay turned to gather supplies to create a protection lock for their book.

"Gala, sweetheart, one more thing about Dark Magic, I'm not an admirer. I don't care if it's understood and you have good intentions, I just want you to stay away from it, plain and simple. This way we'll all be able to sleep, soundly. Do you understand that?"

"Yes ma'am. Don't worry, Mom. I was only wondering. Besides, I doubt that'll ever happen."

In unison, Conkay and Faithin raised their voice and said, "Good!"

"Son, we're still learning. Remember what your mother said. Anything is possible. Never take anything for granted."

"I'll remember, Father. I've been learning a lot these days."

Conkay set all the ingredients for their book's *Protection* spell on his workbench. He walked over and gave Gala a few pats on his shoulder and said, "Don't stop. Even when you think you've learned it all, you haven't, so keep learning."

"Yes sir."

"Okay, the potion's ready, let's zip-zap to it. Bring your wands. Conkay, shrink Force to fit in the container. It says here we have to hold them while they're submerged in the solution and read the incantation at the same time."

Gala's body stiffened and his hands became clammy. "How, I mean, what if I mess it up and things go wrong and—"

"Calm down, Son; this spell isn't like other spells. Your mother and I, including you, can't mess it up. It'll work. Our magic tools will soak up the solution; we will read the incantation; the spell will be intact. Therefore, when you point your wand and begin speaking, the words to the spell will roll off your tongue. It's automatic."

"Mystic wonders! I wish all spells were like that."

Conkay paused, gave Gala a stern stare, and changed his tone down to a slow reprimand. "They're just like the ones you have done in the past. Regardless of lost confidence, regardless of acquired nightmares, learn the words. Practice, study, visualize, feel it, and believe in yourself. Do I make myself clear?"

Before he tucked his head and looked away from his father's debilitating stare, Gala answered, "Yes sir. I will, Father. I promise." Gala thought, "I'd better because if I don't, I'm dead wizard meat! Father isn't as lenient as Mother, and she can be tough." Gala wished he didn't have nightmares and wished he had the confidence he had a year ago.

While Conkay shrank Force, Faithin reached her arm out, waving her hand for Gala to join them. "Dear sweet fella of ours, it'll be all right. Come on."

Gala joined his parents. They held their magic tools in the azure-colored potion while resting a free hand on the container's rim. Each Lakinshire read the incantation. After a few seconds, the potion started to bubble. Their magic tools drank the potion in equal amounts until there was no more to drink. Conkay lifted his tools and permitted Faithin and Gala to use them. Faithin and Gala did the same. They read more from the book, and when they finished, they walked outside to the entrance of Bridge.

They pointed their wands straight up, following the instructions they had read. Their wands turned from their original color, burnt sienna with a sunset orange tint, to azure. From each tip, their unique energies shot out. Faithin's energy was sparkling gold dust particles. Gala's energy was a sparkling gold light, and Conkay's was a rainbow light. Their energies combined above Bridge and created part of the *Protection* spell. They pointed their wands downwards towards Bridge then upwards above the castle. The clear azure dome was taking shape. While they kept their wands pointed upwards, they walked back across Bridge. The protection dome grew as they walked around the wide walk and reached the east side of their castle. They pointed their wands to the outside bottom edge of the castle's wide walk, then above the castle. They repeated the procedure around the castle back to Bridge's entrance. The dome was sealed together and became invisible. The Lakinshire's energies stopped shooting out from the tips of their wands and resumed their natural color. The *Protection* spell was complete.

"Look! It works!" Gala pointed at a fluttery. It flew above his head and continued upwards. When it flew about twenty feet above the castle, it, and its shadow, bounced off the protective dome.

"Other than the Bluewing clan, no one, not even a **Shadow**, can enter unless they're on our guest list," Conkay noted with certainty. "Okay. Let's decorate and create a gift for Acub and Ashlin. I'll put the protective lock on our Spells-Charms book before I lock it up. And son, while we're decorating, you can practice your dragon in the great hall if you'd like. Tell me about your accomplishments this morning. What'd you name your dragon?"

Gala looked over at his mother. She answered, "His name is Redtalon. I'll tell you about our experience while we decorate. But, before I do, let me tell you this, Gala and I learned a valuable lesson."

"What? What do you mean?" Conkay furrowed his brows looking back and forth from Faithin to Gala. Gala kept his eyes on his mother.

Faithin reached over, touched her husband's cheek to keep his eyes on hers then said, "I'll explain while we decorate. For now, just know that we will not, I repeat, we will not make the same mistakes we made this morning. Furthermore, Gala cannot practice in the castle. His Redtalon will not fit in the great hall. His dragon form is impressively massive. He'll have to practice on the wide walk or do his red ruby instead. Gala, show your father your sketch."

Gala reached inside his pocket, pulled out his sketch, and handed the worn parchment to his father. His dad's entire mannerism changed from tense, about ready to jump down Gala's throat, to calm. Conkay smiled and praised, "Wow! This is an impressive drawing, Son. Redtalon is a great name, too. But, what's this red ruby? That's new."

"Yes," Faithin interjected. "That's part of our experience this morning. So, when I tell you about it, I want you to understand." Faithin looked at her husband with an unyielding stare.

"Faithin, as you know, I've made some grave mistakes. You're both safe and right here with me. I just hope my time traveling hasn't harmed us. I should have listened to my gut feelings. Believe me, I'll understand. I tell you what. If you want, you and Gala can tell me about your morning experience during story time tonight. We'll tell Acub and the rest of the clan about the **Shadow** tomorrow. I don't want to worry them while they celebrate their soul mate joining and coronation. This is their night and I want it to be a meaningful happy one, unforgettable."

"I agree," said Faithin.

"Me too," added Gala.

"Also, no one, not even Ddot is to know of my ability to time and realm travel. Okay?"

"Okay, Father. I won't tell anyone."

"Good. Tell Acub to meet you at the kitchen door when the sun is half a measure above the western trees. Tell him we won't be setting the platforms under the orchard canopy. Instead, we're moving the celebration inside the castle. Also, tell him we have the decorations under control. All they need to do is get ready for the ceremonies. If he asks why, tell him your father said he would explain tomorrow, and then hurry back. Also, when our guests arrive, tell them the celebration is inside."

"Okay, Father. I'll be right back." Gala transfigured into his Bluewing form and flew to the Bluewing's cave. After he told Acub his father's plans, he hurried back to help his parents.

Unfriendly Guest

Gala and his parents finalized their gift for Acub and Ashlin. Conkay locked it up with their Spells-Charms book in the door behind the shelves of books in the library. He returned to the great hall to help his loves finish decorating. They filled a long table with fruits, vegetables, and nuts. They filled enchanted pitchers with three different kinds of juice. They set the pitchers on another table. Gala placed several jugs of Fairy Honey along the long table. Faithin used a spell to add napkins, cups, and condiments that their guests might need. Gala reached for a pitcher to pour himself a cup of juice. The enchanted pitcher's handle turned into an arm, reached out, and slapped his hand. "Ouch!" Gala jerked his hand back and dropped the cup in the process. The slap didn't hurt as much as it startled him.

The pitcher's hand pointed its finger upwards, moving it side to side to say, "No, no, no."

Faithin laughed. "Go ahead. Get yourself a drink. Tell the pitcher what juice you want, and then let the pitcher pour it for you."

After the pitcher poured Gala a drink, Gala walked back over to the stage. The rays from the evening sun shone a golden light through the beveled glass window panes. Elongated diamond shadows stretched across the hall. Conkay used his wand to light the last candle on the chandeliers. Faithin used her wand to fashion enough enchanted benches to seat one hundred guests. Gala finished decorating the stage with curtains of soft pink and violet flowers. He dared not use magic for fear he would flub things up. The flowers swayed to sweet music coming from an enchanted harp. Gala packed flowers in a thick circle. He staggered them upwards at different levels against the back wall of the stage for seating. In the middle of the stage, he placed two miniature willow-like plants in decorative pots. The plants formed an archway of white flowers. Tiny violet flutteries flew from one flower to the next, keeping rhythm with the harp. After Gala closed the flowered curtains, he heard Bridge announce their first guests.

 Inkle and the guest list were on a tall slender table next to a matching stool outside the front doors. While Inkle lifted from the table to put a green checkmark by the guests' names, Gala propped open the doors. He welcomed, "Come on in. Glad you could make it. We're holding the celebration indoors. Mother and Father are inside. Make yourselves known; I hope you have fun." Gala sat on the stool. When the guests walked past, he thought, "Ah ha. There go a few jolly wizards that don't live far from us. They're older wizards of wisdom. I don't think they have much magic; I don't think they have wands or wizard robes. They do know some fascinating tricks and are wearing bright-colored clothing. They're more like court jesters than wizards." Gala chuckled but cut it short because he figured his magic wasn't going to win any kind of wizard's prizes or trophies. He swallowed his pride and became humbled quickly.

Gala spotted something flying in from the distance. As it approached, he could see three white-winged Gentalsteeds pulling a rounded carriage. Gentalsteeds resemble giraffes without spots. Their necks were much shorter. Most Gentalsteeds had diverse colors and were born without wings. Gala didn't look down to see Inkle check off the guests' names. He thought out loud, "Now that's the way to make an entrance!"

The dark metallic-blue carriage had rounded corners adorned in white trim. The wheels were dark blue, also trimmed in white with white wings. After the carriage landed, the wheel's wings folded down. The coachman was a tall Elfkie. Gala lifted his brows and thought, "That's the tallest Elfkie I've ever seen and talk about looking sharp! I've never seen one dressed so nice."

Elfkies were humble, loyal creatures who could do many things to keep a home running. Most Elfkies live in the forests. They have large round eyes that change color to their surroundings. Branch-like extremities stick out from their bark-like skin. These attributes keep them camouflaged while they forage. If a predator is near, an Elfkie will stop moving. The predator can't smell them or see them.

Gala examined the coachman. He wore a dark blue, tall-brimmed hat over his round ears. His cloak and suit matched. They sparkled in the sunset's light. His boots were pure white, his reins, dark blue.

The coachman had laid his extremities flat, hidden under his suit. He drove his team of

Gentalsteeds a little past the castle's doors to stop the carriage in front of Gala. Another Elfkie was sitting on the back of the carriage. He was a footman dressed the same as the driver. He was much shorter, about as short as all the Elfkies Gala has ever met. The footman used his left hand, which had three fingers and one thumb, to pull down steps tucked under the carriage.

After the footman stepped up and opened the carriage door, Gala's eyes widened. To his surprise, an enchantress stepped out. Gala thought, "It's Lidee! She's beautiful, and so is her daughter, Floreena. I hope she's—" Right before he finished his sentence, he saw her; his heart thumped. "Oh, my wizard wonders there she is! For the sake of beauty, she has blossomed."

Gala pointed out every detail. She and her mother dressed alike. They wore dark blue gowns with speckles of silver and gold throughout. Their sparkling gowns hung close to their shapely bodies. Their gowns fanned out to the floor; their hems trimmed in white lace. They looked like slender Bellflowers covering their white short-heeled shoes. Their sleeves were the exact length of their arms and trimmed in lace. At the base of their wrists, their sleeves were loose and wavy. The bottom parts of their sleeves extended down a bit longer. The delicate white lace trimmed their scooped necks, as well. Floreena and her mother had thick, long white hair that swayed as they walked with poise and grace. They wore silver and gold circlets imbued with gems secured in place by tiny braids.

Gala's strict gaze attended to Floreena. "She's irresistible! Her white skin no doubt feels softer than Furhoppers' fur. Her shapely lips are pink and thin. I bet they taste sweeter than fairies' honey. Her thick curly white lashes; her big eyes; her dark, big, blue, beautiful eyes steal my heart. They twinkle in the light. Her smile, her gorgeous smile, it makes me melt. Goodness giver of life and love, she's the most mesmerizing sight to gaze at!" Gala seemed hypnotized in love.

Floreena and her mother turned to thank and wave goodbye to the Elfkies. Lidee exclaimed, "We'll send for you if or when we need you."

Both Elfkies waved back. The coachman whispered to the winged Gentalsteeds. They, along with the wheels, spread their wings and flew in the direction from where they came. Faithin walked out to greet Lidee and Floreena. They exchanged hugs, then turned towards Gala and said hello. Nothing would come out of his mouth. All he could do was nod with a smile stuck to his face. Faithin chuckled. She led her guests through the castle's front entrance while Gala sat and stared. He thought about the first time his mother met Lidee, how instant they took to each other. They had a lot in common. Faithin was always interested in the magical fabric of Lidee's clothes. Both loved to sew. Gala wondered if Floreena liked to sew. Right about then, Floreena turned back to look at Gala. He was taken aback. "Oh, my wizard wonders! She just winked at me! What? What's this? Father pushed my chin up! I can't believe it! Seriously! How embarrassing! I bet she's laughing at me! I must have looked ridiculous hanging my mouth wide open! That's why she winked! Gee wizard-bum! Did I drool? Mystic magic, hide me!" Gala turned away. He wiped his mouth in case of slobber. He focused his attention on greeting the rest of the guests who began pouring in.

While Gala waited for the last of the guests to arrive, he could hear the merriment coming from inside. Guests were talking, laughing. Children played, but after fifteen minutes, outside had become still and quiet. Gala looked at the guest list and thought, "There's only three unchecked. I guess they're a no-show. Fine by me. No sweat off—" A loud whistling wind caught Gala's ear; a dark twirling twister came roaring across Bridge. The wind whipped Gala's clothes and hair around. It blew the guest list up off the table. Gala reached up and snatched the list, held it down, and watched Inkle check off the guest's name. "Oh no," Gala thought as his stomach sank. He looked up. Helsin calmed his winds so Gala could see him. Helsin's hair nor his clothes moved about in his *Twirlwind* spell. Helsin slanted his eyes and wore a half-smirking grin. Gala was not impressed with Helsin's pretentious behavior. "Good evening Helsin. Are you alone or will your aunt and uncle be coming?"

Before exhausting himself, Helsin stopped his spell. His black cloak, clothes, nor his sandy color hair were out of place.

"Hello, Gala. No. I seldom see my aunt. As for my uncle, he's hardly worth spending time with. He's indulging in a wiz-forsaken drink tonight. He calls it 'Wiz-Bonker.' Ever since he discovered

Wiz-Bonker, he hasn't done much else. I don't need him to hold my hand. He can stay indulged."

"Oh. Okay then. So, how have you been?" Gala was being polite; he watched Inkle put a red X by Helsin's aunt's and uncle's names.

"Could be better I suppose; hope this isn't a waste of my time. I could be elsewhere practicing and perfecting my mystique powers. How about you? Will you be performing any new TRICKS tonight?" Helsin smirked with a sarcastic grin. He stroked his newly grown mustache. It grew around his lips down to his clean-cut sandy colored beard.

Gala thought, "You could leave, you aren't really welcome. He caught himself before he got carried away by his gruesome imagination. Gala replied, "I might perform a 'trick' as you put it. But Helsin, I'm interested in Acub and Ashlin having a fantastic ceremony. Wouldn't you agree that this is their night?" Gala clenched his fists.

Seeing Gala's irritation pleased Helsin with another smirking grin. "Of course, you're right. I hope they have a wonderful night." He nodded his head and turned, combing the room for an empty seat. "Think I'll sit next to Floreena. She gets sexier every time I see her; wouldn't you agree? I hope you don't mind." He turned back around and saw flame throwers in Gala's eyes. "If your eyes could shoot fireballs, I'd be ashes. May the best wizard win." He gave Gala a sarcastic bow and headed toward Floreena.

"Helsin!"

Helsin stopped and turned back towards Gala. "What do you want, Gala?"

"Why are you angry at me? I thought we were friends?"

"Gala, you know as well as I, jealousy and friendship do not mix. We cannot be friends when you are clearly jealous of me."

Gala pushed air out between his teeth making a shish sound then said, "I'm not jealous of you. I have never been jealous of you."

"At the last gathering, when I saved Eric from the spider and got his wings out of her web, you acted jealous."

"I wasn't jealous of you. I was angry at myself." Gala put his hand on his chest.

"Are you still feeling inadequate?"

Gala's body tensed, his face wrinkled, his lips pressed, he shook his head and snapped, "No! I don't feel inadequate! But for some reason, I'm lacking in confidence, and you know of my nightmares!"

"Yes, I know. Nightmares mean you have some type of fear. Perhaps you feel inadequacies. If so, these have made you weak and without confidence. This can only lead to destruction, and of course, whether you admit it or not, jealousy. You and I have grown apart. We can no longer be friends, especially since we share the same interests."

"What do you mean?" Gala squinted with a glaring stare.

Helsin bent his head down and brought his eyes up. He looked through his top lashes and wore a half-evil grin. He said, "We desire the beautiful Floreena. Like I said, may the best wizard win." Helsin lifted his head and turned back around. He raised his left hand. With a jerk of his wrist, he gave half a wave. Helsin walked over to the empty seat next to Floreena and bowed. Floreena gestured for him to sit.

    Gala stared at Helsin, trying to contain his anger. He put Inkle and the list in his pocket, then slammed the front doors. BAM! Everyone turned to look. "I'm sorry. Phew wee, that unexpected gust of hot air, I-I mean wind, got the best of the doors." Gala chuckled. He hurried to the kitchen. On his way, he darted a daggering glare at smirking Helsin. Gala wondered, "Why is Helsin so mean? Maybe he's right. I won't be able to win Floreena's heart with my so-called magic. I can't protect her. I'm no match against Helsin. He's even built better, taller, handsome. Floreena must think I'm a fool after she caught me staring at her with my drooling mouth hanging to the floor. Oh well. She's better off without me. She's not the one for me anyway," Gala justified as he hurried to greet the Bluewings at the kitchen's back door.

Coronation

Gala opened the kitchen's back door and transformed into his Bluewing form. He greeted the clan. Ddot was in the front of the line, grinning from ear to ear. Standing beside him was his twin brother, Dahc, whose grin matched that of his twin's. Their close friend, Eric, who is now known as Lucky, stood beside Dahc. Lucky and his parents were from another clan of fairies. A year after Lucky's parents became members of the Bluewing clan, Lucky was born.

"Hey, Chum!" Ddot reached his hand out towards Gala's.

"Hey, Bud!" Gala reached his hand towards Ddot. They did their special friendship handshake. Gala exchanged the same handshake with Dahc and Lucky. "Hey, guys! Can y'all help?"

"Certainly," Ddot said with a smile.

"At your service," offered Dahc with a bow.

"Anythin' to help a pal," agreed Lucky as he patted Gala's shoulder.

Gala thanked his friends then addressed the clan, "Okay everyone, let's get started."

The clan was excited; some were a bit restless, especially the young Newlass girls and Newlad boys. Gala explained the seating arrangements and the procedure that was about to unfold. Nobody had any questions, so he and his friends led the clan inside to the stage. Dahc and Lucky led half the clan to their seats through one side of the stage. Gala and Ddot led the other half through the door on the opposite side.

Before long, the stage filled with fairies fluttering above their seats. The sounds of their wings were in accord with the harp. Gala transformed into his natural state, walked to the front of the stage, and opened the curtains. The audience oohed. After they quieted down, Acub and Ashlin flew in from opposite sides of the stage and met under the archway. Acub wore white, leather-wrapped boots covered by his violet pant legs. He had his long-sleeve white shirt tucked in, and he wore a violet vest over his shirt. Ashlin wore a short-sleeve white bellflower dress. It had a V-neck and layers of ruffles from her tiny waist to the floor which covered her violet slipper shoes. She wore a violet scarf belt tied in a bow behind her back; the tails of her bow reached the bottom of her dress. Faithin and Lidee exchanged smiles, pleased because they tailored their clothes. The back slits of Acub's and Ashlin's garments were a perfect fit for their wings. Acub bent an elbow to Ashlin. She put her arm through his, then they faced the audience. Everyone, other than Acub, Ashlin, and Gala's parents, took their seats.

Conkay and Faithin faced the audience as they stood at the front of the stage. Conkay began, "We're happy everyone is here to help us celebrate. May Acub and Ashlin live a long, happy life. May they give birth to a Newlad, a Newlass, or both!" The audience clapped, hooted, and hollered. Ashlin giggled; her skin turned a shade pinker. Acub smiled. He hugged her, then kissed her cheek.

Faithin added, "Conkay and I have known Acub's parents, Trill and Quo, for many full moons past. Most of you know that the four of us met when we were youngsters. We became good friends while Conkay and I lived in Whittlewood Forest. It was before the four of us had any young ones of our own. It was before the Ultra Storm and before the Great Battle of Dragon Slayers. We are proud and honored to be here as part of your family. We know this is not the clan's normal way to celebrate. You are aware of the unknown circumstances to the whereabouts of Acub's parents."

Acub hung his head to hide his watery eyes. The audience wore long faces. Their mouths drooped, and they muttered with occasional drawn-out sympathy sounds of, "Aww." Ashlin reached over and hugged Acub. He looked up at her and managed a small, yet grateful smile.

Faithin continued, "We have taken the liberty to act on their behalf. You honor them, and you honor us. Thank you for accepting our invitation. So, with no objection, we give you Acub Fluttering and Ashlin Phobe!" The audience followed Faithin's lead when she applauded. She and Conkay sat down next to Gala. Gala did his best not to think or even look at Helsin sitting by Floreena. After Acub began to speak, Gala found it easier to keep his focus off Helsin. Acub and Ashlin expressed how much they love each other. They shared what happened when their eyes first met, and how they felt during that special moment. When they finished, they proclaimed their joining avowals. The congregation applauded. Gala clapped and whistled. He tried to be nonchalant as he turned to look at Floreena. Helsin seized the moment. He put his arm around Floreena's shoulders. He kept his eyes locked on Gala's while he whispered something in Floreena's ear. Gala jerked his head back around.

As the congregation continued to cheer, Acub drifted. His face turned blank, with no expression. All surrounding sounds faded from his consciousness. Acub heard nothing but his disturbing thoughts, "I wish I knew what happened to my parents. They've been gone for a year. We looked everywhere, including the old owl's hollow. There's no trace of them. I hope Gala didn't have anything to do with their disappearance. I'm ashamed that I'm even thinking he might know something. I could be wrong. But Gala lost his confidence. His newer spells are wacky. On top of that, he started having nightmares about the same time my parents disappeared. My parents wouldn't have run off, never wanting to return. They went on their moonlight tryst like always. Then they came back. Something serious could have happened to them." Acub lifted his brows at his dreadful thought then switched gears. "I could be wrong. Maybe they're living happier somewhere else. I shouldn't blame Gala especially not knowing all the facts. I'll continue to keep it to myself. I'm sure Gala's parents know there might be a connection, but they're without facts. If they knew, I'm certain they'd tell me. My parents trust the Lakinshires. They've been friends long before Gala and I were born. I must stop worryi—"

"Acub," whispered Ashlin as she gave him a tender nudge and interrupted his thoughts.

He felt her elbow push against his side. After he saw her expression, he looked out at the audience. Everyone was as quiet as a realm without life. Acub cleared his throat. With a sorrowful air, he began the coronation rights. But he couldn't speak without choking. Two adult clan members flew above his head and flapped their wings. Their wings released their glowing blue specks of calming essence over Acub. It stopped the irritating frog in Acub's throat and the interfering tears in his eyes. Acub nodded thank you before his two clan members flew back to their seats.

Acub referenced wonderful things about his parents. After he finished, a Newlad and a Newlass flew down from their seats. Faithin and Lidee made their garments the same as Acub's and Ashlin's. The two young fairies carried a violet feather pillow with a gold crown set on top. Crafted within each crown were sparkling gems. Ashlin lifted one and placed it on Acub's head, then Acub placed the other crown on Ashlin's. Ashlin hugged the two young fairies and sent them back to their seats. Acub embraced Ashlin and gave her a big long kiss. It caused the congregation to erupt into joyful jubilee. After the newly crowned couple stopped kissing, they bowed to the audience and their clan members. Everyone bowed back. While Acub and Ashlin held hands, Acub raised his free arm, balled his fist, and shouted, "Come on everybody let's party! Whoop! Whoop!"

Show Some Courage

Guests were mingling, enjoying the party. Gala was hanging with his pals, who listened to a lovely couple tell a funny story. The couple sat on a loveseat in one corner of the great hall with several chairs surrounding them. Gala sat in a chair that faced the refreshment tables while his friends sat on the arms of his chair. In the center of the great hall, between tables, there was a section for dancing. A couple of Gala's other Bluewing friends, Charmer and Saxy, had a band. They played music and sang songs that the guests asked of them. Gala scanned the mingling guests as he tried to listen to the lovely couple tell another story.

The husband started, "My wife always lights my fire. All she has to do is sit next to me. See, here she is, sitting next to me. Now watch what happens." He drew the attention of his engrossed audience to his cupped hands, one on top of the other. When he pulled his top hand upwards, a yellow-orange flickering flame appeared. As he put his hands side by side, palms up, the flickering flame split and became two flames, one in each hand. One of the flames resembled himself. The other took the shape of his wife and looked like it wore a yellow-orange Southern Belle dress. The yellow-white tip of the flickering flame that bounced around was her hair. It swayed, hissed, and sparked. The husband looked around at his audience. He could tell he had their undivided attention so continued telling his story, "I asked my wife if she'd like to dance; she accepted. This beautiful flame said she would dance with me for the rest of her life. This kindled my fire even more!" The audience oohed when they saw the husband flame bow and the wife flame curtsy. Ddot mused that the flames didn't burn the man's hands. Dahc's eyes widened when the crackling flames burned hotter and turned blue. Lucky smiled wide when he saw the husband flame put a flickering hand up, so the wife flame could place her hand in his. Then, the husband flame took his other hand and placed it on the small of her back; she put her other hand on his shoulder. The flame couple danced and twirled on the husband's palms.

 As the blue flames danced, the husband looked over at his wife. He winked; she nudged him with her shoulder and said, "Go on. Finish your story."

 The flame couple stopped dancing. The flame husband drew the flame wife close to steal a kiss. Right about then, the husband's wife stood up from her seat and cupped her hands over the flame couple. A gushing waterfall spilled down from her hands and put out the flames. She said, "I can put his fire out just as fast as I can light it."

 Everyone cracked up laughing except Gala, who was fidgety. His attention was on Floreena. Ddot saw Gala's uneasy squirming about. He encouraged, "Gala, just go ahead and ask her to dance. She keeps looking over at you. Come on, show some courage, Chum. Can't you see it? Look at her." Ddot stretched out his arm to point. "She wants you to talk to her. She wouldn't even look at you if she wasn't interested." As Ddot pulled his arm back and put his palm on his chest, he said, "Trust me."

"He's right," interjected Dahc.

"It's true," added Lucky. "Remember what happened with Charmer?"

"No," admitted Gala. "And because you're pacing the arm of the seat, I can see you're aching to tell me, so go on ahead. Tell me what happened with Charmer."

"Okie Dokie. One day, while cleanin' his harp, Charmer heard Saxy playin' soothin' sounds. She was playin' her flute, praticin' a new tune. Charmer couldn't concentrate. When he tried to go talk to her, those dag-om Tinglebugs danced in his tummy. He couldn't get up anuff courage. So, me, Dahc, and Ddot decided we oughta help. Dahc and Ddot got Charmer's attention on playin' them one of his music pieces. I flew over to Saxy and introduced myself. I told her that she played beautifully. She thanked me. Then I told her I had a friend who played the harp that they could join their music. It would be interestin' to hear, I told her. Although she knew of Charmer, they hadn't met. So, she agreed to meet him. We flew over to Charmer, whose eyes were closed like they usually were when he played. I led Saxy right in front of him. He was playin' and singin' the one called, *Eyes Meet*, the song he always loved to play because it was so relaxin' and all. Saxy had a contented smile. She listened and watched Charmer's face. When Charmer finished, his eyes opened real slow like. There was no avoidin' it. Charmer's eyes met Saxy's. Just so happened they were soul mates and are together to this day. Ya just never know what'll happen unlessin' ya try."

"Maybe that's how it works for fairies. Besides, I think Floreena is more interested in Helsin. I mean, look at 'em laughing. Helsin has better magic powers, he has more muscle, and—"

"That's all he has," Ddot interrupted. "'All brawn and no brains,' that's how I heard it said. That's a wizardly truth concerning Helsin. You have muscle and magic. You just haven't finished developing yet. Remember that Helsin's older than you. Besides, it's not muscle and magic that gets the attention of a good girl. It's more than kindness too. Just cause she's laughing doesn't mean a hill of magic shrooms. She's just being polite. I'm telling you, if she wasn't interested, she wouldn't even look at you. Come on; show some gumption; stop arguing and being so negative. Besides, what's the worst that could happen?"

Gala rolled his eyes and lashed out, "Well, if she says no, it'll please Helsin, and he'll never let it down, that's what!"

"So, what?! That would only show his smallness like I said, all brawn and no brains. And, if she can't see that, she's blind. No one wants a blind love. But you'll never know if you never try, and that could be your loss."

"Okay! Okay. I'm going." Gala swallowed hard, "gulp." With each step he took towards Floreena, his sweaty hands became clammier. He worried he might trip in front of her or fall on her. He could feel her watch his every move. As soon as he reached her, he bowed. She gave a curtsy in return.

Then Gala stuttered, "W-w-would you like t-t-to dance?"

Helsin laughed, "Ha-ha-ha! With you? Who'd want to dance with you, a feckless wannabe wizard that doesn't deserve the title?" Helsin saw that Gala wanted to bash his face in, knock his teeth down his gullet, and burn him to ash with the flamethrowers Gala held in his eyes. Floreena hurried and intervened.

"Would I?! I mean, yes! I would love to dance." Her cheeks turned a couple of shades redder. After she looked into Gala's handsome violet eyes, she got lost in a realm of romancing. Surprised and rapt, Gala offered his hand to her. She placed her hand in his then they started towards the dance floor.

Helsin turned red, embarrassed, pissed. He couldn't believe, let alone accept, that Floreena wanted to dance with Gala. In Helsin's opinion, Gala was a wizard who didn't perform great magic, a weakling. No girl, especially Floreena, wants a weak or clumsy wizard hanging around her. Helsin stuck out his foot. He wanted Gala to fall hard. To his disappointment, Gala only stumbled right into Floreena's body. They were face to face, lips almost touching, feeling each other's breath, and loving each other's scent. Floreena wanted to kiss Gala as much as he loved to kiss her. She looked past Gala straight into Helsin's eyes. Her darting stare pierced his heart. Floreena looked back at Gala, softened her gaze, and gave Gala a sweet, tender kiss on his cheek. Although ravished with enchanting delight, Gala regained his stance. He floated on a pleasant breeze, feeling as light as a fairy's wing. He thought he would never wash the kiss of sweet tender lips from his cheek. After that kiss, ignoring Helsin became easier. Gala escorted his beautiful love to the dance area holding his head high. He didn't see Helsin's turned-up lip, rolling eyes, or scouring retreat, but he did see his friends.

They had their hands cupped and shaking—switching from both sides of their heads, gesturing, "Way to go!" Gala grinned a big, contented grin. He turned back around to face his beautiful dance partner. At this point, she was his only focus.

Charmer and Saxy watched them walk to the dance area. They agreed to play one of their soothing slow dance tunes. Gala's parents and Floreena's mother exchanged glances and smiled. They were happy for Gala and Floreena.

Floreena put her left hand on Gala's right shoulder after he had put his right hand on her left hip. When he held his left hand up, Floreena placed her right hand in it. Gala led with a one-step right, one-step forward — one-step left, a one-step back — one-step right, a one-step back — one-step left, then repeated the steps. Their bodies were about four inches apart from each other.

Those who were watching smiled as the young couple danced. But Gala and Floreena felt they were the only beings alive. Without much stuttering, Gala complimented, "Y-your eyes bring out the color in your dress. Well, what I mean is that they are beyond compare. No, no..." Gala shook his head. He took a deep breath, looked into

Floreena's eyes, and started again, "Your eyes steal my heart. You are beautiful."

"Aww, Gala. That's the best compliment ever. Thank you. I have always found your eyes handsome, dreamy, mesmerizing." Floreena smiled. Gala found a bit of courage. He kissed Floreena on her cheek; when her smile broadened, he melted, then cleared his throat, "Ahem. Thank you. So, I haven't seen you since the last gathering. How have you been?"

"I've been doing good, busy learning alchemy and trying to complete my first real project. How about you? How's your transfiguring coming along? Have you perfected Phin?"

"Yes. I can transform into Phin without any thought. I'm working on a new one and did another without any help."

Floreena moved her left arm around Gala's shoulder. It brought their bodies closer together and slowed Gala's step to a short one-step left and one-step right. His right hand moved from her hip to the small of her back. They were barely moving. Floreena asked, "Will you be showing your new transformations tonight?"

"I don't know, maybe. Tell me about alchemy. Do you like it?" Gala took Floreena's right hand and brought it into his chest next to his heart, which brought their bodies even closer, and now they were rocking in place, stepping side to side.

"Oh yes! I'm not as good as your father, but I hope to, at least, come close. How about you? Do you like alchemy?"

"Yes. Although I don't know much about it, I'd like to learn more; it's interesting. What's the project you're working on?"

"A crystal. So far, I have it waking up and going to sleep. With a little more time and practice, I'll get it to downsize. After I master that, I'll work on it revealing things to me."

"Father created one about a year ago. He got it to sleep, downsize, and return to its natural state. It also shows him what he wants to see. But it doesn't show much of the surroundings. And for some reason, he can't hear anything; he's having a rough time getting it to perform correctly. He threatened it would end up in shards if he couldn't get it to work." Gala and Floreena laughed.

"I'm sure he'll figure it out. Your father's a genius." Floreena smiled. The music stopped. She reached up and kissed Gala's cheek. "Thank you for the dance."

"I'm happy you accepted. Would you like something to drink?"

"Sure."

Gala held out a bent elbow. After Floreena put her hand inside the crook of his arm, he led her to the refreshments. Gala got over his initial fear. He was in love. His internal happy thoughts rattled on, "Wow! Our castle is full of interesting magical people. I don't remember having so much fun. Our guests are dancing, enjoying themselves and showing off tricks, spells, and potions. I wish Helsin wasn't a jerk. Oh well. I'll never give Helsin another thought. I'll never allow his negativity to rule over me. Being here with my sweet Floreena is pure magic. My friends are the best friends anyone could hope to have. Acub and Ashlin look great with their crowns. They're happy. Floreena is my—"

"It's story time!" Conkay interrupted Gala's pleasant thoughts. He announced, "Acub and Ashlin asked that Faithin and I share our story first. But, before we do, we want Gala to show you one of his newest transformations." Helsin rolled his eyes while everyone else urged Gala on. Conkay and Faithin motioned Gala to stand on a table between them. Gala walked Floreena next to her mother. He gave her a light kiss on her lips then they hugged before he turned towards the table. The audience was quiet.

As soon as Gala stepped onto the table and closed his eyes, Faithin felt something strange in the air. She chanted, "*Hide and protect my sweet child from this wicked wile.*" A thick, silky purple fog engulfed Gala, then POOF! he and the fog vanished from the table.

Taken!

Conkay was puzzled why his wife cast a *Hide and Protect* spell on their son. After he and Faithin watched Gala disappear, they smelled a strange odor. Everyone began to cough and choke. A gust of wind blew out the candles to the grand chandeliers. An echoing thunderbolt shook the entire castle. Everything went dark. No one could see. Children screamed and cried with fright. In the blackness of wicked pitch, someone wrestled. There were growls and evil sniveling snarls. Conkay felt woozy. He summoned his magic tools, but someone knocked them from his hands. Then he and Faithin passed out. After a few minutes, the only sounds in the castle were the moans and groans of guests. The odor lifted; the chandeliers ignited, and the black pitch lifted. Some guests were wandering about, except for Lucky, his parents, and the Bluewing clan. They felt no effects and had flown to the top of the ceiling. Gala's friends looked for him. Acub and Ashlin scanned the great hall for Gala's parents, but they were nowhere in sight.

"Gala! Gala! Where are you, Chum?" Ddot yelled, darting around searching. He saw chairs turned over, food slung across tables and the floor. Dazed guests held their heads, comforted frightened children, or helped each other stand. One was puking. Some were still coughing. Some guests lay on the floor, trying to wake up.

"Here I am." Ddot's head jerked around. He saw Gala unwrapping the drapes from around himself.

Ddot flew straight over to him. "My chum, are you feeling all right?"

"I'm not sure. What happened? What's going on?" Gala scanned the hall for his parents and Floreena. His brows turned upwards and inwards, and his jaw dropped at the sight of chaos. He saw tossed furniture, everything disordered. "Where are my parents? Where's Floreena? Where's her mother? Look at this mess!"

Ddot scanned the entire room. He shook his head and shrugged his shoulders. "We're not sure what happened. Let's look for whoever's missing, check behind drapes, everything. Come on! Let's split into groups and search everywhere, including outside!" The Bluewing clan helped search inside the castle. The remaining dazed and confused guests headed outside to look.

Gala didn't move. He was stiff, fearing the worst. Acub and Ashlin flew above and released their soothing essence over his head. Although he was still bewildered, he felt better. Gala tried to gather his wits. He and the clan searched the castle calling for his parents. Gala called out for Floreena and Lidee. All they heard were their echoing voices bouncing off the walls. They searched the muddled laboratory. It looked as if someone had been searching for something. Gala unlocked the chamber that held their crystal ball. He chanted a *Shrink* spell, "*Downsize*," the ball and its pedestal shrank down to a grain of sand. Gala opened his cloak to reveal a tiny wooden trunk concealed within his cloak's hidden pocket. After he watched the ball and its pedestal float inside, he scanned the lab. Gala found his father's wand and scepter under a large hardwood table. He blurted out, "I can't find my mother's wand! I have got to find my parents somehow, some way! Giver of goodness, life, and love, protect them; do not let wicked sorcery harm them!" Gala's voice choked up while his red eyes watered. He swallowed hard, doing his best to fight off tears. Clan members flew above him, releasing their essence. Once again, Gala felt better and wiped his wet face with his sleeve.

Lucky touched Ddot and Dahc on their shoulders. "Come with me. Let's help the other guests look around outside." Acub and Ashlin stayed close to Gala inside the castle. The twins and Lucky searched everywhere outside. They looked in their forest and across Bridge. They asked the guests when they last saw Gala's parents, Lidee and Floreena. The guests said they saw them standing around the table, ready to watch Gala.

"Lidee?! Floreena?! No! It cannot be!" An old wizard panicked. While holding his head, he staggered to his feet, wobbling as he called out, "Lidee! Floreena! Conkay! Faithin! Where are you?!"

Gala's friends followed the wizard. Ddot flew above his head and flapped his wings. After the wizard calmed down, Ddot hovered in front of him and said, "We've searched everywhere. They're gone. Do you remember seeing them?"

"Yes! I saw them standing together around Gala. But hold on a second." The wizard paused for a moment before he continued. He remembered, "Now that I think about it, I did see something. It was strange."

"What'd ya see?" Lucky asked.

"Well, I thought I saw a **Shadow** standing alone. It didn't have a body to cast it. It looked like it was standing straight up, unnatural, not a normal shadow. I thought I was seeing things because I'm an old wizard with bad eyesight. No sooner than I saw the unusual **Shadow,** an odd odor came in on the wind, followed by a cracking thunderbolt. Then everything went black. I felt woozy. I wandered outside for some fresh air and sat, trying to regain my senses. I still feel woozy."

Lucky urged, "Old wizard, come with us. We want Gala to hear what ya told us about the **Shadow**. Everyone else, y'all may as well just go on home and keep safe and secure. We'll let ya know when we find those who are missin'." The guests gathered their Gentalsteeds and carriages, preparing to leave. The Newlads bowed to the old wizard, then led him inside the castle.

Lucky yelled, "Gala! Acub! All y'all come here and listen to what this wizard says." Lucky gestured for the wizard to sit on a bench and explain what he saw.

Gala could not believe what he was hearing. "Wizardry wizards! How did that dark, evil **Shadow** get in? I thought for sure we secured the castle with our *Protection* spell! The entire castle, including Bridge, was within our protective dome!"

Acub's heart jumped into his stomach, dumbfounded at what Gala said, but he remained quiet. He and Ashlin flew down and stood on the back of a bench next to clan members. Other members found a seat while the rest fluttered in place, listening.

The wizard slightly shook his head. He said, "You mean I did see a **Shadow**? I'm glad my eyes weren't playing tricks on me, but I'm not happy it could be the reason for all this gloom. Do you know anything about the **Shadow**? It sounds like Magic of Menace, Dark Magic, or what I call Wicked Do-wicking."

"My parents told me it could be Dark Magic. They told me it can be dangerous in the wrong hands yet useful in the hands of a sorcerer with a pure heart. They said magic is magic but turns dark if used for ill intentions. Other than that, I don't know anything about Dark Magic. Tell me, Mr. Wizard, what do you know of it?"

"I know some things, not much. I know it can be dangerous in the wrong hands and helpful in the right hands. Like you said."

"Father discovered a **Shadow** in the castle this morning and watched it glide out the window. He thought the **Shadow** might have been lurking around for about a year. He's not sure. Mother couldn't find anything about the **Shadow** in our Spells-Charms book, so figured it could be Dark Magic."

"Yes, yes, now I remember. If I recall correctly, Dark Magic and Magic of Light can create a potion called Shadow potion. It can render its consumer into a **Shadow**. If I'm not mistaken, change will not occur by drinking the potion alone. After drinking the potion, I believe a verbal incantation is in order. Only then will the potion work."

Without coming up for much air, Gala turned his attention towards Acub and spoke fast. "Father didn't want to upset your ceremonies, Mother and I agreed, and Father was going to tell you about the **Shadow** tomorrow, and that's why we didn't mention it, so we put a protected dome around the castle and celebrated indoors. Either the spell didn't work, or there's another way in that the dome didn't protect. I just don't know. I'm so sorry, Acub. We should've said something."

Acub thought the **Shadow** may have had something to do with his parents' disappearance. But he didn't mention it. He sighed, then assured, "Gala, please don't worry. We understand and heartily appreciate you and your parents for your thoughtfulness."

"I'm just, so sorry, Acub. I'm sorry all this happened. I got to think of something. I gotta get some things." Gala went through the rooms, gathering supplies. Before getting the Spells-Charms book, he looked to see if anyone was watching. His parents and himself were the only ones who knew about the secret compartment in the bookcase. He also didn't want Acub and Ashlin to see their gift. Gala was hoping he and his parents would be able to present the gift together. When he saw everyone preoccupied, he grabbed the book. He shut the door with the gift inside. Gala hurried. He locked the door and hung the key back in its hiding place. Then he started asking questions, "Who would want my parents? Why would they want Floreena and her mother? How can anyone be so wicked? Where do I begin to look? I have a gut feeling they're alive, but where are they? Oh yeah! Sheesh! I can't think straight." Gala took a deep breath. He sat next to the wizard and summoned his father's crystal ball using their Sorcermizic language. The tiny trunk inside his cloak's hidden pocket opened. After the crystal and its pedestal floated onto his lap, he spoke a spell using Sorcermizic language. The crystal and its pedestal returned to their natural state. Every clan member flew up and hovered around Gala and the old wizard. Gala explained that the crystal would show anyone in the present. He put his palms face down over the ball, moving them in a circular motion. He asked the crystal to show him his parents. A golden antique glow suddenly surrounded the outside of the crystal. A swirling purple fog filled the inside. After it dissipated, his parents appeared. "LOOK!" Gala's brows rose high. His eyes about popped out of their sockets, and he almost choked on the bucket of air he sucked down his lungs. His feelings were so mixed that his voice cracked and squeaked. He yelled, "Black sacks are covering their heads! They're sitting in a barred carriage that's moving along kinda bumpy! For the sake of goodness, life, and love, they're breathing! Look at those heavy chains binding their wrists to more heavy chains around their ankles. Why can't they free themselves?"

"Enchanted chains would be my guess."

Gala looked at the old wizard and agreed, "That makes sense. Mother and Father could have freed themselves using their *Unfetter* spell."

Ddot flew closer to the crystal to get a better look. He pointed and said, "There's a glowing light flickering on them, but I can't see the rest of their surroundings."

Gala looked back at the crystal. "Father did say the crystal wouldn't show much. But wait a minute; what's that there? It could be a clue! See the Berrybells on the floor of the carriage and Father's cloak? Never mind. That's not a good clue because Berrybells grow in many places."

"This is true, Gala. Yet, Berrybells do not grow in the north."

"You're right, Mr. Wizard! It eliminates the possibility of my parents heading north. It also proves that the Berrybells fell after my parents were in the carriage."

The old wizard patted Gala's shoulder and said, "That's a good observation." After Gala said thank you, the wizard asked, "If you don't mind, ask your crystal to show Floreena and Lidee."

"Oh, yeah, sure, you read my mind." When Gala asked the crystal to show Floreena, he felt the old wizard's hand squeeze his shoulder. Gala quizzically glanced at the wizard before he looked back at the crystal. The fog dissipated. "Oh, no, look! There's my sweet love beside her mother with black sacks over their heads. Thank the giver of goodness, life, and love they're breathing." After Gala told the crystal and its pedestal to sleep and downsize, they shrank and floated down into the tiny trunk inside his cloak's hidden pocket. Gala gave his head a little shake as he thought out loud, "I've gotta tell The Wizard's High Council, but they're in the north. It'll take days to get there. What am I gonna do?"

As the old wizard patted Gala's shoulder, he offered, "I'll travel to The High Council and tell them what has happened."

"You will?"

"Yes, I'll leave tonight."

"I'll go with you."

"No young mage. But there's something you can do. I know someone who might be able to help. Gnome Bloom is an old friend of mine. Bloom might be in the direction that leads you to your parents. He might know who took our loved ones. He hears the whispers of trees. The trees in his realm whisper about what they see around them. And Bloom can hear your thoughts. He also knows of legends and history of our realm's past. Although his village is quite a trek, you'll reach him before I reach the mountains of The Wizard's High Council."

"Thank you, so much, Mr. Wizard," After Gala stood up and shook the old wizard's hand with vigor, he looked for more supplies. He gathered charms, potions, and parchment paper. As he entered the kitchen, he yelled out and asked, "Where can I find your friend, Gnome Bloom?"

"I'll point out the vicinity of his home from your castle's watchtower. He lives northwest of the Boggy Swamps."

Gala stopped dead in his tracks. "Oh! No! No! No! I can't go there. I don't know enough magic, not with my hands or my wand. What'll I do? How can I defend myself against those nasty Boggy Gob-Diggers, Nixies, and Harpies? What about those blood-sucking Gurgling Mudlumps, and, and, and what about those Sharp Teeth Gullies, or, or those other flesh gobblers lurking and flying about, they'll suck the blood out of me? That domain is forsaken; goodness does not dwell in such a realm as the Boggy Swamps. It's filled with wickedness! Oh, my shaken-up wizard fear, I have no magic! I'm a flub-of-a-wizard! I can't do it! I'm doomed! For the goodness of life and love, my parents, doomed! My sweet Floreena and her mother, doomed! I gotta go to The High Councils with you Mr. Wizard. The Elfkies aren't far. They can carry us in their carriage with their winged Gentalsteeds!"

Gala's friends and a few clan members flew above and released their essence over his head. The old wizard walked over, reached out his hands, and cupped Gala's shoulders to provide added comfort. "Calm down, my young wizard friend. I'll find the Elfkies and have them take me to The High Councils. You'll not go anywhere near the Boggy Swamps. Gnome Bloom's village is in the forests northwest of your castle and north of the swamps. Come. Take me up to your castle's watchtower. I want to show you the layout of the land beyond yours."

"Gala! Chum!" Ddot called out. "I'm going with you to find your parents!"

"No! I can't protect you. If something happens to you, I'll never forgive myself. No! It's—"

"Stop right there! I'm my keeper. Although you and I are about the same age, I was born first. I've lived longer than you. Not my parents, nor Acub and Ashlin, can tell me what I can or cannot do when it comes to something like this. This is my choice."

"Me too! Ddot and I are twins. I'm coming along whether you like it or not. Ddot and I are two of the best archers in the clan. Our arrows hit exactly where we want them to. We have sharp ears and eyes. And let's not forget, we've been taking care of ourselves way before you and your parents moved into the castle." Gala chuckled because that's the most Dahc has ever said in one sitting.

"High jumpin' Glow Juneys! Count me in! Y'all ain't goin' nowhere without me. Everyone knows I'm the fastest flyer, runner, and knife thrower in the entire clan. It's fairy truthfulness, and I ain't braggin'. My dagger's blade is sharp and sure. Just like the twins' arrows, my dagger will hit whatever I aim it to hit. My ears are keen; my eyes are sharp. And Gala, ya need to remember that yore transfigurin' abilities will help us if needin'. Besides, I know yo're powerful whether ya lost yore confidence or not." Lucky pointed his hand, palm up, towards Ddot, Dahc, and then back at himself. "Trust that we, yore trusted pals and the entire clan, have faith in ya. But I'm sure we can survive without yore magic powers. Yore transfigurin', along with our abilities, is all we'll be needin' ifin' we're even needin' protectin'. And I'm older than all of y'all, just sayin'." Lucky cleared his throat, "Ahem."

Gala chuckled at Lucky's last statement.

Ddot considered Gala's abilities. He thought about what Gala was going to demonstrate before their loved ones were taken. He said, "Chum, I'm sure I speak for everyone when I say we can't wait to see your newest transformation. Right guys?"

"Ooooh yeah!" Dahc agreed with a nod.

"That's downright fairy truths," Lucky gave a thumbs up.

"I hope we have time to see your new transformation while we're out looking for our loved ones. I totally agree with Lucky. I can vouch for all of us when I say you're a powerful wizard. Right guys?" Ddot looked back over at Dahc and Lucky and around the whole clan. The twins' parents sat on the kitchen table with Lucky's parents and other clan members. Some sat on the backs of benches or in alcoves. Others sat on windowsills, some sat on the castle stones that weren't flush with the walls. Some fluttered in place next to the old wizard.

Gala heard some members yell out, "That's for sure! —You bet! —It ain't no wizard's tale! —Yeah, buddy! —There isn't any doubt in my mind!" And to Gala's joy, Acub even agreed.

Lucky reassured, "I wouldn't say it ifin' it wasn't so. Trust us, 'cause we ain't brewin' up a witch's deceit, let alone makin' up some ole wizard or fairytale lies."

"Personally," added Ddot, "I enjoy watching your *Rock Skipping* spell. Talk about far-out mystics, it's one of the top-flight spells ever!" Ddot held his hand, pretending he was holding a stone, and acted like he threw it. "I wish I could do that. That has got to be one of the hardest spells to perfect. At least that's what your father said. I remember his exact words. He said, 'I didn't perfect the *Rock Skipping* spell as fast as Gala. It's a hard spell to master. Gala doesn't know how powerful he is regardless of lost confidence.' Your father's right, Chum. You just don't know how powerful you are. Listen, Gala. In the goodness of magic light and Bluewing essence, I'm not saying this due to being best chums. I'm saying it because I know it. You'll find your confidence someday." Ddot shook his finger at Gala, then put his hands together. His fingers interlocked. He pulled his palms towards each other until they closed. "But we're not putting any clan—clamp pressure on you. When you're ready, you'll know it. Let's not even think about it. Let's focus on finding our loved ones."

Gala was beside himself. His whole body lit up when he smiled. Although he figured he was a flub-of-a-wizard, he was one of the most fortunate beings ever. "You guys are the best! It's settled. Let's go see the layout of the land and gather what we need for our journey. And, if it's at all possible, I'll show you guys my new transformations. I have two."

His friends shouted, "All right!" Then everyone followed the old wizard to the top of the castle's tower.

"Excuse me, Mr. Wizard. I'm, so sorry. I wasn't trying to be rude, and I did see my pen, Inkle, mark your name off our guest list, but I wasn't paying much attention. What do we call you?"

The old wizard smiled and replied, "My name is Sparktinian, but you can call me Spark as my friends do."

"I've seen you before, but I never knew your name. Guess I should have paid more attention to the guest list. It's nice to put a name on a friendly face. Thank you, Mr. Spark."

"Spark will do," implored Sparktinian. "I'm not sure what the 'Mr.' stands for. It sounds like reverence, but Spark or Wizard Spark will do."

Gala put his hand to his chin, squinted, and furrowed his brows. He thought about where he heard 'Mr.' "You know, I'm not sure where I heard it, and I'm not sure what it means either," he chuckled. "Okay then. We'll call you Spark or Wizard Spark."

After they reached the castle's lookout tower, Sparktinian pointed out the lands. "There's the Treeagers' village. Beyond that, you have the northern snowcapped mountains. Further north, the mountains are bigger, taller, and colder than cold. It's so cold that waterfalls froze and that's why they're called Frozen Falls. The Wizard's High Council resides in those mountains. To the east of your castle, beyond your gardens and forest, is a vast land filled with gentle creatures. Beyond that lies a mystical forest called—"

"Whittlewood Forest," Gala finished Spark's sentence and added. "It's where I was born and where my parents were born. We lived there before we moved into the castle." Gala was nostalgic; he tried not to show it.

"Yes," Sparktinian looked at Gala. He placed his hand on Gala's shoulder and paused. After a couple of seconds, he patted Gala's shoulder and reached out his arm. Spark pointed towards the south of Whittlewood Forest. "Look there. Down from Whittlewood Forest and to the south of your castle, you can see the rolling hills and valleys. Although there are streams, lakes, and rivers in all the lands, here they are abundant. They flow into one large body of water, which is too far for us to see from here."

Lucky flew up above the castle. "I can see one of the streams yo're talkin' 'bout from up here, but, just as ya said, I caint see that large water." Three clan members flew up next to Lucky. One pointed his hand in the direction of the stream while one shook her head and the other nodded. They squinted as if it would help them see better.

Spark chuckled, "You can't see from there either. You'd have to be extremely high where the air is thinner or be close enough to see it. We're just too far. It's a spectacular sight to behold. You might venture there someday. It's called Big Water. But I call it Salty Dragon Water because the water tastes salty. Legend has it that many years ago, enormous dragons, bigger than this castle, lived in the depths of the Big Water. It's possible they still exist. Salty Dragon Water stretches wide and far. It's so large that if one were to stand on its bank, they could not see its end in any of its three directions."

Although Lucky was serious, he humored, "Oi! Just in case the legend's true and enormous dragons are lurkin' in the deep, I ain't never goin'. Unlessin' I was as big as this castle. But someday I'd like to visit the rollin' hills. My parents used to live there. Accordin' to them, the Ultra Storm wiped out the rest of their, rather our, clan even their protector. The Ultra Storm's strong winds swept Ma and Pa up and carried them here. The Bluewing clan found 'em, almost dead and fixt 'em up. They've been here ever since, and then I was born." Lucky and his clanmates flew back down.

"Lucky, that's how I heard the story. And for some unknown reason, The Wizard's High Council has not assigned a new protector. I wouldn't visit unless you have a mage go with you, someone like Gala," Spark suggested.

"Me? Why me?" Gala squinched up his face.

"Because you'll become a great mage. Your friends are right. Every gathering I've ever attended I've seen the power in you."

"I don't want to argue, but I really don't think—"

"I agree. I don't want to argue either. We'll discuss it another time. Let me show you the rest of the land."

"Yes sir."

"Look on the west side of your castle. Here you can see more mountains. As we all know, some of these mountains dwindle to a flat wide area of swampland. This is where Gob-Diggers, along with other foul creatures, dwell." Spark pointed towards the mountains on the other side of Crystal Lake. Everyone could see where they declined down to the swamp. Then Spark stretched his arms straight out in front of him. His left arm pointed towards the decreasing mountains. His right arm pointed toward mountains that seemed to lead to the horizon. "And these mountains to the right do not dwindle. They are the Rigid Mountains, also called The Ridge. They run parallel to the dwindling mountains and the swamplands. One of Crystal Lake's streams pours down between them. Over time the stream created another gorge like the one on the south side of your castle. The Ridge runs east and west. It's one long stretch of mountains that separates the swamps from all the forests on its north side. On the swamp side, south side, The Ridge is a darker color with steep, sharp cliffs. On the north side, The Ridge is lighter in color, not as steep, and not near as many cliffs. But instead, its terrain grows green trees with pink or white flowers. Tall grasses and spectacular wildflowers grow everywhere in a colorful display. The High Council assigned a protector, Wizard Tiaff, for The Ridge. Tiaff protects the surrounding territories on the north side of The Ridge. His fortress was carved into The Ridge just as your castle was carved into your mountain. One particular forest, on the northwest side of The Ridge, outside Tiaff's care, has a mind of its own. This realm is the home of Gnome Bloom. If you're anywhere near his realm, he'll find you. When he does, tell him I sent you."

Gala sighed, "Phew! Thank the gracious giver of life and love that your friend doesn't live near the swamps!" The entire clan joined in with agreeing nods and affirmative yeses.

Gala and his friends thanked Wizard Spark, and although it was nightfall, Spark didn't waste time. He began his journey. After he left, the entire clan helped Gala gather more of what he needed from the castle and gardens. When they finished, Gala transfigured into his Bluewing form. He followed the clan home to their enormous cave behind the waterfall. Blue illuminating mushrooms shone on assorted gems creating a shimmering display throughout. The large cavern always gave Gala a feeling he was entering a world of magical wonders.

Gala flew over and sat on an emerald. He brought out his crystal ball and asked it to show his parents. Everyone gathered around. They were attentive and quiet. A golden antique glow encompassed the outside of the crystal, and a purple fog swirled within. After it dissipated, Gala's parents appeared. Faithin's head was resting on Conkay's shoulder, and Conkay's head was resting on her head. They were sitting with their backs leaning against the barred carriage. Gala's eyes turned red. He told the clan, "They're sleeping. The ember glow is flickering around them. It looks like they're going to camp because the barred carriage isn't moving." Gala became quiet. Tears fell onto the crystal and rolled down over its sides. He wiped them off with his sleeve after he wiped his eyes. He asked the crystal, "*Show me Floreena.* Look! Floreena and her mother are sleeping too. Too bad I couldn't send a spell through the crystal. At least they're sleeping. You know, if we're lucky enough to head in their direction, we could catch up with them tonight!" Gala put the crystal away.

"Wait a minute, Gala," Acub interjected. "I know you're anxious. That's a big 'IF' that we ought to consider. Our borders are more vulnerable without your parents. But Bridge, along with our charms will help keep us safe. However, outside our land, in the dark, where none of us have ever been, is where I wouldn't want any of us to be right now. I insist you get a good night's rest and start early in the morning." Acub was adamant about his decision.

The whole clan joined in with their agreeable words of wisdom. Ashlin added, "Yes. Listen to Acub, to all of us. We can't take that chance. It's risky enough traveling during daylight hours. At least in the morning, after plenty of rest, you'll get a good start, not to mention that you'll be able to see."

Gala grit his teeth and balled his fists. Tears rolled down his cheek. He couldn't argue their reasoning, "You guys are right. I'm helpless." Gala folded his arms across his bent knees and put his face down on his arms. Some of the clan members flew above and flapped their wings. "Thanks, guys," Gala lifted his head and wiped his wet face and eyes. "Morning isn't soon enough; let's go to bed."

Ddot patted Gala's shoulder. "Come on Chum." Gala followed Ddot to his and Dahc's sleeping crevice located in a large grotto off the main cave.

After everyone went into their sleeping clefts, Ashlin helped Acub. They put protective charms on the entrances of their home then they went to bed. Acub was lying on his back. Although he wasn't too hopeful, he did think, "I hope Gala and the Newlads find my parents along their journey." Acub rolled over, snuggled up to Ashlin, and closed his eyes.

 Gala quietly wept. Under his breath, he asked, "Gracious giver of goodness, life, and love, help us find my parents. Help us find my beautiful Floreena, and her mother, including the whereabouts of Trill and Quo. Watch over them." Gala pulled out a handkerchief, wiped his wet eyes and face then blew his nose. He rolled over, pulled his knees up to his chest, and was the last one to fall asleep.

Getting Ready

It was early morning when, "Nooo!" echoed throughout the waterfall cave, breaking the morning silence. Ddot and Dahc sprung from their beds to find Gala tossing and turning in his. They flapped their wings over Gala's head, releasing their calming essence, then flew down and stood by his bed. Their parents rushed inside, followed by Acub and Ashlin. The rest of the clan gathered outside the twin's sleeping crevice.

Ashlin flew beside Gala. Her voice was soft, "It's time to wake up. Wake up, Gala. You're having a bad dream."

He slowed his tossing, put his hand on his forehead, blinked his eyes open, then looked around. "Thank the giver of goodness, life, and love I'm here and not where I was a second ago!"

Acub's brows lifted. "You remember your nightmare!?"

"Yes, but I don't think it's the one I can't remember." Gala sat up. "I'm pretty sure this one is new because I remember it. My parents were falling down a dark hole that was closing in on them, and no matter what I did, I couldn't pull them out. I figure it's because of what happened last night, not to mention I feel helpless.

"Yeah, you're probably right." Acub's brows lowered; his eyes relaxed; his hopes dampened. He suggested, "If you eat your Sweet Dream Charms, they might keep the new nightmares away."

"That's a good idea. And although I've never heard of a fairy having nightmares, I'll make extra for everyone. Sweet dreams never hurt anyone." Gala winked. He was trying to make light of his nightmarish condition. He cupped his hands and said something using Sorcermizic language. Out of thin air, the crystal with its pedestal appeared in his hands. He set them on his lap, faced his palms over the crystal, and moved them in a circular motion. Gala instructed, "*Show me my parents.*" A golden antique glow encompassed the crystal. A purple fog swirled inside. After it dissipated, the crystal revealed Conkay and Faithin. They were sleeping with black sacks still covering their heads. Gala asked to see Floreena and Lidee. They were sleeping, and black sacks were still over their heads too. Gala told the crystal to sleep. The golden glow stopped; as soon as the crystal became clear, Gala said, "*Conceal.*" The crystal and its pedestal vanished from his lap. Poof!

Everyone was quiet until Ashlin suggested, "Let's eat before you leave for your journey. I'll cook pancakes and try to make them as yummy as your father's. We have a fresh jug of your favorite Fairy Honey. How's that sound?"

"That sounds delicious." Gala licked his chops and smiled.

"Okay! Let's get winging," Acub cheered everyone on but stopped Gala. "I want to have a word with you."

Gala gave his shoulders and wings a slight shrug. With a little shake of his head he started, "I know you're mad at me for something and—"

"Wait." Acub gave Gala a friendly pat on his shoulder before he sat next to him. "I need to say something. I've been thinking. There could be a connection between your nightmares, lack of confidence, and no offense, but your wacky spells."

"None taken."

"I realize you're not responsible for my parent's disappearance. I-I had my doubts, and I am truly sorry for that." Acub paused. He and Gala hung their heads. Their eyes turned red and watery.

Gala used his sleeve to wipe the water dripping from his nose. "I'm glad you don't blame me."

Acub pulled a handkerchief out of his pocket and wiped his own tears, and said, "I repeatedly turned it over in my head. About a year ago, my parents left on their tryst the day before your nightmares started. After they left, Ddot went looking to hang with you. Your mother said you were practicing your Bunt and Nix at Crystal Lake or in our forest. Ddot said he didn't want to bother you, so he came home. No one knows for sure where you were. This is why I had suspicions. I realized that if you knew what happened to my parents, you must not remember. You and your parents would've told me if you knew anything."

Gala leaned over and rested his forehead in his hands. "Much of that day escaped my memory. The next morning, I woke up in sweats from nightmares I couldn't remember. Mother and Father have tried everything to help. Mother said that a frightened lock wouldn't let her or Father inside to see my nightmares."

"Look here, Gala. Now your parents are missing. I know the nightmares are as frustrating for you as it is maddening for me not knowing what happened to my parents." Acub cleared his throat, then patted Gala's back. "What I'm getting at is this. If there's a connection between the **Shadow**, your nightmares, and our loved ones, you're in danger!" Acub bent down to look into Gala's eyes.

Gala put his hands down. As he lifted his head and brows, he looked at Acub. "That makes sense! You could be right. Yesterday, before Father saw the **Shadow**, Mother told me that my nightmares, wacky spells, and lost confidence might be connected. I bet the **Shadow** is too. I gotta figure this out."

"Listen, Gala. Don't let nightmares or lost confidence get in the way of your powers. While you're on your journey, do your best to practice simple magic along with your transfiguring. No matter how frustrating or difficult it seems, don't give up. You'll solve this mystery. I know it. I can feel it in my gut. You'll find everyone. Hopefully, you'll find out the whereabouts of my parents. That would give me closure. I'm scared to ask, but do you think your crystal will show me, my parents?"

"Oh, yeah! Good thinking, Acub! Gee, wizards! Why didn't I think of that." Gala summoned the crystal ball and its pedestal, "*Appara Comforte*" POOF! Again, out of thin air, they appeared in his hands. He and Acub looked at each other, took a deep breath, and let it out. Gala set the ball and its pedestal in an alcove beside the bed. He moved his palms in circular motions over the crystal and instructed, "*Show me Acub's parents, Trill and Quo.*" Nothing happened. Then he asked, "*Show me Acub.*" A golden antique glow encompassed the outside of the ball while a purple fog swirled inside. The fog dissipated. Acub and Gala saw themselves looking at the crystal ball. "This doesn't mean anything. Your parents could be blocked from the crystal's vision for some reason. Father did say the crystal was a work in progress."

Acub hung his head and gave it a little shake before he looked up at Gala and said, "It doesn't matter. It's okay. I'll continue dealing with it the best I can. I'm loved and have everyone's support to help me through tough moments. Let's forget it for now and go eat breakfast. I can't hold you up any longer." Acub put his hand on Gala's shoulder to make sure Gala looked him straight in the eyes. "I want you to be careful," he said. "I want all of you to return safely. The clan and I love you, Gala." Acub's eyes watered up again.

At that moment, Gala knew they shared the same pain and faced the same fears. Although Faithin explained Acub's pain the day before, Gala didn't fully understand until now. He told Acub, "I love all of you too. We'll be careful. There's this thing about me and my friends. We're strong, all right. But we're strongest when we're together. Try not to worry." Gala gave Acub a hug. It was his turn to be strong and comforting.

"Thank you, Gala. Let's go join the others." Before they flew out to the kitchen, Gala changed his shirt, and Acub wiped his tears.

After breakfast, Gala flew to his sleeping crevice and readied himself. When he was done, he flew back to the kitchen and started making charms. His friends were still in their crevices getting ready.

Lucky packed the things he needed, then sharpened his knife. He and his father welded it quite some time ago. After Lucky finished, he placed his dagger in the leather sheath his mother had designed. She sewed a red ruby in its flap the night before. Engraved in the ruby was her handwriting. It read, '*May the Giver of Goodness, Life, and Love watch over our Eternal Love.*' Lucky smiled, then turned around. His mother was standing there, and his father was beside her.

"Our dear, sweet, swift flyer." She put her fingers through his jet-black hair. "Ya know how much yore father and I love ya." She cupped his chiseled face beneath his chin and looked in his dark, almost black, brown eyes. "Ya know how much we worry. Promise you'll watch where yo're goin'. Yo're rightly named Lucky by the clan, but yore Father and I named ya Eric. Eric means Eternal Love. After ya were born and we first laid eyes on ya, we felt an everlasting love. We don't wanna hear about spider webs with ya in 'em. We want ya to be eternally lucky. Do we make ourselves clear?" She fought back all her tears except for the two that escaped down her cheeks.

"Oh Ma, Pa, I love y'all with all my heart. I promise. I promise I'll watch where I'm flyin'." Lucky pulled his Ma and Pa to him, creating a group hug. "We'll find everyone and come home. No one will know we were ever gone."

Lucky's Pa tried to sound cheerful. "We're holdin' ya to it. Anuff now; the sooner ya git, the sooner ya git back. Let's go meet yore pals and see if they're ready." Lucky and his parents flew out into the great hall. The rest of the clan was there except for Gala, the twins, and the twins' parents. Gala was still in the kitchen making a few different types of charms. The twins were in their chamber with their parents.

Ddot's and Dahc's parents hugged their handsome, white-haired, freckled face twins. They reminded them to use the sleeping secretion from a Scarlet Leprechaun Frog. That is, of course, if they found any along their journey. Their father handed them an empty vile to hold the frog's secretion just in case they did happen to find any.

The twins' father began his farewell, "May you find a Scarlet Leprechaun. But, if you do not, may you find a safe journey without one. But, if you do not, may your bow and arrows not fail you. But, if they—"

Dahc put his hand on his dad's shoulder. "Father, we love you, too. We'll be on our guard, alert at all times."

"Dahc's right. I know I'm wasting my breath when I tell you and Mother not to worry, but please do your best. Dahc and I will do our best not to worry about you. You only have the Keep Safe Charms and the clan to protect each other."

Their father interjected, "Newlads, we still have archers. They're not as skilled, but skilled, nevertheless. Besides, we have other abilities. Our waterfall cave is hard to enter. After Wizard

Sparktinian tells The High Council what happened, they'll send constables. They'll help find our loved ones."

Ddot gave his head a little shake and rolled his emerald-green eyes. He grunted, "Hopefully, they'll be more successful with this search than with Trill and Quo."

His mother defended, "Some of us think they came up empty-handed, without clues, because of Dark Magic. You may find Trill and Quo on your journey."

Their father added, "Be on your guard, always alert. Keep one emerald open while you sleep. We know you can manage yourselves, especially if you stick together. Come." He and his wife reached out and gave their twins a long hug.

Before she started crying, their mother raised her head. She kissed her twins on their cheeks and said, "Okay, our Newlad chaps, let's join the rest of the clan."

Gala finished in the kitchen and met his friends in the great hall. As he handed them charms, he saw a vile attached to Ddot's and Dahc's belts. Gala tilted his head to get a better look. He asked, "What are those for?"

Ddot did the explaining. "This is a container to hold a sleeping secretion."

"What's a sleeping secretion?"

"It's the secretion from a Scarlet Leprechaun Frog. Father gave us a vile in case we found a frog along our journey. When we scavenge, we hunt for many things; the frog was one of them. We haven't been able to find a frog for many full moons past.

The secretion's effects could kill small creatures and make some sleepy. Some aren't affected. Neither is our clan. We're immune."

The clan agreed, saying, "Yep. —Yeah. —Good thing, too."

Dahc nodded agreeing with his brother. Ddot continued, "In the past, we used the secretion in defending our clan. We also used it to ward off intrusive creatures that would invade our gardens. We'd dip the tip of our arrows in the secretion and shoot, hitting our targets. For other creatures, we used crafted darts and hollow blow tubes. Like these." Ddot pulled out his blow tube and a dart then handed them to Gala.

"Nice." Gala inspected the intricate design before handing them back.

"There used to be a lot of frogs. We were able to keep our nook replenished. But there aren't any more frogs around here. We've exhausted our supply. Rumors say dark witches ate the frogs. First they extract the frogs' secretion for some evil doings. Then they bleed the frogs before they devour 'em."

"YUCK!" Dahc squinched up his face. He added, "But since you and your parents became our protectors, we haven't needed the secretion." The twins smiled wide.

"Oh! That's good to know. I hope we find one or two. Talk about protection. I'm leaving Father's staff with you, Acub. You and Ashlin can use it. It'll help protect you and the clan." Although Gala was anxious to start their journey, he needed to show them how to use Force.

"But, won't you need it on your journey?" asked Acub.

"No. I know some hand and wand spells if we need them. I also have my Spells-Charms book. I'll practice my spells like you suggested and my parents commanded. I have Nix, eight other forms, and some assorted charms I can use. Don't worry. We'll be all right." Gala tried to sound positive for their sake.

Gala wants to get rid of his nightmares, regain his confidence, overcome his fears. He decided he'd make an honest effort perfecting his magic powers. He also thought that if he gets his spells down pat, he'd like to learn Dark Magic because it could help fight against evil.

Acub suggested, "We'll be all right without your father's staff. Take it with you."

"No. I'll feel better if it stays here with you. I'm sure Father would want me leave it with you. Besides, like I said, I know a few spells. I have my wand and some charms. I also have a transformation that'll help us if we need him. That is, as long as I can get him down pat. I haven't perfected him, but I doubt we'll need him." Gala held out his arm and said a word in Sorcermizic. His father's staff appeared in his hand. Poof! He asked Acub, "Are you ready?"

"Hold on there, Gala. I'm sure we're all curious. Tell us about your newest transformation that you haven't perfected yet." Clan members cheered Gala on.

"I call him Redtalon. He's an impressive dragon that—" Gala stopped. He smiled wide.

Clan members sounded out, "Ooh!" — "Dragon?" — "Pixie wonders!" — "Aah!" — "Impressive!"

Gala chuckled. "Yes, he's impressive. Mother's the only one who has seen the likes of such a dragon like my Redtalon. He's a mixture of Mother's and Father's dragon forms and other dragons I learned about. I'm telling you what, when y'all see him, you'll probably do pixie flips. I hope to perfect him along our journey. But I'm not sure I can because I usually need one of my parents to help me when I begin a new transformation. I'll give Ddot, Dahc, or Lucky permission to use my wand if I have time to practice. That's enough about me and my Redtalon. Let's get the scepter lesson started."

"Okay. We're all ears." With an attentive ear, Acub was ready to learn. He was more interested than the rest of the clan because he had always wanted a staff. But little did anyone know, so did Ashlin.

"Come on, follow me to the gardens. Father's staff, or what he calls 'Force,' is helpful in other ways. I'll show you how to use the *Hold* and the *Contain It* spells. Besides, those are about the only ones I know how to use with Force. They'll be the easiest to use, but hopefully, you won't need them."

Ashlin cupped her cheeks. "Fairy hearts and springy tummies, I sure hope you're right."

Clan members agreed. They shook their heads or nodded. One yelled out, "Let's hope not!"

Acub asked, "Do you perform these spells often?"

"No. But they're some of the first spells I learned in my magic career. I have them down pat—to a T. They're simple." Gala smiled and led everyone to the gardens. "I'll have to give you permission to use Force. After that, if there's anything you want to hold or contain, Force will do as you command. Let me show you. Gala tapped the bottom of Force on the ground and commanded, "*Force, Hold.*" He pointed Force's ruby amulet at a yellow fluttery pollinating Sweetie Flowers. Force turned azure then a steady beam of rainbow light shot out from its amulet. The light surrounded the fluttery. The fluttery fluttered in place, unable to fly about.

Although the *Hold* spell is like the *Congeal* spell, they are different. The *Congeal* spell stops objects, making them as stiff as a statue, and prevents them from making noise. The *Hold* spell keeps something in one place without restricting movement or sound.

When Gala pointed Force over another part of the garden, its beam moved the fluttery to that spot. Gala smiled at the astonished expressions on his attentive audience. Then he commanded, "*Force, Release.*" Force's beam retracted into its amulet, and the fluttery resumed its pollinating task.

"Okay. Now it's time to contain it." Gala tapped the bottom of Force on the ground and commanded, "*Force, Contain It.*" The amulet shot out its rainbow-colored beam of light. But this time, after hitting the fluttery, the fluttery disappeared, and the amulet's light stopped. The clan oohed and aahed while scanning the garden for the fluttery.

Gala told them to follow him into his father's laboratory.

They flew over the mess from the night before and hovered in place. Gala pointed at a holding crate. Acub shouted, "There's the fluttery!"

"This is our holding crate created with the same types of gems and gold we used for Father's pedestal to his crystal ball. The holding crate is made with thick beveled crystals. Its top and bottom are pure gold embellished with magical gems. The gold along the edges seals and strengthens the crate. Its gold legs are fashioned as dragon claws, and so is the lock on its door, which were my ideas." Gala grinned big. Everyone chuckled. "Watch what the lock does after I tell the crate to release its captive." Gala touched the lock and told it to release. The claws unclasped, and the door opened. A breeze inside the crate carried the fluttery out the laboratory's opened window. After the crate's door shut, the claws clasped back together." The clan murmured admirations with occasional oohs and aahs. "When I give both of you permission, it'll open for you. Let's lock the fluttery up again to show you what happens when you don't have permission." They flew back outside. Gala handed Force to Acub.

Acub held Force and did what Gala showed him to do. He commanded, "*Force, Hold,*" but nothing happened. Gala took Force and whispered to its amulet using Sorcermizic language. The amulet shone. He handed Force back to Acub. Acub tapped the bottom of Force on the ground. He ordered again, "*Force, Hold.*" This time Force turned azure. When Acub pointed Force, its rainbow beam of light surrounded the fluttery. "All right, look at that!" Acub told Force to release. The rainbow light retracted back into the amulet. Acub did two pixie flips, then relaxed and cleared his throat. "Ahem. I couldn't help myself." After everyone stopped laughing, Acub continued, *"Force, Contain It."* The fluttery disappeared, and the beam retracted back into the amulet. Everyone flew back inside the lab. Acub touched the lock and told the crate to release its captive, but nothing happened. Gala touched the lock and said something in his Sorcermizic language. He motioned his hand for Acub to try again. This time the claws unclasped, and a breeze carried the fluttery out the opened window. Gala and the Clan followed. Acub pointed and exclaimed, "There's the fluttery! It's back in the garden pollinating flowers. Wow! This is magnificent! Thank you, Gala. You won't have to worry about us. Force and your holding crate are great tools. I wish there was something we could do for you while you're gone, like clean up your castle. Put everything back in its place."

"Actually, Force can do that too. Gala gave Ashlin and Acub permission to use Force for the *Straighten Room* spell. "Now all you need to do is think of how you want the room to look, point Force at the room, and speak the spell. Force will straighten the room the way your mind sees it."

Ashlin grinned, "Well fairy wishes do come true. I'll be happy to oversee that task. Your mother shared a desire to change things around. I know exactly what she wants."

"Mother will like that. Thank you, Ashlin. Before I forget, there's something you need to keep in mind about Force. We can't go around holding and containing things just to do it. It's against Wizard rules and regulations. There's no telling what could happen. The fluttery was for demonstration, so no harm was done. If you hold something still for too long, Force will drain your energy. Also, the holding crate is big enough to contain something the size of Father's dragon but only for two days. After two days, the crate will return its captive or captives back to where they came from. If you need to keep something contained longer, tell Force to contain it before the two days are up. The crate will keep it locked up for another two days. When you release something, it can ride on a breeze or vanish back to where it came from. And, it can come out into the laboratory. So, think of where you want it to go, then release it. And Ashlin, you'll get exhausted if you straighten more than one room. It's best to do one a day or do a little in the morning, take a break, and do a little more in the evening. Do you guys have any questions?"

"Those are the only spells we can use?"

"Yes Acub, why do you ask?"

"I wouldn't want to accidentally give Force a command that could endanger us."

"It's not possible because Force only has permission for you or Ashlin to use three spells—

Hold, Contain It, and *Straighten Room.* There's nothing to worry about. Okay?"

"We understand, and we won't slipshod."

"I trust you. And, just so you know, while we're gone, I'll use the crystal to look in on you."

"Thank you, Gala."

"Well, guess we'd better get going." Although fear kept his nerves shaking, Gala was anxious to get started. He transformed into himself. He walked over and took a supply bag from a hook next to the castle's backdoor. He gave out a whistle past their livestock towards the forest. The clan saw Gala's whistle leave his lips and travel through the air, creating ripples like a heat wave. His whistle reached the paisley-shaped ears of a Hobbgie. The Hobbgie lifted his head from the Sweetleaf. He sped towards Gala like a streak of lighting creating a winding trail of himself behind him. The winding trail caught up to his body a second or two after he stopped in front of Gala.

Gala patted his Hobbgie's neck. "Good morning, Trusty," he greeted. "We need your help. Are you up to traveling, carrying supplies, and facing grave danger?" Trusty nodded his neck and head yes. He sounded out grunts like a dragon and whickers like a winged Gentalsteed. "Thank you, Trusty. Wish I was as brave as you." Gala took a brush out of the supply bag and brushed Trusty's chocolate hair. Then he brushed his silky white mane and his long white tail. Trusty's coat was shiny and just as soft as Furhoppers' fur. Furhoppers resemble bunny rabbits. After Gala finished brushing Trusty, he put the brush back in the supply bag and draped the bag over Trusty's back.

    Hobbgies resemble a mixture of dragons and Gentalsteeds. Except they don't have scales, thin legs, or long thin necks. Male Hobbgies do not have wings, females do. Males have four strong legs with feet and claws shaped like the hind legs of most dragons. The back legs of a female Hobbgie are the same as males. But a female's front legs are more like the forearms of some dragons. Their snouts are also like dragons. Female and male Hobbgies alike have paisley-shaped ears. The outside parts of their ears fan out and cup. They have big round eyes with a hazel brown-green hue color or a grass-green color like Trusty's. The rest of their body resembles that of a horse on Earth. Hobbgies are plant eaters, so their teeth are flat. The Sweetleaf plant is one of their favorite floras.

    As Gala patted Trusty, he looked up at everyone and said, "Okay. I guess we're ready. Let's go, guys. We'll be back with our loved ones before you know it." The clan followed Gala around the wide walk across to the entrance of Bridge.

    The twins' father reminded them, "Remember to be on your guard, sleep with one eye open."

    Their mother added, "Yes, and keep an eye out for Leprechaun Frogs."

    "Be eternally lucky," Lucky's mother held back her tears then his father wrapped his arms around her.

    "Practice your spells," Acub held Force up towards Gala.

Then Ashlin yelled out, "May the giver of goodness, life, and love protect you!"

The entire clan waved and wished them well. Gala and the Newlads waved back then turned away. After they crossed Bridge, the Newlads found a seat on Gala's shoulders. His body was shaking. The twins flew above and flapped their wings over Gala. After they sat back down, they couldn't feel him shaking. About midway across the open field of wildflowers, they turned to wave. They did this until they could no longer see the clan.

The four companions were quiet and scared. They know that if they do not try or do not take the journey, they may never find their loved ones.

Redtalon

Gala and his pals traveled for more than half a day. Their fearful thoughts muted the harmonious sounds of nature. Gala sat slumped astride Trusty. His friends sat on his drooping shoulders. They were quiet. Each one wondered what danger they might face. But  the loud silence was too much for Lucky. He couldn't take it any longer. "Y'all know what Quiet said to Silence?"

Ddot answered and asked, "No. What did Quiet say to Silence?"

"Be QUIET! Yo're makin' too much NOISE!"

Ddot chuckled. Gala smiled, still sitting slumped. While trying to understand the joke, Dahc lifted one side of his mouth; his brows went inwards and upwards. And then he got it. He burst out, "Bah ha, ha, ha! Bah ha, ha ha!" everyone cracked up over Dahc's laughter, and then an avalanche of jokes erupted.

Ddot asked, "Do you know the difference between a big bird and a little bird?"

"No. What?" They asked in unison.

"'TWEET!' 'tweet,' 'TWEET!' 'tweet,' 'TWEET!' 'tweet.'"

Gala held his stomach; laughter poured out from his gut. Dahc slapped down on his knee, bent over, belly laughing. Lucky laughed so hard that he rolled off Gala's shoulder. He flew up and around and then sat back down.

Gala stuck his tongue between his lips and blew out hard. His lips flapped against his tongue. Between his chuckles, he managed to say, "That's a big gassy bird!" Then, as fast as he could, he stuck his tongue between his lips again and blew out soft, "And that's a little gassy bird!" Everyone cracked up!

Laughter turned fear into hope. Finally, they became aware of the beauty around them. They saw yellow and purple flowers amongst green grasses swaying in the breeze. Birds perched in tall trees cheerily singing their songs. Furhoppers ate pink flowers off clovers. This is when they felt hunger pangs jabbing at their stomachs. All they had to eat were the pancakes Ashlin cooked that early morning. They decided to stop, get some rest, and have a bite to eat.

Gala found a perfect spot for a picnic. He hopped off Trusty and told him to lie down. While Gala spread a blanket and put rocks on the corners to keep the wind from blowing it around, he thought about drawing a map. He told his friends, "Although the sun, moons, and stars will guide us, I'm drawing a map with a compass rose to help keep us on track. I'll draw everything along our journey. First, I'll draw our homes. We'll name the undiscovered lands." Gala spread a piece of brown parchment paper across a smooth flat rock. Lucky and the twins stood on the blanket to watch.

Gala was about to use Inkle to draw from a high perspective. But then Ddot asked, "Hey, Chum, we've seen your magnificent artwork, and we know you can draw, but we've never seen you do it. Can you draw the castle without using Inkle?"

"Oh, yeah. Okay." Gala put Inkle away and summoned his charcoal then started drawing the castle. Next, he drew Bridge then himself on Bridge. He drew Ddot sitting on one of his shoulders, Dahc on his other shoulder, then he drew Lucky on top of his head. This made everyone laugh. Finally, Gala drew Trusty standing next to them.

"Drawin' wonders! Ya ain't kiddin'. There ain't no doubtin' it, ya can draw." Lucky smiled big, showing his straight pearly whites.

Dahc closed his slacked jaw and said, "That's realistic!"

"Yeah, it's like a real miniature castle that you can pick up off the map. Can you teach me how to draw like that?"

"Sure Ddot, that'll be fun. You guys are the best. Thank you, for all your compliments.

Gala put his charcoal away, summoned Inkle then commanded, "Draw and color." He released his pen but held his hand as if his fingers held Inkle. When Gala's hand and fingers moved, Inkle followed in motion. Its nib changed colors when appropriate. Gala moved Inkle over the charcoal castle, himself, his Hobbgie, and his friends. Everything became colorful and more realistic. It moved, in motion, as if living, waterfalls fell to Crystal Lake, and fairies flew around in the gardens. Gala explained, "I call this live mapping. And look at this, no matter which direction I hold the map, the arrow on the compass rose always points to the

N for the north. Try it." Gala downsized his map and handed it to Ddot.

Ddot turned and faced all directions. "This is amazing, pure magic!" When he finished admiring the map, he looked at Dahc, then Lucky.

Lucky offered, "Go ahead, Dahc, ya can try it next."

Ddot handed the map to his wide-eyed brother. Dahc's mouth formed a wide grin that filled his entire face. He didn't have words. His expressions usually did all his talking. When Dahc finished inspecting the map, still grinning from ear to ear, he passed the live map to Lucky.

"Jumpin' Jingle Beetles! Would ya look at that! This is a great map, Gala, and it gits me to thinkin'. Imagin', writin' a story with Inkle, each page livin', movin', how interestin' it would be to see." As Lucky handed the map back to Gala, it returned to its original size.

Gala rolled up the map, put it away, and agreed, "Lucky, you're a genius! That would be interesting. That's exactly what we'll do, all of us. We'll all write the story of our journey, as we see it, in our own words. We'll express our individual experiences and feelings. Inkle will draw a picture on each page that depicts those words. We'll keep a journal. After we return home, we'll put it all together, make copies and give them out to our family and friends. Here, put these in your satchels and write whatever, whenever you want." Gala handed them some parchment paper and charcoal.

They put away their writing tools, got a bite to eat, rested awhile, then packed up and started back on their journey. It was late afternoon when Trusty stopped to a dead halt. Gala fell forward. The Newlads fell off Gala's shoulders and fluttered next to him. Trusty's head turned towards the north, ears straight up.

"Shhh! I think something's moving over there. I heard a twig snap," Ddot pointed into the shadowy forest.

"It could have been anythin', animals, dead branches fallin', who knows. Let's look and see if we see anythin'," Lucky suggested with a hint of anxiety in his voice.

Gala got off Trusty and motioned his friends to follow. The Newlads stood on a branch of a tree that Gala had crept up and hid behind. Gala peeked around trying to discern any movement in the direction Ddot had pointed. At first, he only saw the forest until his eyes came upon a mist that seemed to glide through the trees. He transformed into Nix, and shook his head, shaking off the wicked faces that flashed in his mind. Nix perched on a separate branch next to where the Newlads stood. He looked towards the north. Nix had a sight as sharp as an eagle's so when his eyes finally focused, he saw what it was, or rather, who it was. "Shhh, do not say anything. Do not move; lay down your wings; do not flutter — Stealth Dragon Slayers."

Six pair of fairy eyes popped out of their sockets. Dahc put his hands over his dropped jaw. When the dragon slayers were out of sight, Nix flew down and transformed back into himself. His voice shook along with his body as he whispered,

"Goodness giver of life and love, if Trusty didn't detect their scent, we wouldn't have seen them. They blend right into the forest like vaporous water, eerie looking."

"I reckon that's the reason they're called Stealth Dragon Slayers," Lucky pointed out. His friends nodded.

"I saw Oxies pulling a humungous crossbow with hefty arrows. Another Oxie was pulling a gigantic apparatus of some sort, and I saw six dragon slayers. They're huge, like the size of twenty-foot giants. Four of them were pushing a cart with a cage on top that had something in it. I bet they're hunting dragons. I gotta think." Gala paced, tapping his thigh as he thought.

Although Gala has never seen a real dragon, he has always wanted to. There were many species, with different likes, dislikes, markings, shapes, and sizes. Some had special powers. Many were caring whereas others were cruel. But the cruel ones were mean due to the training they got from dragon slayers. These dragons helped dragon slayers kill good dragons during the Great Battle of Dragon Slayers. Their grisly massacres practically extinguished dragons from the face of the planet. Gala felt the need to defend all dragons. It's one of the duties of a wizard. But dragon slayers scared him.

Lucky was flabbergasted. "Dragons!? You mean real live dragons?"

"Yes." Gala sounded stern. "I have to stop them."

Lucky had mixed feelings. He had a passion to see an actual dragon instead of a mage in the form of a dragon. He had a curiosity to see if dragons still existed and if so, a fear of what they ate, like fairy meat.

"Chum..." Ddot paused. He knew how much Gala loved dragons, so he chose words that didn't sound discouraging. "I'm not being negative, but what are your plans? How do you expect to stop them? What if they're not hunting dragons?"

Gala stopped pacing. "Ddot, they're dragon slayers; hunting dragons is what they do." Ddot ignored Gala's curt tone knowing his Chum was worried and scared. Gala hurried. He tried to recover his rudeness towards Ddot and said, "But you could be right, Ddot; they might not be hunting dragons. We'll follow them; see what they're up to. If they're hunting dragons, we'll think of something to stop them. My Redtalon could help, but there's no telling what I'd look like without my parent's help. I might be wingless or without scales. It could be disastrous.

"Yeah, easy pickins' for killin'," warned Lucky.

"If only I had time to practice."

"How about one of us? Didn't you tell Acub you could give me, or at least one of us, permission to use your wand?"

"Yes, Ddot. I did, and I'm sure it'll work. I don't see why it wouldn't. But I was hoping we could do it at leisure, so we could practice, but I suppose this is as good a time as any. So, if we need my dragon and there's enough room, I'll give you permission; we'll see what happens. I bet those dragon slayers are on the prowl, getting closer to their target. I'm going to transform into Bunt instead of Nix. Bunt's smaller, swifter, and can whip through dense trees, whereas Nix can't. Bunt flies faster than you guys, so y'all can ride on his back. It'll be a tight fit, but we'll manage. Just hang on tight. I'll tell Trusty to stay here. He can disguise himself, and if we don't come back for him by morning, or if I don't whistle for him by then, he'll go back home."

"Why don't you downsize us to fit on Bunt or fit in your cloak's hidden pocket the way you downsize everything else?"

"That's a good idea, Ddot, but the spell I use to downsize objects might not work for living things. I accidentally cast a *Grow* spell on a living thing once. I shrank it back down to its original size, luckily. But I never tried the *Shrink* spell on anything living. There're too many vibrational elements like cells, chemicals, and all the parts we have in our bodies. That's different than shrinking something solid like wood. It's made up of only a few vibrational elements. If I try it on you, anything could happen. Something unspeakable could go wrong. I'd never forgive myself. Besides, you know that some spells don't affect fairies unless it's a fairy sorcerer casting them. On top of that, Father warned me not to cast it on anything living."

"What about Charms?"

"Ddot. My friend. Some charms don't have effects on you, either. I don't mean to sound rude, but the more we stand around discussing it, the closer the dragon slayers get to their destination, and—"

"ROOOAAAARRRR, ROAR!"

"Never mind! That's a roar of a dragon! I'll transform into Nix and fly above the tree line while you guys hang tight to my neck feathers!"

Gala told Trusty to stay put and disguise. Trusty took the shape and appearance of a large rock like certain dragons can. He blended into the colors of the forest, greens, yellows, browns, and grays. Gala transfigured into Nix. Again, he shook his head because of the wicked faces he saw while transforming. His friends held tight to his feathers as he flew towards the horrifying bellows.

Just ahead, an enormous mountain flourished in the center of a massive lake. A spacious dell surrounded the lake, and a large forest surrounded the dell. The gigantic mountain was a half mile wide as it was high. Nix spotted an adult Lakairian male dragon flying amongst the clouds. The dragon looked about thirty feet in length from its snout to its wavy, feathered, fanned tail. Its blue and green scales gleamed in the sun. He let out another raging bellow which made his scales shimmer. Nix and his friends shuddered.

Nix shook off the chills that ran down his back. He scanned the landscape below and spotted the Stealth Dragon Slayers. They were standing on the west side of the mountain, on the edge of the dell, close to the lake. "Look, guys! The slayers are jabbing a defenseless Lakairian whelp. Her scales are still soft. They locked her in that cage."

"Wicked slayers, those no good for nothing— I feel like...like jabbing them and see how they like it!" Ddot grit his teeth.

Lucky's eyes popped. "Look!" he yelled. "That giant monster of a slayer is doin' it again, jabbin' and cutin' that poor baby with that razor-sharp arrow!"

"Sweet little helpless baby! Shame on them!" Dahc shook his head and spat a dry spit.

"I can't stand it! Her cries are too painful! I need my wand!" Nix flew to the east side of the mountain to hide. After he landed on the dell, his friends flew off his back so he could transform into himself and summon his wand. Gala said, "*Downsize.*" His wand shank to fit into Ddot's hands. While handing it to Ddot, Gala instructed, "Okay, Ddot. Listen carefully. After I close my eyes, point my wand at me and say, Dreckinshire. Got it?"

"Dreck-in-shire?"

"Yes! Dreckinshire."

"I got it!"

"Okay, guys, y'all stay right here. I need some room."

Gala ran to the lake's bank and turned to face his friends. The Lakairian dragon roared with more intensity. A few seconds later, Swoosh! Gala's skin almost leaped off his bones. He felt a powerful force from behind. A startling gush of cold water splashed over his body, soaking him from head to toe. Gala spun around. To his surprise, barreling out of the lake was another adult Lakairian dragon, a female. She whizzed up to join the male dragon who circled the colossal mountain. About that time, the baby dragon shrieked.

Drenched, anxious, fists clenched, and gritting his teeth, Gala turned around and yelled, "Ddot!" Ddot's, Dahc's, and Lucky's attention were on the two fearsome dragons flying overhead. Gala yelled again, but louder, "DDOT!"

"Yes! I'm ready. Hurry, Gala, Hurry!" Gala closed his eyes. Ddot held the wand tight with both hands. He pointed it at his chum and yelled, "*Dreckinshire!*"

The wand vibrated. It turned azure. Its tip shot out a golden beam of sparkling light. It encompassed Gala and filled his entire body. His Redtalon transformation was slower than all the forms he had down pat. The Newlads watched with wide eyes. They saw Gala's golden body and magical clothes change. Gala and his clothes twisted and warped into the shape of an S. The water that had soaked him became a mist before it finally evaporated. Gala's golden S shape body sparkled and popped as he grew, and grew, and grew! With each growth spurt, a little more of Redtalon appeared. His hind legs and forearms expanded into massive muscles. His four paws became equipped with retractable webbed claws. After his transformation, his golden light vanished.

Ddot exclaimed, "Pixie wonders! Gala's Redtalon is huge!" Dahc and Lucky nodded, not able to say anything.

Redtalon was about a hundred feet long from his head to the tip of his razor-sharp, arrow-tipped tail. He was huge. He was bigger than any dragon that ever lived on Mageus. Each wing spanned out approximately forty feet wide. His armored scales glimmered a crimson color. The colors of his clothes, creamy gold—green—brown—red, streaked throughout. However, a lot of his scales were incomplete. Although Redtalon's thick skin is as tough as leather, he was still vulnerable to the elements. His scales aid in protecting him from extreme heat, freezing air, and not to mention, sharp weapons.

    In his baritone voice, Redtalon told his friends to fly to the edge of the forest where the trees butted the dell. He told them to stay hidden until he called for them. After they were at a safe distance, Redtalon jumped upwards. With much vigor, he flapped his wings to gain momentum. The wind from what his wings had generated flattened the grass on the dell and caused the lake's surface to ripple. Redtalon flew above the Lakairian dragons and was unaware that they saw him. They felt threatened, so they flew up to attack him from behind. The Newlads gasped.

    "We have to warn Gala!" Ddot yelled

    "How?" asked Dahc.

    "I don't know! Oh, no! They're flying to the other side of the mountain!" Ddot flew upwards.

    "Hold on!" Lucky grabbed Ddot's foot and held him back. "We caint be in the open. Gala said to stay here until he calls for us. We ain't gonna do him, or us, any good ifin' we're seen. Let's calm down and wait. Ifin' we don't hear or see anythin', we'll make haste up into those trees on the top of the mountain."

"You're right." Ddot landed back down on the branch.

While Redtalon focused on the slayers, the dragons closed in behind him. They sparked their craw and let loose a fiery flame straight towards him. Redtalon roared. Their flame singed his tail. No sooner than Redtalon turned to face them, another burst of fiery breath shot straight for his face. He dove, escaping what could have been severe burns. He flew into a thick cloud to hide, hoping he could lose the dragons. He didn't see them, so he focused on the ground. He gauged the situation and decided to scare the slayers away from the cage. As he flew towards the slayers, the two dragons came behind him, about to let loose another flame. But, when Redtalon swooped close to the baby, they held back their fiery breath. Instead, they flew up and circled overhead to watch.

Redtalon flapped his wings, which hurled the two slayers standing by the cage, and a few others, to the ground. He swooped back up into the sky. The male dragon crept close behind and followed as Redtalon dove back down. Two slayers held tight to a gigantic ballista, cocked, ready to shoot. They had Redtalon's chest in their sites. Redtalon realized what they were about to do. He swooped upwards, and without knowing, he exposed the male dragon into the slayers' line of fire. They pulled the trigger. An immense, four-sided, razor-sharp arrow bolted through the air; it was a hit!

The Lakairian dragon sounded out a most deafening shriek. The arrow had sliced through his thick armored scales. It carved a wide hole deep into his shoulder, a few inches to the right of his neck. The slayers covered their ears and ducked. The dragon flapped one wing over their heads, trying to get away.

The Newlads heard the dragon's cry and couldn't help themselves.

Lucky yelled, "NEVER MIND! Follow me! Let's flap our wings as fast as possible up to those trees." Lucky pointed to the top of the mountain.

"Okay! Lead the way, Lucky. We're right behind you. Come on, Dahc!"

They stood on a large leaf at the top of the mountain. They saw the injured dragon flap fast yet wobbly past the slayers. The arrow sliced inside his shoulder. He shrieked and stopped flapping. He fell aslant towards the lake, skid across the water surface, then across the dell. He crashed and knocked down forest trees before he came to a complete halt. The female dragon flew down and sat next to him.

Redtalon flew towards two dragon slayers who were preparing another apparatus, an enormous net launcher. They hurried, pointed it at Redtalon, then pulled the trigger. "BOOM!" It bolted a large, roped net that spread out like a gigantic web with weights lined around its edges. Redtalon couldn't swoop upwards or dodge the incoming net. He tucked into a ball to prevent any damage while ensnared. The weights twisted around each other, enclosing Redtalon tight within the net.

"NO! Gala's falling!" Dahc yelled, then put his hands over his dropped jaw.

The Newlads hovered above the leaf, flapping their wings one hundred miles a minute or more. They watched their friend cannonball straight into the lake.

The water splashed high like a tidal wave sending slayers into the air and their Oxies across the dell. Two slayers landed in trees while others, along with their weapons and devices, landed in the lake.

The female dragon let out a fearsome roar. She watched the cart and cage holding the baby drift towards the lake. Two slayers swam over and stopped it before it fell in. While the Newlads tried to figure out a way to save Redtalon, the slayers began to regroup.

"Oh no! What are we gonna do? Ddot's voice trembled. They could see Redtalon sinking toward the bottom of the deep dark lake.

"Brother! Use Gala's wand!"

"I don't know how!"

"But you're his best friend; you must have learned something watching him over the years!"

"Listen, Dahc! Gala tells me many things, but the Lakinshires never reveal their secret language to anyone, not even me." Ddot flew back down on the leaf, pacing back and forth. He threw his hands up, down, all around, and huffed, "Today was the first time I ever heard the word, Dreckinshire, let alone held or even used Gala's wand."

"Well, Ddot, why don't ya stop, wavin' that wand 'round so dangerous like ya are. Ifin' ya point it at 'em and say Gala's name, he might switch back into himself!"

"Yeah, maybe he will, Lucky, but not if he's not ready; I'm pretty sure he has to start his transfigure first. It's a two-way communication thing. That's why he told me to wait until he closed his eyes. I don't even know if that's the word he and his parents say to help him turn back into himself."

Lucky held up his clenched fists and opened his hands, stiffly, and yelled, "No! But it's better than doin' nothin'! For all we know, he could be drownin'."

"Okay, fine! Let's just calm down a second. From what Gala's told me about dragons, they can hold their breath for a long time. Follow me." Ddot led them down to the water's edge and stood. They peered into the lake, waiting, debating what to do.

As they debated, Redtalon tried to free himself from the net. But he couldn't open his maw to let loose his fiery flame, nor could he get the net inside his maw to snap it with his teeth. He thought about his other transformations. Several would fit through the net but might not make it to the surface without drowning first. His dolphin form, Phin, was too big. He thought, "I haven't got Redtalon down pat yet. I'm not able to transform into anything new without help. I know I transformed into a ruby without any help, but I didn't do anything to change back into myself. I think the ruby did it for me, and that's the first time I ever transformed into a solid substance. I could flub things up if I try to transform into myself or water. I could drown. I can't use the *Shrink* spell either."

Redtalon racked his brain and adjusted his eyesight to see through the dark water. A silver glint caught his eye. It was a large, two-bladed axe that sank to the bottom of the lake. Redtalon stretched and stretched his tongue, but the axe was out of reach. After three more tries, he was about to give up, but then the axe slipped down a groove his tongue had dug into the dirt floor. He contracted the tip of his tongue to a needle-like shape and wrapped it around the axe.

    Redtalon wiggled, scooted, and adjusted himself next to a large rock. He pushed his snout against the net and stretched it out as far as possible. He swung the axe with his tongue. The blade came down as fast as it could and cut a small strand of the rope. More swinging was needed. This was a difficult task underwater, let alone with the tip of his tongue. It was especially difficult cutting with an axe Redtalon could use as a toothpick. He decided to use the axe like a saw, which seemed to work better. He sawed and sawed until finally the rope snapped making the hole a little bit bigger. But not enough, so he continued sawing. His moving around stirred up a lot of mud, making it difficult to see anything. He also created air bubbles that popped on the water's surface causing panic for the Newlads.

    Ddot screeched, "AIR BUBBLES! Gala's drowning!" Ddot pointed Gala's wand and hoped for the best. "*GALA!*" he yelled. The wand vibrated and turned azure. It shot out its golden light straight through the water and encompassed Redtalon.

    Redtalon felt funny. When he looked up through the cloudy water trying to focus his dragon eyes, he saw the golden light. His eyes followed the light up to his friends who were standing on the bank. He vaguely saw his wand in Ddot's shaky hands. "What in the realm of realms is he doing?" Redtalon felt himself shrinking. The axe got heavier, so he released it. He felt nauseous and confused. He squeezed through the hole he had cut. Like a torpedo, he swam up to his friends without comprehension of how he did it. The Newlads examined the thing that came out of the water. It resembled the friend they knew and loved.

"Jumpin' spookism's! Gala, is that you? I'm so, so, sorry pal. Yo're sure lookin' kinda funny. Yo're lookin' like one of those swamp creatures from one of our spook stories. You have slit pupils settin' in violet eyes with shiny orange, red, and yellow star speckles. Ya have webbed feet, webbed hands, scales here and there, and get a load of yore long arrow-tipped tail. I'm just so da-gom sorry for ya, pal. Are ya feelin' all right?"

"Actually, no. I'm feeling kinda odd and I don't know what the heck you're going on about. 'lookin' kina funny' what's that mean?" Gala touched his face, his stomach. He looked down at his hands, legs, and feet. He twisted at his midriff to look at his rear end. "No wonder I'm feeling mixed up, and you guys are giving me weird gawps and saying I look funny. Thank the giver of life and love I'm a transfigure. If I wasn't, I could be stuck like this!"

Ddot put his hand on his chest. He rejoiced, "Thank the giver you're not jammed between Redtalon and yourself. I could never forgive myself for trying to change you back without you being ready. But if you were stuck looking like you do, you'd still be my best chum."

I'm happy ya ain't gonna be stuck lookin' like that either. Like Ddot, you'd still be my pal ifin' ya were." Lucky was so happy that he felt like laughing, but he held back.

Dahc's brows lifted high above his wide eyes. He pressed his smiling lips together holding back his own snickers.

Ddot saw something behind Gala's ears. He flew over to see what it was. "Well, pixie wonders, would you look at that. You have gills!"

"Yes," Gala jerked his head to the side, showing his gills, then he asked, "Why'd you try to change me back?"

"We didn't know you had gills. You didn't tell us anything about your Redtalon other than he's impressive, to which we agree. When we saw you transfigure, we didn't see gills, so we didn't know. We thought you might drown, especially when we saw air bubbles. So, we decided I should try to change you back into yourself." Ddot felt relieved that his chum wouldn't remain a weird-looking swamp creature. He felt so pleased that he couldn't help himself. He couldn't hold back; he snickered. Dahc and Lucky joined in.

"Okay, guys! Save the laughs. But I admit, if y'all didn't try to help me, I'd still be at the bottom of the lake trying to get out of that net. So, thank you. Let's get back to it. The slayers are regrouping. Ddot, help me change back into Redtalon. I have to stop those dragon slayers and do my best to save the male dragon from bleeding to death."

"But I have to ask."

"Yeah?"

"Well, Chum? How do I use your wand if you fall back into the water in one of those contraptions?"

"They won't catch me again. I'll be alert. Besides, I didn't see another apparatus like that one, and it, along with its net, is at the bottom of the lake. Okay, fellas, back up. And Ddot, point my wand. Remember, you'll know I'm ready when I close my eyes."

Still snickering, the Newlads flew back to give their funny-looking friend room. When Gala closed his dragon eyes, Ddot chuckled, "*Dreckinshire.*"

With more speed and more scales intact, Gala transformed into his impressive Redtalon. He took flight and flew over the dragon slayers. They were busy examining their wounds. He swooped down closer than before and let out an earsplitting roar. The slayers winced and covered their ears. They took off, scattering into the forest, leaving everything else behind. Redtalon landed a distance from the baby before he walked up close to her. He watched the dragon slayers flee for their lives. He heard them exasperating, spatting things like, "Where on Mageus did that beast come from? — It has to go! — Never have I seen the likes of such a monstrous beast! — We'll have to devise a new strategy if we want to catch him! — Catch him! You mean kill him before he kills us! — No one is going to believe us! Let's keep it to ourselves and figure out how to catch him! — Or kill him! — Yeah! Okay, or kill him! — Now we need another blasted whelp! Maybe we'll get that one back! — Let's just get as far away from that beast as possible, keep running! — I don't think it's following us! — I don't care; keep running! Don't look back! Run as fast and as far as you can!"

With that last statement, Redtalon spread his maw, smiling. His pointy teeth sparkled and reflected the orange sky as the sun set across the western sky above the tree line. He turned his gaze towards the two dragons. The female paced back and forth in front of the male. Redtalon could hear her buzzing then the baby cried out. Although the male was in pain, he and his mate called back.

Redtalon called out to his friends, "Guys! Come here! It's safe!"

The Newlads hurried over and fluttered in front of Redtalon's face. Chum? You think those slayers are coming back?"

"No. I heard one say, 'Run as fast and as far away as you can, and don't look back.'"

Ddot wiped his forearm across his forehead and blew, "Phew."

"Yeah. You said it. 'Phew.' I couldn't face them without my Redtalon form, that's for sure."

"What'll we do now?" Ddot asked.

"I need to pull that arrow out of the dragon's shoulder. After I remove it, I'll need to try and stop the bleeding by what Father called cauterizing; I helped him do it once."

"Okay, Chum. But how do you plan to get close? And look! The female keeps looking over here. What happens if you go over there and leave the baby?"

"Good question, Ddot. With all fairy truthfulness, I don't wanna be near any of 'em just in case they wanna spitfire. Ifin' ya know what I'm sayin'."

"Me either, Lucky. And y'all gave me an idea. Just so you know, dragons are no threat to fairies. Actually, they never bother anyone unless they're threatened. Well, except for the ones brought up by dragon slayers. But none of them were around, so we can relax."

"Phew wee! My jumpin' nerves need some relaxin'." Lucky took a deep breath and let it out.

"Me too!" Ddot agreed.

"Me three!" Dahc blurted.

"Well, it isn't over yet, but we'll be all right. Now listen, guys. See the healing moss growing at the edge of the forest?"

"Yeah." The Newlads answered in unison.

"Get enough to cover the baby's wounds. I'll keep the baby's attention while y'all put the moss on her. After you're done, fly back over to the mountain. It'll be safe there.

"Are you sure? What if the female dragon thinks we're hurting the baby while we're inside the cage?"

"Don't worry, Ddot. I don't think she'll attack us while I'm Redtalon.

"But Chum. They attacked you in the air."

"Yeah, they did. But Ddot, they snuck up behind me. They can't sneak up behind me on the ground. And I don't think they want to risk spitting fire around the baby." Redtalon snarled a little under his breath.

"Ddot raised his hands and said, "Okay. Whatever you say, Chum. I just hope you're right."

Lucky brought another thought to Gala's attention. "I'm guessin' the female is the baby's ma, and a mamma can be highly protective of their youngins'. They'll do just about anythin' to protect their babies. My ma and pa were always protective, and they ain't never stopped."

Dahc nodded and said, "Yeah, you're right, Lucky! Ours too."

Redtalon sighed in a low dragon hum and acknowledged, "I agree that the baby is their offspring. But, as I said, I don't think the mother will come over without her mate while I'm anywhere close. Trust me because I have a plan even if she does. After you guys tend to the baby and go over to the mountain, I'll walk over and gather enough moss for the father. Then, I'll get away from the baby. That's when the mother will come to her. When she does, I'll hurry over and put the mother on ice. She'll never have a chance to light her craw. Even if she does, my ice-cold breath will freeze her fire.

"Your craw spits out an ice-cold breath?" Ddot was impressed.

"Freezin' icicles! Yo're a transfigurin' master!" Lucky clapped his hands.

Dahc just grinned.

"I bet you can spit fire, too?"

"Thank you, guys, and yes, Ddot, you bet right. I can spit fire too."

"Dragon wonders! That's impressive! So, Chum, what part of her are you going to put on ice?"

"Good question, Ddot. I thought that I'd put her tail, head, wings, and legs on ice, but leave her nostrils and eyes free. Then I'll fly over and do the same to the father. They won't be able to move until the ice melts or I defrost them."

"Won't the ice hurt them?"

"It could. But don't worry, Ddot. I'll be sure to thaw the ice before they freeze. It shouldn't take me long to craft a rock rod. Then I'll pull that arrow out of the dragon's shoulder. I'll hurry and put the hot end of the rod in, which should sear the inside of his wound and stop the bleeding. I'll cool the rod with my icy breath, pull it out, and put the healing moss on his wound."

"Owie! That sounds like it'll put a hurtin' on 'em."

"Yes Lucky, it's going to hurt. The whole procedure will be painful. The healing moss will stop some pain but that doesn't get put on until the end. So, on second thought, think I'll ice his whole body, keep him from moving. With any luck, by the time the process is over, they'll understand our good intentions."

"Goodness pixie wisdom! That sounds like a great plan. Hopefully, it works. You're amazing, Chum! Your Redtalon spits fire, and ice, and has gills! You're remarkable!"

Dahc slapped down on his knee, "You said it brother."

"Yo're mighty powerful that's for sure, and there ain't never a dull moment! Come on pals, let's git goin'. I see a star startin' the night." Lucky pointed at the sky.

"Okay, guys, let's do this. We have about four hours before the waning light of the day gives way to the night. And Ddot, I'm sorry for snarling at you. I know you're concerned for our safety."

"Apology accepted, Chum. Nerves are shaking in all of us." Ddot and Redtalon smiled at each other. Then Ddot said, "Okay, fellas, let's execute this plan."

The Newlads covered the whelp's wounds, then flew to the mountaintop and sat on an enormous tree branch. They watched Redtalon begin his strategy.

Redtalon gathered large pieces of moss, then flew around to the other side of the mountain. He could see the mother, but she couldn't see him. The baby cried out to her parents. Her mother hurried over. She made clicking noises as she inspected the moss and the strange object that held her baby captive. When Redtalon saw the mother engrossed, he flew above the clouds until he was directly over her. He pointed his head downwards, laid his wings to his sides, and dropped. The mother could hear the wind as it passed around Redtalon's enormous body. She spotted a shadow on the ground circling her. She jerked her head upwards. Before she sparked her ferocious flame, Redtalon had already clicked his right craw. Out from his maw came a blue and white freezing breath; an icy snow shot straight towards the mother's face. He iced her head, leaving her eyes and nostrils free. Redtalon hurried. He iced her legs, wings, and tail in place. She thrashed her neck and bowed her back. Redtalon encased her neck and back to prevent her from injuring herself.

The male dragon mustered all his strength to stand. But fell hard to the ground jogging the arrow. Its razor-sharp tip cut more of the tender tissues deep within his shoulder. An unbearable pain shot throughout his body. A great deal of blood spilled from his gaping wound. He got weaker with each passing moment.

Redtalon flew towards the father, who had released a flame from his maw straight at Redtalon's face. Redtalon reared his neck, ignited his ice-cold breath, and blew. After his icy breath hit the hot flame, it turned into a significant amount of water, which fell to the ground. Redtalon released another burst of freezing breath. Ice covered the father's entire body except for his eyes, nostrils, and the area where the arrow had punctured. Redtalon didn't waste time. He scavenged the stones around the dell, then placed them in a long line. His fiery breath welded the rocks together, making them one complete rod. He cooled one end of the rod, grabbed the arrow, pulled it straight out, and tossed it a few feet away. Then, he picked up the cold end of the rod and stuck the hot end down into the wound.

The dragon let out a growl which muted within his frozen encasement yet caused the ice to crack around his face. The vertical slits of the dragon's pupils dilated and tripled in size. Redtalon narrowed his maw to a tiny opening, ignited his icy craw, then blew on the hot rod. It cooled straight down to the bottom of the wound. Redtalon pulled the rod out and threw it next to the arrow. The father's eyes rolled to the back of his head before they shut. Redtalon saw that the deep hole in his shoulder had stopped bleeding.

After he packed the father's injury with healing moss, he flew over to retrieve the mother and her baby. While carrying them in his forearms, he flew back to the father and gently set them beside him. The father's eyes were still closed.

The Newlads couldn't sit still. They fluttered above the mountain, anticipating Redtalon's every move. They watched as he took the baby out of the cage and set her in front of her mother. The baby lay still. Redtalon picked the cage up with his mouth and walked in front of the dragons, keeping his distance. By using his fiery craw, he incinerated the cage. He collected a few more patches of healing moss and carried it back to the dragon family. He placed a patch on one of the baby's cuts where a piece of moss had fallen off. Redtalon set the rest of the moss in front of the mother, hoping she would understand his intentions. When he finished, he walked behind them, lit his fiery craw, then blew out a warm heat, defrosting them.

After the ice melted, the male's head fell on his mate's body. Filled with fury, she nudged him and roared, thinking he was dead! Luckily, her reactions stirred her mate, which caused him to wake up and come to. His eyes blinked open. After a second or two, he felt the pain in his shoulder and recollected everything that had happened. He lifted his head and nuzzled his family. Before he turned to look at

Redtalon, he saw the deadly arrow lying next to the rock rod.

The male's eyes looked gentle when he sounded a low click and grunt. Redtalon remained cautious. He walked around the dragon family until he faced them, keeping his right craw ready. They didn't shoot fire, so he tilted his head downwards to bow. After they returned his bow, they produced a low humming noise. It came from deep within their diaphragm. They made a click with their tongue against the roof of their maw. Redtalon stepped back, spread his wings, then flew over to the edge of the dell and landed. The Newlads flew down to Redtalon.

"Unbelievable! I'm beside myself, Chum."

"Ya ain't a kiddin' there, Ddot ole pal! Jumpin' Juney's and Tummy Jingles were dancin' 'round in my gut! Talk about intense!"

All wide-eyed Dahc could say was, "Wow!"

"Come with me. I want the dragon family to know we're friends. Y'all can ride on my head and hold tight to my spikes."

The Newlads held on to Redtalon's spikes while he flew over and landed in front of the dragon family. They were calm even when Redtalon walked closer than he had before.

"Okay, Chum, now what?"

"I need you to help me transform into myself."

The Newlads flew down next to Redtalon. "Okay, Chum," Ddot said. "Ready when you are." Redtalon closed his eyes. Ddot held Gala's wand with both hands. He pointed it and said, "*Gala!*" Ddot noticed that Gala's wand shook less than it did before. It turned azure, and a golden light shot out from its tip. The light encompassed Redtalon and filled his body. His body twisted around, reshaping, and shrinking. Gala and his friends could tell that this transformation took less time. Gala smiled as he watched the Lakairian family tilt their heads to one side. They saw a tiny two-legged wizard take the place of the gigantic dragon.

    Ddot handed Gala his wand. After it returned to its original size, Gala concealed it. Poof! It vanished from his hand. He transfigured into his Bunt, Nix, and back into himself. He used Sorcermizic language and said, "*Appara Comforte.*" Poof! His wand appeared in his hand. He pointed it at a stone and chanted his *Levitation* spell. The stone hovered for five seconds before Gala put it back down. He wanted the dragons to know he was a Mystique Transfigure. But more than anything, Gala wanted them to know they could trust him and his friends. He put his wand away then bowed. The mother and father returned the bow. The baby made breathy, throaty noises as if she were giggling.

Mystique Blueblood

Although the Lakairian father staggered to his feet, he managed to walk across the dell to the lake. His webbed feet spread out when he stepped into the water. Like a magnificent swan, he sat on the lake. He used his left forearm to keep him steady, and by using his hind legs, he paddled around to face his family. From deep within his throat came a low grunt. His mate held their baby with her forearms and flew over to him. She landed on the water with grace. She looked over at their rescuers and sounded out a few clicks.

"Hey, guys. I think they want us to follow them. I'll try to transfigure into Redtalon on my own. I'll walk between you and the dragons and give it a go." Gala walked between everyone. He closed his eyes, and with a clear image of Redtalon, he transformed into his magnificent dragon like a pro. His dragon smile spread wide. Without making much of a ripple, he slipped his webbed feet into the water and sat. "Come on, guys!" He called out to his friends in a tenor voice, "You guys get on my head! Let's follow them!"

"Well, look at that! Your Redtalon floats on top of the water as they do." Ddot pointed out.

"Yes. My Redtalon is a mixture of several dragon types. These are Lakairian dragons, also known as Waterswan Dragons. They have webbed paws like me but no gills. They're exceptional swimmers. They remind me of the white Swanian birds that come to Crystal Lake on the nights we have two full moons. Of course, the dragons are way bigger. Look, guys! The dragons are headed towards the mountain."

The dragon family swam close to the mountain and stopped. They stretched and rubbed their necks together. As they hugged, a humming noise came out from their diaphragms. Finally, the mother and her whelp dove into the lake and swam under the mountain. The father made clicking noises toward Redtalon and the Newlads.

"That's the same sound the mother made after she landed in the lake. I think he wants us to follow him. I'll swim closer." They followed the dragon around to the north side of the mountain. He carefully stepped onto its bank.

"I know ya said dragons don't bother anyone, but what do they like to eat?" Everyone heard Lucky gulp hard.

"Ha-ha! It's okay, Lucky. If they were going to eat us, they would have done it after I transformed into myself. You don't have anything to worry about because they only eat certain things, and we are not on their menu. Remember, they're no threat to fairies."

The male dragon walked through roots about half the size of himself. He stood still among flowering shrubs larger than the four companions had ever seen. He turned his head and looked up to meet Redtalon's eyes. After their eyes met, the father dragon made the same click sound he and his mate had sounded out twice prior. Redtalon nodded.

Beyond the flowering shrubs came a rumbling resonance, like an earthquake. The four companions shuddered. They heard sandy, scraping noises. The mountain moved. It extended outwards right in front of the father dragon. Its dirt and rocks ground together as they folded up, out, and back on each other. Like magic, an expansive cave expanded in every direction. It stopped after its width was a bit wider than Redtalon's body, and its height reached far above his head. With fixed expressions, wide eyes, and raised brows, the Newlads looked back and forth at each other. Dahc's mouth agape.

Redtalon followed the father dragon into the cave. After they walked through and out the other end of the cave, rumbling noise came from the mountain. Redtalon turned his head to see what was happening. The Newlads jumped off his head and turned around, fluttering in place. Rocks, roots, and dirt were grinding together, folding back down and in on each other. The cave's opening closed as if there had never been a cave.

The Newlads continued to flutter in place. Redtalon froze while his wizard self mused. "Maybe I'm wrong to trust the dragons. Maybe something terrible is about to happen." But his dragon senses said something different. He looked at his friends and pled, "Ddot and Dahc, PLEASE release your wing's essence over us so we can calm down. I'm sure we're safe."

"Sheesh! I don't know why I didn't think of that."

"Me either, brother." Dahc agreed while he and Ddot released their essence.

"It's called Fairy-Forgetfulness. It happens sometimes, especially when those ole Jitterbugs git a hold of ya. And believe me, they were hoppin' in my stomach creatin' a heapin' havoc. Thanks to y'all, they're gone, for now, that is."

"You're welcome, Lucky." Dahc patted Lucky's shoulder.

"Yeah. Thanks, guys. I feel better, too."

"You're welcome, Chum. I'm glad you thought of it because I'm not thinking straight." Ddot patted the top of Redtalon's head.

Redtalon turned his head back towards the father and was dumbfounded. "Whoa! Guys! Get a load of this place!" The Newlads turned around.

Ddot felt like he was dreaming. His words came out slow, "W o n d e r o u s W o n d e r s!"

"Jumpin' Juneys never jumped higher! No limitin' to this vastness!" Lucky sounded out a long whistle.

Dahc's jaw dropped further, but he closed it long enough to say, "WOW!"

Redtalon remembered when he was a youngster, and his father read him a story titled The Wizard of Oz. At one point in the story, his father said, 'Todo, we're not in Kansas anymore!' Redtalon didn't quite understand what he meant until now. His father would have called this place a realm within realms.

Thinking of his father made him anxious, but he brushed the feeling off. It's a wizard rule that if someone needs his help, he's not allowed to ignore it. He was obligated to serve the dragons and save them from the Stealth Dragon Slayers if he could. Besides, he had no clue where his loved ones were. The dragon family captured his fascination. Regardless of where the father dragon led, Redtalon followed. He wanted to learn more about them, be sure they were out of danger, then he and his friends would continue their quest.

Ddot interrupted everyone's thoughts, "Look at the size of those flowers!"

"Yeah, and get a load of those roots!" Redtalon pointed with his snout.

Dahc yelled, "It's raining!" Then his mouth hung back open.

Lucky's mouth hung open, but not as long as Dahc's. He expressed, "Quaffin' roots drinkin' rainwater like they're thirstin' to death."

Glittering rain drenched the soil. The roots lifted, up and down—up and down, gulping the sparkling water inside the tree's trunk. Water traveled into the tree's large veins. Then, its veins carried the glittering water throughout its branches and leaves. The entire tree shimmered.

"My winging wonders, would you look up at that canopy!" Ddot pointed his finger. "You can see the sky through some of those humongous leaves! The mountain must open wherever or whenever it needs to. In this case, I suppose it opened there to let the rain in. I couldn't see down inside the mountain from outside when we flew over. How about you guys? Dahc, Lucky? Did either of you see inside the mountain when we flew over?"

"All I saw were trees the size of our planet," Dahc exaggerated.

Then Lucky answered, "Come to think of it, I waden payin' attention, too many dragons flyin' 'round."

"Speaking of dragons, look up ahead." Redtalon motioned his head and neck toward a white dragon lying down. His head rested on moss—he wasn't moving. "There's the mother and baby dragon that we rescued. They're standing next to that white dragon. Look! More dragons, several types of dragons, sitting and standing behind them. They're beautiful. The orange-red dragons have spiny tails. The dark-green dragons have pointy tails. And look there. The rustic-gold dragons have arrow-tipped tails. They're a tad bigger than the blue-green Lakairian dragons!"

"And look over there!" Ddot pointed beyond the dragons. "It's a water spring. It must lead out under the mountain and into the lake. That's probably what the mother and baby swam up through."

The father dragon stopped in front of the white dragon. He bent his head down, nudging him with his nose while sounding out a few soft clicks and a low growl. The white dragon blinked his weary eyes open. He lifted his head and looked up at Redtalon.

"You are the wizard Drameer has informed me of. She said you saved her baby, Chizel, and her mate, Dreamster. She said you are a young wizard."

Redtalon and his friends were speechless. Their eyes popped, and now all their jaws dropped. The white dragon spoke to them in their language. Redtalon regained himself but stuttered his first few words, "Y-yes. A-actually, I-I'm a Mystique Transfigure. My name is Gala Lakinshire. I call my dragon form Redtalon, and these are my friends, but they always call me Gala no matter what shape I take." The Newlads flew off Redtalon's head and hovered beside him so he could transform into himself. Redtalon's body filled with sparkling golden light. The light shrank as he transformed into his wizard self. Gala's transformation took less time than before. He pointed his hand, palm up, and continued his introductions. "These two are Newlads of the Bluewing Fairy Clan, Ddot, and his twin brother, Dahc. This is our good friend, Eric, but we call him Lucky. Lucky's a Southland fairy. As far as we know, he and his parents are all that's left of their clan called the Tuberous Tribe."

"I know those names. Please forgive me. My eyesight is not like it once was. Come closer so I can see you."

Gala and his friends moved closer. The white dragon made out their faces and was happily surprised, "It is you! All of you! I thought so!"

"What do you mean? Have we met? I don't remember meeting you. How do you know us?"

"Yes, Gala. We have met. I should show you. However, I need you to promise complete secrecy that what you see here stays here."

"Of course, you can trust us. We promise to keep your secrets." Gala nodded his head and motioned his hand toward his friends. They were also nodding in agreement.

"Thank you. Our mountain and our lake, and the forest that surrounds the dell, is our home. We've lived here before the Ultra Storm and the Great Battle of Dragon Slayers. Our three moons will be full soon. I've protected this domain for several of those occurrences. I've kept it hidden with my spell and the foliage covering large boulders surrounding our land. However, it has been breached, and it's due to the recent attack on my life. I grow weaker with each passing moment, so I need to transform before I cannot. My transformation is going to take longer due to my injuries. So, bear with me, and don't become troubled or uneasy at what you're about to witness." After Gala and the Newlads nodded, the white dragon closed his eyes. His scales began to merge. His wings blended into his body, followed by his legs, claws, neck, and tail. Everything melded together. His entire body became a substance that formed into a thick white blob. The blob bulged outwards, protruding a neck, a head, and facial features with closed eyes. Arms, hands, fingers, feet, and toes jutted outwards. A body resembling a stone statue took shape. A rosy-pink color appeared in the center of his forehead. It expanded across his face and the rest of his body, bringing life to his skin. Salt and pepper hair grew from his head and stopped at his shoulders. Fingernails grew in. White leather-wrapped boots, a white cloak and a wizard's white gown, came to fruition. The wizard opened his eyes.

"SPARK!" Gala and his friends yelled in unison.

"Yes. It is me. The very same wizard you met yesterday." Spark leaned back on a soft pile of moss-covered leaves and coughed a wet cough, "Cou, cu, cos." Gala fumbled as he reached into his pocket for a handkerchief. When he knelt to hold it over Spark's mouth, Spark coughed up blue blood.

"You're a wizard! I mean, not just any wizard, but a Mystique Blueblood Wizard! What happened?" Gala's voice broke up. He felt sorrowful yet excited that he stood in the presence of a Mystique Blueblood.

Dragons, Bluebloods alike, have become scarce. But Gala doubted Mystique Bluebloods still existed. They are unique male or female sorcerers who are half-dragon.

"Have a seat," Spark said while adjusting himself into a more comfortable position. The Newlads sat on a nearby plant. Chizel lay with her head next to Spark's stretched-out legs. Her parents were behind her, and the rest of the dragons were still standing, sitting, or lying down. "Before I tell you what happened, let me introduce you to my friends."

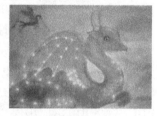

"Oh yeah, sure," Gala humbly complied. He placed his handkerchief into Spark's hand, then sat next to him on another soft pile of mossy leaves.

"You've met Dreamster, Drameer, and Chizel. Here are the others." Spark extended his arm, palm up, sweeping it towards the other dragons. He smiled, then continued, "There are twenty-five dragons. I've given names to each and written a book describing their biographical attributes. I depicted their uniqueness with detailed drawings. They are my friends, my family, or I sometimes call them my thunder."

The four companions nodded and said hello. Dahc waved at all the dragons. They reciprocated by making clicking noises or sounding out a few short hums. After their greetings, Spark shared what had happened. "Yesterday evening, I told you that I would seek the Elfkies. A little fib on my part to protect my identity. After I left your castle, I had time to check in on my thunder before traveling to The Wizard's High Council. As you now know, my dragon form is solid white. My scales reflect the colors around me, which enables me to hide amongst the clouds. I would have reached The Wizard's High Council much faster than the Elfkies could have carried me.

"I told my thunder of our missing loved ones. I told them to go out early for their nightly hunt. While they hunted, I checked my protective spell as my dragon form. A loud crackling startled me. I didn't see anything at first, but shortly after, I heard a loud whine and trees whirring. Then a powerful force tugged at me. My scales felt like they might rip from my body. Another crackling sound that was much louder, directly behind me, jarred my entire body. I turned and saw a dark Twirlwind heading straight for me. It shot out bolts of lightning. They were thicker than any I've ever seen, unnatural, like the work of a wizard."

Gala's heart thumped. "A 'Twirlwind,' you say? '...the work of a wizard?'"

"Yes. A fierce Twirlwind. Try as I might, I couldn't escape or cast spells. It appeared I was under attack. It sucked me in, twirling me into trees while its bolts crashed. I became sick and dizzy; my head hit something hard. Next, I was coming to, lying against one of the boulders surrounding our forest on the north side border. The boulder had fallen and left an opening. Dreamster, Drameer, and a few other dragons were there. They managed to help me inside the safety of our mountain.

"Morning was drawing near, and some dragons were still hunting. They hunt through the night into the morning hours. This and my *Protection* spell protects them against Stealth Dragon Slayers. It also stops wicked sorcerers from discovering their existence. Shortly after they brought me inside, the other dragons came in from hunting. I told them about the Twirlwind and what happened to me. Drameer laid her head on Dreamster's neck and cried uncontrollably. We love and care for each other, but I knew it was not only my injuries that caused her hysteria, so I asked what was wrong. They told me that Chizel was missing. I gasped!"

"Sniff, sniff," Dahc moaned. His red eyes and nose watered. Ddot put his arm around Dahc's shoulders as they continued to listen.

"After Drameer calmed down, she told me what had happened. She said that when she had heard the thundering crack, she and Chizel were swimming in the lake. Dreamster was hunting. Drameer hid Chizel on the bank of the dell and flew up to see what had caused the noise. She called out to Dreamster, then looked down at Chizel, who had curled under a tall patch of grass. After Drameer called out to Dreamster again, she saw the Twirlwind pass. However, she did not see my limp dragon body twirling inside. She yelled for Dreamster a few more times, still checking on Chizel. The last time she looked down, Chizel was gone!"

"Oh no! How terrifyin'! Forgive me for interruptin'. Those disturbin' feelins' are what I felt not seein' Gala's parents, Floreena, or Lidee. That scary darkinin' of the castle last night was terrifyin'! Please, tell us what happened next."

"You're correct to say 'terrifying,' Lucky. Not finding Chizel horrified Drameer. She searched for Chizel throughout the grassy dell. She flew across the forest, calling out to her baby but finding no trace. Drameer screamed a mournful gut cry. Dreamster and a couple other dragons had heard her between the bursts of thunder. Like a flash of light, they were at her side. They searched for Chizel until early morn, but instead, they found me. After they helped me into the safety of the mountain and tended to my needs, they told me about Chizel. I told them to continue their search. They searched most of the day, then Dreamster heard his baby girl scream a dreadful cry."

Ddot interjected, "Yeah! We heard her too! It was awful."

Dahc nodded his head in agreement and sniffed. He wiped the tears from his face with his hand, then used his sleeve to wipe his nose. Ddot patted his brother's shoulder.

"Gala saw the dragon slayers walkin' through the forest with somethin' in a cage. He figured they were huntin' dragons and ifin' they were, he should try to stop 'em. Although we had some shakin' nerves, we went along. Glad we did. Please continue, Wizard Spark."

"Thank you, Lucky. The dragons followed Dreamster as he flew toward Chizel's cries. Her cries led them to the edge of the dell and the lake, where they saw her caged. Dreamster dove down into the forest to hide. Drameer and the other dragons followed behind him. He told the dragons to retreat into the safety of our mountain. Although Drameer was reluctant, she went with the others. When Dreamster saw they were safe within the mountain, he flew back up, then down towards Chizel. As he approached, a dragon slayer stabbed Chizel with the sharp tip of an arrow. He taunted Dreamster. Dreamster roared at the slayer, then flew back up."

"We saw Chizel get stabbed, too. It was after I transformed into Nix. That's when I flew over to the other side of your mountain. Right before Ddot helped me transform into my Redtalon, we heard Chizel squeal. Her father let out a roar more dreadful than before. About that time, right behind me, Drameer came barreling up out of the lake."

"Yes. Everyone inside heard Dreamster roar. Of course, Drameer could not contain herself. She had to help save Chizel; she dove into the spring, swam under the mountain, then up and out of the lake. I'm certain that's when you saw her."

"Yes. I was standing on the bank of the dell when Drameer came barreling out of the water. Please, Wizard Spark, go on."

"Some time had passed, which seemed like an eternity. We heard the loudest dragon roar ever bellowed, which we now know was your Redtalon. I wanted to see what was happening, but my dragon friends rightfully stopped me. If the slayers had discovered the dragons, they'd seek to destroy every last one. Except, they'd keep their hatchlings or eggs and raise them for evil purposes. But if they captured Bluebloods, they'd keep them captive for their blood. A Blueblood held captive will die before their natural transcendence.

"Mystique Bluebloods are rarely captured by Stealth Dragon Slayers. A Mystique Blueblood, like me, is born as you are born, not as an egg, but as a baby. After we reach a certain age, from childhood to adolescence, our blood will morph. We will no longer bleed red blood, but instead, we will bleed blue blood. It's a painful transition. While our blood goes through this transition, we'll transform into our dragon half for the first time. All Mystique Bluebloods endure this. I was fortunate because my parents performed what is called a Bloodra Ceremony. It helps relieve the pain. You may not have read this in your studies, Gala. Some books are not accurate."

"You're right. I don't remember reading anything about the Bloodra Ceremony. My parents might know, but they never told me. Spark, I speak for myself and my friends. We're sorry the slayers found their way into your home."

"If you four hadn't come along— Let me just say that we were relieved when Drameer and Chizel came up through the spring. Drameer told me how you helped save them and mended their wounds. The moss you applied had fallen off after you saw them dive into the water. Drameer picked healing moss from within the mountain and put it on Chizel to show me what you had done. Shortly after, you and the Newlads entered the mountain, following behind Dreamster."

"We're so glad you're okay, Chizel." Gala looked down and gave Chizel a rub on her head.

"We're indebted to you. I cannot inform The High Council of our missing loved ones. I'm fading and may not see another day. I'm truly, sorry."

"That's okay, Wizard Spark. My friends and I can travel to The High Council and—"

"No young mage. You'll need to continue your journey to Gnome Bloom. Day or night, the way to The High Council is long and arduous. You will not, I repeat, you will not be able to use your Redtalon in the open, especially during the day. Stealth Dragon Slayers dwell throughout. You cannot risk them seeing you. Cou, cuf," Spark coughed. He was tense, adamant, and concerned.

"I understand. But my Redtalon is much larger than any dragon that ever lived, and if they know I'm a wizard, they won't bother me."

"Yes, but not while you're flying in your dragon form. Do you remember your studies about flight differences between Bluebloods and dragons? Bluebloods and Mystique Bluebloods have the same flight style, and dragons have their own flying pattern."

"Oh yeah. I'm not thinking straight. That's one of the main subjects all mystics have to study. You're right, Wizard Spark; they fly differently, in their own unique way."

"The dragon slayers also know the difference. They are experts at what they do. Your Redtalon is a dragon and flies exactly like a real dragon. Gala, I took the risk to travel to The High Council because I know those lands. I easily blend in with the clouds. If the dragon slayers knew you were a Mystique Transfigure and I was a Mystique Blueblood, they might not harm us. I say 'might' because their main goal is to capture dragons and Blueblood dragons. But they don't care for the likes of us, Mystiques or Transfigures." Gala sighed. "When you scared them off today, they had no idea who you were. They only saw a dragon. Some of them might want to capture you. Some would rather see a dragon of Redtalon's magnitude dead." Gala gulped. "If they were to capture you and find that you were a Mystique Transfigure, they still might kill you. They would fear your magnificence. Do not take that risk. My strong intuition tells me your loved ones are in the opposite direction of The High Councils. They are closer to you than you might think."

When Gala shrugged his shoulders, he bent his elbows, held his palms up, and said, "For some reason, I have that feeling. Sometimes I feel like I just know things."

"This is true. We all have intuitive abilities, some more than others. The Intuitive Ones live throughout our planet. Their insight developed at birth. They are rare beings. You may not understand, or you don't trust your intuition. It could be that it's undeveloped. Do your best to trust your gut."

"Okay. I'll do as you suggest."

"Good. I want you to find Gnome Bloom. It's up to the four of you to find our loved ones, and as I said, I'm sure Bloom can help. I know you need to make haste, and I want nothing more than to urge you on, but now we need more of your help if you can?"

"Of course, right guys?"

The Newlads nodded. Dahc said, "Yeah!"

Ddot said, "We'd love to!"

Lucky added, "Anythin' we can do to help!"

"The Twirlwind knocked down the boulder on which I was lying unconscious. But it also knocked down others. More than likely, this is how the slayers found their way in. Also, my *Protection*, or *Cloaking* spell, has stopped working."

"We'll put every boulder in place, then collect the things the dragon slayers left behind and burn them."

"Thank you, Gala, Newlads. Putting the boulders back will protect the dragons for a while. I doubt the slayers will be returning anytime soon."

Gala spread his lips into a satisfying grin and agreed, "I don't think they will either. According to what I heard them say, they won't be back for a long time. But...," Gala stopped grinning. "I did hear one of them say that someday they'll come back looking for me, or rather Redtalon."

"This is why it's important to know your surroundings. Do not transform into Redtalon, or anything, until you know your surroundings."

"I'll remember. My father told me the same thing. Sometimes I'm hurried by my feelings. I need to calm down and think."

"That happens. In time, you'll learn to calm yourself before becoming too hasty. Cou, cu, cos," Spark coughed and used Gala's handkerchief to cover his mouth.

Gala reached out and touched Spark's shoulder. "Is there anything else we can do?"

"We need my *Cloaking* spell around the entirety of our home. Although the mountain helps to protect us by having a mind of its own, it's not enough. You saw it open an entrance large enough for your Redtalon. It knows the motives or intentions of others. It won't allow dragon slayers to enter. As you can see, vegetation and spring water are abundant inside the mountain. However, dragons need more than this to survive. They need the protein of Cofish, Furhoppers, and Burrowsnipps, which are plentiful in these parts, but outside the mountain. They must hunt outside the mountain at least once every five suns. Cou-cu-cos-couss." Spark's wet cough was raspy, and his breathing abated.

Gala could hardly believe that he may never see another Mystique Blueblood. "Isn't there anything I can do? Or can't you drink your blood? In my studies, I learned your blood heals. Anyone injured who drinks your blood or the blood of a Blueblood dragon will heal."

"Yes. This is true for all beings. But my injuries are internal throughout, irreversible damage. My insides are torn. My stomach will not digest my blood."

Gala and his friends hung their heads and sighed.

"It's okay, young mage, Newlads. I've lived a happy and successful, long life in this body. I'm thankful to the giver of goodness, life, and love. The journey I'm about to take is a journey that comes with birth into this realm. All will face it. Although, I doubt you'll be facing yours any time soon. At least, I hope not. There's much to see and learn. But for now, let's talk about my *Cloaking* spell that I want you to perform."

Gala grimaced at the thought of his so-called wizardry powers he hadn't mastered. He thought of his inability to cast new spells, let alone unfamiliar ones. Gala wondered about the botched *Protection* spell he and his parents put on their castle. He nodded, shook his head, shrugged his shoulders, and used his hands as he spoke without coming up for much air.

"Yes, no. I mean, I don't know if I can because I never heard of a *Cloaking* spell until tonight. I doubt I can perform it because our protective dome didn't work during the celebration last night. We saw a six-winged fluttery bounce off it, not able to pass. Our spell may have only prevented small creatures or insects from passing through. I don't know, but I do know it was supposed to keep our guests safe and those not on our guest list out, but something went wrong. Our spell must have failed." Gala took a breath and started up again. "Heck, Wizard Spark, you thought you saw the **Shadow** right before the chaos happened, and everyone else saw the pitch and smelt a strange odor, but me, I didn't know anything except that one minute I was getting ready to show everyone my new transformation, next thing I know, I hear Ddot yelling for me as I'm unwrapping my mother's drapes from around me without a clue of how I got there." Gala took another breath and continued, "After that, my friends and I discovered our loved ones missing, and if our *Protection* spell did work, then maybe there's another way into the castle, a way in that my parents and I didn't know about." Gala clenched his fists and grit his teeth. His eyes watered, and his voice grew louder as his words hastened even more, "My father does have secrets! Maybe he knows about another entrance, a secret passage!" Gala stopped speaking. His eyes shifted from Spark's to the floor, his mood pensive. His eyes glazed over as he stared for a moment. Then he spoke quietly as if to himself, "On second thought, Father couldn't have known because if he had, I'm sure he would've said something. There can't be a secret passageway, or we would have protected that too. I just don't—"

"Hold on there, young mage. Relax." Spark patted Gala's clenched fists. Ddot fluttered above his chum, releasing the soothing essence from his wings as Spark comforted, "I know your father well. Don't be suspicious of him keeping secrets. If he does, he does it for good reasons. Your father would have protected any secret passage if he knew of any."

Gala wiped the wetness from his eyes and looked back at Spark's gentle gaze. "You're right. I'm just worried. Thank you for helping me calm down. Thank you too, Ddot."

Ddot flew down next to Gala. "Anytime, Chum, anytime."

"May I suggest another scenario?"

"Sure," replied Gala. The Newlads nodded.

"Last night, while I was checking my *Cloaking* spell before the Twirlwind came upon me, I thought it possible, and although the four of you may find it hard to consider, please do, that someone invited to the celebration was responsible for taking our loved ones."

A quiet pause filled the air. Gala's face turned red. The vein in the middle of his forehead bulged as he started to stew. His voice snarled, "He wouldn't." Then Gala blurted, "No!" Gala shook his head while trying to convince himself, "I know he's capable, and I thought that maybe he did, but it's just ridiculous for me to even think such a thing." Again, Gala shook his head then he jumped up from his seat. His body stiffened. He stomped over to a rock seat and plopped down. He bent over, put his elbows on his knees, then placed his forehead in his hands.

"Enlighten us. Who wouldn't do what?" Ddot asked as he flew over to his chum.

Gala looked up, put his arms down, and without coming up for air, he explained, "Well, when

Helsin showed up to the celebration, he came across Bridge as a Twirlwind but without bolts, then you guys felt a wind right before I attempted to show everyone my new transformation, and I know that Helsin has been mean to me lately, but I can't see why he would harm or even take anyone, let alone my parents or my girlfriend and her mother."

I wouldn't put it past him!" Ddot sternly disagreed, "He's jealous of you. And come to think of it, I didn't see him after the black pitch lifted."

"Neither did I," added Lucky.

"Me either." Dahc shook his head.

"I don't remember seeing Helsin or even thinking much about him after I danced with Floreena. Wizard Spark, you mentioned that the Twirlwind you encountered could have been an angry wizard. Although Helsin isn't a Mystique Transfigure, he is a wizard. And as I said, he came across Bridge as a Twirlwind. But it has be a coincidence. It just has be."

"I wouldn't put anythin' past Helsin. He caint be trusted. I saw him trip ya after Floreena accepted to dance with ya."

Ddot flew next to Lucky and said, "I agree with Lucky."

"Me too," Dahc nodded.

"Helsin wouldn't have taken them. Would he?! If I find out he had anything to do with it, he'll-he'll regret it!"

"It sounds plausible, but, as you said, it could be a coincidence. More facts are needed. Although you want to consider all avenues, don't rack your brains on wondering, and don't make assumptions.

Use your energy to concentrate on getting to Gnome Bloom. Remember what I told you. Bloom can read minds. Sometimes the trees speak to him, show him things, and...cuf, cos, couf." Spark couched up more blood.

    Gala jumped up and ran over beside him. "Okay, Wizard Spark. We won't rack our brains. We'll put the *Protection* spells around your home and burn all the equipment and weapons that belonged to the dragon slayers. We'll get going and be back as soon as we're finished. I need to call my Hobbgie after we're done."

    "What's your Hobbgie's name?"

    "Trusty."

    "A fitting name for such a loyal creature." Spark smiled, then added, "Dreamster will show you where the down boulder is and the perimeters of our land. I'll inform the dragons of Trusty. But first, I want you to do a couple more things. One of them involves my *Cloaking* spell."

    "Sure."

    "I want you to walk over to that tunnel."

    "That one?" Gala pointed.

    "Yes. Inside, you'll find a desk. To the right side of my desk, in the third drawer, are a few of my books. Take the one titled *Dreamster's Language* and bring it here."

    "Okay." Gala walked into the long tunnel lit by glow bugs and blue illuminating mushrooms. A few feet in, on the left side of the tunnel, Gala saw Spark's cedar desk. Above it was an alcove covered by a cedar door engraved with an intricate dragon design. Its handle was a star-sapphire shaped into a crystal ball, setting on a silver pedestal. To the left of the door was a small hole which resembled a keyhole. Gala reached down and opened the third drawer on his right as Spark had instructed. Several books were neatly stored with their spines upwards, displaying their titles. Next to *Dreamster's Language* book was the book Spark wrote, *Dragon's Biographical Uniqueness.* When Gala pulled out *Dreamster's Language* book, he saw a book that heightened his interest. Its title read *Mageon Language for Baby Dragons.* Gala closed the drawer and returned to Spark.

When Gala attempted to hand Spark the book, Spark held his hand up and said, "Keep it with you. If you have time and you're interested, study it along your journey. And you can reveal our secrets to the wizard or enchantress you find to protect my thunder. Don't fret, young mage; you'll know if they are worthy and willing before revealing our secrets. Don't ask how I know just trust me. When, or if you do, find someone, you can give this book to them after you make a copy and keep it for yourself. You can copy or borrow any of my books anytime you wish. Maybe you'll make copies when you come back to visit. Which, I have a good inclination you will after you rescue our loved ones."

"Thank you. I hope we find them. I hope they're unharmed. After that, you can bet your lucky-charms we'll visit. And thank you for allowing me to copy this book. I've always wanted to speak dragon." Gala shrank the book; it floated down into the trunk within his cloak's hidden pocket.

"Did you see the niche above my desk?"

"Yes sir. And I saw the hole next to the door."

"Good. And yes. I'll explain the hole in a moment. Inside the niche is a chill box. Open it and retrieve one bottle of my blood. There are empty bottles, as well. Please bring two and set all three bottles here beside me." Spark patted the ground.

Gala nodded, then did what Spark asked. After he got the bottles, he asked, "Is this what you wanted?"

"Yes. Thank you. I'll use my blood to heal Dreamster's and Chizel's wounds while you four retrieve my spell book." To do that, reach your finger inside the hole you saw located on the left side of the cedar door and push. A lever will spring out from the wall about twenty steps to the right of my desk. Do you understand?"

"Yes sir. You haven't lost me."

"Good. Once you locate the lever, push it down flush with the wall. The wall will move inwards. It's a hidden door. The movement will cause sparks due to friction. The sparks will ignite two sap fuel torches inside, one on your right and one on your left. After the door completely opens inwards, it will give way to a decent size foyer. You will see two large passages, one on your left and one on your right. The foyer's left entrance leads to three large rooms before coming to a flight of stairs. The stairs lead down into a spacious cavern. Take the entrance on your right. It is narrower and leads to a spiral staircase. The staircase descends to a wide circular floor into the same cavern but is closer to my laboratory. Straight across from the spiral staircase, you'll see an open door. That's my laboratory and where you'll find my spell book. Are you still with me?"

"Yes sir. I'm not lost yet." Gala and the Newlads chuckled along with Spark.

"Are you sure you can remember my directions?"

"If Gala can't, I can. I have an excellent memory." With a humbled demeanor, Dahc flew up next to Gala. He lifted his head, puffed out his chest, and wore a proud, gleaming smile.

Lucky and Ddot flew over and joined Dahc. "We can help."

Gala chuckled. He was grateful. With a nod, he said, "Thanks, guys."

"We're in this together, Chum." Ddot gave a quick nod along with a wink and a click of his tongue on the roof of his mouth.

Spark recalled Gala's reluctance the night before. His friends insisted on accompanying him on his quest. After their deliberations, Gala gave in. It was refreshing to see Gala's new attitude of acceptance to their offers. Spark said, "It seems that the four of you are inseparable. It's good to share the bond you have."

The four comrades looked at each other, agreeing with smiles, yeses, and nodding heads.

"It's settled then. My spell book is titled *Wizard Spark's Magic Wonders*. When you say the title out loud, the title will light up. After you retrieve my book and return the torch, look for another hole. It's beneath the torch next to the entrance that leads to the three large rooms. Stick your finger in and push. This will spring the lever back out of the wall. After entering the tunnel, push the lever up and flush to the wall. The door will move forward, creating wind, which the mountain helps to generate, extinguishing the torches. Once again, as soon as the door shuts, it will blend into the wall. Are there any questions?"

The four companions looked at each other shaking their heads no. "We'll be back before you know it." Angst attached to Gala's voice.

Spark not only heard it, but he saw the sorrow on Gala's face. "It'll be okay, young mage. There's time; I'll be here when you return.

Gala pressed his quivering lips together, forced a smile then nodded. He turned and headed towards the alcove; the Newlads flew close by. After they got to the niche, Gala hesitated. "I hope there aren't any spiders inside the hole." He bent over to look inside.

"Hold on. I'll look." Gala moved out of the way while Ddot peeked inside. "It's all clear, Chum."

"Thanks."

"It's nothing. But I've never known you to be afraid of a tiny ole spider. Lucky's the one I would think might have a fear of them, getting stuck in webs as he does, but not you."

"I ain't gonna argue that one with ya, Ddot. I'm scared of spiders, and that ain't no lie. But just so ya know, I only got stuck once."

"I know. I'm kidding. But I am curious, Chum. Is this a new fear?"

"Well, sorta. One night, when we gather to tell stories, Mother and I will share that story with everyone. How's that sound?" Gala's eyes watered up. He worried about their loved ones. But he also thought about his flubbed-up spell that almost cost Lucky his life. Gala was happy Helsin saved Lucky from the spider and saved Lucky's wings.

Ddot's eyes watered when he saw the pensive expression on Gala's face, so he hurried to change the subject, "Sure, Chum. That sounds great. Okay then. Let's find Spark's spell book."

Gala stuck his finger in the hole. He felt a peg in the back and pushed it inwards. "CLANK" The sound came from within the tunnel about twenty steps past the desk. The Newlads followed Gala down the tunnel. No one saw the lever until they were smack-dab in front of it. It was well camouflaged. It had the same cream and tan colors as the rough, bumpy wall. No sooner than Gala pushed the lever flush, the wall began to vibrate and rumble, then it moved inwards.

Lucky slapped down on his knee and joked, "Good golly, what a clever lever." He and his pals chuckled.

Sparks flew between the cracks of the door. After the door opened, Gala and his friends stepped into the foyer. Gala took the torch from its sconce on his right and held it up. He walked to the spiral staircase to his right, then stopped.

Before them was a large circular cavern. Its lapis walls, lined with jasper crystals, sparkled. Juneyglow bugs lit the cavern like tiny stars with wings. The floor below glittered. Gala looked down at the top step. To be sure the stairs were slip-proof, he scooted his left foot until the toe of his boot touched the edge. It had grit, was firm, and was not slippery or steep. He started down the staircase that seemed to jut from the mountain. "Gala thought, "Who knows? The way this mountain moves, it could have created these stairs because we needed them. It created a cave for us to enter. It has secret passages. Heck, what if we have a secret passage at home that Mother and Father don't know about, and what if—"

"WOW!" Ddot interrupted Gala's thoughts. "A mountain with a mind of its own. It creates caves. It has a secret passage, dragons, humongous trees, and plants. Since we entered this mountain realm, it seems that all we can say is the word Dahc always says, 'Wow!'"

"I'll share it; we can all say it." Dahc grinned. Everyone returned his smile.

Ddot got to wondering and asked, "You know, Chum? What if your castle has a secret passage? I mean, look at what we entered. We would've never seen that door. It looked just like the wall!"

"Ddot, you must be telepathic because I was thinking the exact thing. If there is a secret passage, The High Council doesn't even know about it. If they did, I'm almost certain they would've told my parents before they agreed to move in. The High Council told my parents everything about the castle. They told them about Bridge, about the lands Father and Mother would protect. The wizard who lived in the castle before me and my parents could have created hidden passages. I can't help but think that whoever took our loved ones had to come through a hidden passage. I have a tough time thinking it was anyone at the celebration."

"It's hard to imagine, but as Spark said, we ought to consider other scenarios."

"I already know this, Ddot."

"I said, 'we ought to consider,'" Gee wizards, Gala, I wasn't just referring to you and—

"I know I ain't in any positin' for givin' out scoldins'. But let's try to focus on the task at hand, and as Wizard Spark suggested, don't rack our brains 'bout it. We ain't gitin' nowhere if we start carryin' Bitter Sprite's Bickerin' Squabbles with us."

"You're right, Lucky; you are too, Ddot. I'm sorry, guys," with shame attached to his apology, Gala sighed and shook his head.

"That's all right, Chum. Heck, you're not the only one ever agitated. I've expressed Bitter Sprite's Bickering Squabbles with all of you. Once, I held on to that sprite for about a week. Thank the giver of goodness, life, and love that I got rid of it."

"Ya ain't kiddin'. I remember when I carried that ole Bitter Sprite 'round. It ain't good for nothin'."

"You're right, Lucky. I'm guilty too. Those kinds of sprites are never good to hold on to-oo-oo! WOW WEE! Would you look at that!" Dahc pointed at the floor.

Gala stopped before stepping onto the transparent floor. Tiny shimmering water creatures swam beneath it. Without the torch, it would seem like they were floating in space amongst flickering stars. The whole cavern blinked from Juneyglow

Bugs, sparkling crystals, and shimmering water creatures.

Gala used the staircase railing for support as he removed his boot and touched the floor with the tip of his right toe. He gradually put the arch and heel of his foot down before adding body weight. It felt soft yet firm, so he stepped on it with both feet. "Oh, my wizard wonders! You gotta feel this! It's soft, squishy like, and stout all at the same time." The Newlads flew down and stood on the squishy floor, feeling its texture while Gala put his boot back on.

Lucky jumped up and down. "Whee! It's got a spring to it!"

"Aaaah!" Dahc screamed. It echoed off the cavern walls. Juneyglow Bugs darted for a couple seconds, then calmed. Three Newlads about jumped out of their skin. And, like a flash of lickity-split before an eye-blinked quick, they dashed above Gala's head.

"Ha! Ha! Ha! Why the big fuss, fellas? It's just a teeny weenie, itty bitty, colorful fish with lights coming out its oversized and protruding eyeballs." Gala made fun by widening his eyes.

The Newlads caught their breath. "Well, it didn't look 'teeny weenie' from where we stood, but it does look a bit smaller from up here. Embarrassing, really," Ddot chuckled with a feeling of relief.

"It came up outa nowheres' with some spookin' eyes lookin' like it was wantin' somthin' to eat. I ain't never been so scared. Well, maybe when I saw my first real live dragon today." Lucky chuckled.

Dahc had his hand on his chest. "I thought we were goners. Phew!" He giggled a short, quiet giggle. Then he giggled a longer giggle and louder, and then he couldn't stop from giggling. They all giggled.

Their laughter finally slowed as Gala hurried to the open door of Spark's laboratory. He stepped inside. "Wow!"

Dahc followed and chuckled, "WOW!"

No one could contain themselves. They laughed so hard their stomachs hurt.

Between his chortles, Lucky said, "Ha, ha, I reckon that's the word, ha, ha, for today. There just, te-hee, ain't no other words to say but 'Wow' for this place."

Everyone nodded, trying to stop laughing. After quieting down, Gala said, "Phew wee! Come on, guys, let's look around."

Illuminating mushrooms emitted a misty blue glow around the room. Three openings in various locations high above their heads shone light from outside and from the mountain, revealing a spacious laboratory. There were books, herbs, and potions sitting on shelves and tables. Gala thought how familiar Wizard Spark's lab was to his father's. The labs were unique in their arrangement. They had a lot of the same alchemy tools and supplies. And they both had an appealing ambiance that resonated with Gala's love and respect for his father.

Gala spotted a small crystal ball that sat in a solution. It reminded him of the project Floreena said she had been working on. He sighed, then walked three feet inwards from the entrance to a large bookcase on his left. "Do y'all remember the name of the book we're looking for? Wasn't it, *Sparktinian charms and wonderful spells* or something like it?"

"Yeah. Something like that," Ddot answered.

"Let's spread out. I'll start at the other end, flyin' from top to bottom," offered Lucky.

"Dahc and I can search the middle," added Ddot.

"Okay. That leaves me at this end," Gala smiled.

Then Dahc reminded, "I think the book's called *Wizard Spark's Magic Wonders*. Wait! What's that over there? It's glowing! It's on that podium." Dahc flew over to the podium, and everyone followed. "This is it! WOW!" A burst of laughter boomed throughout the lab.

"Yeppers!" Lucky Hollard, 'Wow' is the only word for this place." He patted Dahc's shoulder.

The title shone a light that spread upwards and outwards from the book to the top of the ceiling. The words on the ceiling shone larger than what they shone on the book. Gala put his hand over the word Spark's. Spark's was bigger on his hand than the other words on the book's cover, yet smaller than the words shining on the ceiling.

Gala told his friends, "I'm no expert. I don't understand it. But light does this because it has something to do with the distance light travels."

"Travels?" questioned Ddot.

"Yeah. Father knows why, but when he tried to explain it to me, I didn't grasp the concept of light traveling. It sounded like whacked-out wizard spells to me."

"It's like magic," Lucky thought out loud.

"I think Father—" Gala choked up. His eyes turned red and watery. He swallowed hard, then started his sentence over. "I think Father called it optic physics. It has to do with reflection, refraction, and things I don't understand. Father said that physics is all around us, that we use it all the time." Gala wiped his eyes while he cleared his throat, "Ahem. Well, guys, let's get this book back to Spark. We need to hurry." When Gala picked up the book, the title stopped shining. He concealed the book in his cloak pocket while the Newlads flew over and sat on his shoulders.

After stepping back into the foyer, the Newlads hovered beside Gala as he put the torch in its sconce and pleaded, "Ddot? Will you look in that hole for me, please?"

"Sure, Chum." Ddot flew under the left torch and peered into the hole. "All clear."

"Thanks."

"I can't wait to hear about you and your mother's spider story."

"Believe me, Ddot, you'll know why I'm scared of spiders." After Gala pushed the button inside the hole, they heard the lever make a loud clank noise. He stepped out into the tunnel. The Newlads flew close behind. Gala pushed the lever up into its slot. Again, the floor vibrated; the wall rumbled, and this time, the door moved forward. A suction of air pushed through the edges of the door before it shut flush to the wall just as Spark said it would. The air extinguished the torches.

The four companions looked at each other, waiting for the other to say it. Dahc obliged and blurted, "WOW!"

Ddot slapped a friendly slap on Dahc's shoulder, "You said it, brother." Ddot held his stomach, bending over with laughter.

Lucky slapped down on his knee. Between each chuckle, he exclaimed, "Ha-ha! WOW! WOW! Ha-ha! WOW!"

Gala shook his head, "There's got to be a Giggle Sprite in the air. I'll take that over that ole Bitter Sprite any day. Even though my stomach hurts, it sure feels good. I haven't laughed this hard since the last time we all camped out in the backyard."

"Oh yeah, I remember that night. We had a lot of fun," recalled Ddot.

"Yeah, that was fun, especially the joke Dahc told. Remember, Dahc?"

"Yeah, Lucky, I remember that night. You're right. It was one of the best nights I ever had."

"I waden askin' that. I was askin' if ya remembered the joke ya told us."

"Oh! The joke. Well, umm, let me see…" Dahc thought a second, then said, "Actually, I don't."

"Ha-ha-ha! Te-hee-hee! And ya told Spark ya had an excellent memory! Ha-ha-ha!" Lucky held his stomach.

Dahc's face turned beet red, and his veins popped out of his head and neck. He laughed so hard that the only thing that came out of his mouth was a wheezing sound. It was like he couldn't breathe, which made his brother and friends laugh even harder.

Before they knew it, the four giggling companions rejoined their new friends. Their giggles had slowed down to plastered smiles. After Gala handed Spark the spell book, Spark read the title. It lit up then he turned to a page titled '*Hide and Confine.*' "Here it is. This is my *Cloaking* spell.

"I hope I can cast it. We know I'm not good at casting new spells."

"No need to burden yourself with those fears, young mage. My spell will work for you. Where did you find my book; was it on the bookcase?"

"Actually, Dahc found it on your podium."

"So, tell me, Dahc, did you say the title out loud, as I instructed?"

"Well, Gala asked if your book was titled *Sparktinian Charms and Wonderful Spells*. My brother told him that it was titled something like that. We started to look for it in your bookcase, but I remembered—" Dahc stopped talking. The sounds of quiet snickering coming from his brother and comrades interrupted him. He gave them a sharp look. His brows creased, and his face squinched, holding back giggles. With a quick shake of his head and pursed lips, he told them to shush.

Their brows lifted, moved inwards, and their foreheads crinkled. Their grinning lips pressed together, holding back their snickers. Gala finally tucked his lips inside his mouth and sat down. Ddot put his hand over his mouth. Lucky tightened his neck and stretched his lips outwards. He showed his pearly whites before saying, "Oops." Then he and Ddot took a seat without making another sound.

Dahc looked back at Spark and started over. "As I was saying. I told them your book was titled *Wizard Spark's Magic Wonders*. No sooner than I said it, light shone from your book."

"Well, well," Spark grinned and winked. "You do have an EXCELLENT memory regardless if you forgot your joke." Four jaws dropped. Spark admitted, "One can hear just about anything coming from the tunnels." Everyone cracked up laughing. Then Dahc flew over and sat down next to Ddot.

"We all agree with Lucky. So far, everything about your mountain home is magical." The Newlads nodded. "Although my father tried to explain it to me once when I was younger, I still don't understand how light travels. He said it has something to do with wavelengths, refraction, and reflection. I don't know. But I figured the words on the ceiling were bigger than the words shining from your book because of the distance between them."

"This can be a lengthy subject. I'll try to simplify it. Light has wavelengths like a ripple in the water. The spreading of light has to do with the size of its wavelengths, equaling the size of the gaps or objects it passes through. The gaps in my spell book's title caused the light's wavelengths to spread across the ceiling. However, I added magic. I also added magic to the light of my *Cloaking* spell. The light will diffract and spread out on anything I choose. The wavelength does not have to match the length or width of the gap or the object it passes through. The same will happen once you cast my spell. First, you'll need to absorb it. You'll read the spell, then face your palms over the words. The words will light up, seep into your skin and seep upwards into your brain. The spell will remain within you until you cast it. When you do, the words will shine out from your palms on whatever and wherever you face them. The further your hands are from the object, the larger the words become."

"Does the size of your hands matter?"

"No."

Gala took a deep breath and let it out. "How will I know your spell worked after I cast it?"

"Fly about a thousand feet or more above our mountain's summit. Not as your dragon. Cast the spell, then look down; if all you see is a gray cloud, the spell worked. The cloud covers whatever the words touch. No one, not even the one who cast the spell, can see through the cloud. However, the one who cast it, and only the one who cast it, can see through if they say *Show What's Hidden*. To see the cloud again, say, *Hide and Confine*. Anyone looking up from the ground, even the one who cast the spell, will never see the cloud. This allows the dragons to always see what's above them."

"Now that's magical! I have another question. You said that after I read the spell and absorb the words, the words will stay in me. How long will they stay there; will they ever seep out or fade away? Sorry! That was sorta like two questions."

Spark chuckled, then replied, "I'm its creator, so the spell remains in me even after I cast it. In other words, I do not have to repeat the procedure to cast the spell. Because I'm giving you the spell, it'll remain in you. For anyone else, after they cast it, they must repeat the procedure to cast it again. However, the spell will not work when anyone who owns and absorbs the spell becomes ill or if death transcends. I cannot cast my spell. I'm too weak. Remember to read the title correctly and out loud. This unlocks the book; otherwise, the book is useless. Anyone can cast this spell if done the way I mentioned."

"I can cast it?"

"Yes, Ddot, anyone can. If you forget how to cast the spell, refer to the detailed instructions outlined in my spell book. Do you have any more questions?"

They looked at each other, shook their heads, then looked at Spark and said in unison, "No sir."

"Okay. Let's get the *Hide and Confine* spell in you so you can be on your way. Gala, you read first. Leave the book open when you're done."

"Yes, sir."

Spark closed his book and handed it to Gala. Gala read the title out loud. When the title lit up, he opened to the *Cloaking* spell page and read; then he put his palms over the words. The words shone a golden light with sparkling specks of magic dust that rose off the page and onto his palms. His palms acted like sponges that soaked the words into his skin. Everyone saw the golden words travel up Gala's arms, shoulders, neck, face, and temples. The words dimmed out as they seeped into his brain. "Okay, Lucky," Spark announced. "You're up."

After Lucky absorbed the spell, Dahc and Ddot did the same. Gala picked up the book, handed it to Spark, and asked, "Would you like me to put this back?"

"No. You keep it. If you find someone to take my place in protecting my thunder, make a copy for yourself. Give this book, along with the language book, to them. Will you?

"I sure will."

Spark reached the book out to Gala and told him to put his palm flat on its cover. After Gala placed his hand down, Spark waved his free hand over the book. He said something in a language unfamiliar to Gala and his friends. The book, including Gala's hand, lit up with a flickering blue light. A warm sensation engulfed Gala's entire hand. The light, along with the warmth, moved up and filled his arm, then his body, all the way up to the top of his head. His eyes twinkled like violet gems. Gala's entire body glowed blue. The Newlad's mouths were agape matching the width of their bulging eyes. They felt the soft vibrations emitting from their friend's body. They could hear the vibrations humming.

Gala felt a new awakening, a connection to Spark's Mystique dragon lore. He had a deeper understanding of dragons and their kind. He even understood the word Spark said. The word meant Spark bequeathed the book's entirety and its essence to Gala. Gala would know anyone worthy enough to take Spark's place. Finally, the light throughout his body flowed straight into his heart. It settled there before it dimmed out.

Spark released the book and said, "Now my book is yours, which means you can cast any of its spells. Your book will become the property of whomever you give it to. Remember, before giving it, make a copy for yourself. The copy will be exactly like the original, with every spell intact. As long as you live and stay healthy, the spells will follow your command."

Gala opened his cloak. Using his Sorcermizic language, he muttered his *Shrink* spell. The book shrank to the size of a grain of sand and floated into the tiny trunk within his cloak's hidden pocket. Gala humbly thanked, "Wizard Sparktinian, these are great gifts. I can't thank you enough."

"No Gala. It is I who thank you, all of you. Okay now. Off with you." Spark spoke to the dragons and motioned Dreamster to lead the way.

Interment

The mountain rumbled. Again, its rocks, dirt, and roots folded over one another and created an opening. Before setting foot in the cave, Gala looked back. Spark coughed, then closed his eyes to rest. Gala turned around and joined his friends. All of them sympathetically waited outside the mountain while rocks, dirt, and roots folded down, grinding, and scraping against one another. The mountain closed its opening. Entering the quiet night felt somber. It was as if it knew a loss was at hand. A full moon and two crescents were shining brightly. Gala transfigured into Nix, ignoring the wicked faces that flashed within his mind. The Newlads flew onto his back and held tight to his neck feathers. Nix followed Dreamster around the perimeters of the dragons' homeland. Two boulders had fallen on the north side near the one Spark crashed into the night before. The lighting from the Twirlwind had left a deep crack in each boulder.

Dreamster landed and sat clear from the boulder. After Nix landed next to Dreamster, the Newlads flew off Nix's neck and hovered. Nix transformed into his Bluewing form, then summoned his wand. He told his friends, "Okay, guys, I'm using my *Levitation* spell to move the boulders. You guys direct me while I steer them into place. I'll follow your directions and lower the boulder when you tell me. We'll start with this one. What do y'all think?"

Ddot pulled his chin up to his lips, nodding his head. "Sounds like a good plan to me, Chum. I'll get over on the right side." Ddot flew into position."

Lucky put two thumbs up. "That's some good ole wizardry thinkin'. I'll git on the left." Lucky clapped his hands, then flew to the other side.

Dahc nodded with a grin on his cute, freckled face and said, "Guess I'll take the top."

Gala pointed his wand at the boulder; it glowed azure when he said, "*Elevor Eeup*." A golden light shot out from its tip, encompassing the twenty-ton, oblong boulder. It was lighter than a fairy's wing as it rose off the ground. Gala moved his wrist to turn the boulder straight up and down. The Newlads pointed their fingers or waved their hands showing Gala where to steer it.

Dahc yelled, "Stop!"

Ddot yelled, "Perfect!"

Lucky yelled, "Put 'er down, pal!"

Gala lowered the boulder in place. Rocks grinded together. The boulder fit snugly between two other boulders. They matched the dense foliage around them, black, brown, yellow, and mossy green. Gala praised, "Excellent teamwork, fellas! Come on. Let's put the others in place, then I'll cast my parent's *Protection* spell and Spark's *Cloaking* spell."

Lucky blurted, "Okie Dokie! Let's git wingin'!"

After putting the boulders in place, Gala flew over to the outside perimeters. His friends stayed inside and waited. Gala pointed his wand at the ground about two feet away from the base of a boulder. He chanted the *Protection* spell. The spell spread like a circle, covering the boulders on the entire north perimeter. Gala flew upwards, pointed his wand above the treetops, and over to the mountain. As the protective dome took shape, he hurried around the vast perimeters. When Gala returned to his starting point, the azure-colored dome became invisible. Pleased, he nodded and concealed his wand. He flew back over the boulders and motioned his friends to follow him to the center of the dell.

After they landed, Gala explained, "Okay, guys. I'm flying above the mountain about three thousand feet. That's a good distance to cast Spark's *Cloaking* spell. Let's hope it works." His friends nodded. Lucky put his thumbs up. Ddot interlocked his fingers and rested his lips on his thumbs. It looked like he was praying. Dahc crossed his fingers. Gala gave a half-assuring smile then summoned the dragon's language book, "*Appara Comforte.*" POOF! It appeared in his hands. He thumbed through the book and found the words to explain. Dreamster understood because he sat next to where the Newlads stood and crossed his forearms.

Pleased, Gala concealed the book and transformed into Nix. He flew three thousand feet above the mountain's summit and transfigured into his Bluewing. Gala looked at his hands. "Okay," he said to himself. "Here goes nothing." He faced his palms over the land and spoke Spark's *Cloaking* spell. To his surprise, the words rolled off his tongue, "*Hide and Confine.*" They expanded outwards in all directions and covered the dragons' entire domain, including two feet past their perimeters. As soon as the light stopped shining, Gala saw nothing but a large gray cloud. He said, "*Show what's Hidden.*" The land became visible. He said, "*Hide and Confine.*" The cloud appeared again. "Aha! It worked!" He thought, "Okay. Now I want to see how thick and long the cloud is beneath me." Due to zero visibility, he took his time flying downwards toward his friends. At a thousand feet from the ground, the cloud became misty. A few feet below the mist, everything became clear. Gala could see his friends. When he landed on the ground, he looked up. Everything, everywhere, to the starlit sky was visible except for the perimeters. They were still covered in a thick misty fog from the ground up. Gala asked his friends, "Could y'all see me?"

"Yes," They answered in unison.

"Spark was right; that was easy. In a little while, when we leave to search for our loved ones, we'll fly above so y'all can see. Now, I'll gather the dragon slayers' equipment and weapons, then burn them with Redtalon's flame. I need to hurry so we can get back to Spark. Y'all stay here with Dreamster."

Gala used his *Levitation* spell and began with the large ballista. He placed it on the lake's dirt bank that butted next to the dell. Gala piled ropes, spears, shields, and other weapons on the ballista. Then he summoned the items that fell into the lake and put them on the pile. Finally, he pointed his wand at the arrow that had pierced Dreamster's shoulder. It rose from the ground. Gala didn't have time to inspect it after he pulled it out of Dreamster, so he examined its structure before he tossed it onto the pile. Gala flew over the back end of the shaft and studied the design of the half-moon nock. He followed the thick shaft up to the razor-sharp tip. It consisted of four jagged edges, covered in blood. Gala dropped his jaw. He gasped, almost choking. As if speaking to himself, he raged, "Cruel cursid cusses of putrid rot! Gracious giver of goodness, life, and love, this is wickedness!"

The Newlads hurried next to Gala. "What's wrong, Chum?"

"Take a good look at this arrow. This is the one that pierced Dreamster's shoulder." Gala removed some of the blood so they could get a better look at the tip.

"Is that what I think it is?" Ddot Asked.

"Yes!"

Dahc tilted his head and asked, "What is it?"

Lucky spouted, "No good slayers! My blade's achin' for its target, slayer's heads, to be exact!"

Dahc shrugged his shoulders and lifted his hands. "What are y'all talking about?"

"Dahc, Brother. Take a close look. Does that tip remind you of anything?"

Dahc pulled his eyebrows inwards as he examined it more closely. "Aaaah!" He screeched and jolted backward. He gulped hard. He almost choked on his words when he spat, "Sharpened dragons' teeth fused together! Oh, my winging essence! How could they! Hurry! Throw it on the pile before Dreamster figures out what we're looking at."

Gala pointed his wand and flipped his wrist. The arrow flung onto the pile. After it landed, they saw dragon claws melded together on the tip of a spear. The spear lay across a dragon's scale that the slayers used as a shield. When they inspected the rest of the pile, they saw more dragon claws, spikes, teeth, bones, and rawhide. Gala almost puked. He told his friends to back up while he transformed into Redtalon so he could set the pile ablaze."

The Newlads gave Gala room. Dreamster and the Newlads watched while Redtalon let loose his fiery breath. But then Dreamster decided to help. He walked over to Redtalon and looked up into Redtalon's bright, violet reptilian eyes. He saw ferocious reflections of orange-blue flames dance across them, and he noticed that Redtalon's vertical pupils were intense, thinner than they had been. Dreamster made a gurgling noise. Without stopping his fiery breath, Redtalon understood and nodded. Dreamster faced the burning pile. He opened his maw wide, sparked his fiery craw, and let loose a flame as fearsome as Redtalon's.

They burned the heap to ash. But some things, like the dragon scales used for shields, only warped, or blackened. Redtalon made the same clicking sounds Dreamster and Drameer had made earlier. Dreamster understood, so he followed Redtalon's lead. They dug a pit. When they finished, Redtalon used his icy craw and froze the embers to the dragon relics. They pushed the pile into the hole and covered it before Dreamster could tell what they had burned and buried.

Redtalon spoke a eulogy for every dragon who suffered and died. What started as a bond fire for destroying equipment and weaponry ended as an interment. Redtalon mourned the dragons who never got to transcend into the stars. After he finished, he and his friends headed back to the mountain.

Transcendence

When they reached the mountain, the Newlads flew off Redtalon's head, so he could transform. As soon as he transformed into his wizard form, he whistled. Gala's whistle raced through the air. It rippled like heat waves, dodging all obstacles until it hit Trusty's paisley ears within his rock form. It took nanoseconds for Trusty to become himself. He sped through the forest like a speeding bullet forming a streak behind him. He went through a boulder in seconds. He dashed through the dragons' forest. Then he zoomed across the dell like a jet-propelled airboat. He swam across the lake like a torpedo. And, like a vibrating eardrum, he shook the excess water from his body. This exhausted Trusty, but he found the strength to nuzzle Gala's neck. "Good boy." After Gala patted his loyal Hobbgie, he summoned, "*Com'ere.*" Poof! Trusty's brush appeared in Gala's hand. Trusty nickered with pleasure as Gala brushed. When Gala finished, everyone followed Dreamster into the mountain and sat down. Trusty lay between Spark and Gala while the Newlads sat on Trusty's back.

As Gala motioned his hand towards Spark, the dragons, then towards Trusty, he introduced, "This is Trusty. Trusty, these are our new friends."

Spark patted Trusty's neck and complimented, "What a beautiful creature you are. It is an honor to meet you." Trusty nodded and nickered as if he understood.

"Wizard Spark, I need to use my crystal ball."

"By all means, do."

Gala opened his cloak and summoned, "Com'ere." The tiny crystal and pedestal floated from the trunk within his hidden pocket. They floated down onto his lap. Gala said, "*Natural State.*" POOF! They became their actual size. Gala moved his palms over the ball and asked, "*Show me Acub's parents, Trill and Quo.*" Nothing happened. He furrowed his brows while looking at his friends. They shrugged their shoulders. Gala looked back at the crystal and asked it to show his parents. The crystal emitted its golden antique glow encompassing the outside. Purple fog swirled around inside. After it dissipated, Gala's parents became visible. They were still chained and still inside barred carriages. Gala pointed out, "The carriages aren't moving. My parents still have those black sacks over their heads. They're lying down and breathing. And look! There's an ember glow on them from a lantern hanging outside the carriage." Gala brushed his hand on the crystal as if to touch his parents. Then he commanded, "*Show me Floreena and Lidee.* Look, guys! They're sleeping with those same black sacks over their heads. Cursed wickedness. I won't stop looking until I find you. Hang in there," Gala's voice was almost inaudible.

Ddot could see Gala lost in thought, so with a quiet voice, he asked, "Can you look in on Acub and Ashlin?"

"Yeah, sure thing." After Acub and Ashlin appeared in the crystal laughing, Gala's voice turned joyful. "Look, guys, they're sitting next to each other. Acub's moving his hands around, saying something." Gala and the Newlads grinned. "Okay, guys. Now I'm going to look in on Lucky's parents. *Show me Lucky's parents.* Look, guys! Ddot, Dahc, your parents are sitting next to Lucky's parents, and they're all grinning." Gala chuckled.

"It's story time; it looks like Acub's telling a story."

"Yeah, Ddot. It looks like it. I'm sure glad they're having a good time." While the Newlads were smiling in agreement, Gala asked, "Hey, guys. What do y'all think? Think I should ask the crystal to show us Helsin?"

"Ifin' I could, I'd keep my eye on 'em. I don't trust the slimy slug of a so-called wizard."

"We agree with Lucky. Don't we, Dahc?" Dahc nodded.

"Okay, here goes. *Show me Helsin.*" All eyes watched the crystal fill with purple fog. After it dissipated, they saw Helsin lying down. "Look! He's in bed with his hands behind his head, looking up at the ceiling." Gala's body shivered while fighting down a bile taste that had erupted from his stomach. "The site of him makes me sick," he thought. Then, as if to himself, Gala said, "Too bad I couldn't read his thoughts, although it's probably not a good idea."

"Your surmise is correct; it's best to leave thoughts to their creators." Wizard Spark sounded weaker; his breath ebbed. He knew his time for departure was at hand. He saw dismay, fear, and sadness on the young wizard's face. "Young mage," he said as he touched Gala's shoulder. Gala saw a glint in Spark's cloudy gray-blue eyes. "My transcendence is near. Take these bottles filled with my blood; keep them cool. I hope none of you will need its healing power. But if you do, a little sip can heal the largest of giants. That's if their organs aren't completely severed, bleeding internally."

No sooner than Gala said, "*Sleep*," Helsin faded away. The golden antique glow around the crystal stopped. Gala said, "*Conceal*." Poof! Like lickity-split before an eye-blinked quick, the crystal and its pedestal vanished. He took the bottles of Spark's blood and put them in Trusty's supply bag.

Spark continued, "I want to bring this to your attention. Whoever has our loved ones must want them alive. It looks to me like they are staying put for the night. What do you think, young mage?"

"It does look like they're camping. I suppose my parents would be dead by now, as you said. I wonder what they want with them."

"No telling. It's wise if you and your friends stay the night and get an early start when the morning birds awake. Cut yourselves as many pieces of root as you wish from any of the plants or trees within the mountain. Don't worry; the roots grow back. Eat one or two bite sizes every morning or night. They'll give you energy and endurance throughout the day. They also allow you to sleep well."

"Thank you. But Wizard Spark, I have to warn you about my nightmares. I wake up yelling. I might wake the dragons or scare them. The nightmares started about a year ago. My parents have tried everything to help me get rid of them. Nothing seems to work, not even a spell they got from The

Wizard's High Council. My mom said a frightened lock keeps her and Father out."

Spark patted Gala on his hand, "I'll tell my thunder of your dreams. I'm not sure, but the roots might ease your nightmares. A nightmare is a type of fear, you know. You may have blocked an unbearable tragedy from your memory to avoid pain. If you're not blocking your memories, something, or someone else is."

"What?! Someone else?!"

"Yes. It's possible. Gnome Bloom might know a way to reveal your nightmares so you can get past this."

"That would be a relief! I hope he can."

"Me too. Remember what I told you about Bloom's realm. You'll not see it through your crystal ball. His realm is another dimension which is constantly changing."

"Like a realm within realms?"

"Yes, except his is a dimensional realm within realms." Spark gave Gala another pat on his hand and said, "I have faith that you and your comrades will rescue our loved ones. After you do, and you do not find someone worthy of protecting my thunder, would you look in on them?" Spark's weary eyes peered straight into Gala's shiny ones.

While straightening his shoulders, Gala announced, "I'm honored. Thank you for trusting me. I'll look in on them every chance I get. I love dragons. I've always loved dragons as far back as I can remember."

"I can tell. I knew that when I first laid eyes on your magnificent Redtalon. Anyone who creates a dragon as remarkable as you have must love dragons."

"Will your dragon friends need to go out hunting anytime soon? Or were they able to get the protein they needed to hold them awhile?"

"They have enough to sustain them for five more suns. They're well protected, at least for a time. Your *Protection* spell will keep intruders out. My, I mean, your, *Cloaking* spell will prevent the dragon slayers from locating our home again. As I mentioned, they're safe inside the mountain. It has a mind of its own. It's alive and can discern the vibrational intentions of others. I call it Dragon Mountain With-eyes-that-see. Although there may be other mountains like this one, I haven't seen any during my travels. If you'd like, you can give the mountain another name, but be sure to keep our secrets. The Wizard's High Council doesn't know about me, my thunder, or the mountain."

"Wizard Spark, you have our word. We will keep your secrets." The Newlads nodded. "My friends and I can't thank you enough for your generosity and kindness. I wish we had more time together." The Newlads were still nodding with watery eyes. Gala himself seized the tears that threatened to escape down his cheeks. His dimpled chin, along with his lips, quivered.

"I thank you, Gala, Newlads. I'm grateful for what time we have had. Loved ones will miss me here. But, loved ones wait for me on the other side. We never leave, you know. It's only our true vibrational being, or spirit, as it is sometimes called, which discards our physical substance. Each of you will understand what I mean when it is your time. Everything changes and vibrates at different frequencies. Use all your senses, learn, and grow. Do not stop. The more knowledge we gain, the more we succeed. Know that all things connect. This connection remains constant throughout all changes. You remember this. Spark glanced at each Newlad, then looked back Gala. A contented smile shone as he patted Gala's hand one last time. Spark returned his eyes to the sorrowful faces of the Newlads. He honored, "It has been my privilege to have met you, Lucky, Ddot, Dahc, and you too, Trusty. You are a fine-looking Hobbgie. May the giver of goodness, life, and love guide you always."

Ddot sniffed and wiped the wetness off his nose with his sleeve. He cleared his throat, "Ahem. Wizard Spark, I ask that the giver of goodness, life, and eternal love be with you always."

Dahc wiped his watery eyes and said, "Yes. I wish the same. And Wizard Spark, I ask the giver to award a peaceful transcendence on you."

Lucky's voice cracked. "Wizard Spark, I'm sure hopin' we meet again in the life beyond this life."

"It'll be all right, Lucky. We'll meet again." Spark smiled.

Gala wiped his tears. He wished, "And Wizard Spark, may your life beyond this life fill your being with love and happiness."

"Thank you. Because of your generous wishes, my transcendence will be extra special." Spark smiled, then turned and spoke to his thunder. When he finished, the dragons bowed. Chizel hugged Spark's neck. Dreamster nudged his snout on Spark's cheek and made a couple clicking sounds. Drameer did the same, then rested her head on Dreamster's chest. Every dragon walked up to Spark to pay their respects and say farewell. Upon each face was a mournful expression. Spark's sorrow was for his friends, not for himself. After saying his goodbyes, he faced Gala. Spark's gray brows turned inwards and upwards. Concerned lines filled his forehead. "Head west when you leave tomorrow. It'll lead you straight to Gnome Bloom, which could take a day and a half. It depends on how fast you travel. You may have to camp. You're not anywhere near the Boggy Swamps. I trust you'll find our loved ones. Be sure to tell them I said 'Dragamage and Star'ella-love.' They'll understand." Gala nodded. "Farewell, my friends." Spark smiled; his face was soft and content.

 The dragons thumped the ground with their tails or with the pads of their paws, drumming a unified thrum. An unvarying buzz from their throats and their bodies hummed, "Grumm, Grumm, Grumm..." The sound pulsed through the air reverberating throughout Dragon Mountain With-eyes-that-see.

 Spark closed his eyes and released his last breath. His body faded into a golden stream of light. It rose about five feet from the ground and hovered as if to convey one final farewell. After a few seconds, his light swirled toward the enormous canopy of trees. They reverently parted. The expansive opening of the mountain revealed a star-filled sky. The jovial stars twinkled as if they anticipated the arrival of a loved one.

The moon furthest from Mageus, the largest of the moons, had begun to wax. Its thin silver crescent shone overhead, and two waxing moons rested on the horizon. All three seemed to smile.

Trails blazed behind like a comet while Spark's golden light blasted into their galaxy. Then, like a supernova, Spark's light exploded, carpeting the night with a bright white light. Everyone squinted until the light settled into a new cluster of twinkling stars. Gala and his friends stood in awe, mesmerized.

Gala knew how dragons, Bluebloods, including Mystique Bluebloods, transcended because of his studies. But this was the first time he or his friends saw the actual death of a dragon, let alone seen a real dragon. Gala knew what Star'ella-love meant. It meant Spark's cluster of stars would shine upon his loved ones. But he never heard the word Dragamage. Gala hoped Spark was correct that they would rescue their loved ones. He couldn't wait to tell his parents Spark's message. It was another desperate desire Gala added to his list. This was Spark's dying wish.

As the mountain began to close its wide opening, the canopy followed. The humming and thumping from the dragons had faded into a deep silence like a realm without life. Everyone was within their own solitary thoughts. Gala gazed at the moss-covered leaves where Spark had been sitting. A cool gentle breeze brushed against his face. Then, something caught his attention; his peripheral vision saw the movement of light. When his eyes shifted to his surroundings, they widened. Awestruck, he glanced at his friends. They had their heads bowed as if in prayer. Gala waved his hands back and forth to get their attention. It didn't work, so he snapped his fingers. They finally met his expressions of wonderment. Without a sound, while spreading his arms wide, Gala mimicked, "WOW!"

The Newlads followed his arms. Their jaws slacked, and their eyes widened. Before them was a dazzling display of color, dancing, swaying with the breeze. It added a sense of tranquility to Spark's transcendence. Thousands of cells moved up and down, flooding the veins of every tree and plant. They illuminated vibrant hues of blues, reds, oranges, pinks, purples, yellows, and greens. While absorbing the beauty, Gala heard Drameer and Chizel talking but couldn't see them. The dragons blended into the foliage. It wasn't until Drameer gave Chizel a tender nudge that Gala's eyes adjusted and saw them.

Chizel walked over to Gala and rested her head on his chest. She closed her eyes. Her head was a little less than one-fourth the size of Gala's body, so Gala could reach around her neck to return her hug. Drameer sounded out a soft click. Chizel lifted her head and nudged her snout on Gala's cheek before she walked over onto her mossy bed. The rest of the dragons bowed their heads before they retired. Dreamster clicked for Gala and the Newlads to follow. He led them to an enormous tree with lengthy roots that extended high above the ground. Two tree roots created a large circle. Within it was a thick, shimmering green moss bed that could sleep two thirty-foot adult dragons.

Dreamster made the same soft click Drameer sounded to Chizel a moment ago. Without thinking twice, Gala and the Newlads understood this was their bed.

Feeling right at home, Lucky flew onto the mossy bed. He laid his head on a clump of fluffy down feathers, pulled a piece of shimmering moss over his body, and said, "Aha. This is comfy."

The twins followed. Gala chose a spot far from his friends so he wouldn't hurt them during his nightmares. He took the supply bag off Trusty's back, then sat on the edge of the bed with his legs hanging over the large root. Trusty lay next to him. After Gala adjusted his pile of feathers, he took out his knife. He cut a piece of tree root, and sniffed. "Mm! Smells delicious," he thought. He took a bite. His face lit up; his dark brows lifted. He said to himself, "Mm, mm, sweet deal! Tastes exactly like Fairy Honey!" The notch in the shimmering brown root from the piece he had cut out filled back in as if it had never been touched. "Hey guys, look." Gala cut out another piece. The Newlads watched. After a couple of seconds, the root grew back, then Gala ate it and encouraged, "Go ahead, fellas. Cut one and take a bite."

"Come on, Chums; let's try it." Ddot cut a piece, then took a bite. "Pixie wonders! Mine tastes like Butterfair Cakes, yummy!"

Lucky did the same and exclaimed, "Jumpin' fairy tastebuds! It tastes exactly like Ma's Jammin' Berrycreams!"

Everyone looked at Dahc, waiting to hear what his tasted like. All he did was lick his chops, smack, and make mm, mm, sounds.

"Mine tastes like Fairy Honey. Also, it reminds me of my mother's Sweet Charm Bites. Come on Dahc, we're waiting; tell us what yours tastes like."

"Well, Gala, I can't tell exactly. Umm. Mm, yummy. Mine tastes like Butterfair Cakes... Wait a minute... There's something else... Umm, mm, mm. Oh yeah, Buttyerfair Cakes with a mix of Chocomalt Sweeties. Oh yeah, and it's topped with Charmalnut Delights. We are definitely taking some of these with us!" Dahc gave a sharp nod of his head.

Everyone laughed. Dreamster smiled. Gala took out the dragon language book, then put it away after he found the sounds to say good night. Dreamster repeated the sounds, then walked over to lie down beside his family. Gala and the Newlads said good night to each other, but no one fell asleep. Restless thoughts filled their heads which the mountain sensed. A humming of rhythmic heartbeats started emanating from Dragon Mountain With-eyes-that-see. It soothed each one into a hypnotic slumber.

Good Morning

As Morningbirds' kissed each ear, their sweet music rang throughout Dragon Mountain With-eyes-that-see. Their music traveled through the large canopy of leaves to join the symphony the forest sang. Four companions woke with smiles on their faces.

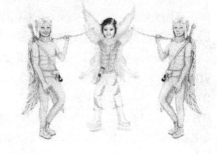

Gala felt good thinking of his new purpose in finding a protector for his dragon friends. As he stretched, he remembered having nightmares. But it occurred to him that they didn't wake him, nor did he wake up yelling. He asked, "Did y'all hear me scream or toss through the night?"

"Not me. I slept like a newborn fairy without a care in the realms," answered Lucky as he stretched.

"Me either." Ddot yawned and stretched his legs. He asked, "How about you, Dahc. Did you hear Gala toss or scream during the night?"

Feeling refreshed and a bit silly, Dahc stretched his arms and yawned. While pondering the question, he scratched his head. He puckered and twisted his lips, moving them left to right. His eyes followed, then he jerked his head towards Gala and stopped all movement. Dahc looked straight into Gala's anticipating violet wide-eyes and sang. "♫ Not a peep. No, not a peep, ♪ I slept mighty deep. Yes, sir, mighty deep ♪." Everyone laughed.

"Wow! Spark was right! The roots reduced the intensity of my nightmares. We are definitely taking some with us, a lot of them. Let's eat a little root every morning like Spark suggested."

"Yeah! And they give endurance, not to mention they taste delicious!"

Ya ain't kiddin', Ddot! They're smack lipin' delicious!"

Dahc cut and plopped a root in his mouth. "Mm, mm! It's amazing how good the roots taste and all the good they do for you." Dahc continued to cut. No one wasted time. They ate one or two roots as they cut themselves enough for their journey.

"I don't have room, and I'd love to take more than this." Ddot showed Gala his satchel.

"I'll shrink what we can't carry and put them into Trusty's supply bag."

"Thanks Chum!" Ddot nodded.

"Thanks Pal!" added Lucky.

"Yeah! Me, too. I thank you too!" Dahc grinned from ear to ear.

Gala chuckled at Dahc's pleasant silliness and said, "No problem, guys."

After they packed their satchels with roots, Gala took out his crystal ball and set it on its pedestal. The Newlads gathered around. Gala asked, "*Show me my parents.*" The golden antique glow encompassed the crystal while purple fog swirled inside. After the it dissipated, They could see his parents sleeping on the floor of the barred carriage. The carriage wasn't moving. Then Gala asked to see Floreena and Lidee. They were also sleeping.

When Gala was about to ask the crystal to show him Acub and Ashlin, Ddot interrupted. "Chum? Look at Floreena's hand. It's sticking out through the bars. The cuff on the chain around her wrist is up against the inside of the bars as if she was reaching out. Oh! Wait! Something's in her hand."

"Oh, yeah! I see. What is it?"

"It looks like a Night Shroomer. It's a delicacy." explained Ddot."

"I'm wonderin' why she's holdin' it while she's sleepin'. She musta' grabbed it before fallin' asleep?"

"Lucky, I bet you're right because I don't remember seeing her hand through the bars last time we looked. Did you guys?" All three Newlads shook their heads then Gala asked, "Where do Night Shroomers grow?"

"My Ma loves 'em. She told me they grow underground where it's dark and wet. Sometimes they grow above ground in dark wet places, but that's rare. She used to find 'em in Mogwarm burrows. Night Shroomers grow where it's not too cold or too hot."

"So Lucky, you mean to say that Night Shroomers can grow in caves?" Gala asked.

"Not if there ain't no wet dirt and not if there's too much light."

"Lucky's right. Our cave has some wet dirt, but too much light shines through the falls for Night Shroomers to thrive. On one of our scavenger hunts, Dahc and I found a Mogwarm burrow on the southwest side of our mountain. We found one Night Shroomer and ate it right then and there. We haven't seen another burrow or tunnel of any type since then. Of course, the last time we scavenged was about three of our two full moons ago."

"So, Night Shroomers do not grow in the cold, same as Berrybells. Night Shroomers grow in dark places. But Berrybells need light to thrive or survive, right?"

Ddot answered, "Well, Gala, that's a yes and no. You're right that neither one will grow in the cold; they both like wet areas. Night Shroomers like water and no light. Berrybells like water and light, and they can live in the dark. The only thing is, although Berrybells flower in the dark and in light, they need light to produce fruit."

"Do y'all remember seeing the fruitless Berrybells on my father's cloak?"

"Yes." The Newlads answered in unison.

"Father could have grabbed the fruitless Berrybells before he fell asleep. If they think I'm using Father's crystal to find them, they might be trying to give me hints. Or, when the sacks are off their heads, they grab things to figure out where they are!"

"Good thinkin', Pal! I'm bettin' yo're right about both. It makes sense." Lucky slapped down on his knees, bent forward, and looked straight into Gala's eyes. "And ifin' yo're right, they're probably in a tunnel or somewhere wet and dark." Everyone agreed.

Gala gave his head a slow nod as he seemed to look out into space, absorbed in thought. Then he asked, "Does that mean they could be anywhere east, south, or west?"

"Likely west," Ddot answered. "Night Shroomers always grow in western areas because they like the climate. They grow in the east but not abundantly, and the south is too hot. Berrybells grow in the east and south, but they're most plentiful in the west."

"Ddot's right," agreed Dahc.

"That means we can bet our lucky-charms we're headed in the right direction. Both grow in the west more than anywhere else!" Gala's voice was loud and hopeful.

"I'm hopein' yo're right," Lucky said. "At least it narrows down our searchin'. I'm figurein' they ain't headin' east. We know they ain't goin' north, and I doubt they're goin' south 'cause it's too hot for Night Shroomers."

"I feel better," Gala concluded with a wide grin.

Lucky put a hand on his chest and one on his stomach. "My heart ain't jumpin' in my gut. I'm feelin' hopeful."

"Me too," added Ddot.

"Yeah." Dahc agreed while he nodded at everyone.

"Okay, crystal ball, *Show me Acub and Ashlin.* Guys look! They're sleeping. Now I'm gonna ask to see Helsin. *Show me Helsin.* He's still sleeping. I'm glad they're all sleeping. It gives us a head start." Gala and the Newlads let out a long sigh. After putting his crystal ball away, Gala took out Dreamster's language book. He went over a few words. "Okay, guys, listen to this. To say the word, good, in dragon, use your tongue to sound out one short, fast click like this." Gala made one click noise, then he encouraged, "Try it."

Everyone used their tongue and made a short, fast-click sound. Ddot said, "This is going to be fun. It seems easy to remember." Ddot was right. It didn't take long for Gala and the Newlads to learn a few clicks and growls of the dragon language.

"Okay, guys. Let's go say good morning to the dragons." The Newlads and Trusty followed close to Gala. The dragons were up putting fresh moss on beds, collecting fruit, or watching their young play.

After the four companions said good morning to the dragons, Gala thumbed through the language book. He sounded out a couple of long clicks, one short, and a low, long, growl, then concealed the book. He must have mixed something up because all the dragons started laughing. Dreamster got up and led his new friends to a wide tunnel lit by blue-illuminating mushrooms. The mushrooms grew out of the walls and were about as big as Gala. The tunnel curved to the left and descended a few feet before it opened into a grand grotto. Several waterfalls fed by natural springs from within the mountain were everywhere. Falls fell into a pool that flowed down a fast-flowing stream, like rapids. It rushed through another tunnel that led into a deep well. Along the fast-flowing stream were different size debits and crevices. Water sprayed within them like showers. Water fell through several cracks, which acted like drains on the floors. Dreamster walked into a large crevice. Everything that came off and out of his body went down the drains, into the fast-flowing stream, through the tunnel, and down the well.

The well, which seemed like a bottomless pit, was much deeper than the lake. The lake was over three hundred feet deep. Dreamster got out and motioned Gala and the Newlads to follow. When they reached the mouth of the well and looked down inside, they couldn't see the bottom. But they did see bright green lights flickering, moving in and out of the walls in the well. They moved faster than the speed of light. Everything in the water that passed down to the light disappeared. Like lickity-split before an eye-blinked quick, the dirty water became clean. Gala took a closer look. He saw that the green, flickering lights were long, oversized Wigglestinks. Wigglestinks devour waste in no time flat. Gala and his friends knew about Wigglestinks. But this was the first time they'd seen them in action, let alone seen any. Although their washrooms have different designs, they work the same. But their Wigglestinks are much smaller.

Lucky started singing. His friends turned and saw him stick his head out from a crevice behind a waterfall. He grinned and said, "The day's a tickin'. Let's git a-movin'. The water's nice, 'n surprisin'ly warm." Lucky parted his lips, showing his pearly whites. It looked like he was gritting his teeth, but he was grinning while moving his eyebrows up and down, up and down. He tucked back inside, then continued singing and whistling. All his friends hurried inside their own crevice and began washing. Gala told Trusty what to do.

Lucky was the first one done. He laid his wings flat, jumped high, then spun fast, like a child's spin-top toy twirling in midair with water spraying from his body. After landing back down, he fluttered his six strong, gossamer, bright green wings. His wings were so fast that you could hear them humming, like a hummingbird. And before you knew it, like lickity-split before an eye-blinked quick, Lucky was dry. Ddot and Dahc did the same. Although their four blue wings are much larger than Lucky's, they spun dry just as fast. When Trusty got out, he vibrated like a jackhammer to dry. Gala decided to attempt drying off by conjuring up a wind using his *Drying* spell.

"Stand back, everyone. I'm going to conjure a *Drying* spell to dry myself. I'm gonna try, anyway." Gala held out his hands.

"Wait!"

Almost jumping out of their skin, everyone jerked their heads around, including Dreamster.

"Gee wizardly nerves, Ddot! You about scared the skin off my bones! What do you mean by 'wait!'?"

"Well, Chum. What if something goes wrong? Shouldn't we hide first? I'm guessing you haven't perfected that spell because you said you would 'TRY' to conjure up a wind."

"You're right. But it can't be too difficult; it's a simple hand spell. But to be safe, you guys sit on Trusty's back and hold tight to his mane. I'll tell Trusty to stand behind Dreamster, and I'll back away. Besides, I promised I'd practice my spells. This one should create a warm wind that blows around me, up through my clothes, drying me in seconds. I'll explain what I'm doing so Dreamster understands.

After Gala told Trusty to stand back, he took out Dreamster's language book and found the correct clicks, grunts, and growls to explain. Dreamster must have understood because he backed away. He sat down and crossed his front forearms. While the Newlads held tight to Trusty's mane, Trusty stood behind and to one side of Dreamster. Gala turned and walked a little distance from them, then turned back around and concealed the language book.

"Well. Here goes nothing." There was doubt in Gala's trembling voice. He thought, "I sure hope this works. I hope I don't hurt anyone. I don't want to conjure up a Twirlwind like Helsin did when he came across Bridge." Gala shook the thought from his head, then whispered three words using his Sorcermizic tongue, "*Ow-a-dy.*" It sounded like one word with three syllables, but it was three words. They meant Blow and Dry.

As Gala cupped the air, pulling it down and around his body, he commanded it to blow him dry. All the sounds within the grotto faded from his consciousness. A loud thumping from his nervous heart echoed through his ears. He felt his heart pounding as if it were going to burst out of his chest, 'Thump-a-thump! Thump-a-thump! Thump-a-thump!' Gala tried to calm himself. But after looking into widened eyes and mouths of his friends, he doubted himself even more. He watched Dahc squeeze off the circulation to Ddot's arm and began to imagine the worst. The air strengthened and became thick; a wind grew, blowing faster and faster. Gala's hair and clothes whipped up and around. His friends saw fear in his eyes; he started spinning like a Twirlwind! Around and around, he spun. Gala felt dizzy, shut his eyes, then became limp and queasy to the point of puking. He rammed into the side of the cavern's wall, then into another and another. Gala spun upwards, downwards. When he finally stopped spinning, the front of his body faced directly above the stream, and then, SLAP! Down he went. The fast-flowing stream took Gala's limp body straight toward the well.

"Hurry!" Dot yelled. All three Newlads flew over to Gala. They grabbed his cloak. With all their might, they grunted and strained, pulling upwards, having no luck.

Dreamster and Trusty hurried over. Gala went down the well with his friends still hanging on! Wigglestinks were chomping while moving in and out from the walls. One large Wigglestink reached out with its mouth wide open. It clamped down on a clump of Gala's hair and began to chew, suck, and swallow! Trusty reached his neck down to grab Gala but missed. Dreamster hurried. He grabbed Gala by the ankle before the Wigglestink sucked Gala's head down his throat! Dreamster pulled the Wigglestink off the nape of Gala's neck and dropped it back into the well. He laid Gala down on his back on the cavern's floor. Trusty licked Gala's face. The Newlads dried themselves again. The twins flew above Gala's head, releasing the soothing essence of their wings. Lucky patted Gala's pale cheeks, trying to wake him.

Lucky pleaded, "Wake up! Gala, wake up! Come on, pal, wake up!" Dot and Dahc flew down to help. With Lucky's last plea, he and the twins gave Gala a hard slap, which got Gala to stir. The Newlads hovered over Gala's face and smiled.

"Glad to have ya with us, good ole pal. How ya feelin'?" Lucky asked.

Gala put one hand on his stomach and the other on his forehead.

"Uh-oh. Back up, fellas. Gala's lookin' like an up-chunk's a-comin'." Lucky flew upwards; the twins followed.

Gala had a tough time opening his heavy eyes. He rolled over to face the rapidly flowing stream. "Oh no! Stop spinn..., HUGK, HUGK, BLAARGH, HUR-HUR..." His vomit swooshed away and rushed down into the well. Gala stuck his face in the water and sucked some into his mouth. He lifted his head, swished, then spit it out before he laid back down. "After all that spinning about, I should be as dry as a parched leaf."

"Ha! Haa! Ha! Haa! Ya was dry all right, but ya ain't now. Yo're soppin' wet there ole pal. How ya feelin'?"

"Better. But what do you mean, Lucky? I knew I was spinning out of control. I got dizzy but felt the wind drying me before I smacked into the wall." Gala sat up.

"Smacked? You were more like SLAMMED into the wall. Then you slammed into another, and another, and thrown, belly slapped, into the stream."

"Yep. You said it, Dot, 'belly slapped.' I mean to tell ya, it was the hardest and loudest belly slap I ever saw or heard. It's surprisin' ya ain't gotta blackin' face and body or any broken bones. All ya got is that little ole bump on yore head. Ifin' it wasn't for Dreamster pullin' ya out, ya would've been sucked to the bottom of that well, drownin' or gobbled up by them there Wigglestinks."

"Yeah, and don't forget, Lucky, we were going down with him."

"That's right, Dahc! I almost forgot. We were hangin' tight to yore cloak, Gala ole pal. We dried off again after Dreamster pulled us all out."

Gala reached up and felt his hair, then his clothes. "Gee, wizards! Flub-of-a-wizard. I knew I'd mess it up, but thank the giver of goodness, life, and love, I didn't create a Twirlwind like I thought I might. You know, the one like Helsin's, or the one that caused Spark's death?" Trusty nudged Gala. After Gala reached around his neck, Trusty lifted Gala to his feet.

"Just so you know, a Wigglestink swallowed some of your hair at the nape of your neck." Ddot tugged on the shorter part of Gala's hair.

"What!?" Gala reached behind his head and felt the short strands of hair. His mouth dropped.

"The top part of your hair covers it," Dahc pointed out. "Dreamster pulled the Wigglestink off before it got to your scalp."

"I-I'm—" Gala paused. He shook his head and started again, "If a Wigglestink...if one of you were...I-I'd never forgive me if a Wigglestink ate you. Gee, wizards! I'm just a flub-of-a-wizard." Gala put his hands on his forehead, covering his watery eyes.

"Hold on there a da-gom minute. Ya caint keep beatin' yoreself up like that. It waden yore fault we hung on to yore cloak."

"Lucky's right, Chum. Lighten up on yourself." Ddot flew over and hovered in front of Gala's face. Lucky and Dahc followed.

Gala thought for a second, removed his hands from his forehead, and said, "Next time I say I'm going to dry myself with that spell, y'all lock me up in a padded room." His friends cracked up laughing. After they quieted down, Gala said, "Okay, guys, back up. I'm gonna spin dry as my Bluewing form." His friends gave him some room. After Gala transformed into his Bluewing, spun, and flapped his wings dry, he encouraged, "Come on guys, the sooner we get going, the sooner we get to Gnome Bloom's." Gala transformed back into himself and let Dreamster know they were done.

Dreamster led them back to the other dragons. They were standing around a pile of vegetation. Drameer put her nose on a round red fruit and pushed it towards Gala. She nudged another towards the Newlads, then a larger one towards Trusty. Trusty sniffed, licked the fruit, then dug in. He didn't stop until his fruit vanished. Drameer giggled in her dragon voice and gave Trusty a few more.

Gala cut the Newlads' fruit into thirds and handed a piece to each. Then, he picked his up.

They sank their teeth in. Juice squirted down their chins and arms. Their faces lit up, followed by satisfying mm, mm, mm sounds. Drameer nudged more vegetation towards Gala. Gala rubbed his tummy to gesture he was full. Dreamster made a clickety-click noise and pushed the same pile closer to Gala.

Gala summoned the dragon's language book, turning pages to see what Dreamster meant. "Oh. I see. They want us to take this with us." Gala thumbed through the language book and sounded a few clicks and growls.

"What'd you say?" asked Ddot.

"I told them we had food and didn't want to take theirs."

"Oh."

Dreamster reached his neck up to the fruit-filled tree. He picked one, then stood there waiting. Like the roots, a fruit grew back.

"This reminds me of Mother's Fig tree. They always produce sweet fruit. Guys, we gotta get going." Gala thumbed through Dreamster's language book. He found how to say they would take the fruit and needed to be on their way. Dreamster and the other dragons nodded their heads while humming and clicking.

Chizel walked over to Gala. In her wee dragon voice, she said, "Hug."

Gala and the Newlads gasped; their jaws slacked, and their eyes popped.

"So, it's true. Stark was teaching the baby dragons how to speak our language. I saw the lesson book in Spark's desk drawer titled *Mageon*

Language for Baby Dragons. When we visit, I'll make a copy of that book too." The Newlads flew over to Gala and Chizel. They created a group hug. Gala told Chizel he hoped to see her soon. After their hug, Gala told the dragons he would be back to visit. They nodded and made buzzing sounds along with a few clicks.

After Gala and his friends were ready to go, the mountain rumbled while creating an opening. Before walking through, Gala and the Newlads turned one last time to see the dragons. The dragons nodded and buzzed. Chizel said, "Bye-bye."

After reaching the outside of the cave, the mountain rumbled again. Its rocks, dirt, and roots folded inwards, adhering to each other until the opening closed. The foliage had covered where the cave had been. It looked as though the cave never existed. Gala and his friends sighed.

"I'll never forget this place."

Ddot agreed with Dahc. "Me either. A living mountain, a mind of its own, and baby dragons speaking Mageon language. You gotta admit, it's unique."

"Ya ain't kidin'. It's a perfect home for the dragons, safe from those wicked dragon slayers," Lucky added.

"Talking about safe, let's see if Spark's *Cloaking* spell is still working." Gala transfigured into Nix and shook his head because of the wicked faces that flashed in his head.

Ddot saw him and wondered, "Gala must've hurt his head worse than I thought. He did slam into those walls pretty hard. I hope he's all right. I'll keep an eye on him." Ddot waited a few minutes. After he saw Gala, Lucky, and his brother hovering above the mountain, he flew up. When Ddot reached the misty fog of the cloud, he could see everything above him. But, when he looked down, and although he could make out Trusty's shape, the mist clouded his vision. The further upwards he flew, the less he could see beneath him. After he reached Gala, he looked down and exclaimed, "That cloud is expansive! We ought to use this over our mountain."

"That's a clever idea. I can't wait to show our parents." Gala transformed into his Bluewing form, took out Inkle and his map, then stopped. He stared at his map.

"What's wrong?"

"I can't do it, Ddot. It's the promise we made Spark, keeping the dragon's home secret. I can't draw it on the map, but I could draw a gray cloud. No better not do that either. We won't be able to write *Dragon Mountain With-eyes-that-see* in our story either. We'll just have to keep it between ourselves for now." Gala put Inkle and his live map away. "Well! Come on, fellas. Let's get Trusty and get going.

Right before Gala landed, he transformed from his Bluewing form into himself. His Bluewing pull-on boots changed into his wizard's leather-wrapped boots. His clothes enlarged to fit, and his cloak materialized around his shoulders. The Newlads like to watch Gala transfigure. The forms he has down pat, he does fast, so all they get to see is a burst of golden light. But sometimes, they get to see his cloak materialize around him. It was a real treat when Ddot helped Gala transform into Redtalon. It was the first time they got to see Gala change shape.

Gala smiled at his friends and asked, "Well, fellas, what will we see and learn today?"

"I hope you can practice some of your spells. Maybe you could show us the other transformation you learned. What is it anyway?" asked Ddot.

"It's a red ruby. It feels different than my other forms. I can't hear anything. If possible, I'll show it to you when we stop to rest and get something to eat."

The Newlads yelled in unison, "All right!"

So far, their journey has been adventurous and although their hearts pounded with fear, they were anxious to find Gnome Bloom and their loved ones.

Stinger

The four companions looked at Dragon Mountain With-eyes-that-see one last time. After a second or two, Gala had an idea. "Come on; let's have fun and ride Trusty across the lake. I'll tell him to run to the boulders at top speed. But then, of course, we all know that if I make him go much further at his highest speeds, he'll have to rest due to exhaustion."

"I didn't know that. I ain't never seen a Hobbgie, except Trusty, and I ain't never learned much 'bout 'em. What else can they do?" asked Lucky.

"Hobbgies can run super-fast for a distance before they need to rest. After a hard run, they can still walk and run but not at top speeds for at least half a day. Trusty can still disguise himself as a rock if he feels threatened. He can even go through rocks and vanish into them. That's how he came through the boulders last night before he met us at the mountain."

"I didn't even think of how he got through the boulders. Too much goin' on. It'll be interestin' to see him do it."

"You got that right, Lucky, 'Too much goin' on.' We'll see him do it after we reach the boulders. Come on, let's get on Trusty." Gala coached, "You guys sit in front and hang on tight." Everyone held onto Trusty's mane. The Newlads laid their wings flat against their backs.

"Okie dokie, Chum. We're ready when you are."

"Okay, Ddot. I'll make Trusty stop in front of the boulders. Are y'all sure you're ready?"

"Yes!" The Newlads shouted in unison.

"GO!" Trusty took off like a shot! Everyone hooted and hollered. The wind pushed their skin flat against their faces, and their eyes watered. They cracked up when Trusty swam across the lake like a speed boat. The dell seemed to appear out of nowhere. Trusty ran through wildflowers where black and orange Stingers were pollinating. "Ouch!" Gala yelled. A Stinger stung him on his forehead next to the bump he got earlier from ramming into the walls, but he didn't stop. Before they reached the boulders, Gala told Trusty to stop.

Lucky belly-laughed, "Ha! Ha! Haa! Ha!" He turned to look at his friends. His jaw dropped, then he yelled, "Poison Stinger spike!"

A red bulge was on Gala's forehead. The twin's legs swelled up like a balloon about ready to pop. And a Stinger's spike, which looked like a gigantic thorn, was stuck in Dahc's side. His side was swollen worse than his leg; he shut his eyes. He was passing out and almost fell off Trusty, but Gala caught him.

"Lucky! Ddot! Hold Dahc! Stay with us, Dahc! Sit right there! I'm gonna give you a sip of Sparktinian's blood, but first, I need to pull out that spike. Understand?"

Dahc's voice was faint. "Yeah."

Lucky sat behind Dahc, holding his arms tight, while Ddot sat in front, keeping Dahc's attention. Gala put his fingers on Dahc's skin next to the Stinger's spike. He put his other fingers on the other end of the spike and asked, "On the count of three. Okay, Dahc?"

"Okay."

"Three!" Out came the spike!

"What happened to one and two?" Dahc asked.

Gala chuckled, "I said, on the count of three."

"Oh," Dahc smiled a weak smile while closing his eyes.

"Stay awake, brother." Ddot shook Dahc a little so he'd keep his heavy eyes open.

Gala summoned a bottle of blueblood and a clean cloth. "Dahc, here, take a sip of this. You'll heal before you know it. Here Ddot, you take a sip too. The Stinger's poison doesn't hurt me like it does y'all. I don't need a sip." Gala patted their wounds with the cloth and apologized, "I'm so sorry, guys. I thought this was going to be fun, but I almost killed you, and look—"

"I had fun," Dahc interrupted. "If I was going to die, at least I had fun doing it." Dahc's voice sounded stronger. He looked down and shouted, "WOW! Get a load of this! Look at my side and my leg! The swelling is almost gone! The pain's gone! Look at the holes! They're closing!"

"Wizard wonders! Talk about fast healing! I've never seen such a quick heal! My healing charms don't even heal that fast."

"Look at my leg! It's healed," exclaimed Ddot. And just so you know, I had fun too. I'd do it again!

"Me too," Lucky added. Ifin' we decide to do it again, we just need to make sure nothins' in our way or use some sorta protectin' spell. Don't be so hard on yore-self there, Gala ole pal. None of us knew. It ain't yore fault, ya know. I bet y'all learned a lesson better than me. I ain't sayin' I didn't, because I was sure scared for y'all's life. I'm sayin' sometimes it takes a painful sting to learn a lesson. We can have fun; we just need to be thinkin' it through, that's all."

Gala agreed, "You got that right. Some lessons are learned the hard way." Gala thought about two days prior when his mother had him practice the *Congeal* spell on a spider. She blamed herself because she thought the spider gobbled up her son for breakfast. Gala blamed himself for casting the wrong spell and not studying as he should have. He told his friends, "I'm glad we had some of Spark's blood. My healing charms wouldn't have healed as fast. Healing moss would have taken some time to suck the poison out, and it didn't look like Ddot or Dahc had much time. Y'all could have died. Geez!" Gala hung his head. Remorse set in.

"But we didn't. I'm still here. Ddot's still here. We're feeling GREAT!"

"Come on, Chum. Dahc, Lucky, you, me, we're all in this together."

"Besides, it ain't their time to be leavin' us. But I'm thinkin' it's time we git goin'," Lucky concluded.

Gala lifted his head. "Okay. Yeah. Sure guys. Come on. Let's fly over the boulders."

"Wait. I wanna see Trusty vanish through the boulder, then watch him come out the other side."

"Oh yeah. I'm sorry Lucky. I—"

"Gala, ole pal of mine?"

"Yeah?"

"There ain't no reason for ya to keep sayin' yo're sorry all the time. Especially about things that there ain't nothin' to be sorry for."

"Okay. I'm sorry...I mean, I'll do my best." Gala smiled; his friends smiled back. Then Gala explained, "We might not see Trusty come through the other side of the boulder. It depends on how fast we fly over and how fast Trusty travels through it. But at least we can see him vanish into the rock." Gala told Trusty to meet him on the other side of the boulder.

Trusty made a low growl sound, "Grrawr, rawr, grr." He put his head on the deep, brown boulder. His head melded with the rock and became as hard. A gradual change took place from Trusty's head down through the rest of his body.

"There he goes! Come on, guys!" Gala transformed into his Bluewing form. They flew up to the top of the boulder. Although the fog was thick, they could see well enough to fly over and back down. The foliage was thick as molasses, so much so that they didn't think they would see Trusty come through. They were right; the foliage concealed the boulders. But their paisley ears heard rocks scraping and grinding. Trusty's head, which was still disguised, came through the thick foliage, followed by the rest of him. His rock disguise faded until all they could see was good ole Trusty.

"Rockin' rock disguisin'! What else can Hobbgies do?"

Gala transformed into himself and answered while he brushed Trusty. "Well, Lucky. As far as anyone knows, that's about it for male Hobbgies, but female Hobbgies do different things. They have wings that can carry them for about as far and as fast as male Hobbgies can run. Females' front legs are forearms like those of dragons. Of course, male Hobbgies don't have forearms. Hobbgie couples usually have one offspring a year. They won't have another until their baby grows and can survive without them. When a mother Hobbgie feels threatened, she can pick her baby up with her forearms and fly to safety. Also, while holding her baby, she can disguise herself and her baby as a rock. She has to touch her baby to do it. The father can do the same. He can touch his baby with any part of his body, and when he changes into a rock, so does his baby. After a baby reaches a certain age, it can disguise itself as a rock. When I rescued Trusty, he wasn't old enough to disguise himself. I'm his parent. That's about it for Hobbgies."

"Hold on a da-gom Mageus mornin' light minute. How'd ya save Trusty, is what I wanna know. Right, fellas?" Lucky looked at the twins.

"Yeah, Chum. Dahc and I haven't heard that story." The twins nodded.

Gala paused. He thought about that sad and joyful day, then began his story, "It was a cold, windy morning in Whittlewood Forest. Snow covered everything. As I was walking home from a friend's, the morning sun tried to warm my cheeks. It failed. But, compared to the dreary snowstorm only hours ago, the sun's golden light was inviting. As we all know, during the cold months, food is scarce for many animals."

"Yeah. Animals don't harvest crops and store food the way that we do before the cold comes. Some creatures stuff themselves before it gets too cold. After they're stuffed, they sleep in caves, hollowed trees, or under the ground until the cold is gone. Squirrlies gather a lot of nuts, so I suppose they harvest food for the cold. Some animals, including Hobbgies, don't hibernate. They eat the Sweetleaf until it freezes or grass until it goes dormant. After that, they'll eat bark to help sustain them. Right, Chum?"

"You're right, Ddot. Unfortunately, there are meat eaters who don't hibernate either. And, although Hobbgies aren't on their menu, their meat is up for grabs. That was the sad fate of Trusty's parents. At least, that's what I thought. I walked up to snow drenched in red blood and found a wee, chocolate, Hobbgie hidden in a burrow. But before I saw him, I readied my wand and followed the blood trail until it ended. Although there were several scuff marks, I couldn't make out the tracks. There were no traces of skin, hair, fur, or feathers to give me a clue. But, as I gave up trying to figure it out, I saw steam coming from a clump of melting snow. I crept up and looked inside. Curled up into a ball was the cutest little, half-frightened, Hobbgie I ever saw. That's when I knew his parents got swept up by something. I told the little guy everything would be all right, and he could trust me. I knew he didn't understand, but I saw that my voice comforted him. I named him Trusty. We've been together ever since. I even learned to speak most of his language." Gala put Trusty's brush away, then took out the crystal ball.

"That's sad and happy," Dahc said.

"Yeah. Trusty lost his parents, sad, but was fortunate Gala found him. He would have died without someone like you to care for him," Ddot pointed out.

"And, it didn't take him long to fully trust me either. Did it ole boy?" Gala patted Trusty's neck. "Let's see what the crystal shows us and see if anyone's awake yet."

Gala asked the crystal to show him Acub and Ashlin. After they appeared in the crystal, Gala yelled, "Oh, look! They're flying over the garden, holding hands. Now they're picking up a bucket filled with nectar. Oh, look, Lucky. Your parents are standing next to the bucket."

"Mornin' pickin' is my favorite time in the garden. For some reason, it doesn't feel like workin'," Lucky chuckled. "It looks like they're doin' all right. Let's look in on your parents."

Gala nodded. He asked the crystal to show him his parents. After they appeared, he saw the glowing ember of light still shining on them. Gala said, "The morning light has slightly opened its eyes, but my parents are still in the dark. They're still in barred carriages, and now they're sitting up. Oh, no!" Gala gasped. A couple of puke-green arms reached into the cage and pulled the black sack off his father's head.

"No! That's a Gob-Digger!" Ddot flew backward, shaking, knowing fairy meat is a Gob-Digger's delicacy.

"Gross! A real live Gob-Digger! Yuck! Look at those nasty black fingernails and disgustin' red bumps oozin' with pus. Get a load of those ugly puce scabs! Are they all over or—? No!" Lucky interrupted himself. He slapped his hands on the crystal ball and asked, "What are they doin'?"

Gala yelled as if the Gob could hear him, "Stop it! Stop cramming stuff down my father's throat! Take your filthy hands off him, you nasty Gob! Mother! Guys, Look! She's hitting the Gob with her head. Oh no! Another Gob is taking the sack off her head! She's yelling! Father's trying to bite the Gob! The other Gob is cramming something down Father's throat! I'm a helpless wizard! There's nothing we can do!"

"Your father's trying to keep his head from going into that sack. But there's not much your parents can do because their wrists are still chained to the chains around their ankles. I can't believe this! What do they want? What are they doing? What can we do?" Ddot screamed!

Gala's heart raced. He was breathing hard, almost hyperventilating. He lifted his eyes from the crystal. The twins flew above his head and released their soothing essence on him, themselves, and Lucky.

"Gala! Look! Your father's startin' to relax! He ain't movin', but he's breathin'. Now your mother's startin' to relax. The Gobs must be givin' 'em somethin' to make 'em sleep."

Gala paced and agreed with Lucky, "You're right. Just like Spark said. They could have killed them by now."

"Or ate 'em!" added Dahc.

"I know they eat fairies, but I don't think they eat Mageons. Well, I never heard or read anything saying they did." Gala stopped pacing and looked into the crystal. "*Show me Floreena.*" Purple fog filled the inside. After it dissipated, Floreena and Lidee appeared. They looked relaxed. The carriage started moving. Gala put the crystal ball away, and without coming up for much air, he rambled, "Come on, fellas! Let's get to Gnome Bloom's as fast as possible! Sheesh! Trusty can't travel too fast, at least not anytime soon. I guess I'll use the *Levitation* spell on him. I'll jog through the forest where it's not so dense. I can run and walk fast through the rest of the forest. Y'all sit on my shoulders. Trusty's too big to follow where Bunt can go. I don't know if Nix—"

"Calm down, Chum. We'll figure something out. I wish we knew exactly where Gnome Bloom lived."

Lucky looked up at Ddot and agreed, "Me too. Wizard Spark said to head west. So, if we keep goin' west, we should find him, unlessin' we pass 'em up somehow."

"Anything's possible. Let's just try to stay p-o-s-i-t-i-v-e." Ddot signaled Lucky. He gave him a quick tilt of his head and moved his eyes down towards Gala.

Lucky got the hint and tried to recover. "Jumpin' trail buster, I shouldn't think it, let alone speak it. Yo're right, Ddot. We need to stay positive." Everyone, including Gala, nodded their heads.

Gala thought, "Too bad we couldn't wish our way to Bloom's home." He negotiated with himself about using his *Levitation* spell and an alchemy mix. If he used it on Trusty, it might help them find Bloom faster. He thought out loud, "I'll try to cast my *Levitation* spell on—"

"What do you mean, 'try'? Ddot interrupted. You have the *Levitation* spell down pat, so what are you talking about?" Ddot and Dahc flew down next to Lucky.

"Oh yeah. Sorry, fellas. No. I'm not sorry. Argh! What I mean is that I do have it down pat, but I was thinking about adding an alchemy spell that might help us get to Bloom's faster. I don't know much about alchemy. But I did a little experiment with Father once. Father called it '*Quantaleap*.' We made a crystal shard vanish from one end of Father's worktable and reappear at the other end of his table. So, because it worked, I'm gonna give it a go on those fallen leaves. But, before I attempt it, we should go sit on Trusty. What do y'all think; sound like a good plan?"

SWOOSH! As the Newlads sped past Gala, he heard them say, "Sounds good, Chum. Go on ahead. —Ya ain't kiddin'. That sounds like a good idea— Yeah, sure thing. We're ready." It took nanoseconds for them to reach Trusty and hold tight to his mane.

"Gee, wizards! Looks like y'all know how to cast a quick speed spell."
"It's called: Move it quick, pal. Like lickity-split before an eye-blinks quick kinda movin'," Lucky

humored. "Come on, Gala, hop on up here behind us and do yore stuff."

Timestill Forest & Gnome Bloom

Gala hopped on Trusty behind his friends and summoned his wand. As he pointed it toward the ground, it turned azure. Its sparkling golden light shot from its tip. The vibration of the planet's energy field rose upwards. Gala pointed his wand over their heads and twirled his wrist around. He created a protective energy sphere encircling everyone. "Okay, fellas. Here goes nothing."

As the Newlad's eyes widened, Ddot encouraged, "Okay, Chum. You can do this."

Gala pointed his wand at the leaves and cast his *Levitation* spell. As the leaves lifted off the ground, he hummed. Vibrations traveled through his arm. While continuing to hum, he reached his left arm out, then clenched his hand. The leaves squished together. After the light from his wand faded, Gala concealed it and pulled his left arm back toward himself. The leaves followed and hovered in front of the protective sphere. Gala placed his clenched hand in his right hand and lowered his arm towards the ground. The leaves followed. In his Sorcermizic tongue, he spoke the incantation to the *Quantaleap* spell. Like throwing a ball up in the air, he jerked his arm upwards and unclenched his hand. The leaves flew upwards. But they only glided back down to the ground. Gala sighed. "Well, fellas, guess I didn't get that right."

"Floatin' magical magic! Those leaves looked more relaxin' than I felt. Can we sit on good ole Trusty while he's levitatin'?"

"Sure, Lucky. I'll keep the protective sphere around him. I've wasted enough time. We need to get going." Gala hopped off Trusty. His friends held tight to Trusty's mane anticipating their guided ride. Gala walked out of the protective sphere; his shoulders drooped. Then he remembered another spell called *Warp Drive* but couldn't remember how to perform it.

Warp Drive can transport someone from one place to another faster than the speed of light. Of course, that's if they know where they're going. Gala knew the vicinity of where Gnome Bloom lived. If only he trusted his powers and remembered the words to the spell, he could cast it. Gala closed his eyes and started daydreaming. He visualized sitting on Trusty behind his friends and thought about using the sphere as a *Warp Drive* transporter. Without knowing, Gala had stepped back into the protective sphere. He used his hand to cast his *Levitation* spell, then clenched his hand to grab the sphere. It, with everyone in it, lifted above the trees.

The Newlads looked at each other, shrugging their shoulders. They wore puzzled expressions like, "What's going on?"

Gala thought out loud, "*Exporalight!*"

"What's happening? Gala! What did you do? The sphere's vibrating!" Ddot's voice shook. A bead of sweat rolled down his forehead.

Gala's eyes popped wide, as wide as all his friends. The sphere glowed a silvery blue color and vibrated with more intensity. The Newlad's clenched tighter to Trusty's mane. The protective sphere became more solid. Gala knew what was happening. At least, he thought he knew. He focused on the *Levitation* spell, visualizing a safe journey. Finally, the sphere stopped vibrating and took off like a speeding bullet.

"Wait! What does 'Exporalight' mean? Are we gonna blow up!?" Ddot yelled, but Gala didn't answer because he wasn't sure.

Gala used his free hand and put a blindfold over Trusty's eyes. Everyone else looked through the glowing sphere. As it sped through the air above the forest's treetops, they saw green, red, brown, and yellow colors streak past. The sphere jolted. It shot down through a clearing, then hit a large body of water. Gala and Trusty bounced off the floor and landed back on their feet. The Newlads held on to Trusty's mane as they lifted, then came back down on his back. The sphere traveled downwards into the depths of the water, into total darkness.

"STOP!" Gala commanded. The sphere came to a complete halt. It all happened within three blinks of an eye. Of course, that's if anyone dared to blink. Gala saw bubbles moving upwards, so he pushed his arm up above his head. The sphere followed. His friends looked up and watched the bubbles travel up toward the light. After seeing that Gala had control, the Newlads began to relax. Gala lifted the sphere from the water. He set it on the bank and released his grip. He removed the

Protective spell and Trusty's blindfold. The sphere dissolved. Everyone took a deep breath and let it out with a sigh of relief. Dahc felt nauseous until he took a couple extra deep breaths.

They looked around their surroundings. Brooks extended out from the expansive lake. One led into a massive forest thick with humongous trees. Other streams flowed into another forest, and colorful wildflowers grew everywhere.

While holding his dizzy head, Dahc asked, "Wow! Gala! What happened?"

"I'm sorry, guys. I had no idea that was going to happen. I wanted to get to our loved ones, but we don't know where they are. So, I imagined us traveling at warp speed to Gnome Bloom's because we know the vicinity of where he lives. I tried to remember the word Father used for his *Warp Drive* spell. I didn't mean to use the spell, and when I remembered the word, I didn't mean to say it out loud."

"So, Exporalight is the spell that means to travel somewhere fast? What I mean is travel somewhere faster than Trusty runs or a bolt of lightning strikes?" Ddot asked.

"Yes."

"And you imagined going fast before you remembered the incantation?" Ddot was getting to a conclusion.

"Yes."

"I hope your imaginations are positive." Ddot chuckled but wasn't joking, and everyone knew it because tension covered his body. He crossed his arms, raised his brows, and had a crook on one side of his mouth, all indications of seriousness.

"I hope my imaginations aren't causing things to happen. I mean, come on Ddot. Do you really think my imagination and not the *Exporalight* spell caused us to travel at warp speed?"

"I don't know. You said you would run, jog, or walk fast while using your *Levitation* spell on Trusty. But instead, you walked into the sphere. You had a look of concentration all over your face. Then you blurted, 'Exporalight' without your wand and no warning."

"That's right. And ya said that ya was tryin' to remember the word for the *Quantaleap* spell before ya did yore *Levitatin'* spell. Ya musta been thinkin' of warp speed before ya blurted, 'Exporalight!' My parents are always tellin' me to be mindful of my thoughts because they can either help ya or hurt ya."

"Yeah," agreed Dahc.

"That's true, Lucky; my parents tell me the same thing. But, as we all know, something happened to me. I'm always messing up my spells. A flub-of-a-wizard, if you ask me. I have no idea why I lost my confidence or why I have nightmares. In this situation, there are different things to consider, different variables. What I mean is, there needs to be more evidence. More facts will tell us if my imagination or the spell, or maybe both caused us to travel at warp speed. So y'all know, I don't have to use my wand to cast my *Levitation* spell because it's a hand spell, too, and so is the *Warp Drive* spell. When I yelled Exporalight, the energy for that spell must have taken over. I'm guessing it had to do with wanting to get to Gnome Bloom's. I don't know." Gala hung his head.

"I reckon ya could be right. But, in case it's yore imaginins' and the spell combined, keep mindful of 'em. Keep 'em positive like Ddot keeps remindin'. And stop callin' yoreself names there pal. Ya ain't no 'flub-of-a-wizard.' And don't say it."

"Say what, Lucky?"

"Don't say yo're sorry."

Gala sighed. He shook his head, rolled his eyes, and blew hard. "Okay, but I am."

Lucky hurried to change the subject. "Let's look and see if Gnome Bloom lives 'round here. His home might be right there in that gigantic forest. But first, I wanna wet my face and wash off these dag-om sweatin' nerves." Lucky flew to the edge of the lake and knelt. When he scooped water to splash his face, he tasted the water. It was warm and sweet tasting. Lucky turned to tell his friends, and instead of talking, he sang uncontrollably:

"♫ Hey pals, the water's warm and sweet, so come on and have a taaaste. ♪Bet it feels good on my feet 'cause it's sure soothin' on my faaace ♫."

His friends stood bewildered. Lucky could not believe what came from his mouth. He stood up, looked at the water, backed up, and began to speak, but again, he sang,

"♪Jumpin' vocals what's this comin' ou-♪"

Lucky covered his mouth. His friends were careful when they walked up beside him. All four companions peered into the water. Lucky took his hands from his mouth. This time he didn't sing when he asked, "Have ya ever heard of such a thing?"

His friends only shook their heads, their eyes fixed on the water. Then Gala whispered, "Guys, don't look around because someone's watching us. Let's get back over by Trusty. I'll put the protective sphere back around us.

They acted calmly. But when they turned around, their hearts walloped through their chests. Woodlanders, gnomes, and elves alike stood at Trusty's side. Hundreds more on foot and astride magnificent Gentalsteeds emerged from the humongous forest. Not one wore a welcoming smile.

Before Gala could retrieve his wand, a Woodland Elf jumped down from his mount and towered over Gala. As the elf looked down on the top of Gala's head, he spoke in a low baritone voice, "Our lake, our home, how did you get here? What do you want?"

Gala felt his heart pick up speed. He threw his hands up, stepped back, then looked up at the angry-looking elf. Gala hardly took a breath as he explained, "Wait a minute! We don't mean to intrude or hurt anyone. I'm Gala Lakinshire, and these are my friends, Ddot, Dahc, Lucky, and my Hobbgie, Trusty, and we're looking for Gnome Bloom."

"Why!?!" Asked a short elf who was more aggressive and had walked up and stood next to the tall elf.

"Wizard Sparktinian told us if we could find Gnome Bloom, he could help us, and that—"

"You lie!" The gnome interrupted and raised his spear to Gala's chest. The spear's tip crackled with blue and white sparks.

The Newlads immediately flew up and stood on Gala's right shoulder. Ddot's brows furrowed. In a forceful voice, he spat, "He's not lying! Sparktinian transcended into the stars last night. We met him the day before. He was going to the Wizards' High Council to tell them our needs. First he had to—"

"SILENCE!" A demanding voice came from the crowd. He purposely interrupted to keep Sparktinian's secret safe because Ddot was about to blurt it out. The demanding voice acknowledged Ddot and said, "You speak the truth. Last night, as I peered into the night sky, I saw Spark's light transcend into the stars."

The crowd made a path. A tall, hooded Woodlander walked through. When the hooded Woodlander stood next to the aggressive gnome, he put his hand on his shoulder. The gnome lowered his spear. His angry body language changed to a peaceful stance, then he stepped back. After the Woodlanders put their weapons away, Gala dropped his arms. The hooded Woodlander pushed his cloak's black hood backward to reveal his face. He was an elf with skin as white as snow. His dark reddish-brown brows and lashes highlighted the intensity of his emerald eyes. He wore a black leather headband around his crown of long, dark-red hair. He had eight braids, four on each side of his head, that hung under his headband past his paisley-shaped ears. After the elf adjusted his hood, he spoke with a softer tone. "Spark is a dear friend."

"'Is'? You mean, was, don't you?" interjected Lucky.

"No. I mean what I say. Everything and everyone transcends yet exists. Elves and gnomes alike know this truth. But, through the years, many Mageons have forgotten. Spark would not have sent you in this direction if he did not trust you. Please come. Let us talk under the forest's protection."

The elf motioned his hand to the Woodlanders. Some got ready to lead the way, while others took up the rear. Before the elf motioned them to go, he placed his hand on Gala's left shoulder. A warmth of energy vibrated throughout Gala's body and up through the Newlads. Gala jolted. He jerked his head to face the elf's piercing emeralds while the Newlads flew off Gala's shoulder and hovered. The elf didn't move his mouth, yet Gala heard him say, "Do not fret. I am the one you seek. After we reach our village, I will introduce myself to your friends."

Within his own mind, without moving his mouth, Gala replied, "I can hear your thoughts! So, you are Gnome Bloom! Spark told us you could read minds."

Gnome Bloom patted Gala's shoulder and continued to speak through his mind. "Yes. I can hear your thoughts through the power of telepathy, mind-reading. However, I need to touch the one I want to communicate with for my telepathic powers to work. Some can read minds without the need to touch. Some mystiques can perform it with a wand crated from the branch of a Whittlewood tree located—"

"In Whittlewood Forest." Gala finished the sentence.

"Yes. Your birthplace. It's where your family's magic tools, including your father's staff, were crafted."

"How do you know so much about me and my parents? Did Wizard Spark tell you about us?"

"Yes. Spark told me stories of the realms outside ours. He also confided his secrets, two of which you and your friends now know."

"Do you mean Dragon Mountain With-eyes-that-see and that Spark was a Mystique Blueblood?"

"Yes."

"Wizard Spark mentioned that the trees whisper to you. Do they tell you what has happened?"

"I'll show you and your friends my Whispering Tree. It's more accurate. Although the other trees whisper, their messages are usually jumbled. Their leaves communicate by creating images of what they are attentive to. They cannot focus on one thing at a time because many things around them happen all at once. Birds create nests in their branches, while animals dig under their bark for food. And then the wind picks up or changes directions."

"Did the trees show you that we were here?"

"Yes. The leaves imitated a large splash in the lake. But, of course, their attention was diverted when they heard a bird singing to another in a nearby tree. Needless to say, their leaves changed."

Gala chuckled and said, "That's funny and interesting."

"After I touched your shoulder, I knew who you were. I know that you and your parents are Mystique Transfigures. You are exceptionally powerful. The Wizard's High Council made a wise decision when they chose your parents as protectors. And yes, I will do my best to help you locate your loved ones. I know your anxious tension and know of your feverish urgency. Relax. In this realm, time moves at a different speed. After spending an hour in our realm, time in your realm would have only moved forward five minutes. We'll talk more later."

Bloom removed his hand from Gala's shoulder. He reached inside his cloak and pulled out a horn that hung on a leather twine around his neck, then blew. Gala thought it strange that he couldn't hear anything. Bloom tucked his horn back inside his cloak, then motioned for Gala to follow the Woodlanders. Gala gave Trusty a tug on his mane and grinned at his friends. They returned the grin and flew down onto Trusty's back.

Along the mossy path where the Woodlanders led, the ground was soft, covered in Hunter Green plants. There were several types of mushrooms growing throughout. The trickling brook flowed parallel to the path. Green, heart-shaped Ground-crawlers grew across the forest floor. They stretched along gigantic roots and trunks of massive Maple, Willow, and Oak trees. There were trees that Gala and his friends had never seen. Some had deep red leaves or yellow and orange leaves. Others had shades of greens and yellows Gala and the Newlads saw in their forest during that time of year.

Gala noticed a slight movement of the roots. It was as if trees were adjusting their weight to a more comfortable position. Branches moved with grace. Leaves swayed as if they were dancing to soothing melodies. Sometimes the forest creaked and groaned. He glanced over the forest and could hear the soft rustle of leaves whispering in their own language. Gala turned and saw that the path behind them had vanished. When he turned back around, he spotted a tree right in front of him. It wasn't there a second ago. Its leaves formed a smile by turning and revealing their lighter underside. Then the smile changed into figures shaped like Trusty and the Newlads riding on Trusty's back, which caused Gala and his friends to giggle.

The forest moved with life. On its soft breath flew glowing Juneybugs, which emitted light on tiny sprites. Glow Sprites, Giggle Sprites, and Gingerly Sprites peeked from around Willow trees. Some emerged from inside the buds of wildflowers. As sprites wisped around, their unique glowing color trailed behind them. An orange Giggle Sprite wisped over to Trusty and sat on his head. He giggled in his neigh-growl voice. Lucky flew up and faced the sprite, squinched his nose, and smiled at her. She reached out and tickled Lucky's stomach, which made him giggle. He did a pixie flip, then flew back down on Trusty's back. Vanishing Sprites vanished from one spot and appeared in a different one. It reminded Gala of the *Quantaleap* spell he didn't know how to cast. A silvery blue Sprite with big blue eyes on her cute round face wisped over and sat on Gnome Bloom's right shoulder. She sat cross-legged, facing Gala. Her smile filled her body, and her aurora pulsed. Gala couldn't help but smile at her.

As they continued along the mossy path, they came upon a mammoth of a tree. Its roots were at least twenty-foot tall as they were wide. Its branches ranged from twenty feet to seventy-five feet in circumference. The length of its leaves expanded out at least ten to twenty feet or more. It would take three Redtalon dragons, from the tips of their snouts to the ends of their tails, to wrap around its trunk. Gala looked up. He couldn't see the top of the tree. He heard a root groan and creak as it moved upwards and around. It extended over the brook and formed a bridge that led straight toward its humongous trunk. When the Woodlanders were close enough to touch the tree, it opened into a gigantic tunnel. Walking through it was like walking through the cave of Dragon Mountain With-eyes-that-see. Except for the mountain, it was rock and dirt, whereas the tree trunk was bark and wood.

At the end of the tunnel, they came upon a village surrounding a large clearing. The brook led into a deep pool on the outside edge of the clearing. Bloom stretched out his arm. As he swept his arm from one side of the village to the other, he said, "Welcome to our home, Timestill Village."

Trees were within the humongous tree. The Woodlanders built their homes inside enormous tree trunks. Some were in trees that had sprouted out from roots. Each had its own intricate design.

Staircases led up around trees and extended over into nearby trees. Hanging down from windows were ladders created out of thick vines. Yellow-orange lights illuminated the windows. The scene was breathtaking.

The village was full of life. Elves and gnomes interacted. Children ran and played. They swung on vines from one tree to the next without fear. Elves and gnomes set food and drink on tables carved from roots and tree trunks. The tables surrounded a stage situated in the center of the clearing. Several Woodlanders created an assembly line up a flight of stairs to a tree house. A gnome inside the house handed an item to an elf outside the door. Each item got passed to the next Woodlander in line. They were musical instruments, flutes, strings, and drums. Their design was different than what Gala and the Newlads had ever seen. After setting the stage, the musicians sat and picked up their instruments. A tall, beautiful elf faced them. She was their instructor and a teller of tales.

Bloom led his guests to a table and said, "You are just in time for storytelling."

Bloom raised his arm towards a distinguished elf. The elf had dark reddish-brown hair with a touch of white running through it. He wore two braids on each side of his crown. They went around his head and weaved into another long braid lying against the rest of his hair. He walked over, pulled out Bloom's chair, then pulled one out for Gala. Bloom didn't sit, so neither did Gala. The elf reached into his pocket. He pulled out a small table with three small chairs and set them on the big table to the right of Gala. Then he put refreshments on the small table. The Newlads flew off Trusty and stood by their chairs while Trusty lay down beside Gala. Everyone thanked the elf.

"You're welcome," he replied, then walked over and stood by a chair next to Bloom.

Bloom introduced, "My name is Gnome Bloom. Everyone calls me Bloom. This is my brother, Celtrek. Celtrek, this is Gala, his Hobbgie, Trusty, and his good friends, Ddot, Dahc, and Lucky. Celtrek doesn't usually pull out my chair, nor is he required to. However, you are my guests, so my brother honors this. I do the same for him and his guests."

After saying hello to each other, Bloom invited everyone to sit. The way the Woodlanders lived in harmony intrigued Gala and the Newlads. It reminded them of their own harmonious life. Gala complimented, "Your home is beautiful, and everyone seems happy."

"Thank you, and yes, everyone is happy. We have our differences. But everything's resolved with a bit of understanding and compromise."

Gala smiled when he saw the sprite still sitting on Bloom's shoulder. He pointed out. "She's so cute and still grinning at me."

Bloom saw her fascination and remarked, "She's a Gingerly Sprite. Her name is Silverlight. She likes you. You must have a pure heart. Gingerly Sprites are quite cautious around strangers."

"That's nice of you, but I've been angry lately. My anger can well up some negative thinking. I don't think that's considered pure."

"Young mage, negative thinking due to anger does not mean you have impurities of the heart. You love your friends and have compassion for them. You have a humble heart. One day you'll learn not to be hard on yourself."

Gala glanced at his friends while he nodded and said, "Okay." The Newlads tilted their heads, looked at Gala through their lashes, and nodded in agreement with Bloom.

"Storytelling is about to begin. Because you are our guests, you can tell a story, or would you rather ask a question?"

Gala pondered Bloom's question for a second before he looked at his friends and asked, "What do you guys think?"

"If y'all don't mind, I wanna know why I sang after tastin' and washin' my face in that lake," suggested Lucky.

"Yeah! Good one. I'm curious about that too. What do you say, Dahc? Ddot asked as he patted Dahc's shoulder.

Dahc smiled a big teeth grin, nodding his head yes to everyone around the table.

"It's settled," Gala giggled at Dahc, then looked at Bloom and Celtrek, who also sounded out bits of chuckles.

"The storyteller loves that legend. She tells it very well. In fact, she tells it so well that you'll see the whole story in complete detail. Her name is Sonata. She is one of the best tellers of tales I have ever heard and watched. Bloom turned to look at Celtrek. Celtrek nodded his head, stood up, and walked over to Sonata. Everyone could see her agreeing smile. After Celtrek returned to his seat, Sonata gave instructions to the musicians. They situated their instruments. The village faded into shadows except for a light that shone on Sonata. She elegantly motioned her hand as if picking up a cup. The Woodlanders followed her lead. Bloom gestured to Gala and the Newlads to do the same, so they did. Sonata put her hand to her lips, then slightly tilted her head. Her audience took a sip of their drink.

    Gala and his friends looked at each other. All of them wore the same expressions, their brows raised. They made little yes nods. Dahc whispered, "This is delicious." A warm sensation spread throughout their bodies. They felt surprisingly relaxed. They smiled and turned their attention to the stage.

    Sonata signaled the musicians. Their mystical instruments soothed each ear. Sonata turned back towards her captivated audience and began humming, her voice sweet. When she moved her hands and arms about, she swayed. The music, her magical voice, and her elegant movement mesmerized her listeners. A luminous scene encircled the stage. Vibrant flowers swayed in a soft breeze. Tranquil resonances came from a lush forest and a trickling brook. Then, Sonata's sweet humming drifted into lucid lyrics while she sang the legend of The Singing Lake:

    — "There is a legend that began not so long ago — when a forbidden mirror revealed the truth of a most devious, hideous, deceitful troll —

    An enchanter whose beauty and wealth are unmatched. Sang of baby birds that were newly hatched. She cooled her feet in a trickling brook, unaware her song caught the ear of a traveling crook. The crook, a hideous Traveling Troll, a bearer of discord, nasty to his core. He followed the voice that made him cringe, the beauty that made his insides twinge. He saw the enchanter as beautiful as her song, then plotted her demise so he could move on. He secretly followed and learned of her wealth; possessing her riches would enrich his stealth. On discovering her assets were under protection, he devised a plan, so they'd be his possessions. He sought help from the Faraway Witches who lived in the swamps and lurked in swamp ditches.

Hearing the troll's request, the Faraway Witches agreed to help. But they never gave out spells without getting something in return. With penetrating glares, they asked the fear-ridden troll, "What will you give us for our generous deed?"

"But I have nothing to give,' snarled the troll."

"No! Not yet!" cackled the Faraway Witches. "We know the enchanter has plenty of gold. If we give you our Potion of Disguise, it will change your appearance into a handsome wizard. It will mask your nasty demeanor with irresistible charm. You will win her love. Certainly, you will wed. Afterward, you will fill these two bags with her gold. You will bring them back to us before the last day of the three full moons or—"

"I'll fill the bags and bring them to you before then. Hurry up! Give me the potion!" he rudely interrupted.

Grock Faraway held his hand out toward the troll. By suggesting his index finger and thumb as a clamp, Grock pinched the troll's mouth shut. He commanded, "Hold your tongue!" As Grock lifted his arm, the troll levitated up to the vaulted ceiling. Grock released his magic grip. The troll fell—his arms and legs flailing—and he crashed hard against the rock floor. After he struggled to his feet, wobbling, he rubbed his throbbing body and mouth.

Faraway's wife screeched, "Keep silent you wretched creature born out from the depths of wickedness! There's more you need to know! You will deliver our payment before the last day of the three full moons, or you will die a slow tormenting death!"

"What happens after I deliver?"

In a deep sinister voice, Grock cackled, "You'll live! But heed our warning. The enchanter must NEVER see your reflection. Your reflection reveals your form, your true nature. If she sees the truth, whether it's before or after you deliver our gold, she can deal with you as she wishes. To remain disguised, you must take a sip of this potion daily. We'll give you a lasting spell after you deliver in full. Understand?"

"I understand."

"One more thing of importance." The Faraways squinted their eyes. They got into the troll's face and cautioned, "A slow tormenting death will befall you if you ever harm her! Do we have a deal?"

The troll thought, "After I have her gold, I'll pay someone else to destroy her." In his desperation, he agreed to the terms. If he had asked, he would know that paying someone to kill her would also get him killed.

"Yes. We have a deal. Now give me the potion," barked the hideous troll.

Grock snapped his fingers. A gooey substance spun in the palm of his hand and formed into a teardrop bottle filled with a red potion. "Hold out your hand," he commanded the troll.

The troll held his hand out, then Grock pursed his lips and blew. The bottle vanished. It materialized into the troll's hand. With his hairy spindling fingers fumbling, the troll plucked the cork from the bottle, then hurried and took a sip. He looked at his arms and hands; his scabby skin turned tan, healthy, and smooth with no bumps or oozing scabs. He touched his face; the bushy hair that once covered his flattened bat-like face was gone. His nose straightened. It took the shape of a handsome rounded nose. The Traveling Troll corked the bottle. With barefaced boldness, he asked for clothes.

The Faraways glared with a smirking grin while pointing their wands at a window drape. It twisted and spun down from its rod, then came down and floated directly in the face of the ungrateful troll. A pair of scissors appeared out of thin air, cutting the drape into equal pieces. A dozen threaded needles zoomed in and out. They stitched together two pairs of pants, shirts, cloaks, and one hat. One set of clothes attempted to dress the reluctant troll. The shirt slapped both sides of his face with its sleeves, and the pants kicked his shins. The toll snarled and screeched from the stings they assaulted. The sleeves of the shirt shook his shoulders hard. The hat squeezed his head tight. The cloak wrapped its corded clasp around his neck and squeezed. It constricted his air flow until the troll finally gave in and stood still.

While the determined clothes dressed him, the other set folded up like a pack that he could carry on his back. The Traveling Troll gave the witches a nod. He said he would return with their payment before the end of the three full moons. With speed, the troll stuck the potion in the pocket of his cloak. He hastened to deceive the unsuspecting enchanter.

Before the first three full moons had passed, the troll won the heart of the enchanter, and indeed they wed. He told her he could not allow mirrors in their home due to sad memories. Nor could he allow reflecting pools or reflecting objects of any kind in or around him. He also explained that because of his work, there were days he would have to travel but would always return to her. The enchanter agreed. However, tucked away in her room, she hid her small looking glass where her husband would never find it.

A troll has no idea how impossible it is to keep a mirror from a woman.

When the night of the three full moons arrived, the troll told his wife he had to travel on business. He told her he would return in a few days. He filled the Faraway witches' bags with gold. He put on his hat and one of his cloaks, kissed his wife's cheek, then said he'd bring her a gift on his return.

As he traveled, he felt well pleased and confident that he would not die at the hands of the Faraway Witches. The deceitful troll reached inside his cloak to retrieve his potion. It was not there. He checked his other pocket. It wasn't there either. He patted his shirt and pant pockets; it was nowhere on him. He remembered he had left the bottle in his other cloak. If his wife found it, being she's an enchanter, she would know what it was. He hurried back towards the cottage.

Meanwhile, the enchanter thought her husband would not return for a few days. She felt safe pulling out her looking glass. The troll returned while she stood in the garden. He saw her standing with her back toward him and noticed she was holding something. His heart thumped against his chest with a punch, fearing she was holding his potion. He tiptoed up behind her, then, with caution, he peered over her shoulder. He saw the looking glass and huffed. The enchanter gasped. In her mirror, she saw a glimpse of a reflection of something hideous behind her. She jerked around; her handsome husband stood before her eyes. Perplexed, she turned back around. She moved to the side so she could get a better view. Once again, she peered into her forbidden mirror and saw the truth. Her mirror revealed every aspect of the troll's malicious intentions. She held her mirror up above her head and let it go. It floated over to face the troll. With great speed, it began circling faster and faster around him. He held up his hands. The mirror circled around him, faster still. Then it shattered into a thousand splintering shards that pierced the toll's backside. It felt as if he had fallen into the quills of a porcupine. He did not dare move.

The sky turned black with thunderous clouds. The enchanter turned to face her intrusive deceiver, who stood in pain and shock. The ground beneath his feet rumbled as her body vibrated and grew—and grew—and grew—and grew! Her inky black pupils flooded across the whites of her eyes. Her veins protruded throughout her skin, face, and neck; her hair turned whiter than snow.

The troll could not move, nor could he speak. He was stiffer than stiff! He tried not to look, but a force drew his eyes to her glare. He saw his tiny reflection in her large, black eyes. Her mouth did not move, yet he could hear her monstrous, thundering voice. It echoed throughout his head while she proclaimed a deserving curse:

"Thieving Traveling Troll, riddled with deceit, Your malicious intent is clear! Using the shadowy darkness, you sought to snip the wealth from a forbidden love. Your heart is black, as black as the pitch from which this sorcery came! You seek to destroy all beauty, all things that make you cringe! I curse your insatiable distaste! No longer will you walk, talk, or have the form of a mindful being! A beautiful lake with many brooks is your fate, forever flowing clean, fresh, and your water sweet! Beings, great and small, who touch or taste your sweetness will sing sonnets of its splendor! All plants growing near will flourish. An unbearable twinge will throb within your watery stomach! You will bend, twist, and turn for eternity. You will flow within the

mystical realm of *Timestill Forest*, where the Timeless Woodlanders dwell! You will persist as a body of water, never to desiccate. Yet! Your insufferable twinging can stop. BUT! It will stop ONLY WHEN you appreciate every form of beauty! From this point forward, you are — *The Singing Lake!*"

The enchanter pointed her fingers at the troll. An intense energy of white light glowed around her body. It filled her protruding veins, which now looked like a web of thick white ropes beneath her skin. The light shot out from her fingertips, penetrating the troll's chest. It filled his body, encasing him while the shards in his back melded with his body. The enchanter felt the troll's breath quicken.

He reached up and touched his chest; his heart pounded through. A peculiar sensation ran through his gut. He reached down. His eyes popped wide. He watched as his hand, followed by his arm, transformed into heavy water droplets, which fell into his watery stomach. It caused ripples throughout his body until the troll was nothing but water.

The enchanter lifted the watery troll from the ground. She commanded, "HOLD FOR EVERMORE!" The ground rumbled while excavating a pit. It expanded outwards in all directions. Long channels, some wider than others, extended into Timestill Forest. Others extended out into the adjoining forests and all their brooks. After the enchanter released the watery troll, he flooded the pit and its channels. He became The Singing Lake.

The enchanter shrank down to her size, veins no longer bulging. Her long hair remained snow-white. It glowed and acquired a silky texture. She disguised herself as a homely woman. But this did not hide her elegance. By and by, when the enchanter sang by the brook, her song caught the ear of a wealthy wizard. He was twice her age yet young looking and handsome. Because the wizard was trustworthy and kind, she allowed their friendship to grow. In time, a mutual feeling of love grew between them. The wizard proposed. Before the enchanter accepted, she revealed herself. She told him about the Traveling Troll and what she had done. The wizard understood and told her the troll deserved his punishment. He told her she was beautiful no matter how much she tried to hide her beauty. She smiled, her heart content. After they wed, they had a child. Before long, they said farewell to their beloved friends, the Timeless Woodlanders. They moved away from The Singing Lake."—

Sonata's arms moved in graceful motion. The musician's hypnotic music and the articulate scene around the stage had faded away. While the audience drifted back to the present moment, Sonata and the musicians bowed. The audience clapped, and some whistled. Gala hooted, and the Newlads hollered as they joined in the applause. After that, the musicians put their instruments away.

An enormous grin plastered across Gala's face. He said, "That was incredible! Everything happened right in front of me. It was as if I was right there! My mother and father are great storytellers. They would have loved this. Their approach and techniques are different, but just as gripping."

"That was magical! I loved her graceful movements. The instruments made specific sounds for every feeling expressed by the characters. I actually felt what they were feeling," added Ddot.

"Me too," included Dahc.

"That was hypnotisin'. What a legend. No wonder I sang so well!" exclaimed Lucky.

"Yes," replied Bloom. "When a being tastes or drinks from the lake, they'll sing a beautiful sonnet, which is unique to each individual. Sometimes they sing in a language other than their own. The singing doesn't last long, although it does last longer on some than others."

"We've heard gruesome stories about the Faraway Witches. Are they still living in the Boggy Swamps?" Ddot asked.

"Good question," Gala said, then he asked a series of questions balled up into one. "Do we have anything to worry about, and is the legend exact, and, well, what I mean is, are all the details to the legend correct, and did the Traveling Troll really get a potion from the Faraways?"

Bloom and Celtrek chuckled. As Bloom explained, he also assured. "There's nothing to worry about. Yes the legend is true. It's a legend because no one has seen a troll or the Faraways for years. So, the truth of the story faded into lore. But anyone who has heard of the legend and has tasted the water realizes the story is not a mythical fairy tale."

"My parents said that The Wizard's High Council banished the Faraways. Grock could have redeemed himself. He could have reclaimed his seat with The High Council if he stopped performing Dark Magic and would take the spell off his wife. But he refused and plotted to take over The High Council. They expected this, so cast a spell using Dark Magic mixed with their Magic of Light to expel the Faraways."

"Your parents were right, Gala. The Wizard's High Council exiled the Faraways deep into the Boggy Swamps years before you were born. It's up to The Wizard's High Council to reduce their sentence. The Faraways cannot venture from the realm of the Boggy Swamps.

"Tell us about trolls. Where do they live? Is there a lot of them?" Asked Ddot.

"Trolls are few in numbers and dwell in the far-off land of Muddy Crud, where it's always cloudy. It's a dreary place where it usually rains, which causes the ground to turn to muck. Its trees are barren of green leaves, and the vegetation consists of Night Shroomers—"

"Night Shroomers?" Gala gasped.

"Yes. And other types of vegetation."

"Where's the land of Muddy Crud?"

"It's in the southwestern land well past the Boggy Swamps. Why?" Bloom asked.

"Because the Gobs who took our loved ones might be heading where Night Shroomers and fruitless Berrybells grow."

"Fruitless Berrybells are more abundant in the west than in the south or east. Night Shroomers are more abundant in western areas. You can find them in the east and the southwest but not in the south. In a few minutes, I'll take you to my place. We'll see if we can pinpoint the whereabouts of your parents."

Gala apologized, "I didn't mean to change the subject. If you don't mind, I'd like you to tell us more about trolls."

"That's quite all right. Trolls stay in their realm because they cannot withstand the sights or sounds of beauty. Those who do happen to venture are Traveling Trolls, hence their name. They venture because most beautiful things do not cause them to cringe. If Traveling Trolls leave the safety of Muddy Crud, they never return home because they either die or end up cursed. It's not likely you'll see a troll or a Traveling Troll."

"Do trolls eat fairy meat?" Dahc asked.

"No. Gurgling Mudlumps and, of course, Night Shroomers. But they do kill things of beauty. Fairies are quite beautiful, so if a troll saw you, it might seek to kill you. Trolls cringe with agonizing pain if they hear or see anything they deem beautiful. They usually do not venture far from home, not even into the Boggy Swamps. Although there is wickedness and danger in the swamps, the swamps are quite beautiful. Does this knowledge help ease your worries?" Gala and the Newlads nodded.

"Come then. Follow me to my abode. Celtrek, will you join us? I may need your help."

"Sure. Lead on."

The Whispering Tree

The Newlads flew up onto Gala's shoulder. Silverlight remained on Bloom's. Celtrek took up the rear while Bloom led everyone to the other side of the village. They walked through a large cluster of roots. Fungi and illuminating mushrooms grew throughout. They came upon a forest thick with Juneybugs twinkling like stars with wings. Bloom walked up to what looked like a dead-end wall of dense trees. Gala and the Newlads finally saw a gap and realized they were inside a shifting maze. It moved as the forest moved. Bloom turned to his right. He walked a few feet between the walls of trees, then turned left and walked a few more feet. He continued forward, passing two pathways, one on his right and one on his left.

Trusty started nodding his head while whickering and growling. Gala patted his neck. They walked up to an enormous tree with a large tunnel carved through its trunk. A tree-lined fence extended out from both sides of the tree and surrounded a field of Sweetleaf. There was an assortment of grazing livestock, Slender Gentalsteeds, and Oxies. But that wasn't what excited Trusty. To Gala's surprise, a female Hobbgie was flying above the Sweetleaf. She is the one thing that can make a male Hobbgie act like Trusty was.

A gnome, whose skin was a darker tan than most Woodlanders, came through the tunnel and greeted,

"Good morning."

Bloom greeted, then introduced, "Good morning, Toma. Everyone, this is Toma. He helps look over our livestock. Toma, these are our new friends, Gala and his Hobbgie, Trusty, the twins, Ddot and Dahc, and this is Lucky."

"It's a grand day to meet new friends; welcome." Toma smiled and bowed.

Trusty neighed and growled. He shook and nodded his head while stomping the ground with his front foot. As Gala patted his neck, he chuckled and said, "Trusty smells the Sweetleaf, but I'm pretty sure that's not all he smells."

Bloom offered, "If it's okay with you, Trusty can stay here until we return."

"That'll be great!" Gala gave Trusty a few more pats and told him to have fun with the others. Trusty nodded. As Toma led Trusty through the tunnel, Trusty bolted straight over to the female Hobbgie. Everyone cracked up laughing.

"Thank you, Toma. We'll be back." Bloom chuckled, then led everyone through the maze.

He took the first left, which declined for about a half mile. The dense walls of branches and the leaves, which were a Forest Green color, lessened as large roots took their place. Eventually, the ground flattened into a lush meadow surrounded by the forest. A mountain stood in the center. Water spilled over its summit. It splashed onto a group of swaying trees that were enjoying the shower. When Bloom stepped into the tall grasses of the meadow, a path formed beneath his feet. It led into the cluster of trees.

Bloom walked to an enormous tree within the cluster. Its protective chocolate bark was thick and stout. It had deep vertical zigzag grooves and ridges. The tree groaned and crackled as parts of its bark moved outwards. It created a spiral staircase with a railing going upwards around the tree. The steps were in the shape of hands balled into fists. The staircase railing was smooth like the mahogany trunk beneath its bark. Bloom walked close to the bottom step; it crackled and creaked when its hand opened. After Bloom stepped up on the palm of the hand step, the staircase moved upwards, allowing the next fist to open for Gala.

Celtrek motioned Gala to step onto the step's palm. So, he did. When the staircase moved up for Celtrek, Gala yelled, "Whoa, whoa, whoa!" His leg jerked upwards, his arms flailing. He tried to catch his balance. The Newlads flew off his shoulders and hovered. Bloom turned to see what was happening. A swift-moving branch reached down like a hand and steadied Gala. After Gala grabbed onto the railing, the bough returned to its position.

Bloom apologized, "I'm sorry. I should have told you to hang on. Just so you know, the stairs move downwards too."

"It's not your fault, but gee wizard! What if I was up high? Will all the trees extend their branches and catch someone if they fall?"

"Yes," Bloom answered.

"So that's why the children didn't fear swinging on vines from one tree to the next," Ddot surmised.

Celtrek considered, "I guess that's true for many. Whereas other children, I suspect, face their fears the way most children do." Celtrek turned their attention. He pointed above Bloom and warned, "Don't be alarmed; we're approaching the entrance."

The Newlads flew back down on Gala's shoulders. They looked up and saw a dense cluster of branches and leaves, which widened into a large opening as the staircase moved closer. Bloom entered through the hole. The staircase stopped. After Bloom stepped off onto a mahogany floor, the bark step balled into a fist, then crackled its way back into the tree. The next step moved upwards and waited for Gala to step off before it moved up for Celtrek.

The tree was carved out around its center trunk, creating a spacious treehouse. Its floor spanned across from the walls of the thick bark to the core and circled around. Books, knick-knacks, large candles, and other items set in nooks. Large flowering plants grew throughout. Flutteries, much bigger than the four companions ever saw, pollinated the flowers. Gala spotted a red fluttery flying through an opened door from within the trunk. He ducked without warning. The Newlads gasped. They held tight to Gala's hair and fluttered in place. Their eyes popped wide when a huge Stinger flew through the threshold. Startled by the Newlad's gasps, Silverlight took off and hid inside a budded flower.

Bloom calmed, "No need for alarm." Silverlight peeked out from the flower. Bloom continued, "All the Stingers in Timestill Forest are docile. Come into my kitchen. Have a seat at the table." Bloom gestured his hands for his friends and Celtrek to come in.

A round mahogany table sat in the middle of a circular kitchen. A couple feet past it was a wooden door that led into another room. Bloom shut both doors to prevent Stingers and flutteries from flying in and out. But for airflow, he left the wide kitchen window open. He whispered something to Silverlight. She bowed, spun in the air, then flew over to face Gala. Her blue eyes twinkled. As she cupped her hands, she bashfully gave her head a slight tilt downwards to one side. Before Gala knew it, Silverlight flew up and kissed his cheek, then flew back in front of him.

"Awe. Thank you, Silverlight. I like you, too, and it was nice to meet you." She spun and bowed, then flew over to the Newlads. She nodded to each one before her silvery blue wispy form glided out the kitchen window. Celtrek reached into his pocket. He pulled out the same furniture he had placed for the Newlads while listening to Sonata. He set them on the table next to Gala. Being less formal, Celtrek motioned the four companions to sit.

Bloom gathered a few items from his shelves. He explained, "I'll use four elements to activate whispers from my Whispering Tree. You'll get a better idea as things progress."

First, Bloom placed a Hunter-Green cloth in the center of the table, then he set a crystal bowl that contained a miniature tree about a foot high on top of the Hunter-Green cloth. Precious gold fused the diamond-shaped crystals together. It triggered an empty feeling in Gala's gut. The bowl reminded Gala of his father's holding crate. Gala hurried and diverted his focus back to the tree. The miniature tree's trunk was thick with branches and colorful leaves. The leaves reflected throughout the bowl.

Bloom placed an empty crystal bowl on top of a small wood burner constructed of rich soil, dry grass, and water. A tube extended from one side of the burner and curved upwards and around to its top. A fan made of bark that faced down over the bowl was attached to the tip of the tube. Bloom put a few tiny wood chips inside the burner. He opened a gold box lined with red velvet fabric. The box had a partition. Each compartment held a magnesium rock which Bloom took out and held close to the wood chips, then tapped them together. The rocks sparked and ignited the chips. Bloom pursed his lips. He blew softly until the chips caught fire.

After he put the rocks away, he walked over to a porcelain basin. Water from the mountain's summit trickled down the trunk of the treehouse. It flowed onto several layers of leaves, then into the basin filling it with fresh water. The basin's bottom was deep and lined with assorted gems.

Bloom dipped a wooden pitcher into the basin and filled it with water. He poured water into the crystal bowl he had set on the burner, then returned the pitcher to the counter. As the water heated up, it formed tiny bubbles along the bottom of the bowl. Steam rose through the tube, causing the fan to spin. Not only was the fan creating a wind element, but it also kept the water lukewarm. Bloom sat down, snuffed the fire out, and took the bowl off the burner. He poured the warm water into the bowl that held his miniature tree.

The tree lit up and glowed. Twinkling colors danced around the room. Gala and his friends smiled wide. Strong, vibrational energy was emitting from the miniature tree. Bloom touched its trunk and instructed, "Gala, touch my arm; think of your parents. In your mind, ask '*Where*' they are."

Gala touched Bloom's arm. While looking at the tree, he formed a vivid image of his parents. Within his mind, he asked, "Father, Mother, where are you?"

The tree swayed. Its leaves twisted and turned, then formed distinctive shapes of Conkay and Faithin. Gala's heart thumped. His parents were lying down. The leaves made a castle, but then, something dark covered it. The dark shape grew and shrank, in and out on all sides as if pulsating. Bloom asked the tree to reveal its nature. The tree's leaves formed the words, and the tree answered in a whisper, "Dark Menace." Gala and the Newlads gasped in unison.

Bloom asked the tree, "*What type of Dark Menace?*"

The tree whispered and formed a word in bold caps, "**SHADOW.**"

Gala's stomach twisted into knots. His body shook, and his hand squeezed Bloom's arm. Ddot nudged Dahc to follow. They flew above Gala, flapped their wings, and released their calming essence. After Gala stopped shaking, they sat back down.

Bloom asked the tree, "*Where is the **Shadow**?*"

The miniature tree swayed; its leaves spelled out, "**Shadow** block."

Bloom thanked the miniature tree before he removed his hands. But before Gala took his hand off Bloom's arm, Bloom heard Gala's thoughts. "I wonder if the **Shadow** was in the laboratory when Father worked on his crystal?"

"Gala. May we look at your crystal? I want to see if what you think might be true?"

"Sure!" As Gala retrieved his crystal, he explained how it worked.

Bloom faced his palms over the ball. While moving his hands in a circular motion, he asked, "*Show me Conkay and Faithin Lakinshire.*" A golden antique glow encompassed the crystal while a purple fog swirled inside. After it dissipated, they could see Gala's parents lying on a dirty floor covered with straw. The black sacks no longer covered their heads. It looked as though they were talking in slow motion. Chains still bound them. The shackles around their wrists were now chained to large iron rings within a stone wall. The manacles around their ankles were chained to iron rings on the floor. Bloom put one hand on his miniature tree and the other on the crystal ball. He asked, "*Was this crystal ball crafted with Dark Magic or the Magic of Light?*"

Bloom's miniature tree swayed; as its leaves formed a word, it whispered, "Both." And at the same time, POOF! A pitch-black fog filled the crystal.

Gala's heart pounded through his chest. After catching his breath, he asked Bloom, "Is that pitch-black a sign of Dark Magic?"

"According to my Whispering Tree, yes. The **Shadow** could have interfered. When I asked my tree where the **Shadow** was, it couldn't detect its location. The **Shadow** and your parents seem shrouded. I do believe the **Shadow** hindered your father's crystal. However, I'd like to be sure. I have a thought. Let me ask the crystal the way I ask my tree. Instead of asking it to '*Show*,' I'll ask it to tell me '*Where*' your parents are. Keep in mind that anything can happen. Is this okay with you?"

Without coming up for much air and merging his sentences together, Gala answered, "Yes. I'll try anything; every time I've asked the crystal to show me my parents, their wrists were chained to chains around their ankles; they were either sitting or lying in a barred carriage, and my girlfriend and her mother were in a separate barred carriage; all of them had black sacks over their heads, and we saw Gobs pulling the sacks off and forcing something down their throats; whatever it was, it made them sleep. Plus, it was always dark, even when morning shined her waking light, and, on top of that, I bet the **Shadow** interfered because my father saw the **Shadow** in his laboratory the same day of the celebration when he was working on his crystal. He said that sometimes he felt like he was being watched, but Father always brushed the feeling off. That started happening about the time I got nightmares. Do you think the **Shadow** had something to do with the crystal, and do you think the Gobs know how to use Dark Magic? I wonder what the Gobs want with them; what if they really do eat—?"

"Rest your mind, young mage. Calm yourself. I want you to take a deep breath and hold it." After Gala took a deep breath, Bloom continued, "Visualize happy thoughts. Hug your loved ones. Now, slowly, release your breath and all negative thoughts. Take another deep breath, hold it, smile, and know your parents are alive. Smile. Release your breath slowly and resume your regular rhythm of breathing. How do you feel?"

"Better." Gala managed a smile.

"First, Gob-Diggers are not intelligent creatures; it is easy to persuade them. I assure you they are not the masterminds behind this violation. You may have learned that Gobs do not venture far from the Boggy Swamps. If they do, it's usually at night, and they're seldom alone. They stir in the late hours of the night into the early morning. A Gob's skin is sensitive to sunlight. It will burn them to ashes if they're caught in it. During daylight hours, they sleep in the shadows of caves, ditches, underbrush, and anywhere there's shade. Furthermore, although they eat fairies, Mudlumps, birds, and many other things, they do not eat Mageons.

Gala and the Newlads shuddered at the thought, shaking it from their minds. Bloom continued, "I will ask your crystal and my tree the same question at the same time. I want to see if we can learn more of this hidden mystery. Remember, anything can happen. Do your best to remain hopeful and calm. Understand?"

"Yes sir," Gala answered while the Newlads nodded.

Bloom put one hand on his tree and one on the crystal, then asked, "*Where are the Lakinshires held captive?*" As the tree swayed, the fog in the crystal became dark purple, almost black. It swirled into storm clouds. They churned above a steep mountain fortress. Sharp rigid peaks were on one side of the mountain, and smooth rocks with foliage were on the other.

The leaves on Bloom's tree rustled and whispered, "Wizard Tiaff's castle—" Lightning burst inside the crystal and interrupted the tree's whisper. Twirling black clouds whirred. Fierce bolts shot out in all directions hitting the inside walls of the crystal. Everything was in slow motion. The golden antique glow of the crystal was now a fiery red glow emitting extreme heat.

Bloom jerked his hand from the heat! He told the crystal to sleep, but the heat intensified, igniting deep red flames. The twirling black cloud was now red. The crystal vibrated faster and faster as if it was about to explode into a million pieces of shard! Its gold pedestal was melting, and the table beneath it charred. The Newlads flew away. Bloom got up, grabbed the miniature tree, and placed it on the counter. Celtrek got up, picked up the green cloth, and dipped it into the basin. Gala sat in shock, imagining Redtalon's icy craw. His eyes popped wide when he heard a cackling, thundering snarl from within the crystal. Tingles shot through the tiny hairs on his neck when an unhurried baritone voice said, "I—see—you."

Ddot yelled, "Gala! Get back!" but Gala didn't hear him. Celtrek was about to throw the damp cloth over the burning crystal when Gala's throat changed form. His throat shot out icy snow, which put out the fire and engulfed the crystal in ice. While Gala sat and stared, his throat resumed its natural state.

The only sounds in the room were the Newlad's fluttering wings and crackling ice. Lucky broke the silence, "Blazin' fireball! By the giver of goodness, life, and love, what was that all about? Gala! Do ya realize what ya did? Yore throat was a miniature Redtalon's throat! It ain't the same as when Ddot used yore wand, and ya were lookin' like a spookin' swamp creature. Ya know, like half dragon, half wizard comin' outta the Dragons' Lake? Heck, I ain't never seen anythin' like it!

"Yeah! Me either," added Ddot.

"Me either!" agreed Dahc.

Gala touched his throat and looked over at his friends. His dark brows pushed inwards and up, forming a puzzled expression. At first, he spoke softly, as if to himself, then got a little louder as he looked around the room, "I'm just as dumbfounded as you. I didn't know I could do that. I didn't even know I did it! All I know is that I wanted to transform into Redtalon. I wanted to use his icy craw to douse the fire, but there wasn't enough room, so I imagined I could transform my throat. By all the wonders of transfiguring, it actually happened. But I'm wondering about the wicked voice inside the crystal. It spoke slowly and said, 'I—see—you.' Did anyone else hear it?"

"No," The Newlads answered in unison, shaking their heads.

Gala looked over at Celtrek and Bloom. They also said no.

"I'm not sure what you heard. The twirling red clouds did sound like a Twister Flame. If you ever witness one, you'll swear the eerie whirring it screeches is saying something. I find it odd. We heard the clouds twirling and the cracks of lightning, but we couldn't hear your parents talking. Yet you heard someone say something to you. We'll see if we can figure this out. Aside from that, I have to say, your transfiguring abilities are far beyond anything I've ever heard of. I have no doubt you are one powerful mage. And I'm certain I'm not the only one who has told you this." Bloom looked over at the Newlads.

"No. You aren't the only one. But I'm beginning to think that my imaginations have a lot to do with some of the things that happen to me, around me. My friends pointed this out and said I needed to be mindful just in case."

"Yes. It seems imagination creates images your mind creates more often for problem-solving. Thinking is the process we constantly do, whether we are aware of organizing them. Some thoughts we produce from what we sense through our bodies. Those types of thoughts pass through our minds. But an imagination lingers with images you put together on purpose to create an image, an idea. Let your inner being, your true self, watch and know your thoughts. In doing so, your being has control and not your thoughts. Your being can replace negative thoughts with positive thoughts. You can replace ungrateful feelings with grateful ones. This will stop your thoughts from creating emotions that can cause fear or sickness. The present moment is all we have, so do your best to live in it. With practice, you'll learn to control your thoughts and your imagination. And, not to mention your ability to transform part of your body." Bloom winked with a smile.

Gala returned the smile. "I understand. I'll do my best to practice. My parents told me the same thing. Having positive thoughts is hard when things don't work out how I expect or want them to. I used to have positive thoughts until about a year ago when I lost my confidence for whatever reasons. I also have nightmares that I can't remember. Wizard Sparktinian gave us some roots to eat. Last night they helped to relieve my nightmares. But I want to know how to stop them. Guess I need to work on feeling positive. Do you think my imagination affects those around me?"

Bloom paused before he answered. He wondered if Dark Magic was part of the reason Gala had nightmares. Bloom thought Gala may have heard a voice from within the crystal. Bloom wanted to find out, but first, he explained what he believed to be true about imagination. He said, "I am no expert in this study. Remember that others have their own set of thoughts and imaginations. You would need to coincide with each other to manifest the same outcome. It might not turn out the way you imagined it. Everyone creates their own life, which details and specifics can disrupt. I find this subject complex. I suppose it's possible to change the outcome of our own future by focusing our energies on what we want. It is best to be happy with what we already have and who we are. If our brain believes what we tell it, we will find a way to make it so. So, do your best to remain positive and grateful."

Gala looked over at his friends, who were nodding. Lucky held up a thumb. Gala smiled, then looked back at Bloom and said, "Yes, sir. We'll all do our best. But do you think I could have caused the disappearance of my girlfriend? I used to imagine saving her from Gob-Diggers." Gala sounded guilty and regretful.

"No. You didn't want this wicked ordeal to become a reality. This act of evil would never be your intent. It happened because someone else with dark intentions wanted to take your girlfriend. I assure you that this has nothing to do with your imagination. You are a good mage with good intentions."

Ddot agreed, "That's for sure. Gala doesn't have a wicked bone in his body."

"No, he doesn't," added Dahc as he shook his head.

"That's the fairy truth. Gala only wants to stop evildoers from hurtin' or inflictin' pain on others. And ifin' it means he has to destroy evil to stop 'em, then he will, and ifin' I can help, I most certainly will." Lucky assured with a nod.

"Thanks, fellas. It's true. I never want to hurt anyone. But I feel vengeful towards the Gobs. I felt like stabbing that dragon slayer for hurting Chizel.

Actually, I wanted to kill that no-good worthless slayer." Gala clenched his teeth and balled his fists.

"But you didn't," reminded Ddot. "You could have killed every single one of those dragon slayers, but you didn't."

Bloom interjected, "If our lives and the lives of others are threatened, it's natural to defend and kill if we must. If someone is tortured, we may feel the urge to torture back. Our innermost feelings, needs, and wants are the things that drive and determine our actions. Unfortunately, there are those consumed with wickedness. There are as many reasons why evil arises as there are leaves on a tree. It's almost impossible to know the exact intent of others. They may not know themselves. What I do know is that you have compassion for others."

With that last statement, Gala relaxed his fists, took a deep breath, then let it out. "Do you think I saw the future?"

"Have you ever seen a vision, and then it comes to pass?" asked Bloom.

Gala thought a minute and replied, "I don't think so. But when I concentrate on a clear image, it helps me accomplish what I want." Like when I cast spells or transfigure.

"That's not the same as seeing the future. That's because you wanted a certain outcome to meet your desires or needs and believed it could happen. Seeing into the future is more like a premonition. It's when a vision from out of nowhere pops into your head, which shows you something that will happen in the future. Sometimes the visions are things and places you've never seen before. It's not the same as when you wish for something to happen, and then it happens or doesn't. And it's not a playful imagination where you are only pretending."

"I understand. But, the other night, when I walked towards Floreena to ask her to dance, I hoped I didn't trip and fall on her. But as soon as she agreed to dance with me, Helsin tripped me. I actually fell into Floreena, exactly what I hoped not to do. It wasn't as bad as I imagined, but I did trip. So, it could be that I knew I was going to trip."

"You do have a point. However, it could have been a coincidence. If you find that this happens to you often, you're either in touch with your intuition or you are an Intuitive One. Either way, it's something you'd want to improve." Gala smiled as Celtrek handed Bloom a towel and gestured the Newlads to sit back down.

"I'm sorry your crystal burned and caused its pedestal to melt. I wasn't expecting that to happen."

"That's okay. It's not your fault. Things happen." Then Gala asked, "Do you know why my father's crystal caught fire?"

"I'll explain what could have happened." Bloom patted Gala's arm. "It's conceivable the **Shadow** was present while your father was perfecting his crystal. It is plausible that while your father tried to perfect his crystal, the **Shadow** placed a curse on it. Both spells produced conflicting aspects. The voice you heard, the lightning crackling, and the whirring of the wind, Dark Magic produced. It prevents you from hearing anyone or seeing their whereabouts. But your father's Magic of

Light allowed the crystal to show you who you want to see.

"That makes sense! It's probably cursed, as you said. Because my father is an excellent alchemist and wizard! The crystal should have worked. Father did say, '...it's a work in progress.' He couldn't get it to work the way he wanted. Now I know why! Father even threatened to break it into shards. At least it worked enough to show us our loved ones."

"Yes. I'm sure it would have worked perfectly. Of course, it can still work if you force the culprit to lift their curse. You could break it yourself with one of your spells. Or you could find the book of Dark Magic from where the spell came, then break it with its reverse spell."

"Break the Dark Magic spell! I can't even perform my new spells without flubbing up! I won't be able to fight Dark Magic or find the spell book. That's impossible."

"Nothing's impossible. Before the crystal caught fire, my Whispering Tree spelled 'Wizard Tiaff's castle.' Your crystal revealed a mountain fortress. The Wizard's High Council delegated this fortress into Wizard Tiaff's care. It was after the loss of his loved ones. Tiaff might know something about your loved ones. He cares for every inhabitant in the area, including the Water Bbeings."

"Spark told us Wizard Tiaff was assigned to that fortress. But not to change the subject, what happened to Wizard Tiaff's loved ones?" asked Dahc.

"Wizard Tiaff fought in defending dragons against the Stealth Dragon Slayers. At the time, his wife, Lovlin, a Mystique Blueblood, was with child. Although Tiaff didn't want Lovlin to fight, she insisted. Dragons needed every ally possible. As she flew Tiaff into battle, Tiaff rode on Lovlin's neck near her shoulder blades. After swooping down toward a dragon slayer, a Dark Wizard astride a dark dragon appeared out of thin air. The Dark Wizard thrust his double edge sword into Lovlin's craw and severed her main arteries! She was bleeding to death. Tiaff immediately cast a *Blood Congeal* spell to stop her bleeding. He held tight to her neck while she tumbled across trees, then crashed to the ground. Several scales ripped from Lovlin's body and landed alongside her. Tiaff jumped off her neck and tried to mend her arteries, but they were unclean cuts, jagged. He looked in Lovlin's eyes. She knew his thoughts and told him it was okay. Lovlin rubbed her tummy; she was in labor. Tiaff had to stop his *Blood Congeal* spell. Lovlin transformed into her enchantress form. The scales that ripped from her body remained on the ground beside her. Tiaff cradled her head and shoulders. He used magic to relieve her contractions and aid in the delivery of their son. He cleaned their newborn, wrapped him in a warm cloth, then placed him in Lovlin's arms. She kissed her newborn's soft cheeks before she and Tiaff agreed to name him Optim. Optim would remind Tiaff to remain optimistic in all situations. Before she became too weak to do so, Lovlin breastfed her precious child until he was full. She cuddled him on her shoulder. As she patted his tiny back to help him burp, she caressed her cheek against his. Lovlin breathed in through her nose to smell her baby's fresh newborn scent. She sang a *Lullaby* spell. After he hears the words, he will know her voice and remember her face. He would know the eternal love she had and has for him. Her lullaby would aid Optim's Bloodra Ceremony if he was a Mystique Blueblood like his mother."

Gala asked, "How about her blood? Couldn't Wizard Tiaff save his wife by giving her a sip of her blood, or were her injuries too severe?"

"While she held Optim on her shoulder, Tiaff was desperate. He tried to heal her again. As he gave her a sip of her blood, he tried to put her arteries together with a *Healing* spell. However, regardless of Tiaff's magic, giving birth is an ordeal. After losing a lot of blood, she became weak. Lovlin became too weak; her blood could not heal her. Her arteries would not mend. After she handed Optim back to Tiaff, she pulled one of her dragon scales close. She told Tiaff to craft a shield and engrave their names on the back, as well as her Star'ella-love and her *Lullaby* spell. She told Tiaff to give it to Optim when he was old enough. Lovlin asked that he show Optim her Star'ella-love within the stars and sing him the lullaby as often as possible. Tiaff said he would sing it to him every night. Lovlin gave Tiaff a parting kiss before her golden light transcended into the stars.

"Tiaff watched Lovlin's Star'ella-love twinkle in the starry night sky. A strong wind blew part of the swaddling cloth over Optim's face. Then everything turned black. SNATCH! The pitch-darkness grabbed Optim. He descended into the dark. Tiaff called out Optim's name, then Lovlin's. His head felt dizzy; with each passing moment, he felt weaker until he finally passed out. After coming to, he found himself in the care of his wizard and Mageon comrades. He told them what had happened. A few wizards immediately took Tiaff and Lovlin's scale to The Wizard's High Council. His other friends searched for Optim throughout all the lands, the swamps, and the forests."

Ddot pointed out and compared, "That sounds like what happened to our loved ones. Except there was a strange odor. Plus, Wizard Spark saw a **Shadow** before everything went pitch dark."

"Yes. Although Tiaff never mentioned an odor or **Shadow**, it doesn't mean they weren't present."

"Did they ever find Optim?"

"No, Lucky. Their extensive efforts were fruitless." Bloom shook his head.

"Oh no! That's wicked upon wickedness!" Lucky concluded.

"That's sad. I hope Optim and Wizard Tiaff find each other. How old is Optim?" Gala asked.

Celtrek answered, "If he's alive, he'll be a bit older than you and your friends."

"I hope he's alive and not mistreated." Gala sighed.

"Yeah," agreed Dahc while wiping his watery eyes.

"I do, too," said Ddot as he looked down at the table with a blank stare.

"We'll keep hopin'," Lucky added as he patted Ddot's shoulder.

Then Gala asked, "I don't mean to change the subject, but what are Water Bbeings?"

Before Bloom or Celtrek could answer, Ddot lifted his head and asked, "Yeah, and what do they look like?"

Dahc jumped in and asked, "What do they do?"

Lucky interjected, "We ain't never heard of 'em. Fill us in so we know what to be expectin' ifin' we run inta any."

"Well, okay then. Celtrek, you've seen Water Bbeings, and I haven't, other than what the trees have shown me. Would you mind explaining?"

"Not at all. First, Water Bbeings are elusive. I was fortunate to see them. As I tried to get a better look, they dove into the lake and swam inside an underwater cavern. But that story is for another time. Water Bbeings are a mixture of Mageons and Water Dragons. From their hips down, is a tail, like a dragon's tail. For comparison, where we have legs, they have a thick tail."

"Like havin' our legs joined together, wrapped all up in dragon skin with dragon scales?" Lucky asked.

"Yes," Celtrek answered. "That's a clever way of looking at it." Celtrek and Bloom laughed when Gala and the twins dropped their jaws. Then Celtrek continued with his descriptions. "At the end of their tail, or if it were, at the bottom of their joined legs, where we have feet, they have a large, strong fin. Their fins are diaphanous like fairy wings. They fan out into a wide half circle, scalloped along their edges. When they swim, their elegant fins sway in the water. They have webbed hands. And, can they swim fast. I believe they're faster than Hobbgies at full speeds. From the Water Bbeing's hips upwards, most have a body like Mageons' bodies. Parts of their skin have the same texture as their tail. Each Water Bbeing has their own markings. The females I saw wore their hair loose and long, whereas the males wore theirs shorter and pulled back. Amazingly, they can breathe in or out of water. Their voices were soothing and could enthrall any weary or heartbroken soul. But, if threatened, their song could cause confusion. Tiaff still visits the Water Bbeings. Their singing eases his pain. Tiaff will never be the same, and he has always been a good wizard."

"I wonder why my crystal showed dark clouds over his fortress. Are you sure he still lives there?"

"Yes. According to Sparktinian and my Whispering Tree, he still resides there. I don't know why my tree spelled out 'Wizard Tiaff's castle, or why your crystal revealed his castle and the storm. Dark Magic is strong, and according to my Whispering Tree, Dark Magic is concealing something. Your loved ones could very well be within Tiaff's vicinity without him knowing. I haven't seen Dark Magic since the last battle against the dragon slayers. Wizard Tiaff doesn't practice Dark Magic, specifically anyway. He does have knowledge of it and studied it after his son mysteriously disappeared. He may use it with the Magic of Light only for good purposes. Wizard Tiaff could benefit you in solving this mystery.

When we're done here, I'll show you which direction you need to travel to find him."

"Thank you, Bloom. We appreciate your help." Gala's voice cracked. "That's a sad story, and as Ddot mentioned, it sounds a lot like how our loved ones disappeared. I didn't smell a strange odor, and I didn't see what happened. I didn't see the pitch blackness either. But I did feel some wind. One second, I'm standing on a table. Next thing I know, I'm unwrapping my mother's window drapes from around my body. I couldn't believe or understand the chaos I saw. The guests were woozy and puking, or passed out. Well, except for the Bluewing clan, including Lucky and his parents. Fairies are immune to many things; whatever happened didn't affect them. I don't know why I wasn't affected."

"It's possible your mother cast a type of hide spell for your protection. Her intuition must have known something was amiss. Let's see if your crystal ball is salvageable, shall we? Suggested Bloom.

"Sure."

Ddot rose from his seat, pointing his finger and said, "Think I'll sit on that flower in the opened window. I can watch from there." Ddot acted nonchalant as he flew over and sat on a flower's large soft petal.

"Think I'll join ya," added Lucky.

"Me too," Dahc said as he hurried past Lucky, then sat next to Ddot.

Ddot shrugged his shoulders and said, "Sorry, Chum. We don't mean to be rude."

"I don't blame you guys. I'd be on guard, too." Gala gave out a long sigh.

After Bloom soaked up the rest of the water, he got up, rang it out, and picked up another dry towel. He handed it to Gala, then sat with his damp cloth beside him. Gala put his hands around the crystal ball to lift it from its pedestal. He gulped hard; his heart sank. The pedestal's bottom half was intact, but the top half had melded and merged around the crystal as one entity. He glanced at his friends. Their lips pulled down as their eyebrows lifted high. Gala dried the crystal and its pedestal, then sat it back on the table, hoping it would work. He sighed, then looked over at Celtrek and Bloom.

Bloom encouraged, "Give it a go, young mage. See if it will '*Show*' you someone. If it fills with dark fog, we'll ready our towels; you ready Redtalon's craw."

Gala nodded and commanded, "*Show me Acub.*" The crystal glowed its golden antique light while purple fog swirled inside. After the purple fog dissipated, he saw Acub with Archer. "It WORKS! Look! Archer's talking! He's pointing at the tip of an arrow! Except everyone looks like they're frozen."

Bloom reminded, "Remember. Our realm does not move the same as yours."

"Oh yeah." Gala chuckled.

"Who is Archer, Celtrek asked.

"Archer is an excellent trainer. He's an expert in defensive and aggressive fighting and instructs the clan's warriors. Archer teaches them to carve weapons like bows, arrows, knives, swords, and other useful tools. He has an impeccable knowledge of our planet's types of wood, rocks, gems, and other materials. I sat through a couple of his lectures. I'm happy the clan is doing okay, and the crystal is still working. Well, at least it's working the way it was."

Bloom suggested, "See what it does when you shrink it and put it away."

Gala nodded and said, "*Downsize.*" The crystal shrank without difficulty. When Gala told it to enlarge, it did so without any problems. He concealed it and brought it back out. It worked.

"That's great. Now see if it will '*Show*' your parents. But remember, ready your craw and the towel," Bloom reminded.

Gala commanded, "*Show me, my parents.*" The purple fog swirled inside the crystal. After it dissipated, Gala's parents appeared. They were still in chains, lying cuddled and sleeping. "It's still working!" Gala blurted, then spoke softly to his parents as if they could hear him. "Hang in there; we're going to rescue you." Gala looked over at his friends. They nodded in agreement. Dahc's eyes watered. Ddot had his elbows on his knees, resting his chin in his hands. Lucky rested his forearms on the top of his thighs. Gala told them, "I'm going to ask the crystal to show me Helsin, but first, I want to see Floreena and her mother."

"That sounds like a good idea, my Chum!" Ddot loudly and excitedly spoke, trying to change the sadness that filled the air.

Gala smiled at Ddot and asked his crystal, "*Show me Floreena and Lidee.*" Purple fog filled the crystal. After it dissipated, it revealed Gala's girlfriend and Lidee. "Look! They're sleeping.

Okay, guys. Let's see what Helsin is up to. *Show me Helsin,*" Gala creased his brows. Helsin wore a gloomy face while standing in front of what looked like a green bush lit by the morning's sun. "Look! Helsin's holding something!" The Newlads flew over and hovered to get a better look.

"I see it!" Ddot shouted.

"Oh yeah! Me too!" exclaimed Dahc.

Lucky pointed out, "He's holdin' it with two hands. It has four sides, two longer than the other two."

"Yes. It does have four sides. Who is Helsin?" Bloom asked.

"He used to be my friend. He used to live in Whittlewood Forest. After his parents died about a year ago, he moved in with his aunt and uncle. They live further north of Whittlewood Forest on its north edge in Black Forest. Since then, he's been mean to me. I don't understand. My mother said he could be jealous and angry because his parents died."

"Your mother has a point. The loss of loved ones can cause all kinds of ill feelings. Have you met Helsin's aunt and uncle?" Bloom asked.

"No. Neither has my parents." Gala started to talk fast and without coming up for air like he usually does when he's anxious or nervous. "When Helsin arrived at Acub's and Ashlin's celebration, he came across our bridge like a Twirlwind. Because of the wind that occurred when my parents disappeared, and the Twister that caused Wizard Spark's death, I thought it could have been Helsin, that he had something to do with it, but then again,

I thought that he didn't have anything to do with it, and I keep wondering that if—"

"Calm down. Let's not worry about that. Let's get back to your crystal." While Bloom put his hands on Gala's shoulders, the twins released their wing's essence.

Gala inhaled a deep breath. After he let it out, he said, "You're right. Okay. Thank you, Bloom, and you too, guys.

Bloom readied his towel and suggested, "Now ask your crystal '*Where*' your parents are. But first, you three better sit over on the flowers in the window." WHISH! Like lickity-split before an eye-blinked quick, the Newlads hurried over to the windowsill and sat back down on the flowers.

Gala cracked up laughing. "Are you guys ready?"

Ddot clasped his hands towards Gala while Dahc crossed his fingers, and Lucky put his thumbs up.

Gala looked back at Celtrek and Bloom, then at his crystal, and asked, "*Where are my parents?*"

The crystal turned orange-red. The purple fog swirled faster and faster. A dark purple, almost black, tornado appeared. Again, it shot lightning throughout the inside of the crystal. After Gala told the crystal to sleep, the lightning intensified as if enraged. Gala's throat and mouth transformed into a smaller version of Redtalon's craw and maw. Out from his throat came a mixture of freezing ice and snow. It engulfed the crystal before it had a chance to catch fire. Like lickity-split before an eye-blinked quick, Gala's throat and mouth resumed their natural state. No one noticed.

"Your crystal is cursed. I'm afraid you can't ask '*Where*' your parents are. At least it'll '*Show*' your parents. Come. We'll clean up your crystal so you can put it away. I'll draw you a map to Tiaff's fortress." After Bloom helped Gala clean the crystal, he put a piece of parchment and a stick of charcoal on the table.

Gala reached into his pocket and pulled out Inklewrite along with his map. "This is my magic pen, Inklewrite. I call it Inkle. This is the map I drew to show where my friends and I have been so far. As you can see, it stops here." Gala pointed at the spot where he and his friends first saw the Stealth Dragon Slayers. "I can't show Dragon Mountain With-eyes-that-see, Timestill Village, or The Singing Lake. They need to stay protected. The dragons need protection from the dragon slayers, and I don't want anyone to see where you live either."

Bloom and Celtrek looked at Gala's map and raised their brows. Bloom praised, "Now this is impressive! Things on your map are actually moving. Look there, Celtrek! Gala and the Newlads are riding on Trusty at the edge of a forest. Oops! Trusty stopped dead in his tracks, and Gala fell forward. Now the Newlads are fluttering beside Gala while Ddot points into the forest. The whole scene is starting over."

Celtrek pointed. "Look up here! They're on a castle's bridge, laughing while walking away from the castle. And look at all those beautiful blue wings flying around the garden. Oh, wait! I see a couple of green wings too!"

"Gala, this is a great map! Your drawings are exceptional. You're right to keep Dragon Mountain With-eyes-that-see off the map. And, although we like our privacy, you can draw Timestill Forest here." Before Bloom touched Gala's map, he asked, "May I?"

Gala gestured his hand and said, "Oh yeah, sure. You can touch it."

Bloom put his finger on an empty spot. "This is a good spot for our forest."

"Okay. I'll put Timestill Forest there."

Then Celtrek recommended, "Add The Singing Lake, as well. If anyone were to follow your map, they would never find our village. They might find the lake and see Timestill Forest, but not us. We are perfectly safe. You didn't find us in the forest; we came to you. If anyone walks into Timestill Forest without our escort, they'll end up back at The Singing Lake. The lake will always be there. And, no one can break the curse on the Traveling Troll."

"Celtrek is right," Bloom interjected. "The troll will remain as the lake even after the enchantress transcends. If the troll has learned to appreciate beauty, his pain will stop. But he'll remain The Singing Lake and continue to move with our forest. Furthermore, the troll is a troll; never will he learn to like beautiful things. Trolls are creatures of pure instinct, unable to change their natural tendencies. The enchantress knew this before she cast her spell."

"So, you mean the enchantress still lives because you said 'after' she transcends, right?" Ddot asked.

"Yes, she went into hiding with her husband and child. In fact, for added precautions, she asked me to have the trees shroud them. This way, if someone forced me to ask my Whispering Tree about their whereabouts, my tree would not be able to answer. She told me it was confidential and of utmost importance that they go into hiding. The enchantress is an expert in disguise; she keeps her identity hidden."

"That's interesting. Is the enchantress a Transfigure like the Lakinshires?" Ddot asked as he flew back over and stood on the table. Dahc and Lucky followed.

"No, her powers can change the appearance of herself or others through illusions. She also uses spells, charms, potions, or a powerful curse like the curse she cast on the Traveling Troll."

"That's amazing! I mean that the troll looks exactly like a Lake!"

"You chose the right word, Ddot. The enchantress is amazing, phenomenal. Her powers have a lot to do with the energies of our planet. I don't understand any more than that. I'm not an alchemist. I haven't studied it, nor do I perform magic, but I'm a mind reader. For some reason, trees talk to me, and I cannot explain that either," Bloom chuckled, then continued. "My parents didn't have magic powers, so there isn't anything to justify my abilities. Yet something happened to me when I was a young elf, which might explain why I can read minds and why the trees talk to me. If, or when, you come back this way, we'll have Sonata tell you that story."

"Okay! Wow! Thanks! We'd like that a lot. Wouldn't we, guys?"

Ddot agreed, "I know that's for sure. I can't wait to watch Sonata tell another story."

Lucky added, "Me either. I can't wait to hear her hypnotic voice, and she didn't even drink from The Singing Lake. She's a natural beauty through and through."

Dahc moved his brows up and down while nodding like a bobble-head doll. He yelled, "You bet!" Everyone cracked up laughing, including Dahc.

When their laughter slowed, Gala asked, "What do we do, now?"

"Well," said Bloom. "After looking at your fantastic map, I realize you don't need this one." Bloom pushed his parchment and charcoal stick over to one side and pointed to another empty area on Gala's map. He suggested, "You may as well draw Wizard Tiaff's castle in this spot after you draw Timestill Forest. When you're done, we'll get Trusty and lead you back to The Singing Lake, so you can continue your journey. I'll blow my horn again to summon our neighbors, the Kelvor Elves."

"Is that what you did the first time you blew your horn?" asked Gala.

"Yes. My horn makes a sound that only Kelvor Elves can hear. They live north of Timestill Forest. They may not have heard my call, but if they did, they'll arrive soon. Their mounts are swift animals, sure-footed, and designed for arduous terrains and snow-covered mountains. They can send word to The High Council of your needs. The Council will send others to join you on your quest."

"Okay. Sure. Thank you." Gala sounded more hopeful.

Celtrek explained, "I should tell you the story about why I was fortunate to see the Water Bbeings. I want you to understand something. Woodlanders cannot leave the protection of Timestill Forest. We're bound to it. We can step outside its boundaries only when our three moons align and are full. Any other time would mean a short lifespan. It's like a pedal after it has fallen to the ground. The pedal withers quickly, while the flower from which it fell continues to bloom for some time longer. Our forest is our lifeline, our beating heart. Looking at my appearance, you might think I'm Bloom's older brother. I'm not. He's my older brother."

Lucky squished up his face and asked, "Are ya sayin' that after ya left yore forest, ya aged?"

"Yes. I was young, curious, and didn't realize I had wandered off. I got lost and got scared. I walked around for a few days before I found an empty cave above a lake where I could sleep. The following morning, I heard water splashing and a beautiful song that woke me. At first, I thought I was dreaming and was back at The Singing Lake. But when I peeked through a brush to see what it was, I saw the beautiful Water Bbeings. I watched them for a while until something startled them. After they dove down into the water, I turned to see what scared them. It was the Kelvor Elves. They found me and brought me home."

Bloom added, "Our parents died a long time ago. We were very young. I was ten and Celtrek six. I was left to take care of Celtrek. After story time, Celtrek was no longer sitting next to me. I panicked. The villagers and I searched the entire village. I searched The Singing Lake hoping he didn't drown. I ran home and asked my tree where Celtrek was. Its leaves revealed a cave and whispered, 'Water Bbeings' lake.' I blew our calling horn. The Kelvor Elves heard it and answered my call. I told them to look for caves, lakes, and Water Bbeings. I wanted to go along, but they insisted I stay behind. If I had gone, I would have grown much older than Celtrek. It took three days for the Kelvor Elves to find Celtrek."

"Wizardry, I'm happy they found you before—" Gala gulped.

Celtrek interrupted, "It's okay. I'm glad too. I learned a valuable lesson, and never again did I lose sight of where I was. In other words, I pay close attention to my surroundings, not to mention my thoughts. Now you understand why we cannot go with you."

"I do. I wasn't expecting you to come with us or go to The High Council. I'm just grateful for your help. We thank you for your offer. We appreciate everything you've done," Gala thanked.

"That's quite all right." Celtrek nodded.

Then Ddot asked, "Is everyone, including your livestock, bound to Timestill?"

Celtrek shook his head and looked at Bloom to answer, "No. Not all. But those who are, they instinctively know their boundaries. Timestill Forest is open to all life. It's a sanctuary for those seeking safety from evil. It's for those who need rest, solace, or shelter. It's for those who need time without losing much time."

"So, anyone wicked with bad intentions can enter your forest? Gala asked.

"Never!" Bloom and Celtrek answered in unison.

Gala gave out a sigh of relief. After a long pause, he smiled, looked down at his map, and said, "Okay then. Let's see now. I'll add Timestill Forest here, The Singing Lake over here, and I'll add Wizard Tiaff's castle in this area." Gala positioned his fingers as if he was holding Inkle. Inkle drew while following Gala's hand movements. After Gala drew the lake and Timestill Forest, he began drawing himself and the Newlads sitting on Trusty. He drew Trusty standing next to the Singing Lake. When he finished drawing, he moved Inkle off the map so everyone could see. Everyone was smiling, amazed as they watched the drawing come to life. Timestill Forest and The Singing Lake shifted on the map while Gala and the Newlads sat on Trusty. Lucky flew over to the side of the lake and kneeled next to the water. They saw water lift off the map as Lucky splashed water on his face. Lucky stood up. He turned to look at his friends and started singing. Tiny black musical notes poured out of Lucky's mouth and rose off the map. They could actually hear Lucky singing. It was faint, but they understood what he sang. When they saw Lucky cover his mouth, the music, along with the music notes, stopped rising off the map. Then Lucky looked back at the lake. He stepped back while his friends walked over and stood by him. After that, the whole scene started over.

"Well done! Well done," Celtrek patted Gala on the back of his shoulder.

"Extraordinary!" Bloom bolstered while he clapped his hands.

"Thank you," Gala smiled and then continued drawing. He drew Wizard Tiaff's castle with a cloudless sky. He explained, "I'll add movement after we get there and see what it looks like. I'll even add what we see between here and there."

Celtrek put his finger on the map and said, "You'll travel through this area. It's abundant with large trees, dense foliage." Gala and Inkle followed Celtrek's descriptions. Celtrek pointed to a different part of the map and said, "After you reach this area, it's less dense. You can run your mount for a long distance. You'll reach a creek where you can rest. From there, you'll ride into a small mountain range, nestled here. It's surrounded by a forest with thick foliage throughout. You'll see cascading waterfalls spill over wide mountain summits into a deep lake. It's where the Water Bbeings dwell. According to the Kelvor Elves, the lake's called Mermary's Lake and Mermary is queen of the Water Bbeings. They're elusive creatures and can be dangerous. They won't harm fairies, but Gala, they might feel threatened by you, so don't get close to the water. They could snatch you under and drown you. It's best you travel in this direction around the mountains through here." Celtrek pointed to another part of the map.

"I can transfigure into my Bluewing form."

"It would be best if you didn't until you know your surroundings. There are other creatures, owls, hawks, and so on, that will snatch up a fairy without warning. And that's not all. There are Wolfers and Black Baris. Wolfers travel in packs. They have jagged teeth, long bushy tails, long hair, long snouts, and four spindly yet strong legs. The good thing about them is they don't bother fairies. You can smell them from two miles away. They stink to the highest mountain. I can't describe their odor, but if you ever smell them, you'll never forget it. As for Black Baris, they don't bother fairies, either. And you can hear them coming. No matter what, they're always grunting. They're huge beasts, tall with fuzzy fur, cute but deadly. They travel alone. They grunt more and much louder than Gob-Diggers. So be alert."

"Okay. Thanks, Celtrek." Gala promised as he shivered and glanced at his wide-eyed friends. Dahc's mouth was agape.

Celtrek changed the subject to help ease the four companions Jitterbugs. "You might encounter fay-folk like yourselves."

"Yes," Bloom added as he hurried to help his brother divert their attention. "The trees, including my Whispering Tree, have only revealed the fay-folk's presence. They've never come to visit, so we've never met them. None of our guests have ever spoken of them. I know that long ago, after the

Ultra Storm, the fay-folk arrived somewhere in this area." Bloom pointed at the map.

"Maybe we'll git to meet 'em."

"That's possible, Lucky. I hope you do. It would be good if they could help you in your quest. They might have valuable information and special abilities like all you have."

"How'd you know we had abilities?" Ddot asked.

"When I first touched Gala's shoulder, and you three stood on his other, I heard your thoughts. You thought you might have to defend yourselves. I know that you and Dahc are exceptional archers. Your aim is precise. Your arrows will hit anything with a deadly blow or to whatever injuries you wish to give. This is true for you as well, Lucky. Your blade is razor-sharp; your aim is precise and can decapitate a giant where they stand. Your dagger always returns to you like a boomerang. You can zip and dodge at lightning speeds. You're a fast flyer. Besides, I already knew fairies had abilities. Spark told me. I'm also aware that fairies avoid violence if possible. They don't like to kill anything. Their natural state of being is love, peace, and tranquility. Actually, that's everyone's state of being. But too much needless thinking has obscured this fact in some Mageons. It's a subject we can discuss another time.

"I hope we get to meet the fay-folk because we could use all the help we can get. At first, I didn't want my friends to come along because I thought something bad might happen to them. But I'm sure glad they came. I needed them, still do." Gala smiled at his smiling companions.

Celtrek and Bloom agreed. Bloom suggested, "Okay, Gala, now that we've covered the routes you can travel and before we get Trusty, I want to try something. It might show me your nightmares. Would you like to try?"

Gala yelled, "Sure!" Before anyone could blink an eye, He snapped his fingers. His map rolled up, then disappeared along with Inklewrite.

Mental Trance-The Curse

Bloom hoped he could find the reason Gala had nightmares. He said, "Come then. Follow me." Bloom opened a door on the other side of the table, across from the first door they had entered. He reminded, "Remember, the Stingers will not harm you. I'll make sure they move." After walking out from the kitchen, they saw a Stinger pollinating a large yellow flower. As Bloom approached, the Stinger moved further away. Bloom opened a door on his right and motioned everyone to enter. Gala stepped inside first. The Newlads followed behind. After Celtrek entered, Bloom entered and shut the door behind them.

    The room was spacious, with assorted flowering plants thriving throughout. And, no Stingers, so Gala and his friends relaxed. In the center of the room, a large device held a cluster of spheres. The spheres were situated around each other. There were bookshelves and a sitting area. The sitting area had two purple velvet chairs and a purple velvet chaise lounge. Between the chairs sat a large end table. Across from the chaise was an open two-framed window. Antique brass sealed its diamond-shaped panes together. In front of the window stood a large pedestal made of brass and gold. Cradled at its top was a brass and gold tube-like structure which extended halfway out the window.

    "What's that?" Gala pointed.

    While Bloom walked over, he explained, "This is a Cosmogazer. Planets and moons appear larger when peering through this eyepiece." Bloom pointed and continued, "I was looking through it when I saw Spark's transcendence."

"So, you can see our stars close up through your Cosmogazer?" Ddot asked while rubbing his chin.

"Yes. It gives me a closer view of moons, planets, and stars. Although we cannot see stars during full daylight, they're still there, which I'm sure you already know." Gala and the Newlads nodded in agreement. Bloom continued, "I've discovered that by some great force, or forces, we are like other planets and stars. We all move, stationed in precise order, perfect synchronization." Bloom pointed out the window at one of the crescent moons, "There's a morning moon. It's closest to our planet and smaller than our other two moons. All three moons look as if they're the same size. The one furthest from us is much larger, but because it is further out, it appears like it's the same size as the other two. The one in the middle is further and a bit larger than our closest moon and smaller than the furthest.

"Also, when our three moons align, are full, and look like one large moon, something mystical happens. My clocks change time, and the trees become quiet as if everything and everyone suspends in time. Things glow that never did before. This is the only time we can walk outside our realm without aging. I don't know why or what it means, but I aim to learn more. This alignment happened many years ago. That's when I created my first Cosmogazer. This Cosmogazer is my sixth one since. It's an improvement from the others."

"Are these our planets and stars?" Gala asked as he pointed at the large device suspending the spheres.

"Yes." Bloom walked over to his display. "These spheres, orbs, or globes as I sometimes call them, are my display of planets." Bloom smiled and stood back while Gala and the Newlads inspected his display. Each planet was set on a separate rod attached to an antique gold and brass base. The planets circled a stationary yellow-orange orb which represented their sun. The sun was larger than the planets. All planets were variant in size, in color, and arranged in assorted positions. They were articulate and embossed with intricate design and color. The gray orbs represented no life. The orbs imprinted with colors represented life. Green and brown portrayed land masses and blues depicted bodies of water. Bloom pushed a planet with his finger. It spun in place. He explained, "This is our planet, Mageus. There are different clusters of stars and planets during our winter cycle. It makes sense to me that Mageus also rotates like this." Bloom touched the rod attached beneath the spinning planet and gave it a slight shove. It, along with the other planets, circled around the sun.

"That one must be the sun 'cause it ain't movin'," Lucky mused out loud.

"That's right." When each planet passed in front of Bloom, he pushed them with his finger so they'd spin in the same direction. He gave another rod a light shove to keep all the planets going around the stationary sun. Bloom explained, "It appears as though each planet spins while rotating around the sun. As I mentioned, moons go around their planet, but do not appear as though they spin in place."

Ddot stared; his eyes glazed over. Then, as if talking to himself, he whispered, "It's like magic."

"Yes. It is. I want an apprentice outside our realm. This way they can observe other planets through my Cosmogazer from other locations. When I'm ready for an apprentice, I'll send word to the Kelvor Elves. They'll take my request to The Wizard's High Council who'll appoint the perfect candidate. One day, when you come back to visit, you and your loved ones can stay until nightfall. You can peer through my Cosmogazer and see the stars and planets.

Gala and the Newlads yelled in unison, "Okay! Thank you, sir! My father would be most interested!" — "Stars and planets are my kinds of things! I can't wait! Our loved ones will want to meet you too!" — "Wow! Thanks! I'd like that!" — "Thanks! It'll be a star-gazin' treat for sure!" Bloom and Celtrek laughed.

"Okay then, sounds like you're all in agreement." Bloom reached out and stopped his sphere display from spinning. "Let's proceed with a hypnotic meditation that could allow me to see why you're having nightmares."

Gala took a deep breath, then let it out and said, "Let's do this."

Bloom swept his arm towards the chaise and said, "Gala, you lie here with your head at the foot and get comfortable. Newlads, sit at the head there." While Gala walked over and lay down on his back, the Newlads flew over and sat on the arm of the chaise.

Bloom sat on the chair closest to Gala's head while Celtrek sat on the other and opened a drawer on the table. He pulled out a bronze object which resembled a candelabrum. Its circular base was black. It sat on four bronze feet designed as leaves. It had a thick bronze stem designed as intertwining vines. A bronze bar, about as wide as its base, stretched out across the top of the stem. An engraved intricate flower and leaf design stretched across the bar. Four branches, or arms, extended upwards from the bar. They, too, were designed as intertwining vines. Each one formed a circle with an alloy bell hanging from its center. The bells were variant in size and shaped like bluebell flowers. Celtrek pulled out a curvy wooden mallet. It had a wooden ball at opposite ends. One ball was smaller than the other. A sweet sound resonated throughout the rooms as he tapped the bells with each end of the mallet. It made everyone feel relaxed.

Bloom looked down into Gala's eyes and explained, "All you need to do is listen. Answer any question you are able or willing to answer. I will only see what is clear in your mind. Understand?"

"Yes, sir," Gala answered.

Bloom brushed his fingers across Gala's forehead. He cupped the sides of his head while Celtrek continued to tap the bells. "Now close your eyes and relax." Gala couldn't help but close his eyes. Bloom's smooth hypnotic voice almost put everyone to sleep. After Bloom saw Gala's eyes dart back and forth beneath his eyelids, he knew Gala was in a much deeper state of mind. So, Bloom led Gala through his memories. He led him back to the beginning before his nightmares and lost confidence began. Bloom asked, "How did your day begin after you woke?"

"I stretched and yawned, got up, and made my bed. Then, by using a *Garment Change* spell, I changed out of my sleeping clothes into my magic clothes. Finally, I put on my purple Wizard's cloak."

Bloom could see every detail of Gala's memories. He asked another question, "How are you feeling?"

"I'm excited and happy!"

"Why?"

"In a few weeks, we'll have a gathering for the Magi Competitions. Floreena and her mother, Lidee, will be there. I really like Floreena, and I hope she likes me."

Dahc put his hand over his mouth to hold back a shy giggle. Gala didn't hear, so he remained relaxed.

Bloom asked, "What did you do after you got dressed?"

"I washed up and met my parents in the kitchen. Mother and I set the table while Father cooked breakfast. He's an exceptional chef. He doesn't even have to use magic."

Bloom smiled and said, "Tell me everything you did after breakfast."

"I went into the library and studied my lessons. I practiced my *Levitation* spell and read one of my favorite books about dragons. I never get tired of reading about dragons. I love them. I love reviewing the detailed illustrations. After I read, I pulled out my drawing of Redtalon dragon. I'm excited because one day, my father will tell me I'm ready to transform into a dragon. My Redtalon has many of the same qualities that the dragons I've studied have. I also added features that my parent's dragon forms have. I even added my own touches. After putting my drawing and books away, I went into my bedroom and worked on a painting. It's a gift for my parents and a surprise. I painted for a while, then decided to go outside and fly around as my Bunt and Nix. I like to imagine my Nix transformation as my Redtalon dragon. Anyway, I cleaned up my paints and told my parents I was going outside to Transfigure.

"Father asked if I studied. I told him yes and that I could cast my *Levitation* spell with my wand. When I was four, I performed the spell without a wand. I didn't know I was doing it. Of course, I wasn't old enough to have a wand then. When I was old enough, my parents wanted me to perform the spell using my wand. It was not as easy as I thought. It felt different. I see why I needed to practice. Father wanted me to show them my spell using my wand, so I did. I lifted a statuette off its base. They were as proud of me as I was of myself. Before I went outside, they reminded me of my boundaries. They told me I could go anywhere on our mountain, including Crystal Lake, but not across it.

My parents worried because my imagination interfered with my awareness of my surroundings." Gala sighed and became quiet.

Celtrek tapped the bells and nodded. He thought about what he told Gala and the Newlads when his boyish curiosity got him lost and caused him to age.

Bloom encouraged Gala, "Go on. What happened next."

"My parents reminded me to be home before dinner. After dinner, we were going to go visit the Bluewing clan. The clan's king and queen, Trill and Quo, left their son, Acub, in charge. Trill and Quo went on their thirtieth moonlit tryst. They asked my parents to look in on the clan. I told my parents I'd be back in time for dinner and to stop being such Worry Sprites. As soon as I went outside and shut the door behind me, I transformed into Nix. I imagined I was a powerful Mystique Transfigure prince. I was on a quest to save the lovely princess, Floreena, from the wicked clutches of the Swamp-Gob king. I pretended Nix was my Redtalon dragon, and when I transformed into Bunt, I pretended he was my scout. Bunt searched the dense forests. My imaginary Redtalon dragon used his exceptional dragon eyes to scan the forests. Bunt found a clue but couldn't figure out what he saw, except for spells flying around and running into each other. I felt uneasy and decided to transform into Nix. As I was transforming, it felt like something struck me. I flew Floreena home and—"

"Wait," Bloom interrupted. The Newlads sat straight up. Celtrek continued tapping the bells.

Bloom told Gala to back up when Bunt saw the spells. "Where is your Bunt when you see the spells?"

"He's, or I'm perched in a tree I've never seen before."

"I want you to stay perched. Look around and tell me what you see, your surroundings."

"I see a lot of trees. I see Maples, oaks, and other trees. But I don't know what they're called, and I see trees growing within wetlands that I've never seen in our forest."

"Describe the trees you're not familiar with."

"They're really tall with long branches near their base and middle. The higher branches aren't as long. The branches twist outwards and extend horizontally from their trunks. The leaves are thick and look feathery or needle-like with different shades of green. And on some of the leaves, there's a hint of blue or a rusty-orange color. Their bark is brown and looks stringy. They have roots that stick up out of the wet ground in dissimilar shapes and sizes. And it has a sweet odor like the moist Sweet Moss that grows along riverbanks. It's mixed with a smoky pine-like odor too." Gala became quiet again.

"Okay. Now look around and tell me what else you see?"

"I see wildflowers growing below me. I don't know whether I imagined flying down to pick flowers for Princess Floreena or stayed perched in the tree. Now I'm imagining that I hear grunting noises. But they sound real. I look towards the noise. I see what looks like a birthday party. Now I see Gobs, but maybe they're my imagination. It's a blur, and it's like I... I can't..." Gala's breath hastened.

Bloom calmed him, "It's okay. Nothing can hurt you. Breathe deep and let it out slowly. You're safe and with friends." When Bloom noticed Gala had relaxed, he asked, "What do you see after the blur?"

"I shot a spell at a Gob. WAIT!"

Ddot darted up from his seat. Dahc and Lucky tensed up with their eyes popped wide. Bloom looked at the Newlads. He motioned his head and eyes towards Ddot to sit, then he pursed his lips in a shush position. The Newlads relaxed, and Ddot sat back down. Gala was quiet. His dark brows turned inwards and upwards, forming creases in his forehead. Bloom encouraged Gala to continue, "It's okay. You're safe. Go on and tell me what else you see."

"I see wicked witches. I can't see their faces, but I know they're ugly. I can't see what they're doing. I see gruesome-looking Gobs. They're holding my Floreena! It's strange because she's a fairy. I cast a spell but don't know where it went." Gala became quiet again.

"What else do you see?"

"I see spells flying around."

"How many and what color?"

"I see a dark cloud-like smoke flying past me. I see a dark purple, almost black, spell and a grayish spell heading toward me. I'm transforming into my Nix. Something hit me before I transformed. Something else struck me in the middle of my transformation. And now, I'm pretending Nix is Redtalon and I'm flying from the edge of the dwindling mountains that are next to The Ridge. I'm flying over Crystal Lake. Floreena is sitting straddled across the crook of Redtalon's neck. I saved my Floreena from the Gob King, and after I flew her home, I kissed her, then I flew home."

"What happened after you flew home?"

"I transformed into myself. Mother opened one of the doors for me and asked if I had fun. I told her yes. She told me to wash up because we were eating dinner early. We talked about the upcoming gathering for the Magi Competitions during dinner. After dinner and cleaning up, we headed to the Bluewing fairies' waterfall cave for story time."

"Did you and your parents go anywhere else?"

"No. We flew as our Bluewing forms straight to the clans' home. As soon as we flew in, I saw my friends. We sat together. Archer started with his story first. He's funny."

"Where did you go after you and your parents left the clan?"

"We flew home, I transfigured into Nix and saw mean ugly faces flash across my mind."

"Did you tell your parents?"

"No. It happened so quick that I didn't think much of it. I figured it was just my imagination."

"Do you see the faces any other time?"

"No, only when I transform into Nix."

"Was it easy for you to fall asleep that night?"

"Yes."

"Do you remember dreaming?"

"Yes. I was saving Floreena when a dark mysterious cloud hid her from me. I saw hideous Gobs and witches. I couldn't see what was happening. It was scary. Something dreadful happened! But I can't remember what it was. Floreena! I can't save her! I can't move! NO!"

"Shh. I'm right here. It's okay. Relax. Breathe deep and let it out slowly. After I tell you to wake up, you will feel happy and relaxed. I want you to see your favorite place where you feel safe. Go there and lie down on a pallet of comfortable moss. Are you there?"

"Yes."

"Nothing can harm you here. Take a deep breath and let it out. Now you feel relaxed, safe, and happy. Anytime you feel you need to relax, go to your favorite spot. You can wake up now, Gala, feeling happy, safe, and relaxed." As Bloom removed his hands from cradling Gala's head, Gala blinked his eyes open.

Gala stretched, smiled, then sat up. "Wizard wonders, I feel great! So, did you figure anything out about my nightmares?"

Celtrek stopped tapping the bells. Everyone looked at Bloom anticipating his findings. Bloom asked, "Gala, can you describe the mean ugly faces that flash in your mind when you transform into Nix?"

"What!? How'd you know that?"

Ddot crossed his arms and said, "I'll tell you how. When you were in the mental trance, you told Bloom about them. Why didn't you ever tell me? I thought we were best chums."

"We are. You guys are the best friends I could ever have or even hope for. I'm sorry, Ddot. I didn't think much about it, so I never said anything. You know I tell you everything, about everything; that is if it's important."

Ddot dropped his arms and turned up his palms while shrugging his shoulders. He shook his head and asked, "How in any realm do you figure this isn't important?"

"I'm sorry, Ddot. I really didn't mean..." Gala couldn't finish his sentence. His face turned to pensive mourning then he hung his head.

Ddot suddenly felt terrible. He felt like a selfish Traveling Troll. He flew down, looked up into his chum's eyes, and apologized, "I'm the one who owes you an apology. All the things we, you've gone through, and, well, never mind, the point is, you don't have to tell me anything. That's selfish of me. Seriously, who wrote the rule that Gala has to tell Ddot everything? Gala, Chum, I'm so sorry."

Everybody smiled. As Gala looked up at Ddot, he transformed into his Bluewing form. He and Ddot did their special handshake. After that, Ddot asked Bloom what he thought about Gala's condition.

Bloom explained what he thought to be true. "In Gala's hypnotic state, he remembered things that might account for his nightmares. Gala, you imagined you were a wizard prince who set out to rescue a lovely princess from the clutches of the Gob king. While you were Bunt, you saw Gobs and witches whose faces were unclear. You thought it could have been your imagination, which part of it was. The other part wasn't." Gala's brows creased while Bloom continued, "You cast a spell and saw spells flying towards you. You mentioned that something struck you before and during your transformation into Nix. Something did strike you. This is the reason the faces flash in your mind during, and only during, your transformation into Nix. As my hands cradled your head, I saw a clear vision of what wasn't your imagination and what was. There is a distinction between both. I saw the spell you cast and the spells coming towards you. One of those spells resembled the fog we saw in your father's crystal ball.

"You thought flying over the Mountain Ridge was part of your imagination. I saw The Ridge. You flew over it." Gala and the Newlads slacked their jaws as Bloom continued. "You were on the west side of Crystal Lake where the dwindling mountains meet the swamp. The Ridge runs parallel to the swamp and the dwindling mountains. You flew up from the swamp, over The Ridge, and east towards home. From your castle, across Crystal Lake, that's about a day's travel down the dwindling mountains on foot. It's less than half a day when flying as Nix or Bunt. You saw imaginary Gobs. But you also saw authentic Gobs as tangible as we are now.

"The trees you described are Swampress trees which grow in the Boggy Swamps. The Swampress trees, wildflowers, The Ridge, spells, Gobs, and witches you saw through Bunt's eyes were every bit a reality." Gala transformed back into himself and walked over to the window. Ddot and Dahc flew up and sat on his shoulders. Lucky flew over and stood on the windowsill. Bloom stood next to Gala while Celtrek put the musical bells back in the drawer. No one said a word as they peered out the window. After a minute, Bloom broke the silence and explained, "The spell that hit you before you transformed into Nix could have been an overlook spell. I assume you saw something they wanted you to forget. This is why you can't remember your nightmares, besides the fact that you're blocking what you saw. It must have been terrifying for you. You blocking this memory, coupled with a spell, adds to why you can't remember. The other spell you're cursed with is a lack of confidence spell. You can break these spells with their reverse incantations.

"Furthermore, this occurred a year and two days ago. It's the same time your father first felt he was being watched. But when he saw the **Shadow** two days ago, he knew someone had spied on him. Gala, your father's suspicions were correct. Wizard Spark's eyes were not playing tricks when he saw the **Shadow**. These are not mere coincidences. What I mean is the **Shadow**, your nightmares, the faces you see, the dark fog in the crystal, Spark's demise, and your loved ones taken are all connected to the same evil doer or doers. I assume they want something. If you heard a voice that said they could see you, which I'm now on the side of agreeing that you did, they know where you are." The four companions gasped. Bloom continued, "Traveling to Wizard Tiaff will lead you closer to your loved ones."

"It all makes sense! I'm sure you're right about everything. I bet I'm cursed. I bet we're getting closer to our loved ones. I can feel it in my heart and my gut." Gala touched his chest with one hand and his stomach with his other.

Bloom raised his brows and said, "That sounds like an intuitive feeling. Don't deny it."

"I'm so happy Wizard Spark led us to you. You, Celtrek, and your Whispering Tree are a revelation to our quest and my conditions or curses. Thank you, guys, for everything. We need to get going."

"If the Kelvor Elves haven't arrived after we walk you to the border of our realm, I'll blow my horn. If they do not show within a reasonable timeframe, you and the Newlads follow my route to Wizard Tiaff's fortress. Is a Timestill ten-minute wait okay with you?" Gala nodded, then Bloom nodded back and said, "Come. Let's get your Hobbgie. If the Kelvor Elves arrive after you leave, I'll send them to The Wizard's High Council."

ONE YEAR AND TWO DAYS AGO
Love, Horror, Curses

Before agreeing to live in their new fortress, Crystal Lake Castle, Conkay and Faithin Lakinshire lived in a quaint cottage in the magical Whittlewood Forest. Because of their mystique powers, The Wizard's High Council assigned them to protect the lands and inhabitants

surrounding the castle. The Wizard's High Council requires that on the nights when a crescent moon shines along with two full moons, Conkay and Faithin are to assemble a gathering of all willing sorcerers to compete in the Magi Competitions. The Lakinshires score sorcerers on their abilities comprising of spells and charms. The sorcerers compete for two weeks. Many sorcerers will drop out or score low against all challengers. They're encouraged to watch the rest of the competition before returning home. On the night of their planet's three full moons, the Lakinshires announce the winners. They will choose a qualified male and a qualified female magus. The Elfkies and their winged Gentalsteeds will escort the winners to the Frozen Falls in the northern mountains where The Wizard's High Council resides.

The High Council receives powerful sorcerers from other competitions around their planet. They will undergo strict training for the duration of their stay. Those who pass their training are selected as protectors, academy instructors, or chosen to sit with The Wizard's High Council. Those who do not pass their training will return home. Many do not pass. When the Lakinshire's son, Gala, is old enough, willing, and interested, he will also go to The High Council.

Gala's parents were proud of their son's innate abilities and talents. The fact that he was compassionate, kind, and forgiving delighted them.

One morning, after Gala helped his parents wash breakfast dishes, he went into the library to study. His parents went into the den to plan for their next upcoming gathering. After his studies, Gala went into his room to work on a painting.

Hours had passed when he decided to go outside. He set his painting on the mantel of his fireplace, cleaned his paint supplies, then called out to his parents, "Mother! Father! I'm going to Crystal Lake to practice my Bunt and Nix."

"Wait!" Conkay walked out to meet Gala in the great hall. Did you study the Spells-Charms book?"

"Yes, sir. I even worked on a painting." Gala smiled.

"Excellent. You'll have to show me."

"It's a surprise for you and Mother."

"In that case, we'll see it when you're ready. What lesson did you study?"

"I finally got my levitation down pat using my wand."

"That's impressive. Hold on. Let's call your mother. Faithin!"

Yes?" she asked as she met her loves in the hall.

"Our son can perform his *Levitation* spell with his wand."

"Oh? Well then, let's see. Umm." Faithin looked around the hall. She pointed, "Lift that sculpture off its base."

"Okay. Here goes." With a hint of humility, which is a quality required for greatness, and a bit of silliness, Gala shook his shoulders back and forth, then puffed up his chest. He lifted his hand and summoned his wand, "*Com'ere.*" POOF! It looked like his wand appeared in his hand out of thin air. When he pointed it at the figurine and said, "*Up*," it changed from its sienna color to gold. Its teardrop diamond tip shot out his sparkling golden light spell and surrounded the statue. As Gala bent his wrist upwards, the five-foot rose quartz sculpture levitated from its base.

"YAY! —BRAVO!" His parents clapped.

"Now watch." A wide grin spread across Gala's face as he moved his arm in every direction, and the sculpture followed. "See? I can set it anywhere, lift it as high as I want, and perform it with my hands. Of course, you know that, but what I mean is that now I can perform it by using our Sorcermizic language. I can summons my wand by saying *Appara Comforte* instead of *Com'ere*, and to levitate, I say *Elevor Eeup* instead of *Up*." Gala set the sculpture back on its base.

"Perfect!" Conkay patted Gala on his shoulder and smiled.

"Yes, that was perfect. You're the most powerful young mage I have ever seen. And I'm not saying that because I'm your mother and love you."

Faithin reached over and gave Gala a kiss on his cheek.

"Thank you, Mother, Father." Gala concealed his wand. It disappeared, vanished into thin air. "Okay. Guess I'll go practice my Bunt and Nix now."

"Remember, Acub invited us to the clan's story time tonight. His parents won't be there because they went out on their moonlit tryst."

"Okay, Mother. When will Trill and Quo be back?"

"In three days. Why?" Faithin asked.

"Ddot wanted me to stay the night with him and Dahc. But I'll wait until Trill and Quo come home. Okay. I'm going out to Transfigure now. I'll be home before dinner."

"Don't wander off to the mountains or the forests across Crystal Lake. Stay on our mountain."

"Yes, sir."

"Pay attention. You know how your imagination carries you away, steers you off track."

"Okay, Mother. Gee, wizards Mom and Dad, don't be such Worry Sprites; I'll pay attention." No sooner than Gala shut the front door behind him, he transformed into his Nix. His Nix was a mixture of a fiery Phoenix and an eagle. Gala loved his bird forms. He loved the wind blowing through his feathers. Gala admired the might and force of his wings. They gave him the courage to escape Gob-Diggers that were in his imagination.

The only Gob-Diggers Gala has ever seen were in his imagination or illustrations. His study books depicted them sitting or standing in the Boggy

Swamps. Gala cringed at how ugly and scary they looked. Some were three times taller than his father at six feet tall. Gala couldn't stand looking at their scabby arms hanging past their knees. Gala figured that was because their backs were hunched over. He couldn't stand looking at their black fingernails. He knew they used them to dig in the muck for food or in rock to excavate a recess where they rest during daylight hours. That's the reason their nails were black. Gala learned that although Gob-Diggers ate different kinds of food, they wouldn't eat a being like him. But they ate birds. So, if Gala were too close to a Gob in his Nix or Bunt form, the Gobs would mistake him for a real bird, snatch him, and eat him.

 Gob-Diggers' favorite delicacy is fairy meat, which is hard to come by. But they also love Gurgling Mudlumps, which were abundant in the swamps. Mudlumps are creepy blood-sucking creatures. Most are small, but some are larger than a Gob-Digger's twenty-inch dingy-looking foot. Mudlumps are black with slimy, slug-like bodies. They have five to ten snail-like eyes extending out from around their mouth. They keep their mouth closed while their eyes stick out of the mud. Their tentacles, some have only one tentacle, stick deep into the muck. When an animal passes close, their mouth opens, revealing razor-sharp teeth. They sink their teeth into the animal's skin. Then their needle-like suction tongue pierces through the skin and immediately sucks blood. This accounts for the sores on Gob-Diggers' scabby skin. The Boggy

Swamp is a perfect domain for Mudlumps and Gob-Diggers because they both like dark wet places.

    Gala never wanted to see swamp creatures, nor did he ever want to get close to the Boggy Swamps. Everything living in the swamps frightened him. But that morning, he was feeling curious. In his Nix form, he soared high across Crystal Lake and the dwindling mountains peering down at the swamps. A chill ran down his back as the thought of flesh-eating creatures dampened his curiosity. He ruffled his feathers, then turned and flew over to the southeast side of the castle, where he felt safe. He flew over the southeastern forest across Crystal Lake. This is where Trill and Quo had gone earlier that morning for their thirtieth-year tryst. They go every year. Nix thought about the story Trill and Quo shared when they first knew they were soul mates. He remembered when they said they conceived Acub.

    Trill and Quo were best friends before they knew they were soul mates and before their son was born. When fairies reach maturity, if they're soul mates and their eyes meet, they know it on the spot. Although Trill and Quo shared commonalities, nature explorations were their interests. During one escapade, when evening was still bright with two full moons and one crescent, they came across an abandoned owl's hollow. It had been vacant for years. They decided it would make a great study hollow. As they cleaned out the old debris, they faced each other. Their soul mate consciousness hit them. That's all it took, that one-time look. They knew they would be together for the rest of their lives. After doing pixie flips, they embraced each other. They couldn't wait to tell the Bluewing clan, especially their parents.

Trill's parents were far in their years as the Bluewing clan's monarchs. His parents hoped to live long enough to perform Trill's soul mate joining and crown them as the new king and queen.

When Trill's parents heard Trill and Quo were soul mates, they did pixie flips. They wasted no time preparing the joining and crowning rites. Trill's parents transcended not long after the ceremonies. When the burial rites and mourning for his parents were over, Trill and Quo flew back to their study hollow. They redecorated. It became their special place for romancing and where they conceived their son, Acub.

Gala hoped he and Floreena would someday have a place to romance. He sighed, then transformed from Nix into Bunt.

Bunt was a small songbird bejeweled in colors of bright red, blue, yellow, and green, his tail solid red. Gala loved to hear the songs his Bunt form sang. He also liked that Bunt dashed through the forest with ease. He could land on branches with dense leaves, whereas his Nix form had a challenging time doing. Bunt can go places Nix cannot, but Nix can reach higher altitudes and see much farther than Bunt.

Bunt flew down into the forest and transformed back into Gala. His imagination sent him on a quest to save Floreena, a princess captured by the Gob king. In reality, Gala hoped Floreena had the same feelings he had for her. She was the love of his life, his beloved princess; in his imagination, she liked him a lot.

Gala transformed back and forth from himself into Bunt, then into Nix. Trill and Quo were in their hollow cleaning out debris while he imagined saving Floreena.

"Look, Quo," Trill pointed up. "Gala's practicing his Nix."

"He's a fine young mage."

"He is. I hope he and Floreena are soul mates. He loves her."

"I can tell she loves him, too."

Trill expressed, "So many years have passed. I'm happy Acub and Ashlin are soul mates. We'll plan their joining ceremony when we return home." Quo smiled as Trill continued, "Remember when my father flew up and hit his head after we told him we were soul mates?"

"Ha! Ha! Yes. Your mother flew up to help him and then hit her head. Ha! Ha! They shook their heads while touching their bumps, laughing between their oos and ows."

"That was funny. They were happy to have lived long enough to curate our soul mate joining and celebrate our coronation. That was their most desired fairy clan wishes. They had always hoped you and I were soul mates." Trill flew over and kissed Quo on her cheek.

Quo turned and gave Trill a tender kiss on his lips, then said, "My parents did too. They knew we were best friends and being soul mates would be perfect, Fairy Honey on Love charms kind-of-perfect." Quo put her finger to her lips, "Shh.

Listen. Do you hear that?" She and Trill flew to the window and looked out.

They spotted a small woodland creature. An Elfkie panted and rested right beneath their hollow. The scared Elfkie lost her way. Trill and Quo flew out to release the calming essence from their wings over her. The Elfkie didn't see them, so she took off through the thick forest. As Bluewing fairies, if possible, they must calm all beings with the essence of their wings. "Come on, Quo! Let's follow her!"

"She's heading towards the dwindling mountains and the Boggy Swamps! I hope there aren't any Gob-Diggers up and about." Quo sighed.

"Me either! I don't think Gob-Diggers like the taste of Elfkies like they do fairy meat. Besides, Gobs should be sleeping by now."

"Oh Trill, I sure hope you're right, and I hope we reach the Elfkie before she reaches the swamps. Other things could eat her or us." Quo gulped.

Trill and Quo tried to keep up, dodging trees, but the Elfkie was quick and agile. She moved through the forest with ease. When she stopped to rest inside the boundaries of the Boggy Swamps, Trill and Quo finally caught up. They flew above her and flapped their large diaphanous blue wings. Their sparkling calming essence covered her. After the Elfkie relaxed enough to listen, Trill and Quo explained that they would help her get home. She agreed, but right before they got started, their eyes popped wide. Trill whispered, "I can't believe those two Gobs are still up."

"Me either," whispered Quo. "And why are they with those witches? Come on, let's hide." They encouraged the Elfkie to follow. As they flew into the bushes next to an old oak and embraced, the Elfkie followed. She leaned still against the oak. Her skin resembled the oak's bark. The extremities she lifted out from her skin resembled twigs with leaves. After she closed her big round eyes, she blended in, hidden and camouflaged like she was part of the oak.

The hideous Gobs had covered their skin with swamp muck mud to protect them from the morning's sun. They stepped off a covered wooden raft accompanied by two evil sister witches. The sister's warlock father, Grock Faraway, followed behind his daughters, Idanab and Terrib. They walked towards a large Swampress tree by the old oak where Trill, Quo, and the Elfkie hid.

While that was going on, Gala had transformed into his Bunt. Bunt darted through the trees unheard and unseen. He landed on a branch in a nearby tree to rest his wings. Gala pretended his Bunt scouted the forest for clues. He imagined he found where the Gob king took Princess Floreena. He didn't realize he had wandered across Crystal Lake down the dwindling mountains. Bunt perched on a branch at the edge of the Boggy Swamps. The one place he never wanted, nor planned, to venture. Bunt had no inclination that Trill and Quo hid in the bushes twenty-five feet from the tree he was perched. While Bunt looked down at an assortment of wildflowers, he heard a grunt, then jerked his head up. His heart thumped through his chest. "Gobs!" he thought. "The Boggy Swamps! Gobs with witches!" Bunt perched still as he watched and listened to the strange gathering.

"Come on, Father. Just a little further, and we're there." Terrib sounded sweet and excited. She walked with a bounce in her step, almost skipping. She and Idanab led Grock to an area where they prepared a table and three chairs to deem as a family picnic. The two Gob-Diggers trudged past and sat on the ground under a shading oak. It was the same oak where Trill, Quo, and the Elfkie hid.

"I wish you girls would at least give me a hint to the surprise." When the girls were little, they surprised Grock with a warlock birthday party. Their mother orchestrated it. Grock remembered the fun he had. But this time, he doubted their sweet intentions. His daughters acted strange. Idanab wore more of a smirk than a smile, and Terrib's voice shook. Just in case his suspicions were correct, he hid his wand to conjure it if needed.

Idanab gestured her hands for Grock to sit. She stood behind the chair and pulled it out. Grock didn't see anything unusual, so he turned to sit. Idanab squinted and said, "You'll see your surprise soon enough."

As soon as Grock sat, the chair's arms wrapped around him like a straitjacket. "What is this?" he demanded as he struggled to free himself and retrieve his wand.

Idanab snarled, "Relax, Father. You're not going anywhere. Do you remember our mother?" Her question rang loud in his ear.

"Of course, I remember her. What are you talking about?" Grock turned his head to look at Idanab, but he could only see her through his peripheral vision. He turned back around to look at Terrib, but she didn't make eye contact.

Terrib turned her back on her father, faced the water and crossed her arms. It seemed she wasn't going to say anything, but then she blurted out, "REMEMBER HOW YOU KILLED OUR MOTHER!?!"

Bunt's little body shook. He couldn't believe what he heard.

He took a deep breath, trying to relax, then the warlock father pled.

"Girls. Please listen."

"SHUT UP!" Idanab screamed.

"Argh!" Bunt screamed in his mind. He almost jumped out of his feathers. He remained perched as Idanab stomped over and stood next to Terrib, who still had her back to her father.

Idanab glared. Her eyes shot daggers into Grock's eyes. She gestured a wave with a quick twist of her wrist, giving him permission to speak, "Don't shut up. Go ahead, spit it out. Let's hear it. But Father, remember, you taught us your ways; we know you're a cheat, a sneaky liar, a murderer."

"You're mistaken. I did not kill your mother." Grock leaned as far forward as the arms of the chair would allow and yelled, "Terrib! Tell her! Tell Ida what happened between me and your mother. Why won't you look at me!?!"

Without turning towards her father, Terrib shook her head no. She brought a fact to his attention, "Actually Father, I was sleeping. I didn't hear anything. I didn't see anything. I didn't even know there was a battle. After I woke up, the next day, mind you, I was the only one in the cottage. You came home without Mother. I didn't say a word. I didn't interrupt you when you told me your story. It sounded like wacky-witchy tales to me. Later that day, I went out into the swamps to find Ida. When I found her, I told her what you said."

"Yeah! And I agreed with Terrib! Your story was wacky-witchy."

"Wait, girls! I'm telling you the truth; it was an accident! It was an unfortunate, devastating incident! Your mother jumped in front of my wand. She didn't want me to kill the fire-breathing dragon. She wanted me to stun it because we thought the dragon was a Mystique Transfigure. During the battle, we couldn't capture or get any blood from a Blueblood, and the—"

"Yeah, yeah, blah, blah, blah! That's un-warlock, you O mighty powerful wizard who once sat with The Wizard's High Council. You're nothing but a necromancer, a liar, and a jealous killer. Why on Mageus would you even think the dragon was a Transfigure?"

Grock sighed, "After your mother and I returned home from the battle, a dragon flew over our cottage. We figured it followed us through the swamps. It flew back and forth. It circled above the roof. We ran from one window to the next, watching then we saw a large bird of prey. We suspected that the dragon and the bird were one and the same, a Mystique Transfigure. So, we devised a plan to capture it, honest girls; that's what we set out to do.

"As we began setting a trap in the Swampress trees next to the cottage, we saw the bird lift from its perch. It transformed into a dragon. Your mother gasped. The dragon jerked his head around. He flew towards us and spit fire. I wanted to kill it. I aimed my wand toward the beast and spat my *Death* spell. Right then...," Grock paused. He hung his head as if warding off tears. He adjusted his hands from the enchanted bonds and conjured up his wand. Then he continued, "...the unthinkable happened! Your mother jumped between the dragon and my spell! She fell in my arms. Devastated, I tried to revive her, but she was gone. The love of my life is dead! I looked back towards the dragon, but it had flown away. I never saw it again. I never want to see another dragon as long as I live.

"I took your mother's lifeless body to our favorite spot in the swamps and gave her a fire burial. This is what she wanted. I read her ceremonial rites. I adorned her with her favorite dress and cloak, including her wand, spell book, and talisman. As I lit her pyre, I begged her forgiveness. I chanted the Witches Passing. I watched as the orange and yellow crackling flames hissed. The fire, its sparks, and smoke turned blue. They rose into the night air and dissipated; her spirit flew into the wind. I laid down and wept, spent all night thinking. If we had not tried to capture—if I had not tried to kill—if only she had not jumped between my spell and the dragon. But there's no turning back. There's no way to make ifs happen in your favor when what's done is done. What is, is what is, and ifs are only wishful, wasteful thoughts. Your mother is our great loss because of foolishness. I have learned to be mindful when angry and think things through before reacting. Girls, I am terribly sorry."

Bunt's eyes watered. He couldn't wait to tell his parents but did not dare move. He heard Terrib sniffle as Idanab sneered at Grock.

"You didn't let us attend our own mother's burial!"

"I didn't have time to wait, Ida! No one knew where you lived!"

Terrib yelled at her father without turning around. "You could have put Mother on ice until we were all together!"

"Terrib, honey, your mother's body had to be warm while I lit her pyre—"

"Warlockries' beguiles and witcheries' garbles!" Idanab interrupted. "I've never heard such a thing as lighting a pyre while the deceased is still warm. You can wiz up a tale of tales, that's for sure! You are a lying piece of wicked warlock muck. I doubt that transfiguring fire-breathing dragon you spoke of was a Mystique Transfigure! I bet he was your friend, a stupid wizard who seduced our mother. He would have taken advantage of me in my bedroom if it weren't for your friend's son, Dectore! Dectore stopped his father. That's why I left home! Terrib was too young. Your friend didn't bother her!" Idanab glared. Grock lied about how their mother died, and she knew it.

Terrib screeched, "Father! Ida and I may not remember everything when we were younger. But we've heard tales about you and Mother, what you did before we were born! You put a curse on our mother to love you! You took her love away from her true love! And you—"

"Yeah!" Idanab interrupted. "You didn't even know she was with child, ME! You only realized it after Terrib was born, and I started to look like my real father. My father is my mother's true love, not yours. When you realized I wasn't your daughter, and after your friend started hanging around, you got yourself a secret lover. Oh yeah! You didn't think we knew, did you! But we knew, so did Mother. We also knew that Mother killed her, and your temper killed our mother!"

"Ida's right, Father. Just so you know, a reliable source told me and Ida the reason you didn't come home after you killed Mother. You tried to raise your lover's spirit from her grave. But you couldn't, could you!?! Another spirit gripped tight to your lover's spirit. That other spirit was our mother! We heard that you condemned Mother past her grave. You cursed her for not letting go."

"Actually, you condemned our mother before you killed her! She was expecting your friend's child! Something she didn't want. When you stole my mother's love from my father by using Dark Magic, you condemned her to this fate. She loved my father, NOT YOU!" Idanab's face turned blood-red.

"Yeah!" Shouted Terrib as she jerked around to face her father. She pointed a stiff finger at him and yelled, "We should condemn you! After you got lit on your woozy concoctions, you allowed your friend to do whatever he wanted. Mother played along, hoping you'd get jealous and stop seeing your lover. It didn't work, so Mother killed your lover."

"Yes!" Idanab shouted. "Mother got pregnant. She let you believe it was yours." As Idanab yelled, she lifted her head and arms into the air, then pointed at Grock. "But one day, after she became exasperated with you, she told you she was carrying your friend's child. You were irate, and yes, you did get jealous! But you tried to hide your true feelings from us. You led Mother to believe you were sorry, that it was your fault, and that everything would be okay. But you lied, you—you sneaky evil knave! You waited until you felt you could kill our mother without anyone ever finding out. Then, on the day of the dragon slayer's battle, you sent our mother and her unborn child to their grave. You murdered her because of your unjustified temper. Terrib and I know your temper! Don't we, Terrib?" Idanab lifted her wand and pointed it toward Grock. Although Terrib was angry towards her father, she was nervous about harming him, so she didn't answer. Idanab jerked her head at Terrib and yelled, "Terrib!?"

"I-I guess," Terrib stuttered. "I-I mean. His temper is about as bad as yours, I-I mean ours," she passively recovered.

Idanab's eyes shot daggers, then her ear caught the sound of leaves rustling in the bush.

Bunt also heard the rustling of leaves, and so did the Gobs. Bunt watched the Gobs get up and lumber over to the bushes. The biggest Gob snatched Trill and Quo from their hiding place. The Elfkie took off running. The smaller Gob chased after the Elfkie, but Terrib yelled for him to stop. He came back and ordered the bigger Gob to share.

"No! No! Me caught. Me keep!" grumbled the bigger Gob. Bunt tried to see what they were fighting over but couldn't see through their backs.

The smaller Gob held out his grubby hand and demanded," Me one, you one, not fair, you two yum, yums!"

"Enough! Give him one!" commanded Idanab. She and Terrib laughed a screechy laugh.

When the Gobs turned around, Bunt's eyes popped wide. He saw Trill and Quo. Bunt transformed into his wizard form. The bigger Gob handed Quo to the smaller Gob. Gala pointed his wand at the Gobs and screamed, "NO! LET THEM GO! LET THEM GO!" His *Release* spell shot towards the Gobs.

Idanab and Terrib jerked their heads towards Gala. Trill and Quo looked at him and shouted, "No! Go home!" But the horrific situation kept Gala from hearing anything.

Meanwhile, Grock freed himself. He sprang up from the chair, pointed his black wand, then cast his *Nightmare Forget* curse at Idanab. Idanab heard him. When she jerked her head toward Grock, she saw his spell coming straight toward her. She cast a *Deadly* spell toward him. They ran into each other, then raced through the air in the path of Gala's *Release* spell. All three spells twisted and combined into one black cloud of energy. Gala didn't see them. His eyes could not leave his friends.

After Trill and Quo yelled at Gala to go home, they looked at each other. Trill managed a smile. Then trying to be brave for Quo, he spoke softly, "Close your eyes, my love. Close them tight. Do not open them. I love you and will see you in our transcendence form."

"I love you too." Quo closed her teary eyes. Her face cringed, but she did not scream. Trill watched Quo as he also felt his wings rip from his body. His wings floated alongside Quo's downwards toward the ground.

Gala's mind screamed, "NO!" He couldn't breathe; everything closed in on him. He watched what seemed like a slow-motion horror story. His friends got stuffed into the mouths of hideous Gobs. The Gobs chomped down. Their sharp pointy teeth crunched and crunched on tiny bones. Fairy blood dripped down the Gob's scabby gnarled chins.

Terrib was watching everything. Her eyes went from Gala to the Gobs to Idanab to her father.

Grock tried to cast the same *Nightmare Forget* curse on Idanab, but again she heard him. She held her hands up and spat a *Lack Confidence* curse. As she steered her curse and Grock's curse toward Gala, the black energy cloud passed in front of Gala's face. It grabbed his attention.

While Gala watched the black cloud shoot past and toward Grock's head, he spotted Idanab's hands. "No!" he thought, "Her spells are heading straight towards me!" Gala hurried to transform into

Nix and hoped the spells wouldn't hit him. But one hit him before his transformation began. The other hit him as he transfigured into Nix. Ugly faces flashed through Nix's mind. He shook his fiery redhead and took flight, not giving the ugly faces another thought.

Terrib dropped her jaw. She watched the dark cloud of spells hit her father's head. Grock let loose his ebony wand. His limp body fell to the ground, then Idanab and Terrib pointed their wands at Gala's Nix and chanted a *Stop* spell. They were too late. Nix was out of reach. Their dusty incantations faded into nothing.

Terrib paced the swamp's bank flailing her arms. "We can't leave the boundaries of the swamp! How are we going to stop him! He'll tell others what happened here. He'll tell The Wizard's High Council!"

"No, he won't! Why don't you just calm down, Terrib. Father cast his *Nightmare Forget* curse on me, but I saw it coming. So, I hurried and cast a *Lack Confidence* curse. I steered both spells toward that Mystique Transfigure. They hit him! That young wizard will have nightmares, but he won't remember anything while he's awake. On top of that, he'll lack confidence in casting new spells. He has no idea he's cursed. If he ever figures that out, he'll have to cast my *Reverse Remembrance* and *Confidence* spells to break them. He can't do that because those spells are my spells, in my spell book. Don't worry little sister. That Transfigure Wizard headed east. We'll figure out a way to find him, but not today. Let's check on Father." Idanab reached down and picked up Grock's wand. She hid it in her cloak without Terrib knowing, then she turned Grock over. "He's not breathing! His heart stopped! That wizard killed our father!" Idanab pretended she was furious.

Terrib jumped to Gala's defense, "Ida. The lad pointed his wand toward the Gob-Diggers. He wanted to stop them from eating the fairies." Terrib's eyes widened. She felt a chill run down the back of her neck. Her sister's face turned fire-red. Terrib hurried and jumped to her own defense, "Besides, I thought that's what you wanted to do. I thought we were going to kill Father for killing Mother." Terrib looked away from Idanab's debilitating stare.

"Not yet! You idiotic dimwitted witch! I was going to kill him, but not yet! I was going to cast the *Blackout* spell, so I could take Father's wand and make him tell us where he hid his spell book. That didn't work because of that stupid wizard! Now Father's wand is lost to us, vanished, and so is the book. Get with the plan, Terrib!"

Terrib's body tensed. Her veins popped out of her neck and forehead. She held her arms stiff, straight down on her sides, clenched her fists, and screeched like a screech owl. "Don't call me an idiot, you sorry witch! I don't know what you're talking about! You didn't tell me anything about a spell book. What spell book?"

"Oh, I didn't? I thought for sure I told you." Idanab tried to recover her slip of the tongue and hid her fear of not telling the truth. She knew she didn't tell Terrib about her whole plan. She didn't want her sister to know about the book because sneaky, wicked witch, Idanab wanted to keep it for herself. Idanab tried to act as if she didn't care, "Oh well. It doesn't matter now. Your father's dead, and we'll never find the book. I've searched everywhere. I don't know where else to look. Besides, we don't need that dark book or his wand. Come on, Terrib. Let's forget it. Help me clean up this mess and tell those Gobs to come help."

Terrib told the Gobs to gather dry twigs and branches for Grock's pyre. She helped Idanab prepare Grock's body for his burial. No one said anything for about five minutes. Then Terrib asked with a hint of sarcasm, "How do you know the young wizard's a Transfigure?"

"Terrib! What in miserable gobs is wrong with you?"

"Nothing! I just want to know how you know he's a Transfigure. He might just be a young wizard for all we know."

"I don't think so. I've never seen or heard of a wizard that young transform that easily. But you could be right. He could be a simple wizard who risked being stuck as a bird. That little wiz got scared half out of his wizard wits. I don't know about you, but for me, the look on his death-gray face was delightful; his eyes were popping out of his skull. I could see his eye sockets!" Idanab cackled as she punched Terrib's shoulder.

"Ow! What!?!" Terrib rubbed her arm.

"Wasn't that funny?"

"Not really."

"Oh, come on. You know that was funny."

"No! I didn't think it was funny."

"Well, I thought so. And sister dear, in case my hunch is right about that scared little ole mage, I want to know how he does it. I want to know how he can transform at will. And if we find a way to leave the swamps, nothing will stand in my way! I'll learn how Transfigures transform if it's the last thing I do! Imagine our possibilities. If we could transform, or at least had a Transfigure do our bidding, we could rule over all other beings!" Idanab raised her arms in the air and yelled. "Those Tricksy Nixies and Lurking Harpies will obey us for once. We won't have to live in the Boggy Swamps with nasty Gob-Diggers. We won't have to step over Gurgling Mudlumps. We won't have to live with foul creatures for the rest of our lives! We'll live in a fine castle like the goodie-do-giver wizards do. It's not fair. Mother said she wanted The High Council to choose her and Grock as protectors. We'd be living in a grand castle if they did."

Terrib interjected. "Mother told us that The Wizard's High Council forced her and Father to live in the swamps because of our ancestors. She said they helped Stealth Dragon Slayers kill Blueblood Dragons for their blood. It's forbidden to kill them because their blood can heal the wounded. Besides, it's wrong to kill dragons in the first place. If our ancestors killed all the Blueblood Dragons, why on Mageus did Mother and Father look for one during the last battle? And you know what? It's not our fault what our ancestors did. I mean, we're not like them. We don't want to kill?

We're not killers just because we let Gob-Diggers eat fairies. The only reason we were going to kill Father was because he killed Mother. That doesn't mean we're killers, right?"

"Mother was partly wrong. She, like Grock, told half-truths or complete lies. One thing she was wrong about is why they lived in these swamps. It's true, Mother wanted to be a protector and live in a fine castle. Yes, she was angry that she wasn't chosen. But she and Grock got banished here because they wanted to overthrow The Wizard's High Council. That's the truth. It had nothing to do with our ancestors being dragon killers."

Terrib shook her head slowly while speaking a rhyme of old, " *Witch's brew, Warlock's stew, evil sorcerers were those two.*"

Idanab shrugged and continued, "Mother was wrong about the dragons. Bluebloods did exist. And the last battle, when you were sleeping, we weren't supposed to know about that. Part of that battle happened over the swamp's boundaries. I bet that the only reason you didn't hear anything is that Mother and Grock gave you something to sleep so they could go without you knowing."

"I bet you're right because after eating breakfast, I felt tired. It was hard to keep my eyes open, so I took a long nap. A long nap. No wonder I didn't wake up until the next day. The sneaks must have slipped me a sleep charm."

"I wouldn't put it past them. And if I still lived there, they would have slipped me one. I knew about the battle. I know that dragon slayers kill for dragon hides and body parts. They don't kill

Blueblood Dragons, well, at least not intentionally. They capture Bluebloods because not only does their blood heal wounds, but it also keeps you young. Some Bluebloods are half dragon and wizard or half dragon and enchantress. They're called Mystique Bluebloods. Their blood has the same youth and healing properties as the blood of a pure Blueblood Dragon."

"How do you know all this stuff?"

"Since I found my own place to live, I've been studying a lot. Terrib, you may not remember or didn't know, but our parents created Youth Potion from a Blueblood's fresh blood. And by the way, their blood is blue, hence their name. Every now and again, Mother would give us a sip. The blood and Youth Potion kept fresh in the cool room. The supplies were running out, and that's another reason they wanted to capture a Blueblood. One sip will keep you young for a long time. After it wears off, you begin aging from that point forward. Unless, of course, you drink more. Just so you know, I went to that battle and stayed hidden while Mother and Grock joined in the fight," Idanab boasted.

"What!?! Aaargh! Why do you keep such secrets?"

"You know why!" Idanab poked her finger into Terrib's shoulder. "You always slip up and tell someone about my secrets! I can't trust my own sister! I would involve you with more things, but you can't keep that big trap of yours shut!"

Terrib dropped her jaw but hurried to close it and said, "You're right. I'm sorry. I only thought that if I said something to Mother or Father, Father would be easy on you. It hurt me to see bloody welts on your back, bruises on your ears, or a knot on your head. I won't do it again. I promise. Please tell me the rest of what you saw at the battle."

"First off, you can't tell Mother or your father anything! They're dead! I'm concerned you'll tell someone else."

"I promise I'll never tell anyone anything you do. Besides, we hardly get visitors in the swamp. Please, Ida. I promise I won't ever spill your secrets."

"I'm not convinced, but I'll try to trust you. So, where was I? Oh, yes. While Mother and Grock fought the dragon slayers on the edge of the swamps, I saw a pregnant sorceress. She transformed into a Blueblood Dragon. What luck! Her wizard husband rode on her back and defended the dragons against the dragon slayers. She took a hard blow to her gullet, and they crashed to the ground. She gave birth right there in her husband's hands. Jitterbugs danced in my stomach, but I managed enough courage to seize the moment. I wanted to get her blood. Instead, I got something better—I got her newborn son." Idanab cackled.

"WHAT!? That's unspeakable!" Terrib covered her ears and pressed her lips tight.

"Let me finish! Listen to me, Terrib!" Idanab slapped Terrib's hands down. "You should agree that the lad's better off with me! A child needs nurturing, something a male figure can't do. Grock proved that point." Idanab gloated with false pride.

Terrib was beside herself. She threw her arms around and shook her head, "Oh, my sorceress ears, you wicked witch of evil witchery doers! Where on the realm's edge is the child now? How old is he? What's his name? What happened to his father? How in the blackest of black magic did you get their son?"

"After the child's mother transcended into the stars, I performed the *Blackout* spell. I used the Lethargic mist I created from the secretion of the Scarlet Leprechaun Frogs. It dazed the father. That's why I was able to snatch the child from his arms. I don't know anything about his father. I named the lad Nam. He's a little older than that wizard we just saw."

"Can I meet Nam? Does he think you're his mother? Is he part wizard and Blueblood?"

"I'll introduce you as his aunt and bring him to you someday soon. And yes, he thinks I'm his mother. He's only a wizard with no transfiguring abilities. Come on, let's finish up here."

Idanab didn't tell the whole truth. She knew Nam's real name and the names of his parents. She also knew where Nam's father lived.

After Idanab had snatched Optim from Tiaff's arms, she took him to her secluded cottage deep in the swamps. She cast a *Sleeping* spell on the child, laid him in a safe box, then returned to where she had left Tiaff. When she arrived, the battle was over. Wizards and Mageons surrounded Tiaff, so she hid in the brush. The wizards told Tiaff that some would search for Optim in the swamps and across the lands. The others would take Tiaff to

The Wizard's High Council. Idanab hurried home. For extra protection, she cast a *Disguising* spell on her cottage. It looked like dense Swampress trees, grasses, and brush. The wizards searched every home in all the swamp villages, even the Faraway's cottage. They never saw Idanab's cottage, and they never found Optim. Idanab was able to raise Optim as her own.

When The High Council banished Grock and Tamian Faraway, they banished any children they would bear together. None of them could ever leave the swamps without consequences. But no one, not The High Councils, Grock, nor Tamian, knew Tamian had already conceived a child with her true love. Tamian was pregnant a week before Grock stole Tamian's love by casting his forbidden *Love* spell on her. Three years after Idanab was born, Grock and Tamian had Terrib.

When Idanab and Terrib were old enough to go outside without a grownup, Idanab led Terrib to the edge of the swamp's boundary line. Sneaky Idanab coaxed Terrib to stick her hand outside the swamp's boundaries. Terrib stuck out her finger. A high voltage shot through her little body and slammed her on her rear. Her red hair stood straight up from her head. Blood had burst out of her ears and nose. Idanab was not about to do the same. But, after she learned Grock was not her biological father, she snuck off to the swamp boundary alone. She paced back and forth, drummed up some courage, then put her index finger close to the border line. She inched it closer and closer until her hand reached over the threshold. Nothing happened, so she stepped across. Since then, she has left the swamps, on many occasions, without anyone ever knowing. On one occasion, twelve years after she stole Optim, she befriended Wizard Tiaff. She introduced Optim to Tiaff as her son, Nam. And now she would introduce Optim to Terrib, but only because she needed Terrib's help.

Idanab and Terrib stood quiet as they watched the crackling flames to Grock's pyre burn. Idanab glanced at Terrib and thought, "I'll never tell Terrib all my secrets. Never!"

After Grock's pyre burn to ash, Terrib asked, "How soon can I meet Nam?"

"I'll bring him over in three days."

"Should I expect you in the morning, noon—"

"We'll be over after dinner."

"Okay. I'll have desert ready. Good night, Ida."

"Night, Terrib. And remember to keep my secret or else." Idanab glared at Terrib.

"I will. Nam is your son, and he's my nephew. That's all I know." Terrib gave a quick nod. She turned away from her sister's awful stare and started home.

Terrib went home to an empty cottage. But Idanab didn't go home just yet. She took a sip of Shadow potion she stole from Wizard Tiaff and glided east in the direction Nix had flown. When she came upon Crystal Lake Castle, she saw Gala transform from his Nix into his natural state. Idanab thought, "So, this is where the young mage lives. And look there, no doubt that's his mother."

While Idanab glided back to her cottage to devise a devious plot, Faithin looked out the castle's front windows. She watched Gala transform from Nix before his feet landed onto their wide walk. Faithin smiled. With a wave of her hand, the front doors opened. After Gala walked in, she greeted, "So, did you have fun today?"

"Yes, ma'am." Gala didn't remember everything that happened.

"Good. Did you practice any spells?"

"I practiced my *Release* spell and freed Floreena from the Gob king."

"O, you silly wizbinker. Come on. Let's go eat."

After dinner, they transformed into their Bluewing forms. Then they went to visit the Bluewing clan. They stayed awhile, telling stories, and playing games before returning to the castle. On their way home, Gala transformed into Nix and saw wicked faces flash across his mind. It happened so fast that he didn't give it much thought. He figured it was part of his imagination. The following morning, Gala woke to a nightmare. When his mother asked if he was okay, he brushed it off. He thought so because he couldn't remember it.

After breakfast, Gala went into the library to study a new spell. He found it odd that he didn't have confidence, and when he tried to perform it, it came out wacky. Gala tried performing different spells several times, but none of them worked. So, he gave up and called himself a flub-of-a-wizard. Gala decided to study his favorite subject, dragons, and practice his transfigure abilities.

The days that followed became more difficult for Gala. Every morning he woke in sweats from a nightmare he couldn't remember. His lack of confidence in casting new spells intensified. He figured he wasn't as powerful as he once thought. Gala didn't know why, nor did his parents. Their efforts to help him conquer his nightmares failed. But they didn't give up, and they didn't stop encouraging him to practice new spells.

Present Day
A New Task for Helsin

Helsin walked the steep steps on the north side of The Ridge, which led to Wizard Tiaff's fortress. Years ago, The Wizard's High Council carved the castle into the mountain's red and black marble rock. Its entrance was an enormous outcrop. It had an arched recess hidden behind drapes of greenery. The greenery grew from the top of the archway downwards to the outcrop's black floor. The floor overlooked the forest and its inhabitants Wizard Tiaff protected. After Helsin stepped onto the outcrop, he gazed at the forest below. Fairies fluttered at the edge of the forest, collecting berries. To the right side of the fairies, Helsin watched waterfalls spill down into Mermary's Lake. Suddenly, a heavy raindrop hit his hand, and a thunderous cloud formed above the castle. Helsin hurried inside the recess behind the green-hanging foliage.

  As his eyes adjusted to the dark, he heard grumbled snoring. He saw two large shapes belonging to Gob-Diggers. They were lying in front of a wooden arched door. They were brothers. The bigger one was Gorg. The smaller one was Durgat. Helsin walked up, kicked their legs, and commanded, "Get up! Act like you're doing something! You're nothing but lazy, useless heaps of rubbish nonsense!"

The clumsy Gobs stumbled as they hurried to their feet. Gorg blurted out, "Stop!"

Durgat snarled, "No, enter!"

As soon as they saw who it was, Durgat said, "You come. Wiz Helsin, you come." Gorg opened the door.

Helsin walked through without giving them another look. After entering Wizard Tiaff's laboratory, he saw his aunt Idanab and a Gob washing long stone tables. He yelled out, "I'm here, Aunt Ida!"

"You don't have to yell."

Helsin rolled his eyes.

"I saw that. Don't you roll your eyes at me! You're the one yelling and scaring the skin off my bones! I should be rolling my eyes at you!"

Helsin shrugged his shoulder and rolled his eyes again.

"Did you get what I asked for?" She asked while gathering her dirty rags off the table.

"I sure hope so."

Idanab ignored his curt reply. She took her dirty rags to a rock basin, then rinsed them under a constant flow of mountain spring water. She hung them over the basin's edge and used a spell to dry her hands. When Idanab turned to walk towards Helsin, she yelled at the Gob, "Keep washing until I tell you to stop!" She reached out towards Helsin, wiggling her fingers, and said, "Here, let me see." Idanab formed a crooked smile with a half roll of her glaring eyes as if she was doubtful. After she lifted the cloth that covered the frame Helsin was holding, she shouted, "Yes! This is it! I can't depend on those Gobs to do much of anything right. At least they helped with my captives and got the weird-looking painting I wanted."

"You mean the one with those machine things you talked about and things we don't have in this realm?"

"Yes."

"I don't understand how all these things will help you?"

"You'll see. But for now, I have another important mission for you."

"What!? I thought I was done."

"I need you to stop anyone that might travel to The Wizard's High Council."

"What do you mean by 'anyone that might?'"

Idanab took the frame and walked into another room, a library. Helsin grudged along. Idanab set the picture frame against the wall. She took a map off the bookshelf and unrolled it onto a table. She put her finger on the map and said, "From here, through this area, you'll come across different villages. They're between Timestill Forest and this place here called Frozen Falls. This is where The Wizard's High Council resides."

"Everyone knows about the Frozen Falls and where The Wizard's High Council resides, Aunt Ida. Stop treating me like I'm an idiot." Helsin furrowed his brows. Before Idanab could snap at him, he pointed a stiff finger at a spot on the map. He asked, "How do you know someone will be traveling through here to The High Council? I already stopped that wizard from going. I drank the Shadow potion you gave me. I recited the incantation. I cast your *Twirlwind* spell. I sprayed the Lethargic mist, then hid in the shadows while you performed your *Blackout* spell. You and those stupid Gobs were supposed to grab Gala and his parents, not Floreena and her mother!" Helsin clenched his fist as he lifted his finger from the map.

Idanab snapped, "Helsin! You know as well as I do Gala disappeared into thin air! Poof!" She raised her fists, and as she popped her hands open, spreading her fingers, she yelled louder, "POOF!" Then she jerked her arms back down and continued, "The Gobs did their best! Besides, they're the strongest, let alone the only help I could get for that task. So enough with that. Tell me a little more about the wizard. Did you hear him say he would tell The High Council?"

"Yes."

"What else did you hear?"

"Nothing."

"You must have heard something; you said you hid in the shadows."

"When you and your half-witted Gobs took Floreena, I got pissed and left out the window. A little time passed, and I calmed down and glided back in. That's when I heard the old wizard say he would travel to The Wizard's High Council. As soon as I heard that, I hurried back out the window and waited for him at the edge of the northern forest. After he left the Lakinshire's castle, I followed him. He walked for a fair distance before transforming into a dragon—"

"A dragon?"

"Yes, and I know what you're thinking, so I'm telling you before you ask. The wizard is not a Transfigure or a Mystique Blueblood Wizard."

"How do you know?"

"Because earlier that evening, I overheard him talking to other guests. They know the consequences of transforming. They know they could get stuck if they're not a Transfigure. I figured the old wizard didn't want to waste time getting to The High Council. So, he took the chance. Maybe he didn't care if he got stuck as a dragon for the rest of his life."

"It might be so. But, things aren't always as they seem, and hidden secrets stay that way, hidden."

"Aunt Ida! Why do you always question me? You don't think I can do anything! And you know I stopped the wizard, so why do I have to go on this mission, especially when you think I'm not good enough?"

"I know you stopped the wizard, and although you're still learning, I know you're good enough. The thing is, I saw a vision of your friend, Gala."

"He's not my friend!" Helsin rolled his eyes.

"Okay then, your old friend."

"What was your vision?"

"I saw Gala in Timestill Forest looking for the whereabouts of his parents through his father's crystal."

"Do you think he was there to get help?"

"I knew you were clever. I'm almost certain Gala was asking for help. I want you to stop anyone traveling to The Wizard's High Council. The High

Council must not get word of what has happened. After you stop them and make sure they're dead—"

"DEAD! What do you mean!?"

"You killed the wizard, did you not?"

"It looked like he was still breathing; if he wasn't, it was an accident! I didn't mean to kill him!"

"Fine, just stop anyone traveling to The High Council. Cast that *Forget* spell you learned at the academy on them so they forget who they are. Cast the *Travel* spell right away. Tell them to journey east-south-east to the Big Water. After you finish, whisper 'Ida' to a Message Raven I'm about to make for you. The raven will return to me while you go home to your uncle. I'll send for you if I need you. Now that you brought me the magical frame, after my first experimental procedure, I'll be able to use it, that is, if I need it."

"First, it's against wizard rules to cast spells on others for evil motives or your own gains. And second, I thought you knew what you were doing. What do you mean 'experimental'?"

"First, taking someone against their knowledge or consent is also against wizard rules. But this is hardly an evil motive when all I want to do is save lives. Besides, no one will know you cast the spells, and second, I do know what I'm doing, but this is my first attempt. If my tools fail or something goes wrong, the magical frame will allow me to enter the weird picture. I can use the equipment it has in it. I saw Gala's father enter it several times over the past year. The frame enables the picture to come to life."

"What about your son, Nam, or your friend, Wizard Tiaff? Are you sure they won't get hurt during your 'experimental procedure'? Isn't it risky to be experimenting on them? And I don't want you experimenting on Floreena."

"I won't touch her. As for Nam and Tiaff, If I don't try, their unknown sickness could kill them. I fear they're dying as we speak."

"Are you sure the Lakinshire's blood will heal them?

"Yes. If I had fresh blood from a Blueblood dragon, I wouldn't need the Lakinshire's. But I don't, so their blood will have to do. The Lakinshire's blood will work just as well as the blood of a Blueblood dragon. Don't worry. I have seen this procedure done several times and know of its success. None of my spells, charms, potions, or anything else will help. This procedure is their only hope of surviving. The Wizard's High Council will not understand and would forbid me from trying. Their spells and potions are no more powerful than mine. They cannot help, and must not know I have Gala's parents."

Idanab lied. She only wants the Lakinshire's Mystique Transfigure gene. Their blood doesn't have healing properties, but Helsin doesn't know that. There's a lot Helsin is unaware of.

"Why can't I stay here and help you while Aunt Terrib goes on the mission, give her the Message Raven? She and those Gobs aren't as useful to you as I can be."

"There are things you don't understand, but you will. I need you to be safe. If you know everything now, your life will be in danger. I cannot let this happen. You're in enough danger as it is. And for Aunt Terrib, she's a dimwit. She's almost as useless as the Gobs. That's why I need you for this task. Aunt Terrib will stay close to me so I can keep an eye on her. Now no more questions. Here."

Idanab pointed her finger at a stuffed raven sitting on a wooden perch. As she twirled her finger, she uttered a spell. A swirling black cloud came from the tip of her finger and covered the entire raven. After she stopped twirling her finger, the black cloud settled. The black raven was now on Idanab's index and middle finger. Idanab blew in the raven's face. The raven took a breath, opened her black beak, and squawked. Then she flapped her large wings and ruffled her feathers before settling down. Idanab introduced, "This is Spyraven. She is a Message Raven and will be your scout. Use her to get close to anyone traveling to the north along the route I pointed out." Idanab placed Spyraven on Helsin's shoulder.

"She's huge; her claws hurt!" Helsin moved his shoulder back and forth.

"When you hold your fingers out, she'll land on them. When you're outside, she'll perch on branches or other things unless you hold your fingers out."

"That's good to know." Helsin wiggled his shoulder again. Spyraven lifted her wings to keep her balance. She settled down after Helsin stopped fidgeting. "So, Aunt Ida, when did you see your vision of Gala?"

"Right before you got here. This gives you time to reach your destination before anyone leaves Timestill." Idanab pointed to the map again and added, "You cannot be anywhere within these areas because the Timeless Woodlanders will know you're there. That's why I want you to start here. Besides that, this is the only path they would take to The High Council from Timestill Forest. If you see someone travel this path, you'll know where they're headed."

"Fine. Just so you know, that Twirlwind spell you taught me, I won't use it for speedy transportation because it wears me out. It takes hours before I can cast it again. At least that's what happened when I stopped the wizard from going to The High Council."

"Helsin dear, about the wizard, you sent me a message using your Wind Communicator telling me you stopped the wizard, that he was 'done for.' I thought you meant he was dead, but you didn't go into detail."

"My Wind Communicator is not the best way to send messages."

"I agree. However, I see you received my message sent through your Wind Communicator. You brought me the frame I wanted." Idanab was being a sarcastic ole witch.

Helsin squinted his eyes and retaliated, "Yes. My Wind Communicator works for simple messages."

"Fair enough. Fill me in. Tell me how you stopped the wizard."

"Talk about fast and stealth. The Shadow potion and its chant allowed me to move quickly, hide in the shadows, and keep up with the wizard after he transformed into a dragon. While he was heading toward the north, I saw a giant rain cloud and decided that was the perfect moment to attack. But when he flew into the cloud, I didn't see him. After a few minutes, I saw him flying over the cloud, so I used the *Twirlwind* spell. It was my strongest yet. I crashed him into trees. He was like a wet rag flipping around. The storm cloud moved away. I looked at my hands. Your Shadow potion was still in effect. That's when I stopped your *Twirlwind* spell and watched the wizard fall against a boulder, hard. He lay motionless. After I saw he was done for, NOT DEAD, I sent you my Wind Message. After that, I hurried home before the Shadow potion wore off. Talk about exhaustion. I could hardly keep my eyes open."

"Do you have any potion left?"

"No. I took the last this morning before I left home. It lasted while I got the frame, but the effects wore off when I reached the forest on this side of Mermary's Lake. Here's your empty vile." Helsin reached in his pants pocket, pulled out the empty vile, and handed it to Idanab."

"We're doing things differently this time. The Shadow potion alone can cause tiredness. Using my *Twirlwind* spell with Wizard Tiaff's Shadow potion caused your exhaustion. By the way, Helsin, the *Twirlwind* spell belongs to both of us. But you're not using it for this task." Idanab put the empty vile in her cloak's pocket and pulled out a full one. As she handed it to Helsin, she instructed, "Now listen. Before you leave, drink one tablespoon of this potion and recite its incantation. The effects will last until you reach your destination. Hide in the brush. Spyraven will scout above the trees between the path and Timestill Forest. This is where you'll watch for travelers." Idanab held the Message Raven still, then plucked out a feather. The bird squawked and shook its body, readjusting her stance on Helsin's shoulder.

"Jeepers bird, do you seriously have to move around like that? Ouch."

"Stop your fussing. You sound like a whimpering Gob. Come, follow me back into the lab. Here, Carry this. Helsin rolled his eyes. Idanab handed him the map and frame while she grabbed the picture and led Helsin back to the lab. "Put everything on this workbench. Now come here." Idanab told the Gob, who was still washing tables, he could go home, and she'd reward him later.

After the Gob left the lab, Idanab walked over to a large stone table. Behind it was a nook with shelves. The shelves were stacked with magic potions and alchemy supplies. Assorted gemstones and charms held in crystal bowls were on one shelf. On the table behind Idanab was a mahogany book stand crafted with magical white hands. The hands had red fingernails and were holding her book of dark spells. On both sides of the book were three fat, black candles.

Helsin saw a wooden perch at one end of the table. He put his fingers out and reached them up to Spyraven. After she stepped onto his fingers, he lowered her onto the perch. Helsin rubbed his shoulder and spat, "Relief!"

Idanab ignored him as she collected a purple cloth, a black Onyx gemstone, and a long piece of twine. She instructed Helsin, "Light the candles. Tell the book to open to the page with the spell, *Through Your Eyes I Spy.*"

While lighting the candles, Helsin asked, "Is this how you saw your vision of Gala?"

"No. Although Gala's father put an alchemy solution and spells on his crystal ball, I cast a spell on top of his. Anytime anyone asks his crystal to find the whereabouts of someone, I can see who's using the crystal. And I know exactly where they are. Gala asked where his parents were. I saw him through my crystal ring." Idanab held her finger out to show Helsin her ring.

"But doesn't that mean he can see where his parents are?"

"No. I reversed the mechanics of the crystal. He can see them all right, but the crystal doesn't show where they are. Well, at least it doesn't show much of their surroundings. Plus, he can't hear what they're saying either." Idanab sniggered.

Helsin told the magical hands of the book stand to turn to the page with the spell, *Through Your Eyes I Spy.* After the hands flipped through to the correct page, Helsin asked, "Is this the right page?"

"Yes. Now I need a teardrop from you."

"How am I supposed to do that?"

"Think of something sad but hurry up because we're wasting time."

Helsin no sooner closed his eyes when tears welled up. "Is this enough?"

"Yes. That wasn't hard to do, now was it?"

Helsin gave his aunt a quick glance. "No. And no, I'm not telling you what I thought about."

"That's fine." Idanab handed Helsin the black stone and instructed, "Wipe your tears on the gemstone. Rub them in while you read the spell." When Helsin finished, Idanab handed him the feather and continued, "Now, warm the feather over the heat of each candle. Then place the feather on the purple cloth, here on the table. Put the stone on top of the feather near its middle. Take the twine and stretch it across the stone out to the full length of the feather. After that, hold your middle finger a half-inch above everything and read the words to the spell."

Helsin warmed the feather over the candles and put everything in place, including his middle finger. As soon as he began reading the spell, things began to happen. The twine wrapped around the stone and the feather. They melded together. The stone absorbed Helsin's tears. After that, both ends of the melded feather and twine turned under and over three times. Then, the ends reached up to Helsin's finger. One end circled over while the other end circled underneath. As it wrapped around Helsin's finger, it formed a black band. Its thick feathery texture covered the gemstone. Idanab chuckled at Helsin's cocked smile and wide eyes. Helsin said, "Tight."

"It shouldn't be. It should fit perfectly."

"No. I mean that it's first-rate. What's it for?"

"Ask your ring, 'What do you spy eye,' and see what it does."

Helsin shrugged, looked down at the feathery-covered gemstone, and asked, "What do you spy eye?" The feathery covering parted like eyelids, revealing the black stone. Helsin saw a solid black eye reflecting a mirror image of himself looking down at his ring. "What's this?"

"Look at Spyraven and tell me what she's looking at." Helsin looked over and saw Spyraven looking at him.

"Now that's tight."

"Yes, whatever she sees reflects in your ring. Now listen, Helsin, as soon as you reach your destination, hide in the brush. Spyraven will scout the area. When you see anyone coming from the direction of Timestill Forest towards this path—"

"You told me that twice already."

"I'm just making sure you heard me."

"Now you think I can't hear."

"I'm sorry, Helsin. Just keep an eye out for anyone coming towards the path and—"

"But what if they're not going to The Wizard's High Council?"

"The only ones who travel this path are those going to The High Council, so when—"

"But what if they're going for some other reason, and it has nothing to do with Gala?"

"Helsin! Anyone who comes from the direction of Timestill Forest, and heads to this path, is going to The Wizard's High Council to tell them Gala's parents are missing! Trust me, I know! Now listen and stop interrupting. I'm telling you again to be sure you get it right." Helsin rolled his eyes. Idanab ignored him as she continued, "Use your wand to cast the *Forget Identity* spell. As you know, it'll last for exactly five hours. Be sure the spell hits straight on their temple. You know that it must hit their—"

"temple or it's not going to work, and I only have one shot at casting the spell for each individual." Helsin finished her sentence. "Wizard's nerves, Aunt Ida. I know this already. I'm the one who learned the spell from Whittlewood Academy, not you." Helsin shook his head.

"I know, Helsin. Just hear me out. You'll have to act fast if there's more than one, which I believe there will be. After you cast the *Forget Identity* spell, immediately walk close to each individual and speak the *Travel* incantation in their ear. Tell them to walk east-south-east until they reach the Big Water. The Travel spell will break after they reach the bank of the Big Water, which is a lot further than five hours. You'll already be home, and my procedures will be over. Don't worry if you think someone will know who they are. By the time the *Forget Identity* spell wears off, they'll be far from home. No one will know them. And if they try to explain who they are, no one will listen. They will think they're kooks and ignore them. The Gobs and I will take the Lakinshires, Floreena, and her mother back to Crystal Lake Castle. Not one of them will have a clue of what happened." Idanab cackled.

You mean they won't remember anything, even what happened at the celebration?"

"No, they'll remember that, but they won't remember me, where they've been, or how they got home. I've kept them drugged, so anything they remember will be vague."

"What if Gala gets here while you're doing your procedures, and I'm stopping travelers, casting spells, or already at home?"

"Remember Helsin, Gala is who I wanted to nab in the first place. If he gets here, the Gobs know who he is and will let me know. I'll wrap my enchanted Fetter Chains around him so he can't escape, transfigure, or use his magic. I'll drug him, lock him in the dungeon until I'm done, then send him home."

"But what if Gala knows how to get out of your Fetter Chains?"

"I'll drug him before he has a chance to escape, same as I did his parents. If they can't escape, neither can Gala. He doesn't know any more than his parents."

"Oh yes, he could. We learned spells from Whittlewood Academy that we weren't taught at home."

"I thought you and Gala were in different classes?"

"Yeah, but he could have learned how to escape your Black Magic in a different class, dah."

"I doubt it, and don't take that tone with me."

Helsin turned his head and rolled his eyes.

"Look at me."

Helsin faced his aunt and said, "You know it's possible Aunt Ida, and you know he might get past the Gobs."

"Yes, but you told me Gala doesn't have confidence."

"I don't remember telling you that."

"Well, you did, but it doesn't matter. The point is Gala has no confidence. The Gobs will let me know if he makes his way here; stop worrying. Now, listen. After you're done with your mission, remember to send Spyraven back to me, but keep your ring on. If I need you, I'll use my ring and send a message through Spyraven's eyes. Your ring's eye will open. You'll see me and hear my message. Do you have any questions?"

"No, let's hope everything works out the way you say and nothing better happen to Floreena."

"Stop worrying. She's fine. Everything's fine. Now get what you need and go."

Helsin took a hard breath. He detested his new task. His resentment was that his aunt took Floreena when she should have taken Gala. Helsin tried to shrug off his anger. He tried to stop thinking of Floreena and Gala.

Farewell

Bloom led everyone back to the open field of Sweetleaf, so Gala could get Trusty. They stood a minute to view the lush green grasses and smell the sweetness of wildflowers that filled the air. Gala whistled. His whistle rippled through the air like a stream of heat waves. It dodged trees and bushes until it reached Trusty's ears. Trusty lifted his head, neighed at his friend, then ran towards Gala with his friend flying beside him. He stopped in front of Gala.  The female Hobbgie landed next to Trusty. She had silky brown hair. Her mane and tail were a lighter brown. Her black lashes brightened her grass-green eyes. Trusty sounded out two low growls, then gave his new friend a little nudge. She lowered her head. As Gala patted her neck, he spoke Hobbgie language, his voice soft and soothing. Gala summoned Trusty's brush. Poof! It appeared in his hand. While he brushed her silky hair, he said, as if talking to himself, "It's going to be hard to take Trusty away from you."

    Toma rode up on a sleek, black, Gentalsteed. He offered, "This Gentalsteed is not winged, but he's strong. His name is Blacky. After watching the Hobbgies get along as they do, I figured you might like to make a temporary trade. You can take Blacky in place of Trusty if you'd like. When you finish your quest, if you wish, you can bring him back and take Trusty and his new girlfriend with you. Her name is Beauty. Or you can keep Blacky and leave Trusty here with Beauty if you like."

"You're generous. Thank you, Toma. I guess it's best if I leave him here for now. I'll take Blacky in his place. Here, this is Trusty's brush. He usually likes to carry it around with him, but I can see he has new interests." Although Gala chuckled at himself, his face said something different, and everyone knew it. They only smiled. Gala took Trusty's provisions from his supply bag and handed them to Toma. Then he gave Trusty a long hug.

"Don't worry Gala. He'll be happy and well taken care of." Toma handed Gala a brush for Blacky.

"Thank you, Toma. It was nice to meet you. I hope we get to meet again." Gala put the brush in his supply bag, then turned and shook Toma's hand.

After Toma handed Gala Blacky's reins, he wished Gala and the Newlads safe travels. They thanked Toma and said they hoped to see him soon.

Gala patted Blacky. He glanced towards Trusty one last time as the Newlads flew down and sat on Blacky's slender neck. Gala gave a gentle tug on Blacky's reins, then followed Bloom through the maze back to the Woodlander's village. Celtrek took the rear. After Gala and the Newlads said farewell to the Woodlanders, they followed Bloom and Celtrek through Timestill Forest. Some Woodlanders followed behind. Everyone was quiet.

A cool breeze brushed across their faces. They listened to the tranquil trickling of water and the whispers of trees. As roots readjusted, trees moved to different locations. Leaves formed smiles. One bush took the shape of a Woodlander Elf waving goodbye. Birds sang. Sprites wisped around. Then Silverlight wisped past Blacky and sat cross-legged on Bloom's shoulder. She faced Gala, smiling. Gala couldn't help but smile at her cute, grinning face.

After reaching The Singing Lake, a horn sounded. "They heard my call," Announced Bloom.

Three Kelvor Elves rode up on stout, brown, and white Woolcoys. Woolcoys resembled wolves and mountain goats mixed in features. Each Woolcoy carried furs and other supplies strapped on their backs. The Kelvor Elves had short red hair but long beards and mustaches. They stood about a foot shorter than Gala, who was five feet tall and as tall as most Woodlander gnomes. All three Kelvor Elves had broad shoulders and thick muscles. They wore Woolcoy's leather skins; horned helmets crowned their heads. One elf dismounted and greeted Bloom. After Bloom kneeled, he and the elf cupped each other's shoulders and exchanged a few welcoming pats. "Hello, Bloom."

"Welcome, Warick."

Celtrek knelt next to Bloom, then he and Warwick patted each other's shoulders. "Good to see you, Celtrek."

"You too, Warick."

After Bloom and Celtrek stood up, Warick presented his companion warriors, "This is Elk, and this is Vek." The two elves greeted. They bowed to everyone. Then Warick asked, "How can we be of service?"

Bloom introduced Gala and the Newlads and explained their situation.

"Understood. We'll make haste. I'll go with Gala and the Newlads. Elk and Vek will take the arduous journey to The Wizard's High Council."

Gala thanked, "Thank you, Warwick. And we thank you too, Elk and Vek." Gala shook Warwick's hand. He hurried over and shook Elk's and Vek's while the Newlads yelled thank you in unison.

Bloom told the warriors, "May you be safe and successful." Then he warned, "Be watchful, Gala. Remember, whoever took your loved ones may have seen you through the crystal. If so, they know you're here."

"We'll be careful." Gala nodded along with the Newlads.

Warick explained to his warriors. "I'll lead Gala and the Newlads to Tiaff's castle and inform Bloom of their safe arrival before I return home. But, if I hear your alert horn, I'll immediately come to your aid." Warick signaled his warriors to start their journey. After they left, Gala put his hand on Blacky's knee. While Blacky knelt so Gala could climb onto his back behind the Newlads, Warick mounted his Woolcoy. Warick told Bloom and Celtrek, "I'll return with news as soon as possible."

Bloom nodded and replied, "We'll expect your return. In the meantime, we wish you safe travels." Bloom and Celtrek reached their arms out to

Warick. They clasped each other's forearms for a farewell shake. Bloom, and Celtrek walked over to Blacky. As Bloom patted Gala's calf and nodded to the Newlads, he expressed, "I hope we meet again. But under happy circumstances."

"Us too." Gala looked at the Newlads, who agreed with yeses and nods.

"Me too." Celtrek wished and reminded, "Remember, always know your surroundings. Do not let your imaginations carry you off."

"Yeah!" The Newlads said in unison as they glanced back at Gala.

Gala raised his brows and widened his eyes. He stretched his lips outwards with his teeth clenched together. Then he said, "It's unanimous. I'm outnumbered. I will definitely do my best."

Silverlight wisped around Gala and the Newlads. She gave each of them a kiss on the cheek. Then she flew back and sat crossed-legged on Bloom's shoulder.

"Aw! Now ain't that sweet. Bye, Silverlight. We thank y'all for everythin'." Lucky waved.

In unison, they yelled, "Thank you, everyone, you too, Silverlight!"— "Thank you for the sweet kiss!" — "Yeah! Thank you! We had fun!"— "Bye, everyone! See y'all again real soon!"

Warick waved and led the way. Gala and the Newlads turned one last time to wave farewell.

Helsin Intercepts

Helsin couldn't kick his agitation that his aunt had Floreena locked in a room or a dungeon. He wanted to see Floreena before he left.

"Aunt Ida, is Floreena comfortable?"

"Of course, she is."

"He didn't trust his aunt, so he pleaded, "Aunt Ida, please let me see Floreena before I leave."

"Helsin, no! She mustn't know you're involved."

"Like I said, I wasn't involved with you taking her!"

"No, but she doesn't know that, and you—"

"Fine!" Helsin jerked up his arms. Why can't I peek in on her?"

"The longer you linger here, the closer someone gets to The High Council."

"Fine! I'll send Spyraven back to you when I'm done. If you hurt Floreena, I—"

"I won't. I'll return everyone to the Lakinshire's castle unharmed."

"Let's hope you know what you're doing, so you can save your son and Wizard Tiaff from whatever threatening illness you say they have."

"I'm sure it'll work. Now go."

Helsin stood with Spyraven on his shoulder. He drank one tablespoon of Shadow potion, then recited its incantation. It took less than a minute for his body to materialize into a **Shadow**. Although the Shadow potion, in conjunction with its chant, causes its consumer to appear as a **Shadow**, their facilities still function. The **Shadow** allows the consumer to glide across the air with exceptional speed. They can hide within the casting shadows of tangible objects. If the consumer drinks more than one tablespoon, exhaustion occurs. This is why Idanab instructed Helsin to only drink one tablespoon.

Helsin glided through the forest while Spyraven flew above the trees. Sometimes she flew down within them. When Helsin reached the path, the Shadow potion wore off. He hurried and hid within the brush. He asked his ring, "What do you spy eye?" The feathery covering opened. Helsin saw Furhoppers, Chipmunkins, Squrlies, and birds. He saw everything Spyraven saw. He stood and stared at his ring for what seemed like an eternity. Helsin thought, "My aunt doesn't know what she's talking about. No one's going to The High Council. If they are, they aren't coming down this path." He sighed. He was about to give up and send Spyraven to Idanab when two Kelvor Elves riding Woolcoys appeared in his ring. They headed straight towards him.

Helsin readied his wand. His nerves jolted at the sound of galloping hoofs. He thought he might miss his target. This would make his aunt madder than mad. The elves were almost upon him. He saw them ride side by side. They ran their Woolcoys at a progressing pace. Helsin could hit the temple of the elf closest to him. But he would have to run across the path to cast one on the other elf.

Helsin gauged the speed of his spell to the distance and speed of the Woolcoys. He pointed his wand just in front, a little past the elf closest to him and spat, "*Knownot!*" Out from the tip of his crooked black and red wand shot a greyish fog-like beam of light. It intersected and hit the elf in his temple, causing the elf to slow his Woolcoy until it came to a complete halt. Helsin hurried to the other side of the path and hid.

The other elf, Vek, stopped his Woolcoy, turned, and asked, "Elk? What's wrong?" Elk didn't answer. He only touched his temple while he stared at the ground. Vek saw the confused look on Elk's face. He immediately blew the alert call on his horn. As Vek tucked his horn within his shirt, he felt a jolt and touched his temple. He and Elk were clueless to who they were, what they were doing, or where they were.

Helsin saw that the elves were oblivious to everything. He hurried close to Vek's ear and cast the *Travel* spell, then did the same to Elk. The elves had no clue who Helsin was or what he was saying, nor did they seem to care. Vek and Elk steered their Woolcoys east-south-east towards the Big Water.

Helsin grinned, pleased he did well and knew his aunt couldn't get mad at him. He held out his fingers. As soon as Spyraven landed, he said, "Ida." Spyraven lifted off Helsin's fingers and flew back to Idanab.

Helsin drank a tablespoon of Shadow potion. He figured that amount would get him home by midmorning, less than an hour.

The potion wore off about two miles from his home, where he lived with his aunt and uncle. Their cottage rested on the north edge of Whittlewood Forest in the Black Forest. As Helsin entered the front door, he saw his uncle Dectore drunk, lying face down in puke.

Helsin shook his head, walked a few feet past his uncle, and stopped. He slumped his shoulders, sighed, and put his forehead in his hand. Helsin turned back, reached for Dectore's arm, and said, "Come on, Uncle Dec. Let's get you cleaned up and in bed. You're drinking your Wiz Bonkers earlier and earlier. It's morning, for wizard's sake. Do you drink like this because you're not happy? Are you worried about your son, Nam?"

As Dectore struggled to his feet, with one arm loosely hanging around Helsin's neck, he slurred, "I'umm maud—*hic-up*—*hic-up*." The puke that wasn't stuck to his sandy-colored beard dripped down the front of his shirt.

Helsin jerked his face from his uncle's mouth. "Woo! The first thing we need to do is wash your beard and rinse your mouth out with Magic Antiseptic Wash."

"I'umm sorwe lad. Mm mad at your—*hic up*—aunt."

"Well, it seems everyone's mad under this roof." Helsin cleaned up his uncle and got him to bed. While he was cleaning up the rest of the puke, he thought about how he hated living there, how different it was when his parents were alive, how happy he used to be. But now, because his aunt is hardly ever around, he takes care of his uncle's drunken episodes, which occurs more frequent. Also, his aunt insists Helsin learns dark spells because she says it's good for him.

Helsin sighed. He went to his room to rest before practicing a new spell Idanab wanted him to learn, more like commanded him to learn or else. While lying in bed, he thought of Floreena and wished she liked him as much as she adored Gala. He thought, "What if Aunt Ida does have Floreena locked away in a damp filthy dungeon?" Helsin creased his brows. It dawned on him, "I never set eyes on Aunt Terrib, Wizard Tiaff, or Nam? Aunt Ida always makes excuses why I have to wait to meet them. It's been over a year since my parents died and I came to live here. Aunt Ida spends more time at Wizard Tiaff's castle than she does here, and why wouldn't she let me peek in on Floreena? It's wicked-washy." Helsin sprang up from his pillow and sat on the edge of his bed. As if speaking to himself, he said out loud, "She's sneaky. She's not telling the whole truth. I'm going back to hide in the corners of Wizard Tiaff's castle to see what she's up to. I'll sneak in through the back tunnel on the swamp side of The Ridge."

Helsin laid back down. He planned to drink two tablespoons of Shadow potion to ensure he wouldn't waste any time getting to Wizard Tiaff's castle.

Vek's Horn

Gala slowed Blacky to a halt behind Warwick's Woolcoy. It took half the morning for them to travel through the dense forests south of The Singing Lake. But, as soon as they reached the forest with less foliage, they ran their mounts hard to gain ground and time.

It was early afternoon when Warwick stopped at a trickling brook to rest. Their mounts drank the fresh water while Warwick and Gala filled their water skins. They set up their cooking gear for a bite to eat.

"A rainstorm's brewing and the wind picked up. We're going to need some shelter." Gala pointed at the dark clouds and decided to practice a simple spell. "I'm going to cast a *Cover* spell. It's an armored hovel. The fallen leaves, twigs, and branches should interlock together. It'll protect us from the elements. Not to mention all those predators Bloom and Celtrek warned us of. They won't be able to see or smell us. The *Protection* spell we use for our castle doesn't conceal us or our scents. It only prevents anything, or anyone, from passing through Bridge or entering our castle."

"Gala?" Ddot paused for a second before he continued, "You said, 'should interlock,' did you mean that you haven't got the spell down pat?"

"Yes. But don't worry. I'll walk far away from everyone and try it on a small scale. Now that I know I'm probably cursed with some sorta *Lack Confidence* spell, I'm more assured than I've been in a long time. Besides, I practiced this spell before the curses happened to me, and I almost had it down pat then, so I'm certain I can do it."

"You're sounding more like the Chum I used to know, the one who knew what he was doing, sure of his abilities."

"Yeah!" added Dahc, who grinned from ear to ear.

"It's good yo're feelin' like yore ole self, pal. We're rootin' for ya, always have, and always will." Lucky clasped his hands together. He raised them to the side of his head and shook them. Ddot and Dahc did the same. Warwick smiled.

While Gala walked further into the forest, Warwick stood by his Woolcoy. The Newlads stayed seated on Blacky's neck, holding tight to his black mane. Gala summoned his wand. He nodded towards his friends with a look of certainty the Newlads had not seen in over a year.

As Gala twirled the tip of his wand towards the fallen debris of bark, leaves, twigs, and branches, he spoke a sentence using Sorcermizic language. A beam of sparkling golden light shot out from the tip of his wand. It swirled over, under, and around the debris, which caused them to wiggle like nervous Jitterbugs. Gala turned to smile at his friends but drooped his mouth instead. Their widened eyes and Dahc squeezing Ddot's arm made him panic. When he turned back around, the debris flung onto him and stuck like he was a magnet. He quickly closed his eyes and mouth so nothing could get in as debris weaved together tightly, interlocking around his body, coving his face, his mouth. He couldn't breathe. Gala looked like a walking bush with arms, legs, hands, feet, and a head. He tried pulling the debris from his mouth, but they snapped back. His heart thumped hard against his chest. He had to do something quickly. He thought, "GALA! You can't breathe! You're gonna suffocate if you don't think! For wizard's sake, use your imagination like you were taught!"

Gala relaxed. He imagined he was showing The Wizard's High Council his *Armored Hovel* spell. He commanded the foliage to form a reinforced hovel large enough to house himself, his friends, and their mounts. Gala visualized The High Council smiling, showing him reverence. As soon as he felt the wind on his face, he snapped out of his imagination but remained calm while he took a breath. When Gala opened his eyes, he saw the debris move through the air away from his body. They weaved together, tight, interlocking until a large domed hovel was created. The Newlads relaxed, and Dahc stopped cutting the circulation off Ddot's arm. They hooted and hollered, shouting in unison, "Way to go, Chum! — Yeah, Buddy! — Ya did it, Pal!"

After Gala walked over to touch the hovel and test its sturdiness, Ddot asked, "Is it solid, safe to enter?"

"Yeah." Gala grinned big, then coached, "Come on guys, let's get inside before it pours." He helped Warwick pick up their cooking gear, then walked over and pulled Blacky's reins. Warwick waved his Woolcoy to follow.

The dark clouds poured down their hard rain no sooner than they entered the hovel. Although the wind whirred through the trees outside, it was quiet and dark inside. Gala pulled a clear gemstone from his right cloak pocket, held it up, and said, "*Light*." The stone lit the entire hovel with an orangish-yellow glow. "Come on, let's get something to eat." Gala laid out a blanket and set his stone in the center. Warwick and the Newlads helped him gather things for their picnic.

"So, Chum, tell us how you felt when you cast the spell; what happened? Why did the debris cling to you?"

"Well, because I'm probably cursed, as Bloom said, I wasn't gonna let that have power over me, ha. After I cast my spell and the debris started jittering, I knew it was working, which gave me a sense of success. At that point, I felt great! That's until I turned and saw the expressions on y'alls face and Dahc squeezing the life out of Ddot's arm." Ddot rubbed his arm as his Chum finished explaining. "Doubt kinda got the best of me. That's when the debris started sticking to me. I tried to pull it off my mouth, but it snapped back, and when I couldn't breathe, I panicked. I knew I was gonna suffocate if I didn't do something fast. I scolded myself and told myself to use my imagination. I imagined that The Wizard's High Council showed me reverence because of my mystique powers. After I felt the air on my face, I knew I could breathe, so I opened my eyes. I saw the debris leaving my body and the hovel taking shape, then I heard you guys hooting."

"When all odds are against you, you still pulled through. I know curses are impossible to break without their reverse incantations. You have got to be one powerful magus to outwit a *Lack Confidence* curse," Warwick said with a tone of conviction.

"Thank you, Warwick. Everyone I know keeps telling me I'm powerful. And now, although I can't break it, YET that is, I'm pretty sure I can beat this cursid curse."

"And we ain't gonna look worried next time ya try a new spell. But ifin' ya can, don't look at us just in case we caint help it. Keep yore focus on what yo're wantin' to achieve. After each success, and ya get more confident, we will, too. Right, fellas?" Lucky nodded at the twins.

"Lucky's right, Chum. After that, you can look at us all you want because we'll be just as sure as you." Ddot gave a quick nod.

"Yeah. I know that's right," Dahc said as he lifted his brows and nodded like a bobble-head doll.

Gala chuckled at Dahc's expression. Dahc always made Gala feel good inside. "Thanks, guys. But it's not your fault I flubbed up. I can't let anyone's expressions, thoughts, opinions, or feelings trigger my confidence." His friends smiled.

After they finished their picnic lunch and while waiting out the storm, Gala summoned his map. Warwick showed them where they were and where the Water Bbeings lived. He reminded them of the routes to Wizard Tiaff's castle. "It's safe to go around the lake here. It's also faster for Blacky to travel. We'll avoid any mishap if we meet the Water Bbeings or if Blacky missteps. Wingless Gentalsteeds are not as agile across mountains as Woolcoys. Gentalsteeds aren't as fast as Hobbgies.

But they're still fast and can run great distances without a break. Their long legs allow them to cover a lot of ground."

"I'm anxious to see if our loved ones are anywhere near or even inside Wizard Tiaff's castle. Bloom's Whispering Tree, my father's crystal ball, and my gut tell me our loved ones are close. And look how far we've come! We don't have far to go! The way we've been traveling, we'll reach Wizard Tiaff's castle early tomorrow morning, if not tonight. We could get there sooner if I cast Father's *Warp Drive* spell."

"NO! I mean, no, thank you, Chum. I don't think my stomach wants to go on that ride anytime soon."

"Mine either," added Dahc.

"Besides, where'd we end up, the swamp's water, the Water Bbeings' lake, or would we crash through Wizard Tiaff's castle?"

"That's a good point, Lucky. Guess we'll stick to riding our mounts." Gala sighed.

"Oh, look. It stopped raining." Dahc pointed outside.

"Good. Let's pack up and get going," Gala hurried. He concealed his map. After they walked outside the magic hovel, Gala raised his palm and said something in his Sorcermizic tongue. When he swept his hand across the air, like using an eraser across a chalkboard, Gala's armored shelter disappeared.

Everyone was ready to ride. But then Warwick yelled, "Vek's horn! Vek and Elk are in trouble! I'm sorry, Gala, Newlads, but I must ride to their aid!"

"OH, NO! I hope they're all right!"

"Me too. I'll send word to The Wizard's High Council as soon as possible. With any luck, if you continue to ride hard, you'll reach your destination before nightfall. Follow this stream. It goes around the Water Bbeings' lake, towards the fay-folk, and Wizard Tiaff's castle. I'm sure they can help you. Farewell, my friends!"

"Thank you, Warwick! Farewell!" After Gala and the Newlads watched Warwick ride off, Gala shouted, "Y'all hold on tight because we're running the rest of the way!"

The Newlads held tight to Blacky's mane as he ran along the stream, jumping rocks, scrubs, and dodging trees. Warwick's Woolcoy did the same. Warwick rode him hard in the direction of Vek's alert call.

Tracks

Three waxing moons accompanied an evening star in the eastern sky as an orange sun began to settle above the western treetops. Warwick made it to the northern side of Timestill Forest. He knew it would be well past dark before he reached the path that led to The Wizard's High Council, but he pressed on.

When Warwick finally reached the path, he slowed his Woolcoy so as not to disturb any tracks. The crescent moons were bright, but he needed more light, so he lit his lantern. Warwick held it out over the path and saw scuffled hoof prints. To get a better look, he jumped off his mount. "Um," he said to himself, "This is where Vek blew his horn. These tracks belong to Vek's and Elk's Woolcoys; they're headed east-south-east, but why? Frozen Falls is northeast of here. Ah. Wait a minute. Here's a set of unfamiliar boot tracks." Warwick followed the tracks. He concluded, "These tracks are on both sides of the path and seem to end here where Vek's and Elk's mounts stood. But there's no evidence of where the individual came from or where they've gone." Warwick looked up into the trees and the moonlit sky. He didn't see any sign of anyone. He hopped on his mount and followed his friends' tracks as far as he could until he and his Woolcoy were too tired to continue and had to camp for the night.

Fay-Folk

Hours before Warwick camped for the night, Gala had slowed Blacky to a halt when he came upon a fork in the brook that Warwick told him to follow. The western sky was dark orange, and a star shone with three waxing moons. The Newlads flew off Blacky to hover and stretch while Gala summoned his map. "Well guys, according to where Bloom, Celtrek, and Warwick pointed out on the map, Wizard Tiaff's castle—"

"Serenity! Serenity! Help!"

Gala concealed his map, summoned his wand, and asked, "Did you guys hear that?"

"Sure did," Ddot said in a low voice.

"It sounded like it came from that direction," Lucky pointed to the east—.

"SERENITY! Help!"

"Now that was louder, listen." Gala put his finger to his mouth as he and the Newlads listened.

"Are you sure?" Serenity asked.

"Yes. We saw Nam transform into a green dragon, then he knocked the sorceress off the cliff when he took flight towards the mountain caves of Mermary's Lake! The sorceress fell and hit her head! She isn't moving! Hurry, Serenity the sorceress—"

"All right, slow down. Show me," calmed Serenity as she put the berries she gathered in her pack.

As Serenity and the two younger fairies flew over to the fallen sorceress, Gala told his friends, "They sound desperate. Come on, guys! Get back on Blacky; let's go see." The Newlads flew back down and held tight to Blacky's mane while Gala rode at a trot in the direction of the voices. When he rounded the corner, at the edge of the forest, he and the Newlads saw three fay-folk about fifty yards hovering over a body at the bottom of a mountain.

"Well, I'll be...," Lucky said.

"They're Southland Fairies like you," Ddot acknowledged.

"Yeah," Lucky replied with a slight nod, his lips parted and his eyes glazed.

Then Gala pointed, "Look up, guys. I wonder if that's Wizard Tiaff's castle." Gala stopped Blacky and had him lie down. "Y'all sit on my shoulders. Let's see if the fairies need help, but I don't want to scare them, so I'll walk up slowly and call out before we get too close." As Gala and the Newlads got closer, Gala called, "Is everything all right? Can we help?"

The three fairies jolted backward, then the oldest asked, "Well, I don't know. Who are ya?" Serenity demanded as she put her arms out in front of the two younger fairies as if she were protecting them.

"I'm sorry. My name is Gala Lakinshire, and these are my friends. We're looking for our loved ones who were taken two days ago and were told that Wizard Tiaff or fay-folk like yourselves could help us."

"Who told ya that?"

"Gnome Bloom," Gala answered.

"I ain't never heard of no Gnome Bloom."

"Have you heard of the Bluewing Fairy Clan?" Ddot asked.

"No!"

Then Lucky asked, "Well then. Have y'all ever heard of the Tuberous Tribe, also known as Plant Fairies or Southlanders? They're fay-folk who once lived in the southern land of the rollin' hills before the Ultra Storm wiped 'em out, except my parents." Lucky flew up off Gala's shoulder towards Serenity. Her eyes popped when she saw him.

"HUH!" She put her hands on her cheeks and exclaimed, "Yo're a Tuberous fairy, a Plant fairy, a Southlander! My parents told us stories about the Ultra Storm and how many were lost. The ones left behind regrouped and traveled here. They made their home there in the forest..." Serenity pointed across the large clearing to the forest behind Gala and the Newlads as she continued, "...I was born about a year later."

"So was I. I'm Lucky. I mean Eric, but everyone calls me Lucky. The two fay-folk behind me..." Lucky turned towards his friends and introduced, "...are twins, Ddot and Dahc. Their tribe, or clan, is called the Bluewing Fairies, and this is our wizard friend, Gala." When Lucky turned back around and flew closer to the three fay-folk, the twins and Gala followed."

"I'm Serenity, this is Bud, and this is Rose. We could use your help, then we'll see if we can help ya find yore loved ones if that's okay?"

"Sure. How can we help?" Gala asked.

"Rose and Bud saw a young mage transform into a green dragon and fly off that crag." Serenity pointed up at the castle. "That's the entrance to Wizard Tiaff's castle. The young mage knocked our newest sorceress off the outcrop. She fell down the mountain and lies motionless, but it looks like she's breathing." Serenity pointed at the sorceress's chest.

The sorceress was middle-aged, short, and a bit chubby. Her long dark-brown hair was silky, and she had a rosy tint to her freckled-covered skin. The three plant fairies had never seen her look so bad, hardly recognizable. She was covered with mud from her head to the bottom of her oversized black boots. She usually wore a tan-colored apron over a long, darker, tan-colored dress. But now she was wearing britches, a tattered shirt, and a sorcerer's cloak.

Serenity flew down to her sorceress and lifted one of her eyelids. Her eye didn't sparkle, and her pupil was dilated, so much so that her light brown iris looked black. Serenity lifted the other eyelid. That pupil was just as big, but her iris was dark blue. Serenity wondered why she never saw the difference and thought it was probably because she rarely saw her face-to-face. As Serenity observed further, she said, "I don't remember her boots being so big."

Gala asked, "What's her name?"

"Idanab. We need to git her inside."

"I have a potion that heals the injured pretty quickly, but they have to sip it, and it doesn't look like your sorceress can swallow, so I'll use my *Levitation* spell to get her into her castle."

"If ya don't mind, use yore spell to git her to our home instead. This is the closest we've ever been to the castle. I'll explain later after we git inside and git more acquainted. But we need to hurry 'cause the night creatures will be stirring soon. Being out after dusk is dangerous, especially in the moonlight." Serenity told Rose and Bud to fly ahead and have a mossy feather bed and pillow ready for Idanab.

"Wait. If it's all right, I'd like to go along," Ddot offered.

"Me, too," Dahc added.

"That'll be great," Bud and Rose thanked in unison.

"I'll stay back with Gala and Serenity and help keep an eye out," Lucky said as he gave his sheath and dagger a pat. Ddot and Dahc held out their bows showing that's what they intended to do for Bud and Rose.

"I thought we could all ride on my Gentalsteed, but his movements could worsen your sorceress's injuries," Gala explained.

Serenity asked, "Yo're probably right. Where's your mount?"

"Over there at the edge of the forest." Gala pointed.

"We won't ride him, but we'll be sure to fetch him when we pass that way. We have a place he can stay."

"Thank you, Serenity."

"Oh no, Gala. It is we who thank all of you." Serenity smiled, then addressed Rose, Bud, and the twins. "It's settled. Y'all fly faster than the wings on buzzing Buzzbees, and be sure to tell Herbal what has happened; she'll know what to do. We'll be there as soon as possible. Now off with ya. Be swift but watchful."

"We're off," Bud said as he waved his hand toward Rose and the twins. Although their six green wings were swift, Rose and Bud didn't fly faster than the twins. Serenity watched them until they flew out of site. She motioned Gala to examine her sorceress.

Gala looked Idanab over and felt a massive bump on her head. She clenched a two-tone ebony and sienna-colored spiral-shaped wand in her right hand. Gala crisscrossed her arms across her chest. As he pointed his wand at the sorceress and cast his *Levitation* spell, his wand turned azure. Gala thought Idanab's wand moved and changed color from azure to gray. He paused to glance at it, but it was the same as he first saw it. Gala shook his head, dismissing the incident, and continued his spell. Using Sorcermizic language, he said, "*Elevor Eeup.*" Idanab jerked her head towards him. Gala jumped back. Her eyes popped wide, peering straight into his. He gulped down a bucket of air and held it. After a couple of seconds, the sorceress closed her eyes. Gala let out his breath with a sigh of relief. When he lifted his wand, Idanab rose off the ground. She was lighter than a fairy's wing. "We're ready," Gala said with a smile.

"That was creepy-creepers the way she looked at ya, pal. Jitterbugs were dancin' in my gut."

"Mine too, Lucky. She must have been dreaming."

"Yeah, she mighta been."

As Serenity led, she thought about how amazing Gala's *Levitation* spell worked. She figured Gala was a good wizard. She also thought how wonderful and exciting it was that Lucky's parents survived the storm. Serenity wasn't the only one having happy thoughts. It amazed Lucky that he and Serenity were the same age. He didn't ogle, but he sure did acknowledge her loveliness. He liked how she wore her thick white hair in a pixie cut, and some strands shimmered like golden sunlight. They matched her golden-colored pants that hugged her long shapely legs. She wore her pants tucked inside a pair of Hunter green boots that came up below her knees. Her shirt was a light golden color. It reached down past her tiny waist to her thighs. A Hunter green satchel rested on her hip. Lucky was happy he and his parents were not the only Southlanders who had survived the Ultra Storm.

After they got Blacky, Serenity led them through the forest. The evening sunset shone through large shading trees. Cool air smelled of sweet Honeysuckle and Mountain Mahogany blossoms. Birds began to calm as they settled in their nests to roost for the coming night. Juneyglow bugs twinkled throughout the forest. Gala's ear caught the trickling of a stream. It forked off into a small pool. Serenity flew over and stood on the stump of an old fallen oak. She asked Gala to hover her sorceress over the water.

"Y'all will like this." Gala and Lucky watched Serenity as she spread her fingers and pointed them toward the ground. Finger-like ferns rose from the rich black soil. They followed Serenity's graceful hand movements. Serenity dipped them into the pool, and as they soaked up water like a sponge, they became plump. Serenity guided the ferns over Idanab's body. She turned one hand forward and the other backward. It was like she was wringing out a rag. When the ferns twisted, water poured out onto Idanab. Mud rinsed off her head all the way down to her oversized boots. The ferns were no longer plump. Satisfied, Serenity wrapped the ferns around her sorceress to soak up the water. They became plumb again. Serenity moved her fingers to unwrap the ferns from around Idanab. Her sorceress was clean and dry. Then Serenity steered the ferns back down to the ground. "I guess that'll do it. Let's git goin'." As Gala and Lucky followed, Serenity explained, "Some members of our tribe can make things smell sweet or sour. Some of us can turn plants into different colors. We all have our own unique abilities. But I'm sure y'all already know this."

"Yes, but this one is new to me. I've never seen a fairy control plants. Have you Lucky?"

"No. This is the first for me." Lucky smiled.

Serenity continued leading the way. They came upon a waterfall centered in the forest. It spewed over a small mountain into a large natural spring. "Your Gentalsteed will be okay here by the spring. He can graze on the Sweetleaf that grows in that area," Serenity pointed.

"This is perfect for him. I know he's hungry and tired." Using his free hand, Gala removed the reins and supply bag. He hung them on a stout tree branch beside the spring. He summoned Blacky's brush. Poof! It appeared in his left hand. After he brushed Blacky's sleek coat, Blacky went straight to the Sweetleaf. Gala transformed into his Bluewing form and put Blacky's brush away.

"What's your Gentalsteed's name?"

"Blacky."

"Fits him. He has a healthy sheen. Looks like he's settled, so let's go inside." Serenity led Gala and Lucky behind the falls through a large entrance into a spacious cavern. It was as beautiful as the Bluewings' cave. Gemstones twinkled throughout, which reminded Lucky and Gala of home. Lucky's eyes popped. Fay-folk flew up to him and Gala. They greeted them with hellos, glad to have ya, hand-shakes, hugs, and pats on their shoulders. Some of them clapped while others whistled, and little ones giggled. Lucky could hardly believe he was among his own clan. He and Gala grinned at each other.

Serenity quieted, "Shh. Okay, quiet down, everyone. We'll join ya after we git Idanab settled." Gala and Lucky followed Serenity toward the back of the cave. Lucky turned back to look at the tribe. They waved at him. Lucky grinned wide, showing his pearly whites, then turned back around. The cave went on for quite some time. They passed several alcoves of different sizes. One had a large table with chairs carved within the mountain. On top of the table were smaller tables and chairs crafted from tree trunks. Finally, they came upon a deep part of the cave. It was a large cavern. It veered off a little to the right. They saw the twins helping Rose, Bud, and Herbal, a healer, finish making a feathered bed for Idanab. Herbal is one of the few remaining elders of their tribe. Her gray hair with thin black streaks surrounded her weathered face. Her black brows and lashes brightened her sparkling brown-green eyes. She wore a dark green apron with many pockets over her dark green dress.

Gala guided Idanab over the large bed. He gently laid her down, then removed his *Levitation* spell while Herbal sat at a table within an alcove. The table held tinctures, healing herbs, and a bowl of the healer's mending mixture, which she had dipped a rag into. Herbal asked, "Rose and Bud, would y'all come help?" They flew over and held tight to the other end of the rag as Herbal twisted hers, wringing it until it was damp. Herbal gestured her head for Rose and Bud to follow. Still holding to their end of the rag, they followed Herbal as she flew over and placed the rag on Idanab's bump. "Thank ya, both."

"Anytime," Rose and Bud said in unison.

Herbal hovered over Idanab's face. She lifted her eyelid and noted, "She's somewhere in the land of LaLa. She ain't got no ability to sip. I'll have to soak my healin' solution in a moss strip and place it around her tongue. This way it'll seep into her body. The first sign I see her tryin' to swallow, I'll see if I can git her to take a sip."

After Herbal finished tending to Idanab, Serenity introduced her to Gala and Lucky.

"A pleasure to meet ya. I hear yo're a Mystique Transfigure, and a powerful one, at that."

Gala sounded modest, "Thank you. I'm doing my best."

"I'm sure you'll git there." Herbal smiled then addressed Lucky, "So Lucky, yore parents are alive and well. This is celebratin' news."

"Ya knew my parents?"

"Yes, I helped 'em enter this realm."

Lucky raised his brows; then, after a short pause, in a high-pitched voice, he asked, "Ya knew all my grandparents?" Lucky cleared his throat.

"Yes. And before ya ask yore next obvious question, I want ya to sit." Lucky took a seat at the other end of the table. Serenity and Gala fluttered down. They stood by Rose, Bud, and the twins. "Yore parents may have spoken of me usin' my real name. I'm yore grandpa's sister on yore father's side."

"Yo're my great Aunt Herbaleen?"

"Yes. Yore father's my nephew. Our bloodlines are all that's left until ya find yore soul mate and have some youngins of yore own."

Gala flew over and put his hand under Lucky's slack jaw, which brought Lucky out of his stupor. Lucky's reddened eyes watered. He asked, "Can I give ya a hug."

Herbal flew up from her seat and fluttered with her arms wide open. Lucky flew into her embrace. Tears rolled down their cheeks. Serenity flew next to Gala, grabbed his hand, and squeezed. Everyone teared up. After Herbal let loose of Lucky, they wiped their smiling faces dry.

"Ya must be tired and hungry, all of ya. Why don't y'all follow Serenity to the kitchen and git a bite to eat? We'll meet in the main hall after yo're done. We'll watch the youngins play their game. After they git to bed, we'll talk more. I wanna discuss our needs and how we can help each other." Herbal gave Lucky another hug before he followed everyone to the kitchen."

Wands

Serenity coached, "Quiet, wee ones. I know yo're excited, but our guests don't know how the game's played. I've asked Rose to explain it to them while I put y'all in pairs. Our guests need to hear what she's sayin', so y'all stay quiet." With plastered smiles on little faces, the children became quiet. Serenity nodded to Rose.

"Ahem," Rose cleared her throat and began. "From time to time, before bedtime, the youngins gather to play a game called *Go Find and Find Again*. There has to be an even number of wee ones to play, but if there ain't, one of the older children will fill that spot. The game leader, usually Serenity, waits until all the children are in line and quiet, then she'll put them in pairs. The main object of the game is to find somethin' worth keepin', remember what it looks like, hide it, then find it again.

"The leader will explain where the children can search, usually within the main hall. When they know their boundaries, the leader will say *Go and Find*. The children take off in search of somethin' they find worth keepin'. After they find their treasure, they'll show it to the game leader. If the leader approves, the child will hang on to it and step back in line. If it ain't approved, which doesn't happen often, the child has to find something else worth keepin'.

"After each child is back in line, the leader will tell them to inspect their object. While examinin' their treasure, they do their best to remember what it looks like. Then, when the leader says *Pass*, the children pass their objects to their partner. At this point, the leader will tell the children to face the cavern wall except for one child of each pair. The leader will tell those children to hide their partner's object. When finished, they git back in line, face the wall, and their partners turn around. The leader instructs them to hide in a different area. Doing this ensures they won't come across their own item while hiding their partner's. After the treasures are all hidden, the children git in line and face the wall alongside their partners.

"The leader tells all the children to *Go Find* their object worth keepin'. After they find it, they step back in line and wait for everyone else to find theirs. This game builds memory skills. Plus, the children git to keep what they find, or they can trade it with their partners. Here is what I found when I played." Rose lifted her hat. Out came a miniature dragon. He fit in the palm of her hand. He had a reddish-orange body and a white patch of hair running along the ridge of his back from the top of his head to the end of his long-feathered tail. His twinkling black eyes were big and round.

"This is my pet. His name is Gekastone, but I call him Geka. When I found him, he just looked like a pretty, little reddish-orange colored gem to me. After my partner, which happened to be Bud, hid my gem and I found it again, I put it in my bed durin' my nap. When I woke up, Serenity and all the members of the tribe were gigglin' and smilin' down at me. Then I felt somethin' on the top of my head. It was my gem or rather Geka. He was fast asleep, and all balled up holdin' on to my hair. I woke him and told him to jump into my hand so I could git a better look at him. He actually understood. He wiggled his whole body, while his tongue was hangin' slightly out of his mouth. His tail moved side to side. He was smilin' at me with his cute big eyes. I kissed his cheek, then I heard him in my head say, 'My name is Gekastone; you are my master.'"

Gala smiled and said, "He's a fine-looking dragon. He is definitely something worth keeping. What does Geka eat?"

"He eats fruits, vegetables, and fish. He can see and hear really well. We're usually always together. Well, guess I'd better go sit down so we can watch the game." Rose put her hat back down over Geka, then sat by Bud.

After Serenity thanked her for explaining the game, she encouraged, "Okay, children, let's play."

Gala and the Newlads enjoyed watching the game. When it was time for the children to find their treasure, one child couldn't find hers. She started to panic, "Where's mine!? I caint find mine!?" Tears welled up in her eyes.

"It's right there," said the young fella who had hidden hers.

"Where? I don't see it!?"

"It's as plain as the twinkle in yore eye and the tear that joins it. Look down where yore tear is 'bout to drop." The young fella pointed towards the ground.

"I see it!" She reached down, picked it up, turned around, hugged her partner, and held her treasure high to show everyone.

The entire tribe, including Gala and the Newlads, cheered. The children showed their parents and tribe members their things worth keeping. When the young Newlad showed Gala his treasure, he said, "I helped my partner find hers. She couldn't see it, but it was under her nose. It even glowed."

"You're a great partner, that's for sure; she's happy, and... it glowed! You gave me a thought. Would you excuse me, their partner?" The wee Newlad nodded. He smiled proud and wide at Gala for calling him a great partner. After the wee Newlad flew to his parents, Gala told the Newlads and Serenity to follow him. Rose, Bud, and Herbaleen went along too.

Gala pulled out his wand. He kept his eyes on Idanab's wand. As he began to chant, his wand turned azure, and so did Idanab's, but only a moment before it turned gray and dimmed out. Gala stopped his spell. He flew closer to get a better look and saw that Idanab's wand was two distinct wands twisted around each other. He began to chant another spell. One wand glowed azure and changed shape. After it dimmed out, it changed back. Then the other wand glowed gray, changed shape, dimmed out, and changed back. "Um," Gala said.

"What is it, Chum?"

"Ddot, look here, come closer, and watch Idanab's wand." They flew in closer. As Gala began to chant, they saw two distinct wands untwist."

"Are ya thinkin' what I'm thinkin'? One of those wands is the same color as yore parents and yores? And it looked like your mother's." Lucky looked at the twins, who agreed.

"I'm glad you guys saw what I saw because I thought I was seeing things. I'm gonna see if they do the same when I use Father's wand." Gala concealed his wand and summoned his father's. Gala's disappeared from his hand, and his father's appeared in its place. When Gala began to chant, his father's wand turned azure, and so did one of the twisted wands in Idanab's hand. "This has got to be a coincidence. That can't be my mother's wand. Serenity, Herbaleen, have you or any tribe member ever seen Idanab use her wand?"

"Actually, that's what I wanted to talk to y'all about. Today was the closest we've ever been to Wizard Tiaff's castle. He always came to see us. We never disturbed him while he was in his castle. Sometimes I went with him to Mermary's Lake. Mermary and I got acquainted. She's the queen of the Water Bbeings. But, after Idanab came 'round, I ain't been back to see Mermary. We've seen Idanab on and off but never seen her use her wand. Wizard Tiaff became friends with Idanab about five or six years ago. He found her and Nam over by Mermary's Lake. The Water Bbeings use ta soothe Wizard Tiaff with their song because he lost his wife and newborn son about sixteen, seventeen years ago—"

"Yes. We heard the story. It's sad." Gala glanced at his friends, who nodded in agreement. "Forgive me for interrupting. Please go on."

"Well, Tiaff told us that Nam was scoutin' and lost his way. He slipped on a rock and broke his leg. The lad couldn't move. By the time his mother found him, he had a fever. About that time, Wizard Tiaff went to visit the Water Bbeings. When Idanab saw him approachin', she asked for his help. Of course, Wizard Tiaff, the good wizard he is, helped them. He brought them up into his castle. Since then, Idanab has visited Tiaff a lot. She's even left Nam in Tiaff's care. Wizard Tiaff seemed happier. We figured it was because Idanab and Nam kinda filled his emptiness. Tiaff introduced us to them once. He told us we were welcome to the castle, and if we ever needed anything, one of them could help us. After some time had passed, Wizard Tiaff stopped goin' to see the Water Bbeings, and here lately, we ain't even seen him. We seldom saw Nam, but sometimes we saw him at the entrance practicing spells. You know that Rose and Bud saw him transform into a green dragon. As he took off towards Mermary's Lake, he knocked Idanab off the outcrop. It was an accident." Serenity took a deep breath and sighed.

"Are ya all right?" Lucky asked as he put his hand on Serenity's shoulder.

"It's just that a lot is goin' on and—"

Herbaleen interjected and finished the story. "And every time that lad, Nam, practiced a spell, we saw mysterious lookin' clouds appear over Tiaff's castle. But they don't stay for long. And that ain't all. Some of our tribe members, includin' Serenity's parents, have gone missin'." Gala and the Newlads gasped. "Yeah! We don't know where they've gone off to. It ain't like any of us to wander off alone, and we're always in before dark. That's why I know there's somethin' not right goin' on, and it started ever since this here sorceress came 'round." Herbaleen glared down at Idanab. "I ain't afraid to say it, but she ain't well-liked by me. And I'm tellin' ya now, I suspect she's gotta lot to do with our members bein' missin'."

"There sure is a lot of that goin' on, loved ones missin' or disappearin'. Whatcha thinkin', Pal?"

"Well, Lucky, I want to see what's going on, why Wizard Tiaff stopped coming around, why that wand looks like my mother's. I want to go up to the castle and check it out. But before I go, and until I know more, I want to be sure Idanab doesn't wake. Herbaleen? Do you have anything that'll keep her sleeping that you can put on her tongue as you did with your healing mixture?"

"Glad ya asked, Gala. When Wizard Tiaff came 'round, he gave me some helpful charms. He even taught me how to whip up different kinds, includin' sleepin' charms and sleepin' creams. The sleepin' charms dissolve on the tongue. I don't want her here, and I don't care for her, not one bit, but at least I can keep her sleepin'. I'll go and fetch the sleepin' cream." It didn't take Herbaleen long to return with a basket of jarred sleeping cream. After she read how much she needed to apply, she rubbed a generous amount on Idanab's temples.

"Pee-ew! That stuff stinks," Lucky complained as he held his nose.

"It is awful to make too. It's made from the secretion of Scarlet Leprechaun Frogs."

"There's Scarlet Leprechaun Frogs around here?" Dahc asked.

"There's lots in these forests. Why do ya ask?" Herbaleen asked while she washed her hands.

"Well, Ddot and I used to scavenge for them back home, but we haven't seen any in a long time."

"Maybe y'all'll get the chance to find some while yo're here." Herbaleen smiled, then tended to Idanab. Everyone else gathered around and discussed what they were going to do next.

"Chum? It's getting dark, and from what we've heard, it could be dangerous going up there."

"Yeah," agreed Dahc.

"Ifin' ya do go, ya ain't goin' alone. But as Ddot said, '...it could be dangerous...;' we need a plan."

"I'm wonderin' where Nam flew off to, how he's doin'. I hope he's all right."

"Me too, Rose. We don't know if he's a Transfigure, a wizard, or what. As Serenity mentioned, we never got to know Nam or his mother. Earlier, when Rose and I saw Nam on the outcrop, he was himself. But then he changed into a green dragon and then back into himself. That's when we saw his mother coming out from behind the green foliage and stood by him. It looked like they were in a disagreement of sorts. Then Nam transformed into a green dragon, spread his wings, and knocked his mother off the side of the cliff. He didn't even look at her, so I don't think he knows what he did. But it sure is odd that Wizard Tiaff never came out to calm them or even see what they were arguin' about."

"Yo're right, Bud. I didn't even think of that," confessed Serenity. "I hope there's nothin' wrong with Wizard Tiaff, and I hope Nam's all right. Nam

could be hidin' in a mountain cavern above Mermary's lake until he calms down. Young folk do that sometimes. Ya know, hide when they git mad. And they always come back home ifin' they don't run into any kinda danger or lose their way."
Serenity put her hands on her cheeks and said, "Pixie limits! What are we to do?"

"I could go look for Nam before I go to Wizard Tiaff's castle," offered Gala.

"Yeah, and I'm going with you, Chum," offered Ddot.

"Me too," added Dahc.

"Ya ain't goin' without me," Lucky interjected.

"I can wake the warriors to go with ya?"

Gala thanked, "Thank you, Herbaleen, but we'll be all right. Which way to Mermary's Lake?"

Serenity explained, "Her lake ain't far. It's northeast of here and north of Wizard Tiaff's castle. I'll lead ya to the path Wizard Tiaff always took to visit the Water Bbeings."

"Okay. Thanks, Serenity."

"Yo're welcome. We're thankful to all y'all too, Gala. But, goin' to Mermary's lake under the moonlight is awfully dangerous. Maybe ya have a spell or know of a way ta hide us from the Night Owls. They're usually out about this time."

Gala tried to summon some charms. He checked his pockets and came up empty-handed. "Wizard-bummer. I wish I had some *Char pro ect* Charms. Those charms make you invisible for about an hour; they take too long to make. I'll just transfigure into my wizard form. You and Lucky can hide on my head under my cloak's hood. Ddot and Dahc, you can sit on my shoulders. You'll have protection from my hair and the lower part of my hood. Should we ride Blacky?"

"No. Yore Gentalsteed is safer where he's at. Besides, the lake ain't far. But Gala, in case the Water Bbeings see ya and think yo're a threat, yo're gonna have to keep a distance from the water."

"I know. But what'll happen if I walk far away from the lake?"

"If they see ya, they could sing their confusin' songs. That'll draw ya close so they can snatch ya under. I'll make ya some earplugs so ya don't hear them. But ifin' I could talk to Mermary, they won't bother ya. The problem is that she doesn't always come to the surface. And Gala, ifin' we find Nam, and he's a fire-breathin' dragon, what'll ya do then?"

"Don't worry, Serenity. I can transform into my Redtalon dragon. He's the biggest dragon that's ever lived. But if there isn't any room for me to transform into him, I'll just transform into parts of him. As for the Water Bbeings, I'll keep my distance and use the earplugs you suggested."

"I'll git my huntin' gear and make ya some earplugs. Rose and Bud, y'all follow me, and let's make sure everyone gits to bed before we leave."

"I'll wait up until y'all git back," offered Herbaleen. "If y'all ain't back in two hours, I'll alert our warriors to come lookin' for ya."

Water Bbeings

It didn't take long before they saw Mermary's Lake. A thick forest surrounded the lake. Cascading waterfalls spewed out from some of the mountains. The light from three crescent moons sparkled across the water's surface. Juneyglow bugs twinkled throughout the forest. Gala took out one earplug to listen. The orchestra of Scrub Chirpers 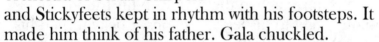 and Stickyfeets kept in rhythm with his footsteps. It made him think of his father. Gala chuckled.

Ddot tapped Gala's ear. After Gala took out his other earplug, in a quiet voice, Ddot asked, "What's the humor, Chum? Fill us in."

"I was just thinking about my father while listening to the night. I think it's funny how he likes to give things another name. Father likes to call Scrub Chirpers, 'Crickets' and Stickyfeets, 'Tree Frogs.' I guess I'm just missing him."

"I'm missing everyone too, Chum," Ddot sighed.

"I'm missin' 'em too, pal," Lucky patted Gala's head.

"Yeah, I am, too," added Dahc.

"Look there," Gala whispered as he pointed towards a cave with an ember of light shining from within.

"That cave ain't got no water comin' outa it. Looks like a fire's burnin' the way that light's jigglin' 'round. That's probably Nam," Serenity guessed.

"There's only one way to find out, and that's to go up there and see for ourselves. Night Owls won't bother my Nix. You guys can hide underneath and hold on to my legs or talons while I fly up to the mouth of the cave's opening."

Serenity and the Newlads flew off Gala. He transformed into Nix, and although the ugly faces flashed through his mind, he didn't shake his head. Ddot noted it and smiled. He knew that his Chum was conquering his fears.

Nix approached the cave with his friends holding tight to his leg and talons. Lucky turned his ear. "Do y'all hear that? Listen."

Serenity and the twins turned their heads to focus on what Lucky was hearing.

"Yeah. I can hear it," replied Ddot.

"Me too," added Dahc.

"Gala!" Serenity whispered loud enough for him to hear her. "Do ya hear anythin'?"

"Yeah. It sounds like a mixture of growls with low tonal moans and singing. It sounds like a dragon."

After Nix landed, his friends flew over to one side so he could transform into himself.

"It sounds like the moans of somethin' big." Serenity raised her brows.

"If it's Nam, he sounds sad." There's no room for me to transform into Redtalon. Maybe that's a good thing because Nam's bones would jump out of his skin if he saw my Redtalon. I'll go in as myself.

You guys stay here and hide in that flowery bush on the right of the cave. It should hide you from Night Owls. Also, if the dragon spits fire, you won't get burned. I'll introduce myself and tell Nam y'all are with Serenity outside the cave. If he listens and accepts our help, I'll call you guys to come in."

Gala's friends watched him as he went deeper into the cave. He gave them one last look before he slipped around a corner. The cave was separated into two tunnels. The moans resonated throughout both. Gala would not have determined which tunnel to take if he didn't see the flicker of light within the right tunnel. As he crept closer, the moans became louder, and the tunnel got warmer.

"I can hear you and smell you," said a curt, wispy low voice. "Who are you? What do you want?"

Gala turned the corner and saw a green dragon about ten feet long lying on a flaming chafe. The dragon held an urn with an inscription that Gala couldn't make out. Gala answered, "My name is Gala. I'm a wizard. My friends and I are looking for my parents."

While Gala acquainted himself with Nam, his friends gazed at Water Bbeings. But the Water Bbeings weren't the only ones being watched. Perched in a tree at the top of the cave, out for his evening hunt, a Night Owl watched. His black feathered ears looked like long skinny horns sticking out from the top of his cone-shaped head. His bright yellow eyes glowed as they fixed on dinner, Dahc. And Dahc, with his fascinated friends, were oblivious to the predator above them.

Pollen filled Dahc's nostrils, which caused an unbearable tickle. He rubbed and squeezed his nose, trying not to sneeze or scare the Water Bbeings. The Night Owl dove straight toward him as Dahc lost the battle with his nose, "ACHOO!" Dahc fell forward when he sneezed, and SWOOSH, six talons clenched nothing but air. Serenity and the Newlads bolted out from the bush. They raced through the forest along the edge of the lake.

The Water Bbeings dove down into the depths, except for Mermary. She swam two feet beneath the water, then up behind an outcrop of rocks. The rocks expanded five feet above the water's surface and down two hundred feet to the lake's floor. Mermary saw the Night Owl swoop up into the sky and circle around before it bombed back down towards Dahc.

Dahc was behind Ddot, who had taken the lead. Serenity followed behind Dahc, and Lucky was behind Serenity. The owl screeched. Lucky yelled, "DIVE!" Ddot and Dahc laid their wings flat, tucked in their chins, and pointed their heads toward the ground. They dropped like an anchor down into the brush, evading their assailant by a fraction of a second. SWOOSH! The owl's claws clasped shut. He swooped into the sky and released the debris from his grasp. Serenity looked up to see where the owl had flown. Lucky shouted, "Serenity! Watch where yo're goin'! NO!"

Serenity flew smack dab into a spider's web along with the twigs the owl had dropped! "Aiyee!!" Serenity screamed. Her body and the debris had made a hole in the web, but four of Serenity's wings got stuck, which caused her to dangle. As a red paralytic spider raced towards her, she panicked. Instead of reaching for her blade, she reached up to remove the web with her hands, and now her hands were stuck. Serenity struggled to free herself, but the more she did, the more she became entangled.

Lucky's eyes dilated. He calculated his target. With swift tactical precision, he threw his dagger. It spun through the air as the spider stretched out to grab Serenity. But Lucky's razor-sharp blade sliced through its silk-steel web. Serenity fell. Lickity-split, with a flap and a flip, Lucky sheathed his blade, and Serenity dropped into his arms.

When they could no longer see the owl, the twins flew out of the brush. They raced to aid Lucky and Serenity. Ddot gave out a couple of short sharp whistles. Lucky returned the whistles. The twins followed Lucky's whistle to the bank of Mermary's Lake. "We'll keep a watch while you set Serenity down," offered Ddot.

Lucky gently laid Serenity under a water shrub growing on the bank. The Night Owl had given up and flown out into the night. About that time, Mermary swam beneath the water's surface over to the edge of the bank. Then, without wanting to scare everyone, she peeked her head out of the water. The twins pointed their arrows while Lucky lifted Serenity back up, but then Serenity said, "It's okay, y'all. Remember, she won't hurt us. That's Mermary." Lucky put Serenity back down, and the twins lowered their bows.

Mermary pulled herself up on the bank and clenched her webbed hand. When she opened it, a clear secretion settled in her palm. Mermary tipped her hand, allowing the secretion to pour over Serenity's hands and wings. Like magic, the web dissolved into bits of dust particles and disappeared. Serenity stood up. She flapped her wings, bowed in reverence to Mermary, and thanked, "Sheanaka."

Mermary gave Serenity a nod with a smile and replied, "Sheanooka." Then she asked, "Sheis-ar shez shos?"

As Serenity introduced, "Her friends," she pointed her palm towards each Newlad. Then pointed her palm towards the cave where Gala entered. She said, "Wizard Gala sheis-a sho nas sheis sheookin-or Nam sheis-a sheena dragon."

"What'd y'all just say?" Lucky asked.

"First, I thanked Mermary by saying Sheanaka, which means thank you. Mermary replied, 'Sheanooka,' which means yo're welcome. Then she asked, 'Who are your friends?' or in her tongue, 'Sheis-ar,' (who are), 'shez,' (yore), and 'shos,' (friends). I finally told her that Wizard Gala is a—"

"Friend," Mermary interrupted and smiled.

"Oh! You speak our language?"

"Yes," Mermary told Ddot. The Newlads smiled and became quiet with their thoughts.

Mermary almost matched Celtrek's descriptions to a T. Lucky thought Mermary favored Gala's mother. She had rosy cheeks, thin shapely lips, and long blonde hair, but her eyes were emerald green like the twins. Her upper body was like any female he and the twins ever saw. But, from Mermary's hips downwards, she looked nothing like any female they'd ever seen. She had a dragon tail with scales that matched the color of her eyes and an emerald gossamer fin.

Dahc broke everyone's muses. "We need to check on Gala, get back up to the flowering bush in case Gala comes looking for us. Or do y'all think we should stay here with Mermary where we're safe?"

BOOM! They jolted, then turned towards the sound of the blast.

"NO!" Ddot yelled. He took off. Dahc followed.

Lucky looked back and forth between Mermary and Serenity and said, "Serenity, you stay here with Mermary. We'll be back!"

Serenity grabbed his hand before he could fly off. Their eyes locked, "Y'all be careful, Lucky."

A glistening sunburst of brownish-orange eyes connected deep into Lucky's heart. Both Serenity and Lucky felt their hearts thump in perfect rhythm. Their soul mate consciousness hit them like a mountain of diamonds. They knew they'd be together for the rest of their lives.

"We'll be careful." Lucky embraced Serenity. "I'll be back before ya know it." Lucky gently pulled away. He nodded, then raced to catch up with the twins.

"Gala! Chum! Where are you!?!" Ddot darted up, down, around, and under rubble but didn't see his chum anywhere.

"Over here!" Dahc yelled. Ddot and Lucky flew down to the cave beneath the one Gala entered. Dahc was pointing at what looked like a fist sticking out from under a pile of granular rubble.

"Gurr!" A voice sounded out, but it wasn't Gala's.

Whoever it was began to cough and stir. He lifted himself up into a sitting position, and some of the sandy rock fell off his body. The Newlads could see it was a fella about sixteen years of age. But they couldn't make out his facial features due to the chalky gray residue sticking all over him. The lad hugged an urn in one arm and had something clenched in his other, which began to vibrate, so he dropped it. It bounced off the side of the mountain onto a crag right below the water's surface behind a waterfall. The Newlads flew down to the outside of the falls and hovered.

"It's a ruby!" Exclaimed Ddot.

The ruby flickered with a red and gold light. Finally, it shone steady golden bright, and made a loud, "ZAP! SNAP! POOF!"

"GALA!" The Newlads yelled in unison.

"Guys! Did you see the dragon? Did he fly off? Where's Serenity? Did the mountain blow up?"

"No, we didn't see a dragon. We saw a young lad at about sixteen or seventeen years old. He was under the rubble holding you, or you as your red ruby," Ddot corrected.

"And yes, the cave you were in blew up," added Dahc.

"We would have blown up with it ifin' it wasn't for that Night Owl chasing Dahc. And Serenity's fine. She's with Mermary over there..." Lucky pointed "...on the side of the bank."

"Thank the giver of life and love that none of us got hurt. Is the boy all right?"

"He's covered in gray and blue residue but seems okay. He's hugging an urn," Dahc answered. "Let's go see him."

As soon as Gala transformed into his Bluewing form, bits of rubble fell from where the lad was sitting. Gala and the Newlads looked up. The green dragon flew off the mountain eastward above The Ridge.

"Was that Nam?" Ddot asked.

"Well, I think the lad was the dragon. When I first saw the dragon, he hugged an urn in one arm. He told me he could hear me, so, in a calm tone, I told him who I was, who you guys were, and that Serenity was with us. He asked what I wanted; I told him we wanted to help him. But he insisted there was nothing anyone could do. Then he said, 'It's all a lie. I've been living a lie.' When I asked if his name was Nam, he got mad, and I mean infuriating mad. He scratched his claws as hard as he could against the cave and told me, 'I'm not NAM! And if you don't leave me alone, I'll crush you with my new claws.'"

"New claws?" Quizzed Ddot.

"Crush you?" Asked Dahc.

Lucky interjected, "And ya were only tryin' to help the lad. My guess there's a lot of hurtin' goin' on inside of 'em. So, Pal, what do ya suppose he meant by his 'new claws,' and what happened after he said he'd crush ya?"

"Well, I figured he had just learned to transform into a dragon. That's why he said 'new claws.' When he said he would crush me, he turned towards me. I saw it in his eyes; he was about to grab me. He didn't even give me a chance to leave. There was only one thing I could do that might stop his grip from crushing me. That was to transform into my red ruby. When he went for me, and I started to transfigure, I saw his spiked tail hit the magnesium vein within the cave's wall. It caused a gigantic bright-white spark. I didn't see anything after that."

Ddot interjected, "So, the dragon and the lad are one and the same. He's a young wizard, maybe a Mystique Transfigure or a Mystique Blueblood. That blue residue could have been blood. From the looks of the rubble, I'm almost certain he had cuts and scratches. We couldn't see them due to the rubble."

"And Gala, because the lad told you he lived a lie, and his name wasn't Nam, I'm more curious. I want to know what's happening in Wizard Tiaff's castle, like right now."

"Me too, Dahc. I'm thinkin' my aunt Herbaleen's suspicions of Idanab are correct. We oughta wake up that ole witch and ask her some questions."

"LUCKY!" Serenity yelled. She flew next to Mermary as Mermary and other Water Bbeings swam towards Lucky.

"Serenity! What's wrong?" Lucky flew over to greet her.

"Water Bbeings are trapped inside an underwater cavern! Gala? Can you help? This is Mermary, queen of the Water Bbeings. She speaks our language."

Gala nodded at Mermary and offered, "I'll do my best. The cavern must have collapsed from the blast. I'll transform into parts of my Redtalon." Gala stood on the crag behind the waterfall. He closed his eyes and thought about the parts he needed. He began visualizing his Redtalon's eyes, gills, and webbed claws. His transformation was fast. This time his friends didn't poke at him for looking like a swamp creature. "You guys stay behind this waterfall until I get back."

Speaking in her own tongue, Mermary instructed one of her subjects to sit with the fairies. Serenity translated so the Newlads would understand. "Shash, you stay here and watch over the fairies." Shash pulled himself up on the crag and sat behind the waterfall with Serenity and the Newlads. Gala dove into the water and followed Mermary and the other Water Bbeings.

They swam through tall, swaying water grasses. Colorful fish swam throughout. After they swam through the grass, Gala's eyes widened at the site of an underground city of caverns. Carved within the caves were articulate designs depicting the Water Bbeings' history. Mermary swam into a cavern beside the one blocked by rubble. She swam all the way around, then came out on the other side through another cavern.

"There's no way out except through here where the rocks are piled." Mermary's voice sounded deeper below the water. She pointed and shouted, "Gala, look! Bubbles are coming out from this tiny hole."

Gala told Mermary to tell everyone to stay clear so nothing falls on them while he removes rocks. When she did, she heard voices telling her they had moved. The bubbles stopped coming out from behind the rocks. After Mermary told Gala to go on, he summoned his wand, "*Com'ere.*" It appeared in his webbed hand like a glimmering spark of golden light. He pointed his wand at the top layer of rubble and tried his *Removal* spell first. No sooner than he said, "*Subtracto,*" a stone shot straight into his torso. The force sent him backward until he smacked into the wall of another cavern behind him. Mermary swam towards him. "I'm all right," he said. "Guess I'd better cast a different spell." They swam back to the blocked cavern. Gala played it safe and cast his *Levitation* spell, "*Elevor Eeup.*" Gala's wand turned azure. Its golden light shot out and encompassed the top row of rocks. He gently pulled his wand back towards himself. The rocks followed his movement, which in turn caused other rocks to fall. The Water Bbeings were free. No one got injured. The Water Bbeings hugged each other and Gala.

"It's okay; you're welcome. I'm glad everyone's all right. Mermary? Is it okay to go inside to see if the cavern is safe?"

"Yes."

After they inspected and found the cavern sound, the Water Bbeings, and Gala swam to the surface. Gala pulled himself up onto the crag. He transformed into his Bluewing form and spun dry before he transfigured into himself and thanked Shash for watching over his friends. Shash said you're welcome in Water Bbeing language, then dove into the lake.

"Thank ya again, Mermary. I don't know how I would've gotten that sticky web off," Serenity thanked.

"Take some with you." Mermary cupped her hand.

"What?" Gala's eyes popped wide.

"Yeah," Ddot said, "It works like magic, Chum. When the Night Owl chased us, Serenity flew smack dab into a spider's web. Lucky got her out with the impeccable aim of his dagger. Mermary poured her body's protective secretion over Serenity's hands and wings. That web dissolved into nothing. I'm telling you, it literally dissolved into nothing."

"Here. You can use my vile until we can put it in something else," Dahc offered.

As Mermary poured her secretion into the vile, Serenity expressed, "I hope Nam, or whatever his name is, finds a safe place to sleep and doesn't hurt anyone or himself."

"Too bad we didn't have a chance to calm him with our wing's essence. I wish we could look for him," Dahc added.

"Me too. But we can't go looking tonight. What do you think, Chum? Think we could look for him tomorrow morning?"

"I'm not sure, Ddot. We need to sleep on it. But, as Serenity said, he might go back to the castle.

I want to know who, or what, the lad had in the urn. And I want to know what he meant when he said he lived a lie. I hope we get a chance to ask him. Well, guess we better get going. Herbaleen's probably worried. I'm sure she heard the explosion."

After saying good night to the Water Bbeings, Gala transformed into his Nix. His friends held tight to his legs as he flew them home. Herbaleen was waiting for them at the entrance and was happy when she saw them return.

"We heard the blast, but I suggested we wait before the warriors went lookin' for ya. Thank the giver of life and love yore all safe. And I sure am thrilled to learn about you two, Lucky and Serenity." Herbal hugged them and continued, "We'll celebrate yore soul mate joinin' when this is over. Let's git some shut-eye; tomorrow's gonna be a big day. I'll sleep here with Idanab while Serenity shows y'all to yore sleepin' crevice." Herbaleen hugged everyone and wished them goodnight.

Serenity showed Gala and the Newlads their sleeping quarters and said, "We'll make plans during breakfast on how we'll approach Tiaff's castle and if we ought a look for the lad. Y'all must be exhausted. I know I am. Get a good night's sleep."

"You too, Serenity." Gala shook her hand.

"See you in the morning; sleep well," Ddot wished and shook her hand.

"Yeah. Thank you, and I wish you sweet dreams," added Dahc as he patted her on the shoulder.

Lucky followed Serenity into the main hall. He cupped her shoulders, gazed into her dreamy sunset eyes, and said, "Love Charm, when this is over, we'll have a proper soul mate joinin' and find a way to bring the clans together to celebrate." Lucky pulled Serenity to his chest, and they kissed. After the tender kiss, Lucky wished, "Good night, my sweet breath of sunshine. I'll see ya bright and early, which doesn't come soon anuff."

Serenity wrapped her arms around Lucky, hugging him tight, then pulled back and gazed into his romantic dark-chocolate eyes. She brushed her fingers across his chiseled jawline and said, "I'll hold ya in my dreams, my magnetic love charm." With that, Lucky watched Serenity fly to her sleeping crevice. Before going inside, she blew him a sweet kiss. He blew one back, then they went inside their sleeping crevices.

Gala and the Newlads ate a piece of root they got from Dragon Mountain With-eyes-that-see. Then Gala sat on his feather bed and summoned his father's crystal ball. He looked in on the Bluewing clan first. "Everyone's sleeping," he said. "I'm going to look in on Nam, then Helsin." After Gala asked the crystal to show him Nam, it did nothing. "I guess I need to ask to see the green dragon or the lad that thought his name was Nam." When Gala asked, the crystal revealed a green dragon flying, looking toward the ground. "It looks like he's searching for a place to sleep. It's hard to tell."

"I'm guessing that he is. He's probably looking for a tunnel or a cave where he feels safe."

"I suppose you're right, Ddot. Guess I'll see what ole Helsin's up to." After seeing that Helsin was sleeping, Gala asked the crystal, "*Show me Floreena and Lidee.*" Purple fog filled the inside, then after it dissipated, Floreena appeared, but not for long because the crystal suddenly filled with fog. After it dissipated, Lidee appeared. But briefly, because fog filled the crystal again. It went back and forth, showing glimpses of Floreena and Lidee. Gala yelled, "Crystal blunders! Wait a blasted magic second. *Show me, my soul mate.*" The crystal filled with purple fog. After it dissipated, he saw Floreena illuminated by moonlight. She was shackled and sleeping on a stone floor covered with dirt and straw. Lidee wasn't beside her. Gala gasped. His brows creased as he looked at his friends, who shrugged. Gala looked back at the crystal and asked it to show him Lidee. Purple fog filled the crystal, dissipated, and revealed Lidee in shackles sleeping on a strange-looking table. Gala surmised, "So that's why the crystal did what it did. It went back and forth because they weren't near each other like before. Why is Lidee on that strange-looking table? What is going on?"

"Hurry, Chum! Ask the crystal to show you your parents. I mean, ask to see one at a time just in case they aren't together," Ddot suggested.

"The Newlads nodded, then Gala demanded, "*Show me, my mother.*" Purple fog filled the crystal. After it dissipated, they saw Faithin illuminated by moonlight. She was still shackled. And like Floreena, she was also sleeping on a stone floor covered with dirt and straw. "Father's not near her. *Show me, my father.*" Purple fog filled the crystal covering Faithin. As it dissipated, an unrecognizable figure appeared. It flickered in and out from a shadow to a bright light. "What's this!?! I gotta go to that castle tonight!"

"I'm going with you," Ddot insisted.

"Me too," added Dahc.

"Y'all ain't goin' nowheres without me, but we have to be quiet so we don't wake the tribe. I'll let Serenity know before we go. Maybe we ought a tell Aunt Herbaleen too."

"Good idea. We'll make plans when you get back. Maybe Serenity or your aunt knows another way inside besides the main entrance." Gala told the crystal ball to sleep, then concealed it.

"Yeah, Chum. A castle usually has two doors. And maybe there's a secret passage."

"You read my mind, Ddot. Okay, Lucky. Ask Serenity and your aunt to meet us here."

"Will do, Pal." Lucky nodded at his friends, then ZOOMED out the sleeping crevice before they could blink. Gala and the twins laughed, knowing Lucky couldn't wait to see Serenity.

It didn't take long for Lucky to return with Serenity and Herbaleen. While they began making plans, Helsin woke from his nap and was making his own plans. He was preparing to travel back to Wizard Tiaff's castle.

Helsin's Discovery

Helsin stretched and made his bed. He looked in on his Uncle Dec, covered his ears, and thought, "I can't believe I slept through this. He's got to be snoring to the furthest galaxies." Helsin cracked his uncle's door and went back to his room. He put on his cloak, then took out the bottle of Shadow potion his Aunt Idanab gave him that morning. "Two tablespoons ought to get me to Wizard Tiaff's castle. Aunt Ida said the Gobs excavated a tunnel on the swamp side of The Ridge. Think I'll sneak in the castle through there."

 Helsin drank two tablespoons of the potion. After his body materialized into a **Shadow**, he shot upwards. He leaned forward, almost horizontally, above the treetops. As he sped, with determined speed, his cloak, clothes, and hair flapped through the cool night air.

 Helsin glided down to the swamp's bank on the cliff side of The Ridge. The sandy ground beneath his feet was wet and soft, not mucky as he expected like other parts of the swamp. Helsin jolted. He heard swamp water smack against something. He turned and saw the outline of an empty raft hidden within tall saw grasses and cattails. Helsin hurried inside the dark tunnel. After he stepped inside, the Shadow potion wore off.

 Helsin summoned his wand and whispered, "*Light.*" The tip lit up like a burning torch. Wet walls twinkled from its light. Crawling bugs scurried throughout, and worms burrowed into deep holes. Dangling roots housed black spiders, ready to pounce on unsuspecting prey. Helsin shuddered.

He followed the tunnel's zig-zag incline up to an excavated stone wall. It led into the oldest and deepest dungeon of Wizard Tiaff's castle. It was a forgotten dungeon. Sealed off centuries ago but now exhumed or dis-entombed. A stale, musty stench emitted straight up Helsin's nostrils. "YUCK!" He commanded a kerchief to block the smell. It floated out of his pant pocket and tied around his head, covering his nose and mouth.

    Helsin tip-toed over the threshold and peered through iron bars to a cell on his right. He jumped; his eyes popped. A skeleton was leaning against the wall in a sitting position. In front of it sat an empty silver plate, tarnished with time. Enormous rats scurried across the damp floor. Cobwebs hung from the high ceiling, the wet walls, and the iron bars. As soon as Helsin regained his courage and breath, he peered into the rest of the cells. Nothing was living except for more rats, spiders, and creepy crawling bugs with lots of legs, lots of eyes, or both.

    There was a narrow flight of spiral stone stairs at the other end of the dungeon. Helsin tip-toed up the stairs, peeking around its center granite wall. At the top of the stairs, he stepped over the rubble that once blocked the entrance to the old dungeon. After stepping over the remnants of the wall, he stepped into another dungeon. Unlike the musty dungeon he walked through, this dungeon had fresher air. It had high windows which allowed moonlight or the sun to shine through. He commanded his kerchief to return to his pocket and stopped the light of his wand.

Helsin stiffened to the sound of someone breathing. Their breaths were steady as when sleeping. He followed the sound to the second cell on his right. Its breath was quick. Light from a crescent moon shone on a small figure wrapped in blankets and sleeping in a makeshift cradle. "It's a wee Treeager baby! What is my aunt doing with him!?!" Helsin yelled in his head. He heard another breath coming from the cell right across from the baby. His eyes glimpsed the twinkling of gems as the moonlight shone on a tiara. "Floreena!" His voice echoed. He ran back to the staircase and hid behind the wall to listen for anyone coming who may have heard him. He peeked around the wall and waited.

An ember of light flickered against the walls of the staircase that led down to the dungeon's entrance. Helsin saw large shadows cast against the stairwell wall. "Gobs!" He thought. Their grunting got louder as they got closer. He grimaced, then ducked his head behind the wall. His heart quickened. The clinking of keys echoed. A loud CLANK-CLANK came from the unlocking of locks. The squeaking of heavy iron doors rang throughout, followed by the unlocking of shackles. A Gob snarled a command, "You carry tree babe. I carry other." Helsin shuddered. He waited until it was quiet before he peeked back around the wall.

The Gobs were gone. Helsin crept up to the open cells and yelled in his mind, "Floreena! The babe! They're gone!" He could hardly contain his rage. He headed to the stairs but stopped. Someone else was breathing. As clouds covered the light from the moons, the dungeon turned pitch black, so Helsin told his wand to light. "Faithin!" His stomach knotted; his heart ached. Over the past year, Helsin became jealous of Gala and figured Gala didn't deserve Floreena. But he liked the Lakinshires. Helsin thought his aunt was treating them with respect and dignity. He thought she had them sleeping in beds with a fire to keep them warm. But instead, he finds them lying in a filthy dungeon amongst rat excretions. His face turned red. Mortified and outraged, he was to the point of vengeance.

Helsin stopped his torch and pointed his wand into the lock. Blue, red, and white-hot light shot out and crackled as it melted the lock. He opened the door and rushed in. Helsin used a *Fetter* spell to release the heavy shackles from around Faithin's reddened wrists and ankles, then he picked her up. She was ice cold. He carried her up the staircase. When he reached the top, he came to a corridor with three doors on his left and a decorative wall on his right. The first door led into a bedroom, the second was a storage room, and the third was Wizard Tiaff's laboratory. Past the laboratory was the castle's great hall, which two other passageways and the castle's front entrance extended from.

Helsin entered the bedroom, then laid Faithin on the bed. He didn't risk lighting a fire, so he covered her with a wool blanket. He hoped the Gobs wouldn't find her and slip her a sleeping charm or potion. He gave Faithin one last look. Under his breath he apologized, "I'm sorry."

Helsin peeked out the bedroom door. He couldn't hear or see anyone, so he carefully shut the door behind him. He followed the light that burned at the other end of the passageway. As he crept closer, he could see the great hall where he had walked through that morning. It was lit by a grand candled chandelier. "Gurr, gr, Gur." The grunting voices of Gobs echoed through the corridor. The Gobs were in Wizard Tiaff's laboratory at the mouth of the passageway. Helsin hurried. He slipped inside a dark storage room that butted next to the lab. Helsin gently shut the door and waited for his eyes to adjust. Light emitted through the cracks of a two-way door that adjoined the two rooms. Helsin headed across the room towards the two-way door. He was careful not to knock anything off the tables or shelves along the way.

He peeked between the cracks, then jerked his head back as a Gob walked past. After his heart slowed and he caught his breath, Helsin pushed the door open enough to see better. He saw parcel parts of a Gob holding Floreena's mother, then POOF! They vanished. Helsin waited and listened, then POOF! The Gob returned empty handed and grunted, "Give him." A smaller Gob was gentle when he passed the Treeager babe into the larger Gob's arms. The larger Gob ordered, "Go. Guard castle front door."

The smaller Gob snarled, "Me yum-yum."

"Yum-yum when Witch Ida done. Go!" growled the larger Gob. The smaller Gob squinted. His eyes set in beneath his bulging forehead and his creased bushy brows. He wrinkled his big bumpy nose and ran his puke-green, scabby forearm across his mouth. He grudgingly trudged out of the lab. Then POOF! The larger Gob and the babe vanished.

Helsin pushed the door open a little more. He saw the frame he had brought to his aunt that morning. It held the picture of strange beds and machines that the Gobs stole from Conkay's laboratory two nights prior. A scuffling of footsteps came towards the two-way door. Helsin hurried and ducked under a table. The door opened. He peeked out from underneath the table and saw a **Shadow** enter the room. The **Shadow** held a candle in one hand and a box in the other. The **Shadow** glided upwards and placed the box on a top shelf next to a cage covered with a thick purple cloth.

Helsin saw a jar filled with tiny Scarlet Leprechaun Frogs, two shelves below the top shelf. Beside it were empty bottles like the one his aunt had given him that morning. Helsin held his breath as he watched the **Shadow** rummage through the empty bottles, then curse. "Wretched witch! No more potion. She told me she had another bottle! I'll have to get my bottle from home." The voice was an unfamiliar witch's voice. She glided back into the lab and commanded, "Gorg! Come with me. I have to get to the swamp before this potion wears off."

Helsin stood up and listened through the cracks of the two-way door. He heard the trudging footsteps of a Gob fade away. He didn't hear anything else, so he slowly opened the door. A large fire burned within a hefty fireplace. He scanned the left side of the lab and saw the picture and frame leaning against a wall. Then he looked to the right. His eyes glanced across candlelit workbenches where his aunt created Spyraven. Perched in the corner, at the end of one work table, he saw Spyraven. When Helsin scanned further to the right, his mind yelled, "Floreena!" She was lying on one of the three stone tables that Idanab and a Gob had washed that morning. There were strange looking tubes lying on Floreena's stomach. Someone rolled up the right sleeve of her blue gown; her elbow pit was facing upwards. As Helsin rushed in and picked Floreena up from the table, the strange tubes fell to the floor. He carried her through the storage room, then out the other door back down the corridor and tiptoed past the room where he had put Faithin.

"Helsin? Is that you?"

Helsin came to a dead halt. He turned and yelled, "Faithin!" Faithin held a candle up in front of her.

"Where am I, Helsin? What's going on? I'm dizzy and confused?"

"I'll explain later. We need to get out of here. Snuff the candle and follow me."

"Is that Floreena?"

"Yes. Please, Faithin, I'll explain when we're somewhere safe away from this castle."

"First, you answer me. Where are we?"

"We're in Wizard Tiaff's castle."

"I know of him. Helsin, I heard a Swamp Gob talking to someone. They passed this room just before you came along. Do you know why Gobs are here, what they're doing, where they're going? And what are you doing with Floreena? Is she all right? Why are we here!?!" Faithin's head started to clear. She furrowed her brows and narrowed her eyes, which frightened Helsin. He knew her wrath was something no one who knew her wished to reckon with.

Helsin stuttered, "F-Floreena is fine. S-she's sleeping. I-I need to lie her down. She's getting heavy."

"Come inside. Lay Floreena on that bed. I'll shut the door and lock it."

After he laid Floreena down, he turned to face Faithin and respectfully hung his head. "I'm sorry, Faithin. My aunt said she wasn't going to hurt any of you—"

"Any of us!?!" Faithin interrupted. "Where's my son!?!"

"I-I'm not sure where he is, but I-I know he was out looking for you guys."

"Who? Me and Floreena?" Faithin's brows creased tighter.

"Y-yes, ma'am. A-as well a-as your husband a-and Floreena's mother."

"Where are they!?!"

"I-I think they're both still here. I-I don't know."

"Why don't you tell me what you do know. Sit." Faithin gestured her hand towards one of the armed chairs in front of the cold hearth. After Helsin sat, Faithin sat in the chair across from him and set the candle on the table between them.

Helsin leaned forward and placed his forearms on his lap. His head was still bent, looking down at the floor. Tears dripped off his nose and cheeks onto his arms and lap. He told Faithin everything he knew, except when he followed Sparktinian. He didn't want to tell her how he knocked Spark around. He felt bad enough as it was. "I'm sor-sorry, Faithin."

"It sounds like your aunt was teaching you Dark Magic. Many have dabbled with it. Most who do become wicked, irritable, negative, hateful; the list goes on. Their actions are illogical, unconscious, and deadly. Your aunt lied to you about our blood! And, she was wrong about the paths leading to The Wizards' High Council. Many will travel those paths to get to other villages. Let's hope those two Kelvor Elves don't run into danger before the spells you cast on them break. There's nothing we can do for them right now. You know the consequences if you cast spells on others without their permission. You know it's wrong to cast spells for malicious purposes. You can cast spells without permission only for defense, healing, or wholesome purposes! Do I make myself clear?"

Helsin shuddered. "Yes, ma'am. I won't do it again."

"Good. We'll look for the Kelvor Elves as soon as we can."

"Yes, ma'am." Helsin wiped the tears from his face. He looked up at Faithin and saw that her face wasn't as angry as before, but her brows were still creased. He told her, "We're not safe here. We should get out of this castle."

"Not until I look around first. I gather your aunt was going to practice her procedure on Floreena. She probably gave her enough sleeping potion to kill a five-ton dragon." Helsin's eyes popped wide. "That's figurative speaking, Helsin. I'm sure Floreena won't be waking any time soon. You're coming with me after you light a fire. I'll grab the key and lock the door behind us. Can you light your wand if we need it?"

"Yes, ma'am."

"Good. Now make a fire." Helsin lit the fireplace and kissed Floreena on her forehead. Faithin snuffed out the candle.

Helsin hurried with caution as he led Faithin to the storage room. After their eyes adjusted, they walked over to the two-way door. Faithin peeked through. The first thing she saw was, Conkay's picture in Gala's magical frame. POOF! Faithin jolted. A witch popped out of it with a baby Treeager in her arms. The witch laid the baby on a table and cursed, "Dimwitted sister is a piece of worthlessness just as them Gobs. I don't have time for this!" She jerked the tubes up from the floor, then POOF! The witch went back into the picture.

Faithin faced Helsin, her brows raised high. She asked, "Was that your aunt?"

"Yes. I recognized her voice."

"Stay here."

"Yes, ma'am."

Faithin hurried into the lab to the picture and removed it from the frame. She held it flat across a workbench and examined it. Idanab was bending over someone lying on one of the weird-looking beds inside the picture. Faithin gasped, "Lidee!"

Idanab stopped what she was doing. She jerked her head towards Faithin, then ran towards the front of the picture. The closer she got, the bigger she became. She looked like she was a foot tall. She scowled her evil eyes at Faithin. With a somewhat squeaky voice, she yelled, "Why can't I get out!?! What have you done!?!"

Faithin only glared at Idanab.

"Why don't you answer me!?!

Faithin ignored the question. Instead, in a deep voice, she warned, "I will deal with you in due time. Do not hurt Lidee." As Faithin rolled up the picture, Idanab cursed. But her voice muted into mumbled garble, unrecognizable. It sounded like that of a wee mouse deep within the castle's stone walls.

After Faithin hid the picture and frame behind a workbench, she cradled the baby Treeager and walked into the storage room. She told Helsin, "This wee one looks unscathed. I'll examine him later. At least he's sleeping. Your aunt and Lidee are stuck in the picture for now. I'll get them out later. Let's look for Conkay."

They searched every room down every corridor, but Conkay wasn't in any of the rooms.

"My aunt may have taken your husband into the picture."

"No. I inspected it in detail. Follow me to the front entrance." After they reached the front door, Faithin whispered, "I'll keep an eye here from inside while you look out the front entrance. If the

Gob sees you, you won't surprise him because he knows you're Idanab's nephew. Besides, Gobs aren't that intelligent."

"I know," Helsin agreed as he rolled his eyes. He put his ear to the thick mahogany door, listening. He whispered, "I can hear the Gob snoring. I'll be back."

Faithin nodded.

Helsin left the front door ajar and kept his eyes on the Gob as he tip-toed past. He gradually pulled the foliage to one side. The moonlight shined through but didn't faze the Gob. Helsin walked out onto the shiny black crag. He squinted when he saw it scratched with deep claw marks and scuffed with boot prints. He whispered to his wand. A round ball grew from its tip and lit like a glowing globe. Helsin pointed his wand towards the side of the mountain and on the ground below the outcrop. He whispered, "*Go.*" The light floated off the tip of his wand and traveled over the areas he had pointed to. Helsin didn't see anyone on the mountainside or on the ground. After his glowing globe dimmed out and dissipated into the cool night air, he snuck back past the Gob and took care when he shut the door behind him.

Before Helsin could say anything, Faithin pursed her lips. She gestured her head for him to follow. They ducked into a dark corridor and listened. Two sets of footsteps got louder and louder. One scuffled across the floor as the other lumbered like a Gob-Digger. Helsin peeked around the wall. He saw the **Shadow** of the witch he had seen earlier. She was leading the Gob named Gorg toward the laboratory. Helsin whispered, "Faithin! Let's run." Faithin held the baby secure to her bosom, but then the baby sneezed.

"Who's there?" Asked the **Shadow** as she and Gorg crept their way toward the sound.

Faithin handed the babe to Helsin and whispered, "After I have their attention and they turn their backs, you run. Take the babe to the bedroom. I'll be right behind you."

Helsin nodded in agreement.

Faithin transformed into her overgrown rat and ran into the great hall. She stopped about twenty feet in front of Gorg and sneezed twice. "Oh, my witchy nerves! It's only a rat! Let's get back to work," the **Shadow** cackled.

"No. Me eat rat," Gorg said as he chased the rat around the large dining table, then across to the adjacent corridor. He grabbed the rat by the tail and lifted her up. Helsin peeked around the corner. He didn't see Faithin, but he saw the backs of the **Shadow** and Gorg. Helsin held the babe close to his chest. He ran across the main hall, down the corridor, and to the room where Floreena lay sleeping. He stood with his back pressed against the locked door and waited for Faithin.

Gorg was about to drop Faithin into his nasty mouth. But Faithin extracted her razor-sharp claws and swung herself upwards. She dug into Gorg's wrist. He yelled, "OW!" and let loose Faithin's tail. He watched as she dropped to the floor. She ran across the great hall, past the lab, and out of Gorg's sight. Gorg looked down the dark corridor. "No see rat. Where rat?"

"I don't care where it went. You're dripping blood all over the place. You fool! Come with me, so I can mend that wound!" The **Shadow** commanded.

As Faithin's rat form ran down the corridor, she transformed back into herself. She met Helsin and handed him the key. After they entered, Helsin pleaded, "Can we leave now?"

"Yes. Put out the fire. Do you know how to cast a *Levitation* spell?"

"No, ma'am."

"That's all right. You keep hold of the baby while I use my *Levitation* spell on Floreena, and then you can lead us out of here."

"Yes, ma'am."

Faithin pointed her palm upwards towards Floreena. Under her breath, she spoke her *Levitation* spell using Sorcermizic language. A cloud of sparkling gold dust began to swirl in the palm of her hand. Faithin blew the dust cloud over Floreena. After it dissipated, Floreena's body rose upwards. "Okay, Helsin, lead on."

Helsin lit his wand. Faithin kept a sharp eye as she followed him out of the bedroom and down the corridor. He hurried down each stairwell, through both dungeons, and to the mouth of the tunnel. Helsin stopped to be sure their way was clear. He saw the empty raft. This time it was tied to a Swampress tree instead of the bushes when he saw it earlier. He nodded to Faithin. She followed Helsin along the edge of the swamp's moonlit bank. They hurried onto a path through the mountains and into another tunnel.

"We can slow down now."

"Is this one of the tunnels the Gobs dug?"

"Yes, ma'am."

"Where does it lead."

"Through some of the caves in the mountains alongside the Water Bbeings' lake. The first cave we come to has two tunnels. One leads up outside to the top of the cave. The other tunnel the Gobs dug. That's the one they used to sneak into your castle. It travels back into The Ridge down under the gorge beneath Crystal Lake. Then it goes up through your mountain and into your laboratory."

Faithin asked, "How far are the caves from here, and what are Water Bbeings?"

"It'll take us approximately one minute to reach the first cave. As for Water Bbeings, they're an elusive, half dragon and half Mageon type of water beings who dwell in the depths of spring water." Helsin described the Water Bbeings in detail.

Faithin's brows lifted. She expressed, "They sound remarkable. Are we safe from them here?"

"Yes, ma'am."

"Good. Now Helsin. Have you used your wand to practice any Dark spells your aunt wanted you to learn?"

"No, ma'am. Not yet. So far, I've only used hand spells and a chanting spell."

"Good. I'll cleanse the darkness from your hands and mouth as soon as I get my wand, but first, I need to find it. Would you trust me to use your wand, only for a moment to locate mine?"

Helsin paused. He knew Faithin. She's made mistakes, like who hasn't, and has yelled, sometimes losing her temper. But she was loving, kind, honest, and did not have a sneaky bone in her body. She was straightforward. She never intended to hurt others with her actions or words unless they deserved it. Helsin trusted her more than he trusted himself. He answered, "Yes, ma'am. Let me use it to make a fire first."

"Do you know how to create a cushioned seat or bed from our planet's resources?"

"Yes. I learned that at Whittlewood Academy."

"Good. After you create a fire and make a bed for Floreena, I'll use your wand."

Helsin did as she asked. "How's this?"

"Perfect." After Faithin laid Floreena down, she faced Helsin. He held out his hand, gingerly offering his wand. Faithin put one hand on his shoulder. When she reached with her other hand, she cocked her head and assured, "It'll be all right, Helsin." He sighed but felt more relaxed when she patted his shoulder.

Faithin turned her hand face up. She pointed the tip of Helsin's wand in the center of her palm and chanted her *Location* spell. Her wand appeared blurry, hardly noticeable, and only for a moment before it vanished. Faithin handed Helsin his wand.

"Did you find it?"

"No." Faithin sighed. "Thank you, though. I'll figure something out later. I'll cleanse the dark from you another way, but that will also have to wait. Helsin, I want to get this baby to the Treeagers' village before he wakes. Then I need to take Floreena to Crystal Lake Castle and put her in the care of the Bluewing Fairies. There's no way this can happen unless I use my dragon form. My dragon wings are strong and swift."

"What if you use the Shadow potion, then glide as your dragon?"

"Isn't the potion Dark Magic that your aunt concocted?"

"No. Wizard Tiaff created this potion. I've never met him, but I'm pretty sure he's a good wizard because when my aunt talks about him, she reeks with envy. She's jealous of him."

"I suspect you're correct. I heard Tiaff was a good wizard. How fast can I travel if I drink the potion?"

"Well, you'll be gliding over the treetops, so you can get to the village, your castle, then back here in less than an hour. You'll need to drink about two tablespoons of the potion. Any more than that, you'll get tired unless it acts different when you're a dragon, that I don't know."

"After we reach the cave, you sit tight and wait for my return. I need to get your aunt and Lidee out of the picture. I'll need your help. Understand?"

"Yes, ma'am." Helsin hung his head.

Faithin reached out and pulled his chin up towards her gaze. With a tender voice, she said, "Helsin, we have always loved you. I don't like, nor will anyone else be happy with what you have done, but we love you. I understand you were under the influence of your aunt. You may have felt obligated to help her, not to mention that anyone subjected to Dark Magic..." Faithin paused to calculate her words. "Well, dear lad, to put it plainly, Dark Magic is not good, period. This is why it is important to wash the dark from you. Also, Floreena likes you. She also likes Gala. She has loved Gala for a long time. If you love her, you will accept and respect her decision. Do you understand?"

"Yes, ma'am."

"I know you're angry and miss your parents. I am so sorry for your loss and your circumstances. We will resolve your living situation. We'll talk more about it later. Is that okay with you?"

"Yes, ma'am." Helsin's face lit up with hope.

"Good. Let's get going." Faithin used her *Levitation* spell on Floreena. As soon as she lifted her from the magical bed, the soft moss, rocks, and other resources went into the tunnel from where they came.

Helsin pointed his wand at the fire and said, "*Snuff*." The fire poofed out, leaving no evidence that it was even there. After he led Faithin to the cave, he pointed at a tunnel and explained, "There's where we need to go. It leads up to the top of the mountain, where you'll have plenty of room to transform into your dragon."

On the top side of the cave, the crescent moons shone bright, allowing Faithin and Helsin to see The Ridge. Faithin kept Floreena afloat while she drank two tablespoons of the Shadow potion. She recited its incantation. After her body materialized into a **Shadow**, she handed the vile to Helsin. He backed up and gave her room. POOF! Her transformation looked like a spark of golden dust particles. Lickity-split, before Helsin could blink, he saw a shadowy dragon standing before him.

Helsin put the baby in Faithin's free arm. "Helsin," Faithin said in her dragon voice. "Go back down into the cave and stay safe. I'll return as soon as I can. After we tend to your aunt and Lidee, we'll search for my husband and son."

"Yes, ma'am." He gave her a respectful bow of his head.

After Helsin started back down to the cave, Faithin spread her enormous wings. She jumped upwards and flapped, but to her surprise, she didn't have to flap her wings to go anywhere. Instead, she glided towards The Ridge like the fast-blowing wind of an Ultra Storm. As Faithin sailed through the air, she thought, "I'll find you, my loves."

Earlier That Evening Before Gala and the Newlads Met Serenity

Conkay started to stir. He felt himself hoisted over the shoulder of a large Swamp Gob and pretended he was still sleeping. The Gob carried Conkay from the dungeon, up a flight of stairs, down a corridor, and into a laboratory.

"Lay him here, Gorg, and be careful with him," demanded a cackling voice of a witch. "Now get your brother. The two of you will fill this jar with Scarlet Leprechaun Frogs on your way to get my sister. Give her this other bottle with these instructions. Then you and your brother hurry back with my sister and the frogs before it gets too dark. Be quick about it. Go!"

Without strapping Conkay to the table, Gorg bolted out of the laboratory to get Durgat. Durgat was watching the front entrance. "Come!" Gorg commanded. They raced across the great hall and down the corridor. They trudged down both staircases through both dungeons. Then they ran out of the tunnel to the swamp, where they left their raft hidden. As they hurried to do the witch's bidding, the witch prepared for her gene extraction procedures.

"Mother," a lad about Gala's age called out to the witch.

Conkay peeked over at the lad. He was lying strapped on the table next to him. And, lying strapped to another table, on the other side of the lad, was a wizard.

"Yes?" The witch asked.

"I feel worse."

"You'll feel better soon. Your Aunt Terrib will be here with more potion. It'll help you sleep. Then when you wake, you and Wizard Tiaff will be healed." The witch kissed Nam on his forehead, then turned towards Wizard Tiaff and gave him a pat on his shoulder.

Conkay almost gasped when he saw Faithin's wand tucked in the belt of the witch's robe. He lay still as the witch past him and toward the picture he had gotten from Earth. Conkay watched the witch enter the picture. He heard the lad express his pain to the wizard.

"Wizard Tiaff, my veins feel like they're on fire. It's like my blood is curling."

"There's only one thing I can do that might help soothe and take your focus off your pain. My wife wanted me to sing this Bloodra Lullaby to our son every day of his life so that he would remember her face. The lullaby would also aid in his transition if he was a Mystique Blueblood like his mother."

"Anything. Please. The pain's getting worse."

Although Wizard Tiaff was weak, he began to sing. His magical voice was soft. Conkay saw a golden-green light come from Wizard Tiaff's mouth straight into the lad's ears. When Tiaff finished singing, he asked, "I hope that helped. Do you feel better, Nam?"

"Yes! And, and, I-I know my mother's face!"

"What?"

"I can see my mother's face! My name isn't Nam. And-and you, you're my father!"

"Optim?"

"Yes! Yes! That's my name. I know my mother's face! That wicked witch is not my mother! Ow!" Optim's body hurt as green scales started to appear. He looked over at Wizard Tiaff, who was crying. Optim changed into his dragon form for the first time. When he called out, "Father!" fire shot from his throat. Wizard Tiaff turned to ash. "NOOOO!" Optim screamed. He changed back into himself, then into his dragon form, back and forth several times. He had no control. After realizing he had busted out of his straps, he got off the table and leaned over his father's ashes.

Conkay had jumped to his feet. He grabbed an urn from a shelf, handed it to Optim, and said, "Here. Put your father's ashes in here. Leave this castle quickly. Do you know where Crystal Lake Castle is?"

"Yes," Optim cried.

"Make your way there, hurry now, and sing the Bloodra Lullaby to help your transition. You are a Mystique Blueblood. After you reach the castle, tell the Bluewing Fairy clan everything you know. I'll meet you there as soon as I deal with this wicked witch and look for my loved ones."

"All right," Optim wailed.

No sooner than Optim left the laboratory, the witch came out of the picture to see why he yelled. She screeched, "You're awake!" Conkay had already reached his hand out and summoned Faithin's wand. It shot from the witch's robe straight into his hand. As Conkay chanted his *Zap* spell that would render the witch unconscious for a couple of hours, the witch summoned her wand. She chanted a *Reversal Disguise* spell. Her spell would allow her ownership of Faithin's wand. At the same time, it would disguise Conkay as the witch, and the witch would look like Conkay. Conkay's spell was fast. It sped towards her and sheared the edge of her spell. His spell hit the witch first. She still looked like herself and fell to the ground. Her wand shot out of her hand, straight towards Faithin's wand. While Conkay watched them intertwine, he was unaware that he now looked much like the witch. He didn't know the witch's wand had reversed its ownership to him. There were only two ways the witch could regain ownership of her wand. She would have to use another magic tool while Conkay was present. Or, Conkay could reverse the spell anytime and anywhere without Idanab's presence.

    Before Conkay left the laboratory, he saw a small pile of Wizard Tiaff's ashes left on the table, so he ran to tell Optim. Optim was standing on the black outcrop to the front entrance. He saw Rose and Bud, the two Tuberous tribe fairies he had met when Idanab first brought him to Wizard Tiaff's castle. Optim wondered if he should tell them anything before he traveled to Crystal Lake Castle. But then Conkay ran beside him and told him to get the rest of his father's ashes. But Optim ignored him because Conkay looked like Idanab.

    Optim transformed into himself, then back into his dragon form. His dragon claws scratched the floor of the crag. He spread his wings, and without knowing, he knocked Conkay off the outcrop. While Optim flew towards Mermary's Lake,

Conkay fell down the mountainside. He hit his head on a rock before he landed on the ground. The blow knocked him unconscious.

Rose and Bud watched Optim, who they thought was Nam, change back and forth from himself into a green dragon before he took off. They saw him knock who they thought was Idanab off the crag. As Rose and Bud flew to tell their leader, Serenity, Gala, and the Newlads got off Blacky and stretched. Gala looked at his map to see if they were close to Wizard Tiaff's castle. Then he and his friends heard someone yelling, so they followed the voices.

When they came to a large clearing, they saw three fay-folk hovering over a body at the foot of The Ridge.

Gala called out, "Is everything all right? Can we help?"

The three Tuberous fairies jolted backward. Serenity asked, "Well, I don't know. Who are ya?" She put her arms out in front of Rose and Bud like a protective mother.

"I'm sorry. My name is Gala Lakinshire, and these are my friends. We're looking for our loved ones who were taken two days ago and were told that Wizard Tiaff or fay-folk like yourselves could help us."

After they introduced themselves, Serenity accepted their help. Gala used his *Levitation* spell to get who they thought was Idanab to the Tuberous tribes' home so the tribes' healer, Herbaleen, could tend to her. In the meantime, Idanab was still knocked out in Wizard Tiaff's laboratory.

Idanab Wakes

The *Zap* spell Conkay had cast on Idanab began to wear off; she started to stir. After her eyes blinked open, she saw her sister standing over her as a **Shadow**. "Terrib? Is that you?"

"Yea. We just got back and found you lying on the floor. Gorg and Durgat put you on the table. What happened?"

"The Lethargic potion wore off that Wizard Conkay," Idanab spat. "We had a witch's dual. He cast his spell on me before I could cast mine on him." Idanab looked over at the other tables. "Wizard Tiaff and his son? Have you seen them?"

"'His son?' Why didn't you tell me you knew Wizard Tiaff was Nam's father?"

"I meant to say, my son."

"Ida! You're a liar!"

"Does it matter if they're father and son, Terrib!?!"

Terrib creased her brows and thought for a second. Then she answered, "I guess not."

"No. It doesn't matter. So, have you seen Tiaff or Nam?"

"No."

To divert Terrib's attention, Idanab asked, "Did you see Wizard Conkay?"

"No."

"Did you see my other captives in the dungeon?"

"Yea."

"That's strange."

"What do you mean? Aren't they supposed to be there?"

Idanab jerked her head towards Terrib and snapped, "You nitwit! Don't ya think that wizard would have freed them after he cast his *Zap* spell on me?"

"Well, I—"

"Don't you remember what I told you, that I have his wife with their friends locked in the dungeon, and I needed more frogs to make more Lethargic potion before they woke up, so I needed you to hurry!?!"

"Well, yeah, sorta, it's just that I don't understand all your planning, Ida. You're not exactly straight with me, ya know." Terrib glided over to the picture as she talked. "Gorg and Durgat caught the frogs for your Lethargic potion. Gorg gave me the bottle of Shadow potion with your instructions that aren't clear. So, I did what I thought you wanted. I sipped some potion, turned into this **Shadow**, and came here with the Gobs." Terrib glided back over to Idanab and handed her the instructions.

The parchment was wet with frog secretion, which blotted out some words. Idanab rolled her eyes and shook her head. She got up off the table. "Gorg! Where'd you put that jar of frogs?"

"On same shelf."

"Fine. Now go fetch me Floreena's mother, Lidee. And Durg, don't you dare eat another one of my frogs!"

"Name Durgat, your witch."

Gorg's eyes popped wide, worried his brother would get hexed by the wicked witch.

Idanab scowled. "Whatever," she snarled and waved her hand back and forth as she commanded. "Now, Durga, bring me some clean rags from the storage room. After Gorg brings me Lidee, you will help him fetch me the Treeager babe and Floreena! Then Gorg, hang those keys back on the hook. Got it!?!"

"Yea'am." Gorg and Durgat said in unison as they stumbled over their own feet. Gorg grabbed the ring of keys to the dungeons' cell doors and shackles. He ran out of the lab while Durgat hurried into the storage room.

"Terrib, I want you to help me wash these tables. Wizard Conkay must have taken Tiaff and Nam with him, and I don't have time to look for them. I'll put the genes in the baby instead of Nam."

As Terrib started to wash the table Wizard Tiaff had been lying on, she stopped and called out, "Ida?"

"Yea?"

"Look at this."

Idanab furrowed her brows when she saw white ashes in a small neat pile. "Um. Wizard Tiaff was lying on this table. I wonder if this has anything to do with him." Idanab walked over to a workbench where Spyraven was perched. She took a box from a shelf and wrote Tiaff's name on the outside of it. She handed the box to Terrib and commanded, "Scoop the ashes into the box. Be careful about it.

When you're finished washing the table, put the box on the top shelf in the storage room."

After Terrib put the ashes in the box, she set it to one side then continued washing the table. It didn't take long for Durgat to return with the clean rags and for Gorg to return with Lidee.

"Lay her here for now." Idanab gestured her hand towards the table she had cleaned. Gorg obeyed. As Idanab took the clean rags from Durgat, she ordered, "Now go fetch me Floreena and the Treeager babe. When you get back, lay Floreena on that table." She pointed with a stiff arm and finger, then asked, "Do you understand?"

Durgat nodded while Gorg choked up and answered, "Huh, huh, yea, ya mighty witch?"

"Enough with the high and mighty kiss-ass crap. You call me Ida."

"Yea, Ida."

Idanab shook her head and huffed. "After you lay Floreena down and Terrib has prepped Lidee, I want you to pick Lidee up and be careful about it. I don't want Terrib's prep job ruined. Be gentle when you carry Lidee into the picture. You do remember how to enter the picture, don't you, Gorg?"

"Yea."

Idanab commanded by using a condescending tone and slow hand gestures. "Now listen here, genius Durg, or Durga, whatever your name is, you hold the babe. Wait for Gorg to come back out of the picture. Then after you hand Gorg the babe, you go and guard the front entrance." She gestured her fingers like they were legs walking to the front entrance. Her eyes slanted, and her top lip curled up. Even though she was less intense, she did the same to Gorg. "And now for you, older and wiser brother to Durgy, I want you to bring the babe into the picture. Do you think you can remember that because if you don't do it right, neither of you will get any yum, yums?" Idanab turned her glare on Durgat.

"Yea," Gorg said. Durgat only gave a curt hostile nod because Idanab didn't care to pronounce his name right.

"All right then, I'll explain what we'll do when I'm done with the babe, so go! And make it quick!" Ida clapped her hands. Gorg and Durgat took off down the corridor like scared oversized rats. Idanab cackled.

Terrib took her dirty rag to the basin and asked, "What do you want me to do with my dirty rag?"

"After you rinse and wring it out, hang it over the rim of the basin, then come here so you can help me with these tubes. I'm going to use these for Floreena. I want you to wash them, and I mean wash them well."

"Can't I use magic to wash them?"

"No. I don't want our magic influencing the equipment or my procedures. Now listen, Terrib. I want you to prep Floreena before I bring the babe back out from the picture. You do remember what I showed you?"

"Yea."

"All right. And remember to put that box on the top shelf in the storage room. I need to prepare those machines and beds in the picture. Be sure Gorg lays Floreena on this table. Remind him to bring Lidee into the picture before the babe, that is, when you're done prepping them."

"Witches' nerves, Ida. Stop worrying."

"I will when this is over."

"By the way, Ida, do you have any more Shadow potion?"

"There should be another bottle in the storage room on the shelf next to the jar of frogs. Why?"

"In case I need it."

"You don't have any left from what the Gobs brought you?"

"Yea. but I left it at home."

Idanab shook her head, "Why do I do this to myself?"

"What!?!"

"Forget it. It's nothing. Just drink some of what's in the storage room. That's what's left of Wizard Tiaff's batch. I'll make a batch when I make more of this Lethargic potion. This is all that's left, and it's for Floreena." Idanab handed Terrib a liter bottle with a long neck, half full of the sleeping potion. She instructed, "After Gorg lies Floreena down, she'll start to wake. As soon as she stirs, I want you to pour the potion down the back of her throat so she swallows it. It works quickly and will keep her sleeping until the early morn. By the time you're done prepping her, I'll be done with the babe and bring him back out."

Idanab went inside the picture. Gorg and his brother returned with Floreena and the Treeager babe. Gorg lay Floreena on the table while Durgat stood holding the babe. And, as Idanab figured, Floreena started to stir. Terrib poured the Lethargic potion down Floreena's throat. It took seconds for it to take effect.

After Floreena fell back to sleep, Terrib continued prepping Lidee. She talked to Gorg in a softer, less demanding voice than her sister. "Now, Gorg, be gentle when you pick Lidee up and hurry back, so you can take the babe to Witch Idanab."

Gorg was gentle for a Gob who usually does things rough. He slipped his arms under Lidee's neck and legs, then took her into the picture. Durgat was also gentle while he stood holding the Treeager babe. As soon as Gorg returned, he held his arms out toward Durgat. After Durgat handed Gorg the baby, Gorg told Durgat to go guard the front entrance to the castle. But Durgat wanted yum, yums first. Grog told him not until Witch Ida was done. Durgat creased his brows. He wrinkled his big bumpy nose and ran his puke-green scabby forearm across his mouth. He huffed and lumbered out of the lab, across the great hall, out the front door, then Gorg took the babe into the picture.

Before Terrib began prepping Floreena, she took the box with Wizard Tiaff's ashes into the storage room. Little did she know that Helsin was in the storage room, hiding under a table.

Helsin peeked out from underneath the table and saw Terrib's shadowy appearance. He watched as she placed the box on the top shelf. Then she rummaged through empty bottles next to a jar of Scarlet Leprechaun frogs. Terrib got mad when she couldn't find a bottle of Shadow potion. By the time she glided back into the lab, Gorg was in front of the picture. Terrib told Gorg to go with her as she went to get her Shadow potion from her cottage in the swamps.

After Helsin heard them leave and everything was quiet, he peeked into the laboratory through the two-way door. He scanned the room and saw Floreena. He ran in, picked her up, and carried her down the corridor to safety.

Present Moment in Time
Wizard Tiaff's Castle

Faithin took the babe to the Treeager's village. While she glided home in her shadowy dragon form, Helsin waited in the cave for her return. Gala and his friends were planning to investigate Wizard Tiaff's castle.

I wish I studied my spells and charms more often like my parents wanted me to. We'd have *Char pro ect* charms that would make us invisible so we could search Wizard Tiaff's castle unseen. I wasn't truthful with my mother when I told her I was studying. And you know what, she knew it and forgave me anyway."

"Yeah. I don't know about some parents, but our parents are good like that. Our parents know what it's like to make mistakes, tell lies, do stuff they shouldn't do or say then regret it afterward.

"One time, I was mad at Mother only because I believed my friends. They distorted what she said, made it sound like she was some mean ole witch, which I knew better.

"Of course, in time, Mother forgave my friends. Plus, after they got counseling, they apologized. But Mother forgave me right away because she loves me with that unconditional love of hers. She didn't come begging for my forgiveness either. She did try to explain things to me, but I didn't listen. I felt shameful. Forgiving myself was hard, knowing I should have stuck up for her in the first place.

"Mother said it's good to forgive others, but I needed to forgive myself. She said it takes a lot of courage to admit when you're wrong. It makes you a better being and helps you gain humility. When you have forgiving parents, it isn't so hard to forgive yourself or others. Right, Dahc?"

"You're right, Ddot. I remember our father told us that we'll make mistakes for the rest of our lives, so we may as well get used to it. He said that all *could haves, would haves,* and all the should haves, including the *ifs,* are things of the past which we are to learn from. They're to be forgiven. Let them go. Be present, be in the moment, aware of our being, senses, surroundings, and what's smack dab in front of us."

As they talked, Herbaleen thought, "If that witch had anythin' to do with my missin' tribe members, I don't think I'll be forgivin' her, ever!"

Lucky rubbed his red eyes and added, "We have some darn good parents, that's for sure. I've heard 'em say, some time or another, that when we make mistakes, we need to make apologies and amends ifin' we can, as long as we ain't hurtin' no one. If we learn from our mistakes and learn to forgive, we'll become better beins'. I love our parents. Now let's stop before I git ta cryin' 'cause I'm missin' 'em."

Serenity hugged Lucky before she flew over and sat at a table. She pulled a parchment and a charcoal stick out from the drawer and told her friends, "Okay, y'all come here so I can show ya the main entrance to the castle and where I think another door is." After they gathered around the table, Serenity began to draw and explain, "Up here on the outcrop is the main entrance. It's covered by foliage. I was figurin' there was an entrance on this side. I saw Wizard Tiaff walk 'round to it, and he never came back."

Gala lifted his black brows. "There's probably a back entrance. Crystal Lake Castle has a back door. We'll look around the side first. It might be safer than the front entrance. No telling what we might find behind that hanging foliage. I'll use Nix to go up to the castle while y'all hang on to his legs."

"But, Chum? What if those Gobs are around? Don't they eat birds?"

"You're right, Ddot. What am I thinking? The Gobs would eat you guys and my Nix. I know they don't eat dragons, so I'll take a chance flying as my Redtalon with you guys on my head, hanging on to my spikes. Hopefully, Stealth Dragon Slayers don't see me. Has the Tuberous tribe ever seen dragon slayers?"

Herbaleen answered, "No. They don't come 'round here 'cause there ain't no dragons. That's the first time the lad transformed into a dragon, and there ain't no other dragons around this forest."

"Well then, after I take us to the edge of the forest, as Nix, I'll transform into Redtalon. If there isn't a door on the side of the castle, I'll take us to the back. If there's a door, I'll transform into myself, and we'll sneak in through the back."

Concerned about Gala's fear of evil lurking in the swamps, Ddot reminded, "That's on the swamp side of The Ridge."

"It'll be okay, Ddot. You guys will be safe. I'll protect you. I'll summon my wand after I transform into myself." Gala smiled.

Ddot realized his best chum had gained some courage. Ddot didn't tell him that he was referring to Gala's fear and not his own.

"I'll stay up 'til y'all git back. How long should I wait before I send the warriors out lookin'?"

Everyone looked at Gala to answer Herbaleen. "Well, I'm not sure. Any suggestions?"

Serenity and the Newlads looked at each other. Dahc paced the floor using his hands while he explained his suggestion. "It won't take us long to reach the castle. Gala will have to transform into himself before we attempt to enter. We'll sit under his cloak's hood, and on his shoulders, under his hair. Of course, while Gala hides in the shadows, we'll keep our eyes and ears sharp and have our weapons ready. We'll be quieter than a family of sleeping mice. We'll be as stealth as dragon slayers. There's probably three or four corridors extending off the main hall inside the castle. Each corridor will have at least two to three rooms. There'll be a laboratory, a few bedrooms, storage rooms, bathrooms, a kitchen, and a library. Um, let me see," Dahc stopped pacing. He counted on his fingers, unaware that his brother and his friends wore wide grins. It was astonishing how much Dahc was talking, let alone calculating, making decisions. After he finished counting, Dahc answered Herbaleen, "Give us about three hours." He looked around and asked, "What? Why are y'all grinning."

Ddot chuckled. He flew over, patted Dahc's shoulder, and teased, "Oh, nothing. It's just that you have a lot to say these days."

Everyone laughed. Gala added, "Yeah. And your calculations sound right if we don't run into any problems or do any lollygagging around, that is. So Herbaleen, give us about three hours like Dahc suggests. Come on, you guys. Let's get going. You too chatterbox." Laughter filled the sleeping crevice, with Dahc being the loudest. Gala flew over and gave Dahc a quick rub on the head.

"It's settled then. Y'all keep yore eyes and ears sharp and git back quick, ya hear?"

"Yes, ma'am," everyone answered Herbaleen in unison.

Herbaleen flew back to where Idanab was sleeping. At least, who she and everyone presumed was Idanab. Gala flew to the edge of the forest as Nix. His friends hung on to his right leg and talons.

Clues

Where the forest butts the clearing, Nix perched on a branch with his friends standing next to him. Their sharp eyes scanned the sky and the forest as they listened. There were no signs of predators lurking about nor Stealth Dragon Slayers. Nix flew over to the clearing and transformed into Redtalon. His friends sat on his head while he flew up and around to the side of Wizard Tiaff's castle.

"There is an entrance. It's a hidden door," Serenity said as she pointed.

Redtalon landed a few feet away from the castle. He complimented, "Good eye, Serenity."

"Thank ya, Gala, or rather Redtalon? But I wouldn't have seen the door if it weren't for the light of our three moons' and the shadows of trees dancin' 'round."

"I didn't see the door, and my Redtalon's vision is superb, so again, good eye, Serenity. And just so you know, I like to give my forms names, but everyone who knows me calls me Gala no matter what form I take."

Serenity flew down in front of Redtalon and patted his snout. "Thank you, Gala."

Redtalon smiled his wide dragon smile. He told his friends, "Okay, guys, stand by the door while I transform into myself." After his friends flew down and stood on the top step, they watched Gala transform from his Redtalon into himself. His transformation was so fast that they only saw a flash of golden light, then Gala. After Gala ran up to his friends, Lucky took Serenity by her hand. They flew onto Gala's head. Gala pulled his hood up until Lucky and Serenity held its rim to where they could see from underneath. They sat. The twins flew onto Gala's left and right shoulders. They hid within his hair and the bottom part of his hood.

 Gala took a deep breath. He reached for the door handle. The latch was locked. He summoned his wand. When he chanted an *Unlock* spell, the door made a loud clank noise; Gala stood still. He and his friends didn't hear anything, so Gala pushed the creaking door inch by inch until it was completely open. A sliver of light shone through a crack in the wall across the small room. There was no sign of anyone. Gala walked in and shut the door behind him. The crescent moons shone through a high window. Gala and his friends spotted a family portrait hanging above a fireplace. The mother was holding their newborn while the father stood next to them. Large candles sat on the mantle. To the right of its stone hearth was a dragon's scale crafted into a shield. It had an inscription of a lullaby and a Star'ella-love. A couch sat in front of the fireplace with a pillow and a blanket, a sign Wizard Tiaff had lied there.

 In one corner of the room was a mahogany desk. An inkwell, quill, parchment, more candles, and an opened book sat on the desk. Gala flipped through the pages of the book. He came to a page with a graphic drawing in motion. It depicted a battle between a dark wizard and a Mystique Blueblood. The wizard's solid white eyeballs had black slivers of diamond-shaped pupils. The Mystique Blueblood was in his dragon form, with his white wings ablaze. The wizard's black cloak waved behind him. He stood with both hands on the hilt of his sword, which he had stabbed into the dragon's heart. As blue blood spilled from the dragon, its three-edge, arrow-tipped tail severed the wizard's gullet. The wizard's head hung halfway off his neck while red blood gushed from his artery.

"Whoa," Gala whispered. "That's enough. No wonder my parents told me battles are terrible and sad." Gala turned the book face down and read the inscription on the back cover. "*In Reverent Memory of Our Ancestry.* I bet the story of Wizard Tiaff, his wife, and their son is within these pages. Look here. There's a request written on this parchment. It reads, '*Giver of life, love, and happiness, please bring my son back to me. Keep him safe. Thank you.*' It's written over and over again. Water stains blotted out some of the words."

"Yeah. I bet Wizard Tiaff cried when he wrote it," surmised Ddot.

Gala nodded, then made his way to the crack in the wall. "This is another hidden door." Gala ran his fingers over the wall, looking for a lever, a button, or a door handle. "Aha. Here's a circular indentation. A hole in the wall." Without a hint of hesitation, no fear of tiny spiders, which Ddot made a note of, Gala stuck his finger in the hole and pushed. The wall creaked. Everyone could see the outline of the door. Gala stood still, listening for sounds on the other side. It was quiet, so he pushed the door open enough to peek through.

Gala saw the great hall lit by candles on a grand chandelier and the light of moons shining through windows. He pushed the door further, then scanned from left to right. A long mahogany dining table sat in the center of the great hall. Carved At the bottom of its six legs were dragon paws. Eight mahogany chairs with velvet red cushioned backs and seats surrounded the table. Carved dragon claws were in the front two legs of each chair. On the tops of the chairs were more intricate dragon designs. Torches burned within stone sconces at the entrance of three corridors. Under each sconce sat a decorative, narrow table against the wall. On both ends of each table sat a chair that faced into the great hall. Light emitted from a room at the front of the third corridor to Gala's right. A little further to his right was the main entrance to the castle. Gala forewarned his friends, "I'm changing the color of my cloak to black." Gala spoke under his breath using Sorcermizic language. His cloak turned black and appeared shadowy.

 Gala hurried into the first corridor on his left. He reached an open door and stood against the outside wall to listen. It was quiet, so he peeked around the door. It was dark. Gala whispered to the diamonded-tip crystal of his wand, "*Light.*" It lit up like a burning torch revealing an empty bedroom. They checked every room down two corridors. There was no sign of anyone. Gala snuffed the light from his wand and tiptoed to the third passageway, where there was a lighted room. He stood still with his back against the wall and listened. Gala took a deep breath, then peeked around the door. He and his friends scanned the room. Gala whispered, "This is Wizard Tiaff's laboratory."

"Yeah. Look over there, Chum. It's a raven sitting on a wooden perch." Ddot pointed.

"Oh, my pixie heart," whispered Serenity, "Is that blood?" She pointed at the basin.

"It looks like it, and it looks like blood on that third table closest to the basin," added Lucky.

Gala gulped. He walked over to the third table, then to the basin. His eyes followed blood splatters on the floor leading to a two-way door. As Gala readied his wand for defense, he crept up to the door and listened. He didn't hear anything, so he took another deep breath and slowly opened the door. He needed more light to follow the trail of blood. He whispered, "*Light.*" The tip of his wand lit up like a torch. "Look, guys, the blood splatters stop here." Gala lifted his arm. "And look. There's blood on the shelves."

"A jar of Scarlet Leprechaun Frogs," Ddot pointed.

"And look up there," Serenity said as she flew out from underneath Gala's hood. "There's a box up top. It has the word *Tiaff* written on it." She flew up to the box. "I wonder what's inside."

"Serenity? Did that wicked witch snatch ya?"

"What? Who said that?" Serenity asked.

There was a short pause before an answer, "It-it's me, St-Stamen. We're inside a cage covered with a purple cloth. Do ya see the cloth?"

"Why yes, I do." Serenity's eyes watered.

"Back up, Serenity. I'll get them down." Gala used his free hand to cast his *Levitation* spell. He set the cage on the table, then removed the cloth. Gala put out his torch. He used his wand to unlock the cage. After the locks cracked open, he lit his wand again. Two plant fairies hovered together with their hands over their eyes.

Serenity opened the door of the cage. She called out, "Stamen! Nectar! Yo're safe. Look at me. Don't be scared. It really is me."

They peeked through their fingers. After seeing Serenity, they ran over and hugged her tight like they would never let go. Serenity asked, "Have ya seen Sepal and Pistil or my parents?" Stamen and Nectar drew back. Tears flooded their red eyes; they hung their heads. They couldn't speak.

The *Nightmare Forget* spell cursed Gala. It kept him from remembering that he saw Trill and Quo get eaten by Gobs. But it didn't stop him from feeling the plant fairies' pain. He began to cry. Everyone cried. Gala wiped his tears and said, "I'll take you guys home, then I'll come back and check the rest of the rooms down this corridor." Creeeak! The front door opened. Gala snuffed out the light of his wand. "Shh. Someone's coming. Y'all get under my hood. Twins, Lucky, ready your weapons to injure."

They readied their weapons, and Gala stepped behind the storage room's two-way door. Trudging steps along with grunt noises got closer. A scratchy voice of a Gob asked, "Gorg? Ida? Terrib? Where you gone?" The Gob yelled through the two-way door, "GORG!" Gala stiffened. He could feel Stamen and Nectar shaking. Serenity embraced them, but they still shook.

"SQUAWK! Squawk! Gala and his friends heard the raven's cries and her wings flapping around the laboratory.

As Gala and his friends listened to the hysterical raven, Helsin sat in the cave waiting for Faithin. He wondered if he would see anyone in Tiaff's lab through Spyraven's eyes.

Helsin's Spy Ring

Helsin looked down at his spy ring. He worried how his aunt would react when she found out he was helping. Faithin. But he knew Faithin would protect him. He worried about what the **Shadow** and Gorg were doing in Wizard Tiaff's laboratory. He wondered if they found the frame and the picture. He asked his ring, "What do you spy eye?" When the feathery part of his ring opened, Helsin jumped to his feet. He saw glimpses of Durgat and the laboratory. Helsin could tell Durgat was chasing Spyraven.

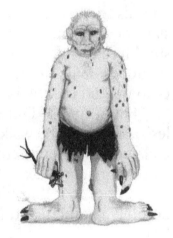

Helsin saw the two-way door, then the storage room. The room spun and stopped. Helsin saw a wide-open mouth filled with sharp greenish-black teeth. Then his ring turned black and fell apart. Its feather, twine, and ebony stone fell to the rock floor of the cave. The magic spell that created Spyraven and Helsin's spy ring had broken. While Helsin paced, he debated whether to go to the castle. He wanted to see what else Durgat was doing or destroying. Gala and his friends saw a different view of the raven.

Spyraven Through Different Eyes And New Clues

Gala and his friends watched the raven flap through the two-way door, then snatch! "SQUAWK!" Spyraven sounded out as Durgat's green putrid arm, with oozing scabs, grabbed her from behind. He twirled her around, stuffed her head in his mouth, and chomped. Spyraven turned into a dead headless raven with stuffing in its head and neck. "NOT MEAT!" Gala and his friends jumped out of their skin. The Gob slammed the bird on the table. Objects on the table shuddered while test tubes fell to the floor and shattered. Gala stood stiff for a short time after the Gob walked out the back door of the storage room.

The sound of Durgat's trudging footsteps lessoned. After he walked down the first staircase, Gala and his friends could no longer hear him. They began to relax.

"I want to follow him, but I'm worried about Serenity, Stamen, and Nectar. They need to get home."

"This is the only corridor we haven't checked. Because we're already here, why don't we find a place for them to hide? Me and Gala can check out the rest of the castle. What do y'all think?" Asked Ddot as he flew off Gala's shoulder.

"I'm going with you. Lucky can keep Serenity and her friends safe while they hide," suggested Dahc as he flew out next to Ddot.

"That sounds like a good idea to me. I'll keep 'em safe in Tiaff's secret den," offered Lucky as he flew out from under Gala's hood.

Gala agreed, "Okay. You guys get back under the protection of my hood and hair; let's go." He and his friends checked the front entrance before entering Wizard Tiaff's secret den. "You guys sit tight." Gala summoned some root. He handed one to Stamen and the other to Nectar. "Eat a little of this. It'll help you feel better. Lucky, if we're not back, let's say, in twenty minutes, take them home. Go out that window..." Gala pointed, "...and flap your wings as fast as possible. Understand?"

Lucky gave a quick nod with his thumbs up and said, "Understood. But just so ya know, my blade's set to kill. Understand?" Lucky patted his dagger's sheath.

"Yeah. My arrows are, too," the twins said in unison.

"Well, Okay then. If we gotta defend our lives, kill if we must. But let's hope we don't have to," Gala pled.

"Be safe, alert," Serenity wished.

Gala and the twins nodded. Gala hurried and shut the hidden door. He kept his hood on with his wand ready as the twins set their arrows in the string of their bows and stood on Gala's shoulders. Gala crept past the laboratory, then stopped to grab a candle he saw sitting on the table in the storage room. He whispered, "*Light.*" The wick of the candle lit.

When Gala reached the room where his mother, Floreena, and Helsin had been, he peeked inside. It was empty, but there was a familiar aroma. Gala asked, "Do y'all smell anything?"

Ddot and Dahc flew off Gala's shoulders and around the room, sniffing the air. With a quiet voice, Dahc announced, "Over here. There's a sweet smell of Honeysuckle and Stargazer on the bed."

Gala inspected the bed. "Look, guys. This wool blanket, it's pulled back." Gala bent down and smelled the blanket. He lifted it. His eyes popped wide. "Mother wore these flowers in her hair the night of Acub's and Ashlin's celebration. She was here!"

"Shh," Dahc quieted, "Let's search the rest of this corridor."

"In a quiet voice, Gala assured, "I'll remember to be quiet. Come on. Let's go. The twins stood back on Gala's shoulders."

Gala stopped at the door. He looked both ways before leaving the room. It was clear, so he walked further down the corridor to the first flight of stairs.

"I wonder where this goes." Ddot gulped.

"We're about to find out." Gala crept down the staircase and stopped on the bottom step. "Guys. This is a dungeon. The moons are shining through those high windows." Gala continued walking, looking in the cells as he passed. He held the candle up to the cell on his right. "Someone melted the lock on this door. And look there, someone melted those fetter chains. This looks like the floors I saw in Father's crystal."

"You're right, Chum. It does look the same."

"Aching pixie's heart, look on your left; is that a cradle?" Dahc asked as he pointed.

Gala lifted the candle towards the cell. He gasped, hardly able to speak, "Giver of life and love. It is a cradle. This cannot be Wizard Tiaff's doings. I don't think he'd put his infant's cradle in the dungeon."

"No. I doubt it. But I wouldn't put anything past those Gobs."

"You might be right, Dahc. Let's keep looking," Gala lifted the candle towards the cell directly across. "Oh, my wizardry nerves." Gala hurried into the cell and picked up a torn piece of a blue garment that shimmered with silver and gold. "This is a piece of Floreena's gown. I feel sick."

"Hang in there, Chum. I don't see blood or any signs of struggle." Ddot flew above Gala and flapped the calming essence from his wings."

"Gala took a deep breath and cleared the swirling thoughts of dread. Thanks, Ddot."

"Any time, Chum, any time. Let's keep looking." Ddot flew back down and stood on Gala's shoulder.

After they reached the end of the dungeon, they saw a hole in the wall and rubble on the floor. Gala held the candle up. He surmised, "I bet that Gob knocked this wall down." Gala stuck the candle through the hole and saw steps.

"Pee-ew. It stinks. I'm using my face wrap," Dahc said. He tied it around his head. Ddot did the same.

Gala said something in his Sorcermizic language. A kerchief floated out of his cloak's pocket, then covered his nose and mouth.

"It sure is dark," Gala said under his breath.

"Yeah. Dark and creepy." Dahc added. Tiny hairs on the back of their necks stood at attention. "You can use your Redtalon's craw if you need to, right?"

"Oh yeah, Dahc. I almost forgot about that. If I need to use his craw, I will."

"That makes me feel safer."

"Yeah. Me too, Dahc," added Ddot.

Gala stepped over the rubble and headed down the staircase. He and his friends cringed at the black spiders in hanging webs. But Gala continued onward despite his nerves. An enormous, scraggly fat rat scurried across his path, which made him stumble. The twins held tight to his hair. When Gala lifted his candle toward the last cell, he jumped backward and yelled, "Whoa!" He and the twins shuddered. Their skin almost jumped off their bones like the skeleton they saw sitting against the stone wall.

"I wonder how long that's been down here and if he was evil or good," Ddot whispered.

"I wonder who it was that closed him inside," Dahc added.

"I bet it was before Wizard Tiaff got assigned to this castle. The more I think about it, the more I think Lucky's aunt is right about that witch, Idanab. When that Gob yelled out, he yelled for Gorg, Idanab, and Terrib. I thought Gorg sounded like a Gob's name. Terrib sounds like a name that would belong to a witch. I bet those were the Gobs we saw in the crystal. They're the ones who helped those witches do something to our loved ones and to Wizard Tiaff and Nam. Or whatever the lad's name is."

"Look there. Someone knocked that wall down." Dahc pointed.

"Oh yeah." Gala held up the candle. And look, there's a tunnel. I bet those Gobs dug that out too."

"Are we going through there? It's creepy."

Gala cringed. "Sheesh! I don't know, Ddot, and I don't know what's creepier, the spiders or those crawling bugs with all those legs and glowing eyes blinking at us." Gala shook off his bone-chilling sensation. He looked down at the ground. "Look, guys, footsteps, and more than one set. Some of them are hard to make out. This tunnel looks heavily traveled." Gala bent down and touched one of the prints. "These must be the Gobs because they're fresh." Gala stood and bent over at his midriff. He continued through the tunnel, looking down at the tracks. "Look, guys! These are small shoe prints like my mother's size. And look at these boot prints; they're much bigger. Let's keep going."

After they reached the mouth of the tunnel, Gala snuffed out the candle, concealed it, and then peeked around the mouth of the tunnel. He and his friends saw Swampress trees, saw grasses, and cattails. Everything glittered under the light of the moons. A cool breeze came off the dark-blue swamp water and brushed their faces. They heard Scrub Chirpers chirping and frogs croaking. A loud plop hit the water. Gala and the twins stiffened.

They saw ripples in the water. A fish jumped up. They jolted, then relaxed after seeing it was the fish that made the flip-plop noise. Fish jumped to the surface, eating insects that landed on lily pads, grass reeds, or the water's surface. As Gala took in the scene with all his senses, he thought, "Gee, wizards. The swamp might have creepiness and evil lurking about, but it sure is pretty."

"Hide. Someone's coming," Ddot warned.

Before Gala ducked back inside the tunnel, he squinted, furrowed his brows, pressed his lips tight, then spat, "Helsin! What are you doing here?"

"Gala! It's you!"

"Yeah, now answer the question!" Gala balled his fists after concealing his wand.

"I'm looking for a Gob while your mother is—"

"My mother!?! Gob!?!" Gala's fists clenched tighter. "Where's my mother!" As Gala charged towards Helsin, his hood fell backward, uncovering his head. The twins flew off his shoulders.

Helsin held out his hands. "No! Gala wait! I can explain!"

POW! Gala punched Helsin across his left jaw. Helsin turned his face back towards Gala and pleaded, "Gala! Let me expla—"

POW! Gala threw Helsin a punch with his other fist. Gala was about to punch him again when Helsin rushed in and tackled Gala to the ground. Gala wiggled his way out of Helsin's hold. They jumped to their feet and exchanged punches. They punched each other in the gut, eye, and jaw. "Where's my mother!"

When Gala swung another punch, Helsin dodged it. He grabbed Gala's arm and twisted it around his back. Gala struggled to get loose. He wasn't about to use magic to fight Helsin. They fell into the swamp water, which caused Helsin to let loose of Gala's arm. Helsin and Gala found their footing. They were about thigh deep in water where the swamp's muck bottom butted the sandy part of the bank. Gala lunged towards Helsin. They fell into the water and wrestled, one on top of the other, back, and forth, water splashing high. Once again, they stood, then Gala leaped toward Helsin, but this time Helsin stepped to one side, and Gala fell face down in the water. Helsin reached both hands around Gala's neck and held his head under. The twins yelled for Helsin to stop, but Helsin ignored them. Gala could tell Helsin was in front of him, so he wrapped his arms around Helsin's legs at the knees. He pulled and pulled to no avail. Helsin's feet were firmly planted. Gala couldn't hold his breath any longer, but he did not give in; his pride wouldn't allow him to transform or use magic. His air bubbles surfaced. Ddot flapped his calming essence over Helsin, then flew down beside Dahc. Gala was on the verge of passing out. The twins pulled back their bows, aiming at Helsin's head. Before they let loose, Helsin put his hands around Gala's shoulders and lifted him to his feet. Gala sucked in a bucket of air and coughed.

Before Gala could say anything, Helsin yelled, "I'm helping your mother! After you hear me out, you can decide if we should continue this punching match."

"Start talking," Gala said between a few more coughs. He slapped Helsin's hands off his shoulders.

"We're sopping wet, and it's cold; can we at least get out of the water and dry off first?"

"Fine!"

"Wait! There's a monstrous Mudlump on your neck!"

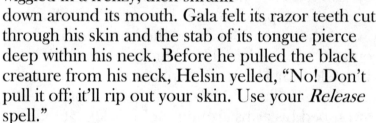

Gala wrapped his hand around the slimy blood sucker's neck. Its ten snail-like eyes wiggled in a frenzy, then shrank down around its mouth. Gala felt its razor teeth cut through his skin and the stab of its tongue pierce deep within his neck. Before he pulled the black creature from his neck, Helsin yelled, "No! Don't pull it off; it'll rip out your skin. Use your *Release* spell."

"Are you patronizing me?"

"No! But if you don't hurry, that thing will make you sick; you and I both know this."

Gala closed his eyes and hoped he didn't look weak in front of Helsin. He imagined the Wizard's High Council applauding. But he couldn't help but imagine Helsin standing amongst them laughing. Gala scolded, "Argh! Focus!" After he shook the image from his head, he yelled out loud, "*Let Loose!*" When Gala felt the Mudlump's tongue and teeth retract, he pulled his arm back and heaved the slimy bloodsucker far into the swamp. He and Helsin hurried onto the sandy bank before anything else latched on to them.

Gala transfigured into his Bluewing form and spun dry. Helsin lifted his hand and said, "*Ow-a-dy.*" He was dry in seconds. It was the spell Gala had not perfected when he and Helsin attended Whittlewood Academy.

Gala transformed back into himself and demanded, "Okay! Start talking showoff!"

Helsin rolled his eyes. He slightly shook his head and said, "I'm helping your mother. She's going to meet me after she puts Floreena in—"

"Floreena!?!" What about Flor—"

"For mage's sake, would you let me finish," Helsin pleaded with open arms.

Gala pressed his lips tight. He gave Helsin a quick gestured nod to continue. But before Helsin could say anything, they heard Gobs grunting. The twins flew onto Gala's shoulders. Gala was about to hide when he felt Helsin touch his arm.

"Follow me," Helsin implored. Gala saw the gentleness he once saw when they were friends, so he nodded for Helsin to lead. As Gala followed, he summoned a bottle of Wizard Spark's blood and took a sip without Helsin seeing him. The wound he got from the Mudlump healed. It was gone in less than a second, and so was the black eye Helsin gave him.

Helsin led them to the cave where he was to wait for Faithin's return. He started a fire and made them comfortable seats.

Helsin ate one of his Healing charms. When he turned to offer one to Gala, he saw that Gala's black eye was gone. Helsin lifted his brows, but he didn't say anything. He put his charm away, took a deep breath, then let it out. He began telling them what his aunt Ida had planned. But he wasn't about to say how he stopped Wizard Sparktinian from traveling to The Wizard's High Council. As Gala and the twins listened, Lucky and Serenity had flown back home with Nectar and Stamen.

Wicked Must Die

Herbaleen waited at the entrance of the Tuberous Tribe's waterfall cave. She stopped biting her nails when Lucky and Serenity came in with Nectar and Stamen. Herbaleen hugged them tight, with tears running down her cheeks. She took Nectar and Stamen into her private chambers where she could tend to their needs. Lucky and Serenity waited for her return in the main hall. Serenity placed her face in her hands and broke down.

Lucky embraced her. When she stopped crying, she looked at Lucky and cupped his cheeks. She kissed him tenderly and said, "I'm feeling better now. I knew it in my heart. It's easier for me because I already accepted what I figured was true. Now I have closure. I'll be okay." After they hugged, Serenity sat on a large fungus growing out from the side of the cavern.

"It's been about two hours since we first left to investigate Wizard Tiaff's castle. I got this urge to be helpin' my pals." Lucky paced across the fungus.

"I wish there was somethin' we could do. It's hard not knowin' and just sittin' here waitin'. What do ya think Gala would want ya to do?"

Lucky stopped pacing and sighed. He sat down beside Serenity. "Gala would want us to stay put and have the warriors go lookin' ifin' they don't come home in about one more hour."

Serenity gave Lucky a tender kiss on his cheek. He put his arm around her and returned a kiss. "Yore friends are wonderful, Lucky. The twins are cute. I wouldn't be able to tell 'em apart ifin' their personalities were the same, or their freckles." Lucky and Serenity chuckled. "Y'all are fortunate to have Gala lookin' after ya. He's a good wizard. I can tell y'all are tight. Wizard Tiaff is good too, and he's a Mystique Wizard. He has several forms. It's fun to watch him transfigure."

"Yeah. Gala's a great friend, and his magic abilities are extraordinary. We like to watch him transfigure, too."

Herbaleen came out to the great hall. After she joined Serenity and Lucky, she said, "I gave them somethin' to sleep and a couple of Sweet Dream Charms that Wizard Tiaff taught me to make. They'll be out for the night and won't have any nightmares. So now, tell me everythin'." Herbaleen sat on a large gem.

Serenity could see Herbaleen start to fidget and seethe as they told her what they had seen. Herbaleen stopped listening when she heard her tribe members were locked up in a cage. She knew how scared they must have been as they waited for Gobs to devour them. The thought that Gobs ate fairies as some mere treat was nauseating. Revenge swirled in her head, "That wicked witch! Wickedness must die. If it's not destroyed, it will kill innocence every chance it gits!" After Lucky and Serenity finished their story, Herbaleen encouraged, "Come, you two. Let's git somethin' warm to drink."

Herbaleen didn't say a word while she was making their drinks. When she set their drinks on the kitchen table, she did so without making eye contact. She walked over to the cookery stove and said, "I'll join y'all after I'm done whippin' up a few charms."

Serenity and Lucky smiled, but deep down, Serenity knew Herbaleen was acting distant.

While Herbaleen mixed ingredients, she glanced over at Lucky and Serenity. They weren't watching, so she hurried and reached inside a cabinet where they store their poisonous herbs and extracts. She took out a vile filled with a tincture extracted from a Death Root plant. Herbaleen poured the whole bottle into her mixture. It was enough to kill a five-ton dragon. She slipped the empty vile into her apron's pocket as she stirred the mixture to her desired thickness. After she puts the charm in Idanab's mouth, it will dissolve and absorb into Idanab's bloodstream. It will cause her organs to slow until they stop functioning. Her breath will still until all life finally leaves her body. No one will know the cause of Idanab's death. Everyone will think she died from her injuries. Herbaleen put her toxic charm into her apron's pocket.

After she cleaned the cookery stove, she sat at the table with Lucky and Serenity. They sat talking while waiting for Gala and the twins to return and hoping they found their loved ones safe.

Meanwhile, after Faithin had flown the baby to the Treeager's village, she flew to the Bluewings' cave with Floreena.

Dragon

Faithin stood on the outside of the Bluewings' cave. She didn't want to frighten anyone, so she yelled for Acub and Ashlin to forewarn them of her shadowed appearance.

Acub and Ashlin recognized her voice, but Acub held Conkay's staff in case witchery was afoot. They peeked outside the entrance. A shadowy figure in the shape of Faithin had Floreena in a levitated state. Acub pointed Force towards the **Shadow**. He demanded, "What dark trickery is this?"

"It's not dark, but those who had used this shadowy disguise have used it for dark purposes. It is me, Faithin. Watch. Faithin transfigured into all her shapes, then back into herself.

"Faithin!" — "It is you!" Acub and Ashlin yelled in unison.

"Yes! Yes, it's me. I'll explain everything later. I need your healer to look after Floreena. I must meet Helsin. He's going to help me. His aunt is the culprit for this mess, and she's trapped until I free her. Lidee is trapped, too, so I must hurry."

"Come in! Come in!" Acub motioned Faithin inside their spacious home.

"I'll get Remedie," offered Ashlin.

"Thank you, Ashlin. I'll lay Floreena in the cavern here to the left. Tell Remedie that Floreena is in a deep sleep. She'll likely sleep until morning due to the amount of sleeping potion forced down her throat."

Ashlin understood. She took off towards their healer's crevice.

After Faithin laid Floreena on the feathered bed, she asked Acub how he came to use Force. When he told her, she put her hands on her mouth. Acub could tell she was about to cry, so he comforted her, "Faithin, your Gala and the Newlads are strong together. Let's keep faith that they're okay, and you'll find each other."

Poof! There was a golden spark of dust particles where Faithin's **Shadow** stood. Faithin's Bluewing **Shadow** flew towards Acub and gave him a hug. "Thank you, Acub. We'll stay optimistic. According to Helsin, Gala was searching for help from the Timeless Woodlanders. They dwell within the realm of Timestill Forest."

"Timestill Forest? I've heard stories about that realm. Gnomes and elves live together in harmony. It's rumored that one elf has telepathic abilities. I heard trees could talk to him."

"Yes. I heard that too." Faithin stopped hugging Acub and said, "Tell Ashlin I'll be back as soon as possible. When Floreena wakes, tell her to stay put and wait for our return." Poof! Faithin transformed into herself and hurried outside. Acub followed to see her off.

"May the giver of life and—OH NO! A fire-breathing dragon! Faithin, don't let anyone come out of the cave. I'm gonna use Force to contain that dragon, so it doesn't destroy anything or anyone!"

"Okay. Be careful!"

"Will do." Acub tapped the bottom of Force on the ground and said, "*Force, Contain It.*" He pointed Force at the dragon. Force turned azure. Its amulet shot out a rainbow-colored beam of light straight toward the dragon. Poof! Force transported the dragon into Conkay's holding case inside the laboratory.

"What's happening?" Ashlin flew up to Faithin.

"Ashlin, call your warriors. I need them to follow us to the castle. Acub used Force to contain a dragon." Ashlin gasped and hurried inside to rally the Bluewing warriors. It took less than a minute for the warriors to get ready.

Everyone hurried into the castle. Faithin saw her furniture arranged the way she wanted it. She looked at Ashlin. "You did this? You remembered what I wanted?"

"Yes." But Faithin. There's something you should know. Acub and I found what looks like a secret passage behind a wall in the laboratory. It's a tunnel."

"Yes. I know. I'll explain it later. But thank you for putting our home in order, Ashlin. That was considerate of you."

"You're more than welcome."

Faithin gave Ashlin a content smile. After they entered the laboratory, they saw an angry green dragon in Conkay's holding crate. The dragon was holding an urn. He hit the glass walls with his fist and tried to scratch them with his claws. He yelled, "Let me out of here!"

Faithin instructed, "Warriors, release the essence of your wings. Acub, use Force to contain their essence inside with the dragon, so he can calm down and we can find out who he is."

One hundred Bluewing warriors released their essence. Glowing blue speck particles fell from their wings. Acub used Force and contained them inside the case with the dragon. After the dragon calmed down, he transformed into his wizard self. He was still covered with grit and dust from the explosion. Faithin asked him his name and where he came from.

"My name is Nam. I mean Optim! All my life, until tonight, I thought my name was Nam. Wizard Tiaff is my father. That wicked witch, Idanab, lied to me. My mother is, was, Lovlin, a Mystique Blueblood enchantress. I didn't mean to, but I burned my father to ashes." Optim cried as he held up the urn. Without any control, he transformed into his dragon, then back into himself. "Wizard Conkay told me to come here to find the Bluewing clan, so they could help me. He said he would meet me here after he deals with Idanab and finds his loved ones. I wasn't going to come here. I found a cave to sleep for the night. But after this young wizard came into the cave and offered to help me, I got mad at him for calling me Nam. I was going to grab him, but I don't think I did. I know that I woke up under rubble holding a red ruby. I dropped the ruby. After a minute or so, I flew away and was going to look for another cave, but decided I should come here instead. I'm sorry if I hurt anyone."

Faithin was speechless for a moment. Then she said, "Conkay is my husband. Did the young wizard tell you his name?"

"I'm pretty sure he said Gala."

Faithin gasped. "Do you know what happened to Gala?"

"No. But I saw two Bluewing fairies and one with green wings. They flew down to another cave, then that's when I transformed into my dragon and flew off."

"Gala is my son, and those were his friends. Do you know the Bloodra Ceremony?"

"No. But my father sang me a Bloodra Lullaby, and your husband told me to keep singing it to myself."

"Yes. Sing the lullaby over and over until your veins stop hurting. Acub will use Force to move you into one of our guest rooms. Your dragon will fit. I want you to direct your craw towards the fireplace. It won't take long before you finally have complete control of your transitions, not to mention your craw. When you do, Acub and Ashlin will be outside the room waiting. They'll show you where you can wash up, then they'll get you something to eat and drink. I'll be back as soon as I can."

"Are you going to my father's castle?"

"Yes. Why do you ask?"

"Well, Idanab said I left some of my father's ashes on the table, but I didn't trust her, so I ignored her. But what if she was telling the truth?"

"I'll look around and bring them back if I find them."

"Thank you."

"You're more than welcome. I've got to go before this potion wears off."

Reunite

Faithin ran outside to the main walk of her castle and transfigured into her dragon. Her shadowy dragon took off like the wind. After she reached the mountain where she was to meet Helsin, she transfigured into herself and headed down the tunnel. She heard voices. "Gala!" She yelled. His name echoed through the cave.

"Mom?" When Faithin entered, Gala gasped. He pointed his wand and yelled, "SHADOW!"

"No! Gala! It's me, your mother. Helsin? Didn't you tell him?"

"I didn't get to that part yet. I was just about to say you trapped my aunt Idanab and Lidee in Conkay's picture—"

"What!? Lidee? Idanab? They're trapped in Father's picture?"

"Then who is that in Herbaleen's care?" Ddot asked.

"Who is Herbaleen?" The Shadow potion wore off Faithin.

"Mother! It is you!" Gala lowered his wand. He ran over to his mother, and the twins followed. They hugged each other, all in tears. Helsin's eyes turned red as he watched their reunion.

Dahc flew back; his jaw slacked. "What is it, Dahc?" Faithin asked.

"It's Herbaleen. She's Lucky's great Aunt. And she doesn't like Idanab! What if Lucky and Serenity took Nectar and Stamen home? It's been over twenty minutes since we left them in Tiaff's secret den. I'm sure they're home by now. We thought that was Idanab in Herbaleen's care. Lucky,

Serenity, and Herbaleen don't know it's someone else. What will Herbaleen do when she hears Idanab snatched some of her tribe members and fed them to Gobs?"

Helsin's eyes popped. Faithin covered her gaping mouth.

"We need to tell them. Now!" Ddot yelled.

"I need to get Lidee and Idanab out of the picture."

"But, Mother? How are you going to do that without having to fight Idanab?"

"I've got a plan, and Helsin will play a big part. Idanab will not suspect anything when Helsin comes to her aid." Faithin looked over at Helsin. He gave her a determined nod.

Gala glanced at Helsin and thanked him. With a tone of regret, Helsin said, "It's the least I can do after all I've done." Gala reached out to shake Helsin's hand. Helsin was happy to exchange the gesture.

"Where's the Southlanders' home? We'll meet you there with Lidee after I bind Idanab."

"It's not far, Mother. It's like catty-corner or northwest of Wizard Tiaff's castle. When you hear the waterfall, you're there."

"Here. Why don't all of you take a sip of the Shadow potion so you travel swiftly. You too, Faithin, although you might be tired from the last amount you drank."

Faithin patted Helsin's shoulder. "I'm a little tired, but I'm all right."

They recited the incantation and materialized into **Shadows**. Gala gave his mother another hug. "Be careful, Mother."

"I will. I've lost my wand, but Helsin has his, and I have a few hand spells I can—"

"Your wand!" Gala interrupted, "That's your wand! If the Shadow potion changes your appearance, the witch could have disguised Faither!"

"What?" Faithin cocked her head.

"We gotta go! I'll tell you later." Gala and the twins glided straight toward the Tuberous Tribes' home.

Time to Rid Evil

Herbaleen excused herself from the table. "I need to look in on Idanab, make sure she ain't wakin'. It's 'bout time for her next dose of sleepin' cream. Would y'all be so kind as to look in on Nectar and Stamen for me? Let's meet back here. If Gala and the twins ain't back by then, I'll wake the warriors to go lookin' for 'em."

"Be glad to, Aunt Herbaleen."

"Yeah, sure. But are you okay, Herbal? I'm upset about what Idanab did with our Tuberous Tribe members, but how do you feel?"

"Well, Serenity, I ain't gonna lie. I'm more upset than a rattled Stinger, alright, and who wouldn't be. I'm sure you and I ain't the only ones upset. There's nothin' I'd like better than to rid Mageus from all evil, but that ain't gonna happen. Don't worry 'bout me. I'll git over this sooner than Nectar and Stamen. They're gonna need a lot of Healin' and Nightmare removal charms before they can return to normalcy of any kind."

"Okay then. We'll meet back here when we're done."

Serenity and Lucky gave Herbaleen a hug. After they were gone from her sight, she thought, "I didn't lie. I said there's nothin' I'd like better than to rid Mageus from ALL evil. That didn't mean I caint rid at least one evil, and that's what I intend to do." When she flew in and hovered over who she thought was Idanab, she snarled, "Cursid witch! Open your mouth!" Herbaleen pulled the Death charm from her pocket, then flapped her wings across Conkay's lips. As soon as his mouth opened, Herbaleen aimed—"

"THAT'S NOT IDANAB! THAT'S MY FATHER!"

Lucky, Serenity and half the sleeping tribe heard Gala holler. Herbaleen's eyes popped out of her head when she heard him. But she had already dropped the charm; she fumbled to catch it and missed.

Gala and the twins glided inside. The Shadow potion wore off right when Herbaleen turned to face them. "Herbaleen! That's my father!"

"I'm sorry. I tried to catch it but—"

"Catch what?" Gala asked.

"A Death Charm. It's in his mouth and—." Herbaleen covered her mouth.

Gala pointed firm fingers at his father's throat and mouth. Using Sorcermizic language, he commanded, "*Dri-Ous-Xpel!*" Which meant to expel and banish anything foreign in his father's mouth or throat. He never cast the spell before. Nothing happened. Gala stood waiting for the charm to expel. Lucky and Serenity flew in. Half the tribe members waited outside the entrance. The room was as silent as a realm without life. Herbaleen held her clammy hands on her cheeks, her brows squinched inwards. Serenity saw Herbaleen's body shivering, so she flew over and embraced her.

Gala shook his head while his mind he screamed, "NO! NO! NO!" He decided to try the spell once more, and right when he pointed his fingers, his father coughed. Out came the charm.

Gala lurched out and caught it, then slipped it into his pocket.

Gala looked at Herbaleen. Her hands were over her heart, her eyes beet red. Gala asked, "Do you have Wake Smells?"

"Yes!" Herbaleen hurried to her healing crevice with tears running down her face. She thought, "I ain't never doin' nothin' like that again."

After Herbaleen returned with the Wake Smells, Gala thanked her and comforted, "And don't fret. I might have done the same if I was in your place."

"That's good of ya to say, young mage, but I ain't never gonna do that again. I'll kill ifin' I have to defend myself. I'll kill defendin' my loved ones from bein' harmed or killed. But I ain't never doin' anythin' like this again." Serenity put her arm back around Herbaleen.

Gala held the Wake Smells under his father's nose. After a few breaths, Conkay began to stir. His eyes blinked opened. When they focused, he asked, "Son?"

"Father!" Although he still looked like Idanab, Gala bent over and embraced his neck. "Oh Father!"

Conkay returned Gala's hug and patted his back. He asked, "When will you introduce me to your friends? They look like Lucky's kin."

"They are. This is Serenity and Herbaleen. Herbaleen is Lucky's great aunt. Most of their tribe survived the Ultra Storm and made their home here."

"Does Lucky know?"

"I do," Lucky answered. He flew over next to Serenity. The twins flew over too.

"You're all here, but where is here?" Conkay looked at the twisted wands in his hand and saw that his hand looked like someone else's. He ran his other hand across his face and felt his nose, cheeks, and mouth. "That witch disguised me. Her wand twisted around your— MOTHER'S! Where's your mother!?! Where's Floreena and Lidee!?!" Conkay tried to get up but fell back down. He put his hand on his head. "Ouch!"

"Lie there and relax. Ya got a nasty bump on yore head. It's gone down some, but ya need to give it a little more time before ya go jumpin' 'round. Hold on a minute. I got something that'll ease yore pain." Herbaleen flew over to her table of healing supplies.

"Wait, Herbaleen! I almost forgot." Herbaleen flew back over next to Serenity. Gala summoned a bottle of Sparktinian's blood. "Take a sip of this, Father." Gala held the back of his father's neck so his head could rest while he took a sip. After his father's head laid back on his pillow, Gala saw the bump shrink down to nothing and said, "Would you look at that. The bump on your head disappeared like lickity-split before an eye-blinked quick."

Conkay felt the wands in his hand move. "Wizardry. Look at these wands. They're unwinding. My hand—" Conkay touched his face. "And my face—" Gala's brows rose. His father looked like himself. "Working wizard wonders, that's mystical mystics. My headache has vanished. Poof! Gone! Just like magic." What is that stuff?"

"I'll tell you everything later. But I can tell you this, Wizard Sparktinian gave it to us, me, Ddot, Dahc, and Lucky. He wanted me to tell you, 'Dragamage and Star'ella-love.'" Conkay cupped Gala's arm. They locked eyes and rested for a moment. Gala could tell his father knew what Spark meant. He could tell his father knew Spark was a Mystique Blueblood.

"We'll discuss Wizard Spark when we find the time. I need to find your mother?"

She should be in Wizard Tiaff's castle by now. She had trapped the witch in your picture, but Lidee is in there too, so Mother planned to bind the witch and get Lidee out. Helsin is helping her. They're coming here when they're done. Oh yeah. Here." Gala summoned his father's wand. "I found it on the floor after you got snatched. I found your staff too, but I let Acub and Ashlin use it for added protection while we came looking for you."

Conkay kept his wand ready and concealed the other two. He complimented, "Good going, son. Wise decision. Now point me in the direction of the castle."

"It's southeast of here, on The Ridge. I'm coming with you, Father."

"Me too," added Ddot.

"I'm coming too," Dahc said.

"I ain't lettin' y'all outta my site," interjected Lucky. Lucky hugged his aunt Herbaleen and embraced Serenity. "Don't ya fret none. The Lakinshires are the most powerful Mystiques on

Mageus. When they're together, anyone against 'em ain't gotta chance." Lucky gave Serenity a kiss.

Conkay lifted a brow and concluded, "So, I see we have a soul mate joining to celebrate. We'll get the clans together when all this is over."

Conkay turned towards Herbaleen and thanked her, "Thank you."

Herbaleen's red eyes watered. She smiled and bowed.

Conkay returned a bow, then encouraged, "Let's go, warriors. Lead on, Gala."

"Yes, sir."

Truth

After entering Tiaff's secret den, Gala led his father across the room to its hidden door. They heard Gobs snarling on the other side. The twins stood on Gala's shoulder while Lucky stood on Conkay's. Gala pushed the button to the hidden door. Inch by inch, it creaked open. To their surprise, the Gobs hung upside down from the rafters. They were back-to-back, wrapped in fetter chains from their ankles to their necks.

Gala and Conkay ran toward Wizard Tiaff's laboratory. After peering inside, they saw Helsin pointing his wand at Idanab. She couldn't move. Helsin used the Lakinshire's *Congeal* spell that Gala hadn't perfected. Lidee lay on a table, unconscious from the Lethargic potion, and two **Shadows** were in the middle of a witch's dual.

"**Shadows**!" Conkay pointed his wand and began his spell, "*Sha–*"

"FATHER! WAIT! One of them is Mother!"

Helsin interjected, "The one stuck against the wall is Faithin! The other one is my Aunt Terrib she snuck up behind us!"

Terrib turned her head around with her wand still pointing up at Faithin. She held her left hand out behind her towards Helsin. She chanted. A red ball of fire formed in her shadowy, clenched, claw-like hand. Her concentration on Faithin relaxed, which allowed Faithin to transform into her eagle. Faithin's shadowy eagle stretched out her claws as she flew towards Terrib. She grabbed Terrib's arm and pulled her up into the air. Terrib started to bring her free hand around. But before she could throw her *Fiery* spell at Faithin, Conkay yelled, "*Soligulat!*" Terrib stilled, froze in time. She looked like a black statue ready to heave a red ball with her left arm coming up from behind. Her right arm stretched out with her wand pointed towards the ceiling.

Conkay had cast the *Congeal* spell using Sorcermizic language. As he lowered Terrib to the ground and held her there, Faithin transformed into herself and ran to Conkay. The shadow potion wore off when she embraced him, and he wrapped his free arm around her.

Faithin gazed into Conkay's dreamy blue eyes and asked, "What do you suppose we do with them?"

"We're gonna bind them good and tight, then get some answers. I'm certain Wizard Tiaff has the ingredients you'll need to whip up your Truth Serum." Conkay winked before he gave Faithin a tender kiss.

"We ought to gag and bind them before we remove your spells. You're not gonna want to hear what comes out of their mouths. Especially my aunt Ida's." Helsin could feel his aunt glaring at him.

"Gala?"

"Sir?"

"Take those Gobs down from the rafters before their brains fill with blood. Keep the *Fetter* spell on them while you use your *Levitation* spell and lock them up. Make sure they can't escape. After your mother and I tend to these evildoers, we'll deal with the Gobs."

"Yes, sir. I'll go ahead and take the Gobs to the swamps and be sure they never set foot out of their realm again. Then I'll seal up the tunnel and both dungeons."

"Great. You can seal the tunnel and the back wall to the castle, not the dungeons. Your father and I need to remove the restless skeleton from that—"

"Hold on a minute. Dungeons? Someone's bones?" Conkay's brows creased, and his head tilted.

"Yes. You'll see. We'll tend to that later, but I can't use my wand because I don't know where it is."

"I have it."

"How'd you— Never mind, you can tell me later," Faithin gave Conkay a quick peck on his lips. She summoned, "*Appara Comforte*" POOF! A spark of gold dust particles appeared in her hand, followed by her wand. She smiled.

What about Lidee? Is she okay lying there?"

Yes, Ddot. She'll be fine," Faithin answered. She walked over and felt Lidee's head. "If you don't mind, I'd like you and Dahc to look after her while we tend to these witches."

"Sure thing," Ddot and Dahc said in unison. With their arrows ready to fire, Ddot stood on the table near Lidee's head, and Dahc stood by her feet.

"I'll go with Gala, ifin' that's alright," Lucky suggested.

"Thank you, Lucky. That was my next suggestion," Faithin said with a smile. Lucky flew over and stood on Gala's shoulder.

"Y'all be sharp and be quick. We may need your help."

"Yes, sir," Gala and Lucky said in unison. They hurried into the great hall to take care of the Gobs.

Helsin shared what he heard his aunts say. "Just so y'all know, I'm wondering what will happen to Aunt Terrib if her potion wears off. Because my aunt Ida yelled, 'Terrib! Return to the swamp before the Shadow potion wears off!' My aunt Terrib yelled back, 'Ida! I drank enough to help you fight this witch and your ungrateful assistant, Helsin! I have time to help you bind them before anything happens to me.'"

"Helsin?"

"Yes, sir?"

"We've never met your aunts before tonight. We still haven't met your uncle. What is his name?"

"Uncle Dec, I mean Dectore."

"What are their last names?"

"Uncle Dec's and Aunt Ida's is Tangler, but I don't know Aunt Terrib's. I never met Aunt Terrib until tonight, and only as a **Shadow**. I couldn't tell you what she looks like. Why?"

"Have you heard the story of the Faraway witches?"

"Yes, sir. I heard The Wizard's High Council banished them to the Boggy Swamps."

"That's right, and so were their children, if they had any."

Faithin interjected, "I see what you're getting at, Conkay. But if they are Faraway's children, then not just one, but both would be bound to the swamps."

"You're right, my gem, but what if they are half-sisters? What if Idanab was born before Terrib? What if the sisters' mother, Tamian, had conceived a child with her true beloved before Grock cast his *Love* spell on her?"

"Oh, yes. That would mean Idanab is the firstborn, not bound to the swamps. Whereas Terrib is. The Wizard's High Council only banished the children Grock and Tamian conceived."

"Exactly. So, the Shadow potion must allow Terrib to leave the boundaries of the swamps."

"Helsin?"

"Yes, ma'am?"

"Do you have enough Shadow potion to keep your aunt Terrib a **Shadow** for a few hours? She might not have much left of her own?"

"Yes, ma'am."

"Good." Faithin pointed her wand at Terrib. She commanded, "*Colatherner*," which meant to collect all the items Terrib had on her. Terrib's wand shot out from her shadowy hand. It glided across the room and landed on the table next to Faithin. Out from Terrib's cloak pockets came a bottle with a small amount of Shadow potion. Next came a jar with three Scarlet Leprechaun Frogs inside. Then a spell book titled, *Faraway's Rituals & Spells* floated out. Faithin gasped, "Conkay! Your suspicions are correct. She is a Faraway. Read this title. Faithin pointed her wand at the book and lifted it so Conkay could read its cover.

"Umm. So, it seems. I'll conceal the book on me. "*Conceal.*" The book vanished from the air and hid inside Conkay's burgundy cloak. "Okay, Gem, get what Idanab has on her."

Faithin pointed her wand at Idanab, "*Colatherner.*" Idanab's spell book and an ebony wand came from her robe onto the table. Then Idanab's crystal ring came off her finger. It floated over and landed on Idanab's spell book. Conkay wondered who the ebony wand belonged to. He concealed them inside his cloak. "Helsin. Let's take your aunts out into the great hall. We'll sit them back-to-back. Faithin and I will bind them with our *Fetter* spells."

"Yes, sir. But remember to gag them."

"We will," Faithin assured. Faithin and Conkay gagged and bound the sister witches. Then Helsin and Conkay stopped the *Congeal* spells. The sisters were mute and paralyzed. They couldn't yell or wiggle loose. "Helsin, do you mind helping Conkay keep an eye on them while I search for ingredients?

"I'd be glad to." Helsin smiled.

Faithin hugged Conkay before she went into the storage room. "I sure hope Gala and Lucky are okay."

"Don't worry, Gem. They made it this far. I'm sure they're okay." Conkay was right. Gala and Lucky were taking care of the Gobs without any problems.

Promises Will Be Kept

Gala levitated the Gob brothers high above the Swampress trees that stood tall in the shallows of the swamp. He thought, "I could just hold them here and let them burn to ash with the coming of the morning sun." Gala shook his head, rolled his eyes, and clicked his tongue, then huffed, "Sheesh. I'd better not. Guess I'll cast a *Ward* spell instead."

"Are ya alright there, pal?"

"Yeah. I'm just wondering what I can do to make those Gobs stay in the swamp and never set foot outside their realm again. I know it's against magi rules to cast spells on others without their permission, but in some cases, we're allowed. If I was to cast a spell on these Gobs for what they've done, I don't think The Wizard's High Council would count it against me."

"I don't know, Pal. They might, seeins' them Gobs ain't got no sense. It ain't their fault they were born that way. How 'bout ya make 'em forget or make 'em scared, so scared that they ain't never gonna leave them there swamps?"

Gala's brows creased. He gave the suggestion some thought and said, "Lucky ole boy, you're a genus." Gala continued to hold the Gobs in his *Levitation* spell. Without fearing them, the swamps, or the creatures in it, he transformed into his Bluewing form. He told Lucky, "Follow me up to the top of The Ridge. I'll transform into my Redtalon and give them a fright they'll never forget."

After they flew to the top of The Ridge, Gala transformed into Redtalon. Lucky flew up and lay on the top of his head. Redtalon pulled his left forearm inwards towards himself. He brought the Gobs close to his enormous maw. As soon as he released his *Levitation* spell, the Gobs dropped into the center of his paw. They trembled; their jaws slacked, and their eyes popped wide. They saw their reflections within Redtalon's vertical diamond-shaped pupils. They felt the heat of his breath. They jolted when he spoke in his dragon's baritone voice, "Gorg and Durgat!" Redtalon felt pleased as he made himself clear. "My hearing is exceptional, my eyesight superb, and my sense of smell picks up the slightest odor. Engraved in my memory is your scent. I will never forget it. If any Gob, you, your family, or friends, EVER sets foot outside the swamp boundaries, I'll have a feast. I'll snap your bodies in half. I'll use your bones to pick your bloody flesh out of my large, sharp, powerful teeth." Redtalon brushed his tongue across his razor-sharp, pointy teeth. He licked the head of each Gob. Their bodies shook like a leaf whipping in the wind. Redtalon stuck his tongue back in his mouth and warned, "If I hear of you, or any Gob, eating another fairy or bird, I will use my claws to rip out your guts." Redtalon took his right index claw and scratched the tops of their potbellies. A fine red line of blood beaded up through the scratches. The Gobs screamed and pleaded. Their voices cracked. Redtalon commanded, "HUSH! If I hear of you or see you talking with warlocks or witches, I will squish your heads until they pop off your necks. Do you understand?"

The Gob's heads wobbled like bobble-heads. They spit out their promises, "Understand, most powerful dragon." — "Understand, mighty master, dominate eminence." — "Never we leave swamp." — "Never we talk witches." — "Or warlocks." — "Never we eat fairy meat." — "No more yum-yums." — "No eat birds." — "You not eat us."

"I'll be lurking in the shadows watching you. If you even think about breaking your promise, I'll devour you. Maybe I should eat you now.

"No! We keep promise! We keep promise!" the brother Gobs yelled in unison.

"You'd better!" Redtalon snarled in his deep dragon voice. He pushed the tip of his enormous claw down on the Gob's potbellies. Durgat was about to pass out, so Redtalon flicked the Gobs far into the swamps. He and Lucky heard them bellow as they hurled through the air. Their bodies flayed across Swampress trees before they slapped hard on the surface of the swamp water. As they swam away, the water splashed until Redtalon and Lucky could no longer hear them.

Redtalon looked at his paw. He told Lucky, "Because of the disgusting excretions they left behind, I don't think they'll ever leave the swamps. What do you think, think I scared 'em enough?"

"Oh yeah, ya had me shakin'. Tinglebugs were dancin' in my gut. Ya sounded convincin'. The mere sight of your magnificence is frightin' anuff. I bet they warn every Gob they know and don't know. We ain't never gonna see a Gob set foot out of them-there swamps again, that's for sure. And they ain't never gonna talk to witches or warlocks. And, they ain't never gonna eat another fairy or bird."

"I bet you're right, Lucky. Well, let's get going. After I wash this shit off my hand, I'll close off the tunnel and seal up the castle's wall. Then we'll go see how my parents are faring."

"Did you say 'shit?'"

"Yeah. I heard my father call a pile of rat excretion shit, so I figure shit means excretion."

"Makes sense."

After Gala and Lucky returned to the dungeon, they covered their face with their kerchiefs. Gala retrieved and lit the candle he had put in his cloak's pocket earlier.

He pointed his wand inside the tunnel and chanted. "*Ose-up Sel-cure.*" It meant close and secure; after the sparkling gold light shot out from the tip of his wand into the tunnel, the tunnel rumbled. It folded in on itself like Dragon Mountain With-eyes-that-see did when it closed its caves. Rocks, roots, and dirt adhered to each other until the tunnel filled in and closed. Gala did the same to the back wall of the castle. It looked as though it was never excavated.

With Lucky on his shoulder, Gala hurried back to Wizard Tiaff's laboratory. Ddot and Dahc were still watching over Lidee. "Where's Gala's parents," Lucky asked.

"They're in the great hall," Ddot answered.

"Let us know what's happening," added Dahc.

"We will," assured Lucky.

After Gala and Lucky entered the great hall, "TERRIB!" Idanab screamed. It boomed throughout the castle. Gala jolted. Lucky shot off his shoulders.

"What do you want, malicious sister!?!"

"You had Father's, I mean Grock's, spell book and never told me! You knew I wanted it! You're a lying sneak, a wicked witch!"

"Me!?! Look at you, you evil doer, you baby snatcher! You LIAR! You had my father's wand all this time. Faithin, thank you. If it weren't for your Truth Serum, I would have never known the extent of my sister's wickedness. I mean, I know she's wicked, but I didn't know—"

"Shut your mouth or else I'll—"

"Or else what!?! You'll kill me like you killed the baby belonging to Helsi—"

"SHUT UP, TERRIB!"

"You couldn't take care of your own bab—"

"Terrib, so help me, when we get out of this, I'll cut out your tongue and slice—"

"No, you won't, you wicked witch! You're the one who killed my father, NOT GALA! You're the stench on—"

"ENOUGH!" Faithin yelled. She clapped her hands loud, then snapped her fingers in front of the witch's faces. Their heads dropped down, chins to their chests, fast asleep. Faithin hurried over to comfort Helsin, who had turned away. When he turned around, he saw Gala, and wiped the tears from his beet-red eyes. But Gala was wiping off his own tears.

After Gala composed himself, he asked, "What else is wrong? I can see it on your faces. Mother, Father?" Gala glanced back and forth from his mother to his father.

"There's quite a bit wrong with these two, especially Idanab. While your mother and Helsin stay with Lidee, you and I will take the witches to The Wizard's High Council. But first, I want you to take the Newlads to the Tuberous Tribe."

"I will, Father, but first, I want you to tell me what else y'all learned about these witches? Are they—?"

"Gala, sweetheart. I don't mean to interrupt, and I know you don't mean to be rude. You deserve to know everything, but we'll discuss it later."

"I don't mean to be disrespectful. I just want to know one thing, just one thing more, before I go. Did those witches curse Father's crystal ball? Did they curse me? And I still don't know where Floreena is?" Gala slung his arm up, then slapped it down against his thigh.

Conkay and Faithin lifted their brows. "That's more than one question. I'll answer one, and your father can answer the other two. Floreena is safe at home with Acub and Ashlin. You'll see her soon enough. First things first." Faithin glanced at her husband.

"Yes, Gala. Idanab cursed you, and she cursed my crystal, but we can reverse the spells." Conkay observed Gala's pensiveness, his narrowed eyes. When Gala turned his gaze towards Helsin, Conkay assured, "Helsin will be all right, and so will you.

Now take the Newlads to the Tuberous Tribe and hurry back. Morning's coming. Lidee will be waking soon, and so will Floreena. I need your help to get these witches to The High Council. After we return, your mother and I have reversal spells to perform. There are other matters to attend to that we'll need your help with. Okay?"

"Yes sir," Gala answered in an enthusiastic voice. "Oh yeah, Father. We gotta tell The High Council about our friends, the Kelvor Elves. Helsin said they're going to the Big Water—"

"Yes. I know. Your mother and Helsin told me. We'll tell The High Council. They'll send someone to aid the Kelvor Elves. Now take the Newlads back to the Tuberous Tribe."

"Yes, sir. Lucky waited while Gala hurried into the lab to get the twins. "Come on, guys. I'm taking y'all to the Tuberous Tribe. Father and I are taking the witches to The Wizard's High Council. I'll come to get you after we get back." The Newlads followed Gala towards the front entrance. Right before they reached the door, it slung open. They jolted backward. Their eyes widened; their jaws dropped.

Optim stood on the threshold, holding an urn in his arm. He wasted no time introducing himself. He apologized. He thanked Gala and the Newlads for trying to help him earlier. Gala stood dumbfounded. Optim hurried passed him, straight over to Conkay, and explained, "I had to come. I mastered my transition and figured I could help, but it looks as though you have everything under control. That's good, that's good. Wizard Conkay?

Did your wife come back? Did she get a chance to see if the witch was telling the truth about the rest of my father's ashes?"

"Actually, I was the one who told you about your father's ashes. Idanab disguised me as herself, which I didn't know."

"Oh. I see. I see."

"I'm here," Faithin interjected.

"You're Faithin?"

"Yes. This is me without the shadow appearance. Here." Faithin held out her hand. After a flash of golden dust particles poofed in her hand, a box with Tiaff's name written on it appeared. Faithin explained, "I found this box on the top shelf in the storage room of your father's lab."

Optim set the urn and the box on one of the decorative tables between the corridors. He took care and removed the lid from the box first. After he took the top off the urn, it began shaking. The box shook, too. Tiaff's ashes rose out from both containers and joined in the air. They twisted around like a storm cloud. Then, to everyone's surprise, the ashes piled together and formed a tall figure. Optim yelled, "Father! I thought I burned you to ash!" Optim lunged toward Wizard Tiaff and embraced him.

"Optim!" Tiaff cried. After a few seconds of embracing Optim, Tiaff put his hands on his son's shoulders. He gently pulled away and said, "Let me look at you. I didn't want to say it before. But the first time we met in the mountains of Mermary's Lake, I could have sworn I saw your mother's eyes.

Now I know I did. Your eyes are the exact color and shape. Oh, son! You've been with me for all these years, and I didn't even know it. That's why I felt contentment that I didn't quite understand. Listen, son, we'll catch up later. Let's attend to matters at hand."

"Yes, sir." Optim smiled and stood beside his father.

After Tiaff introduced himself, he clarified, "I am a Mystique Transfigure like you. My ash form is bits of thin granite that resemble ash. If my granite bits are separated, I cannot transform into myself. Of course, if my bits are close together, I can. When I first realized Nam was Optim, I knew what was happening. He was going through his Bloodra, his Mystique Blueblood transition for the first time. I saw his dragon scales take fruition and saw the flame in his maw. I knew he would not have control, so I transformed into my granite bits." Everyone acknowledged that they understood. Then Tiaff explained Idanab's deceit, "Idanab led me to believe Optim was her son. She befriended me using my weakness, which, as you may already know, was the loss of my wife and son. I have not been myself for some time." Everyone agreed with nods and yeses, including Helsin. Helsin had mixed feelings of anger and sadness, especially towards Idanab. They continued to listen as Tiaff resumed the rest of Idanab's wrongdoings. "Idanab was able to drug and keep me sedated. Half the time, I didn't know what day it was. She told me I had a deadly sickness that no one, not even The High Council, could cure. She said that the only ones who could cure me were the Lakinshires. She showed me a consent agreement from you. It read that you gave permission to extract the genes from your blood to heal us. I'm so sorry this happened to you, to us. I will do what I can to make things right."

"I gather you know me and my wife, Faithin?"

"Yes."

Conkay gestured his hand towards Gala. "This is our son, Gala." Gala walked over, then shook Tiaff's and Optim's hands. "And these are our friends, Helsin, Lucky, Ddot, and Dahc." After everyone shook hands and bowed to each other, Conkay continued. "You know, Idanab. Do you know Terrib?"

"I've never met Terrib."

"She's Idanab's half-sister. Terrib is a Faraway witch." Conkay pointed his wand at Terrib.

"Oh yes. The Wizard's High Council banished her parents and any children they conceived. So that's why Idanab wanted my Shadow potion, so Terrib could cross the swamp boundaries."

"Yes. We figured as much. After the sisters drank Faithin's Truth Serum, they revealed their devious plot. We'll expound on that in more detail later. But I will tell you this, Idanab wanted to put our genes, including yours, into Optim. She wanted him to become the most powerful Mystique Blueblood Transfigure on Mageus. She expected him to do her bidding. But that didn't work. She decided to put the genes into the Treeager baby. When that didn't work, she planned to steal another baby. Idanab is vengeful and angry towards everyone for the life she feels she should have had.

The one Grock stole from her. After Gala returns, he and I will use my warp speed to travel. We must get these witches and their belongings to The Wizard's High Council. We need to get there before the Shadow potion wears off, Terrib. We gave her the last of the potion."

"I'll make more. It's quick and easy. Also, I have a faster way for you to travel. It's a portal, a direct passage to The Wizard's High Council. You'll be there within seconds."

"Now that's interesting and impressive."

"So is your warp speed. I'm sure you and I will become close friends if you'd like."

"Yes. I can learn a lot from you."

"We will learn from each other."

"It's said and done." Conkay and Tiaff shook hands. Conkay turned and told Gala, "Hurry back, son."

"Yes, sir." Before he and the Newlads turned to take their leave, Gala yelled, "Lidee!"

Faithin hurried to help her. "Sit here a few minutes until your head clears."

Lidee looked around the room. Her head picked up speed, and her eyes followed. "Where's Floreena?"

"The Bluewings' healer is caring for her," Faithin assured.

"Here. We can see Floreena in Father's crystal ball." Gala hurried over and sat in the chair at the other end across from Lidee. He summoned his father's crystal ball and set it on the table."

"That doesn't look like my crystal."

"It is, Father. It's just that it went through some heat and kinda melded together. It was an accident, but I could—"

"Save it for story time, son," Conkay interrupted and winked. "Show Lidee her daughter. Afterward, tell her and your mother what Wizard Spark asked you to convey."

"Yes, sir," Gala asked the crystal to show Floreena. When Floreena appeared, Lidee took a deep breath, her smile content. Then Gala told Lidee and his mother Wizard Spark's final wishes.

Faithin and Lidee lifted their brows. Their eyes watered. Faithin bent over and hugged Lidee before she walked over and stood next to Conkay. Lidee looked at Gala and said, "Thank you, Gala. Spark always loved you and still does."

"Lidee, I know what Star'ella-love means, but Wizard Spark didn't tell me what Dragamage meant. I'm guessing y'all..." Gala glanced at his parents, then at Lidee, "...know what it means."

Lidee reached over the table and touched Gala's hand. She held his gaze, then said, "We'll talk when we get home."

"Yes, ma'am."

"Okay, son, take the Newlads and hurry back. Don't lollygag."

"Yes, sir."

Gala took the Newlads to the Tuberous Tribe. Faithin Went into Tiaff's kitchen to make everyone something warm to drink. Helsin kept a close eye on the witches as he went over and sat next to Lidee. Tiaff showed Conkay how to create his Shadow potion and how the portal worked.

One Year & Three Days Later

Conkay and Faithin sat in bed cuddled. Faithin's head rested on Conkay's chest while his arm wrapped around her shoulders. He brushed his hand up and down her soft arm and asked, "How are you feeling, my gem?"

"I didn't get sick this morning, so that's a plus." Faithin rubbed her abdomen.

Conkay kissed the top of Faithin's head and replied, "Good. What do you say if we let Gala announce his brother during tonight's celebration?"

"I say that's a good idea, love. He'll be honored."

Conkay put his other arm around Faithin and gave her a squeeze. He slid down, kissed her abdomen, and said, "Do you hear that sweet little fella? Your big brother is going to announce you to our friends tonight." Conkay kissed Faithin's abdomen again, then sat back up and put his arms around her. She rested her head back down on his chest. Conkay praised, "I'm proud of Gala. Even though Idanab cursed him, he fought through it. He overcame her *No Confidence* curse. My only regret is that I was hard on him. If I had known, I wouldn't have been so—"

"Oh sweetheart, shh, shh." Faithin lifted her head from Conkay's chest. She rested her finger on his lips and sympathized, "I know exactly how you feel. I felt the same. Let's promise not to beat ourselves over that. The past is over. I know you're as happy and grateful as I am that he's no longer cursed. Gala finally has his confidence and is sleeping without nightmares."

"Absolutely. I'm thankful he's no longer traumatized. When we first reversed the *Forget Nightmare* curse, it was unbearable to watch him break down as he did. His uncontrollable tears tore into my gut. Like you, I wanted to take his pain away."

"Yes, our son was terribly traumatized watching Trill and Quo go the way—" Faithin fought back her tears. She gulped twice, then continued, "At least Acub didn't have to endure that. The High Councils' *Healing* spell did wonders for Acub, Gala, and the two Tuberous Tribe members."

"Speaking of Nectar and Stamen, do you think they'll come tonight?"

"Oh yes. The whole tribe will be here with Wizard Tiaff and Optim, except for Lucky and Serenity. They'll come shortly after."

"Good. What do you say, shall we get the day started?"

"Yes. Let's do it." Faithin and Conkay kissed, then got up to face the day.

Announcements

Gala sat at the front entrance of Crystal Lake Castle, waiting for more guests to arrive. Floreena tiptoed behind him. She bent over to sneak a kiss, "Aah!" She screamed. Gala pulled her onto his lap and started kissing her cheeks, eyes, forehead, her tender lips. Floreena wrapped her arms around his neck and giggled. Gala reached his hand around to her sides and gave her a little squeeze. She squirmed and laughed even harder. She drew her arms from around his neck and bent them down to cover her sides. Gala's fingers found another spot. She sprang from his lap and tickled him. He squirmed. Gala leaped from his seat and ran.

"Ha! Ha! Haa! Okay, okay. Ha! Haa! Ha! I give up," he chuckled.

"You promise?"

"Weeell," he said while wearing a mischievous grin and slowly walking towards her. He wiggled his fingers with his head tilted, looking up through his lashes.

Floreena crept backward; she held her hands out and warned, her words measured, "G a l a. Don't... you... do... it." He reached out, grabbed her, and drew her close. They giggled. They kissed. They mingled their tongues and exchanged sweet pecks on the lips with an occasional nip. Then after they hugged, Gala led Floreena to the chair across the table from his chair. No sooner than they sat, Inklewrite lifted from the table and checked two more names off their guest list.

"Good evening Gala, Floreena."

"Helsin! Glad you could come." Gala stood up and shook Helsin's hand.

"Wizard's growth spurts. You sure popped, muscle upon muscle. I almost didn't recognize you." Helsin chuckled.

"I don't know what came over me," Gala laughed along with everyone else, then motioned his hand towards Floreena.

When Helsin turned towards her, she stood. As he offered his hand so she could place her hand in his, he complimented, "Goodness giver of beauty. You grow more beautiful every time I see you." Faithin smiled. After Helsin politely kissed the top of her hand, he introduced, "Father, these are my friends, Gala, and his fiancée, Floreena, and this is my father, Wizard Dectore."

Wizard Dectore bowed, then expressed, "Pleasure to meet you, both. I've heard great things about you."

"Thank you, sir. We're delighted you could come." Floreena said as she returned a bow.

"Glad to meet you, sir." Gala shook Dectore's hand. "My mother and father are looking forward to meeting you. Why don't y'all go inside and get something to drink—I mean, we don't have any—I mean, there's plenty of refreshments, so help yourselves."

Wizard Dectore chuckled and explained, "I don't miss Wiz Bonkers." He lifted a pant leg. "Look here."

Floreena and Gala gasped. "What happened," Floreena asked.

"Well, dear lass, this is the result of foolishness. I'm not a Transfigure wizard. When I was first introduced to Wiz Bonkers, I drank little. That small amount gave me a feeling I could do anything. I knew the consequences of transforming without being a Transfigure. But I thought nothing would happen to me. Over the years, I've transformed several times without complications. I was invincible, or I thought, or rather lied to myself. One night, after my drinking episodes had increased to a whole thirty-ounce flask a night, I transformed into a handsome Swanian waterfowl. When I transformed into myself, my foot remained as you see it now, three yellow webbed toes with claws. I never took another drink, with no desire to either, and I will never practice transforming. I'll leave that to Transfigures."

"I'm so sorry this happened to you," Floreena sympathized.

"It could have been worse. My whole body could have remained as a Swanian bird, or worse yet, I could have been half bird and half wizard. It's a good thing this happened to me. I was an arrogant wizard, and now I'm quite humble. I intend to share my story with others and show them my leg. I hope to deter anyone wanting to use their powers to transform when they're not a Transfigure. And I hope I'm able to deter them from drinking Wiz Bonkers. One drink or two isn't bad. But if anyone guzzles it down as I did, it could cost them their precious life."

"You're an encouragement. If it happened to me, I don't think I would have been as positive," Gala confessed.

"I appreciate that. It wasn't easy, but watching my son pull through the mess me and his mother put on him opened my eyes. I commend you all. It's a good thing we learn from our mistakes as well as the mistakes of others. It's sad if we learn them through some great loss. I'm grateful I haven't lost my nephew-I mean my son. Jeez! After all this time under the impression Helsin was my nephew, I still call him my nephew by mistake." Dectore put his hand on Helsin's shoulder.

"Me too, Father, me too. I slip up and call you Uncle Dec sometimes. It won't take long for us to get it right. And although I'm learning to forgive Idanab, I'm not sure I can ever call her mother." Helsin hugged his father, then suggested, "Let's say we go inside, have some refreshments, then meet Gala's parents.

Gala shook Dectore's and Helsin's hands again and said, "We'll be in as soon as our other guests arrive."

Gala watched Helsin and his father walk inside. When he turned around, he saw Wiley and Wiley's cousin, Vine, coming across Bridge. Vine was holding her wee babe. When they were a few feet in front of Gala and Floreena, Vine knelt and let her little one stand. "Walk to Wizard Gala," she said while she pointed towards Gala.

Gala got up and squatted toward the Treeager babe with his arms open. The babe giggled as he took off. Pitter-patter, pitter-patter went his little feet straight into Gala's arms. Gala kissed the little fella's short neck. He held him up and brought him back down to blow on his belly. The babe giggled. His green grapevine veins went across his forehead and shaped into a grapevine leaf, which covered the right side of his face, and accentuated his emerald eyes. His large pupils twinkled. After Gala blew on his belly one last time, he kissed his soft, chunky cheek and handed him to Floreena.

"Come here, you sweet little fella, you." Floreena kissed his cheek and neck. She wiggled her head and said, "Yum-yum-yum, gitcha-gitcha-gitcha." She held him up and brought him close to her pursed lips. He gave her a wet baby kiss. When she handed him to his mother, she complimented, "He's adorable."

"Thank you. If it weren't for Faithin, well, if it weren't for you, all of you, even Helsin, my baby would not—" Vine paused to gulp. Her eyes turned red.

Gala hurried to stop her tears and said, "I'm happy Idanab revealed where she held your midwife captive. I'm happy Idanab didn't hurt your little fella while she tried to perform her procedure."

"All Treeager veins are hard to puncture. That witch couldn't draw blood, or give it, no matter how hard she tried. I'm thankful to the giver of life and love that she didn't get mad and kill him. I'm surprised she didn't kill my midwife. By the way. Have you heard anything from The Wizard's High Council about Idanab and Terrib about how they're getting along?" Vine asked as she cuddled her baby.

"As a matter of fact, we have. The Wizard's High Council has made some progress in healing the witches. They use healing spells, charms, and counseling techniques. It'll take time for them to heal. Grock was abusive and mean, especially to Idanab. He killed their mother and might have killed Idanab if he had a chance. The Wizard's High Council is trying to find Idanab's biological father. They think that bringing him and Idanab together will help mend her."

"We hope everything works out for them. At least they're in good hands and can't hurt anyone, same as those Gobs," Wiley assured as he put his arm around Vine.

"Yeah. Gala's Redtalon dragon form scared the Gobs, so they would never leave the swamps or talk to sorcerers. But we learned that we still need to be on our guard because we ought never take things for granted." Floreena added.

"That's a fact. But now we want to devise a plan to stop those Stealth Dragon Slayers from killing dragons." Gala pulled his lips up to one side, lifting his right cheek.

"I didn't realize there were any dragons left. I thought they all died in the last battle," Wiley guessed.

"Well, in case there are any, I don't want them hunted and killed. Dragon slayers have killed Mystique Bluebloods too. They might decide to kill me even if they knew I was a Mystique Transfigure. I heard they don't like our kind. I want to transform into my Redtalon without worrying if a dragon slayer's gonna see me and kill me."

Floreena took Gala's hand in hers and squeezed it. She leaned over, kissed him on his cheek, then acknowledged, "Me too, sweetheart, me too."

"We have no doubt you'll come up with a solution. Not to change the subject, but the book you and the Newlads put together is extraordinary. Next time you visit your friend, Gnome Bloom, tell him I'm interested in his studies."

"Okay. Bloom and his brother, Celtrek, will enjoy your company. They'll want to learn about your essential crops."

"Sounds great. Thank you, Gala."

"Sure thing. Guess you guys better get on inside. Everyone's eager to see you."

"You'd better hang on to your little fella. When my mother or Gala's mother sees him, they'll want to indulge him."

"Yeah. Floreena's right. You should have seen them with Acub's and Ashlin's twins."

"I didn't know they had twins. What's their names?" Wiley asked.

"They named their Newlass, Klover, and their Newlad, Lark. The Kloverlark plants were in bloom when the twins were born. So, they named their twins after the plant."

"Clever. We'll congratulate and give our blessing," Vine said as she beamed.

"Yes, just remember to watch out for those coddlers," Floreena and Gala chuckled.

"Ha! Ha! Ha!" Wiley and Vine laughed, then went inside.

As soon as Gala and Floreena sat back down, Inklewrite lifted and marked off the last three guests on their list.

"Warwick! Elk! Vek! So glad y'all came. I didn't think you'd make it."

"We would have been here sooner, but we stopped to see Bloom and Celtrek and lost track of time. Haa! Ha! Ha!" Everyone laughed, then Warwick continued, "They wanted us to give you this." Warwick handed Gala a miniature tree planted inside a crystal bowl. "You can talk to Bloom anytime you want. This is the clipping from Bloom's Whispering Tree. They communicate with each other."

"Wizard Wonders! Magic Joys! This is fantastic! I'll send Bloom a message later! Wait until my father sees this. He's gonna love it. Come on. Let's go inside and join the others."

Everyone was having fun, telling jokes, spoiling babies, and sharing stories. Some danced to the music Charmer, Saxy, and their band members played. Gala and Floreena were about to call everyone's attention but didn't see Lucky or Serenity.

"Mother? Have you seen Lucky and Serenity?"

"I don't think they're here yet." Faithin scanned the main hall and told Gala, "I see Herbaleen and the Tuberous Tribe members. I don't see Lucky's parents, so I'm guessing they're in your father's lab waiting for them. Oh, yes, you two, I introduced Helsin to Constatina. We'll be seeing another love joining soon. I can tell the way their eyes met."

Faithin winked and clicked her tongue against the roof of her mouth.

"That's wonderful." Gala looked at Floreena, who nodded in agreement. "We'll be back, Mother. We're going to see what's taking Lucky and Serenity."

"Hurry back."

"Yes, ma'am." Floreena kissed Faithin on her cheek.

Gala and Floreena found Lucky's parents sitting with Ddot and Dahc. Gala greeted, "Hey, guys!"

"Hey, Chum, Floreena." Ddot flew over and kissed Floreena's cheek, then slapped the palm of Gala's hand.

"Hey y'all, how are you?" Dahc asked as he flew up and kissed Floreena's cheek, then slapped Gala's palm.

"We're doing great. What about you guys?"

"We're good." Ddot and Dahc said in unison.

Then Gala offered Lucky's parents, "Hi, you two. I'll see what's keeping them if you'd like."

"If they ain't here within the next—"

"Wait, Sugar Plum. Here they are," Lucky's father said as he took his wife's hand.

"Hi, y'all," Lucky greeted after he and Serenity popped out from the portal. Everyone hugged each other and shook hands. Lucky expressed, "I tell ya. We're grateful to The Wizard's High Council for puttin' this here portal in. It's convenient and all, but I might miss travelin' on the neck of a Gentalsteed or holdin' on to Trusty's mane." Everyone laughed. Lucky asked, "How is ole Trusty, anyhow?"

"He and Beauty had a young one. How about we go see 'em later."

Everyone answered at once, "Sounds good, Chum." — "Yeah, I'd like that." — "Sure thing." — "We'd love to." — "Yes!" — "Indeed."

"Let's git goin' then. Lead on Gala, Floreena. We're right behind ya." Lucky gave a thumbs up.

"I want to say how beautifully handsome you two look. I love your dress, Serenity."

"Why, thank ya, Floreena. It's one of your mother's designs."

"Mother's an expert in clothing designs, that's for sure. Her fabrics are magical. We'll get together with my mother and design more if you'd like."

"Oh yeah! I'd like that very much."

After they reached the great hall, Gala walked up on stage. Floreena stood to one side of the stage, with Lucky and Serenity hovering beside her. Lucky's parents flew to their seats, and the twins flew to sit by their parents. Gala got everyone's attention. He announced, "Thank you all for coming. First, we congratulate the parents and their most recent adorable wee ones. You know, the wee ones that my mother and Lidee can't stop pampering." Cheers and whistles filled the room, then quieted when Gala continued, "Next, I am happy to tell you I'm having a baby." The audience cracked up laughing. "No! I mean, I am expecting— No! My mom and dad are expecting a baby brother—No! What I mean is, I'm gonna have a baby brother soon." Gala laughed with his audience, who also hooted, hollered, whistled, and clapped. Gala glanced over, shrugged his shoulders, and smiled at Floreena, who was wearing a wide grin. Gala addressed and quieted his audience, "Okay, okay, listen, everyone." He held his hands up. "Now, I want Lucky and Serenity to come over and share their wonderful news. I hope they're better at announcements than I am." He chuckled and applauded, then hurried over next to Floreena.

The crowd welcomed with cheers. Lucky and Serenity flew up and stood on the tall pillar, arm in arm. Lucky started, "Since our soul mate joinin', which we're glad y'all attended, we've been busy." Lucky looked at Serenity. In unison, they proclaimed, "We're expectin' a wee one!"

The crowd hooted, hollered, and whistled. Serenity's cheeks turned a darker red. Lucky calmed the cheers down to make another announcement. "But now—" Lucky paused as he looked at Serenity to finish.

"But now, we invite y'all to our coronation as the new king and queen of the Tuberous Tribe. We'll celebrate in three months." Both Bluewing fairies and green wing fairies fluttered above their seats. The rest of the congregation stood. They all cheered and bowed. Lucky and Serenity bowed back. Herbaleen and Lucky's mother cried. Lucky's father hooted and whistled. Everyone sat back down. Lucky and Serenity took their seats next to Lucky's parents and Herbaleen.

Gala and Floreena walked up to the center of the stage. The crowd became quiet. This time Floreena spoke, "As you all know, Gala and I will wed soon. What you don't know is when and where. First, I'll tell you when. We will wed two weeks from tonight. And now for the where. Floreena paused." After another moment passed, she surprised everyone with the location. "Our wedding will be held in Timestill Forest, where the Woodlanders dwell." The crowd applauded, oohed, and awed. Gala heard someone say that they always wanted to meet the Woodlanders. Floreena continued, "We've arranged travel accommodations for everyone. There's no need to worry about how you're going to get there or how you're going to get home. Now I turn you over to Gala and his parents."

The audience applauded Floreena as she went and sat next to her mother. Gala's parents joined him on stage. Conkay started. "It's been one year and three days since we celebrated Acub and Ashlin, which was interrupted, and we never got to finish. So, tonight is a celebration for the wee ones that have come into our lives. It's for the wee ones on their way. It's for our newfound friendships, accomplishments, and the ones we mourn. But it's also to continue our celebration for Acub and Ashlin. We, Faithin, Gala, and I, created a gift we'd like to present to them."

Faithin added, "It's a gift that will aid in protecting their Bluewing clan. It will aid in other things, as well."

Gala concluded, "It's a gift any sorcerer would love to have. Come on up here, Acub and Ashlin."

They handed their twins to Ddot's and Dahc's parents, then flew up on stage and hovered. Gala held out his hand and summoned, "*Com'ere*." A golden light flashed in his hand. A staff, taller than Gala and holding an emerald on its hilt, appeared.

Conkay said, "Hold your hands out, Acub, you too, Ashlin.

After they held out their hands, Gala turned the staff sideways. As he went to place it in their hands, it shrank and split into two.

Acub and Ashlin looked at each other. Their eyes widened, their jaws slacked, then they grinned. "Pixie wonders! Magi surprise! Acub has always dreamed of having a staff. Thank you so much, but how'd you know I wanted one?"

Faithin transformed into her Bluewing form. She looked at Ashlin and said, "Because I could see it in your eyes every time Acub mentioned that he wanted one." Faithin hugged Ashlin and Acub, then transformed back into herself. Conkay and Gala also transformed into their Bluewing form and hugged Acub and Ashlin.

After they transformed into themselves, Conkay explained, "We'll show you how to use your gifts later. For now, let's party." Conkay, Faithin, and Gala snapped their fingers toward the high ceiling of the great hall. Fireworks popped, twirled, and whistled. Laughter, excited screams, oohs, and aahs resonated throughout the castle. After the fireworks, everyone mingled, danced, told stories, and played games.

Gala and Floreena walked outside for some fresh air. Lidee stood on Bridge gazing into the night sky at Spark's Star'ella-love formation. When Lidee felt her daughter's presence, she turned and gazed into her eyes. After a moment, she looked at

Gala and said, "Gala. You now know that no one knew Spark was Floreena's father. No one knew Floreena was a Mystique Blueblood. Wizard Spark didn't even tell you. The only ones who knew were your parents and Gnome Bloom. I had Bloom make Timestill Forest, including his Whispering Tree, shroud our whereabouts. That was in case someone forced him or his trees to reveal our secrets. No one else ever saw me and Floreena with Spark. You knew we couldn't and cannot let others know of Dragon Mountain With-eyes-that-see, or what you now call Dragons' Mountain." Gala smiled as Lidee continued, "We cannot let others know Floreena is a Mystique Blueblood. Nor can anyone know that I am the one who turned the Traveling Troll into The Singing Lake."

"Yes, ma'am, I understand."

"Spark was a great Dragamage, Intuitive one, a magnificent Mystique Blueblood Wizard, husband, and father. He knew what he was doing when he bequeathed his position to you. You'll make a fine Dragamage. Spark and I knew, and know, you and Floreena love each other. You and Floreena will make a powerful couple. As for the Stealth Dragon Slayers, we'll stop their cruelty. When we do, the dragons will be free to live without fear."

"I can't wait for that to happen. I'll be free. I won't have to hide who I am." Floreena hugged her mother.

"I'm sorry, dear."

"It's okay, Mother. I've always understood the dangers and knew I had to hide my identity." She hugged her mother again, then changed the subject,

"Oh yes, Gala. I almost forgot to tell you. Chizel can't wait to see you again. She's learned some more words. Can you guess what one of them is?"

"Give me a hint."

"First word starts with 'W.' The other starts with 'G.'"

Gala chuckled, "That's more than one word." Floreena and Lidee laughed. Gala grinned and guessed, "Wizard Gala?"

"Brainy Wizard. That was too easy."

Gala laughed harder. He kissed Floreena on her cheek and admitted. "When you told me Chizel couldn't wait to see me, I figured she learned to say my name, especially after you practically spelled it out for me." Everyone laughed. After they quieted down, Gala said, "Tell Chizel I look forward to seeing her too. I can't wait to see all of them again."

"You'll see them soon enough. Come on, soul mates. Let's go in and join the party."

THE END

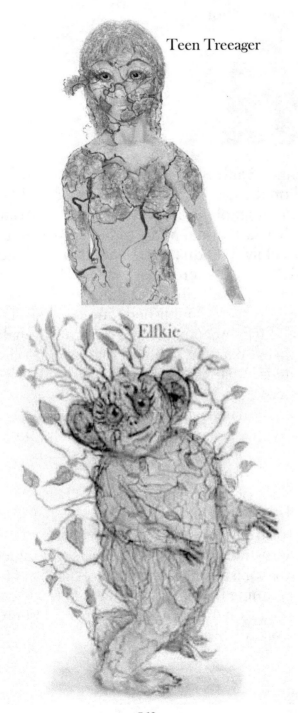

About the Author

Constance Faith Koehler was born in Alabama and raised on the east coast of Florida. Connie has spent years photographing and writing about the wildlife in Vero Beach, Florida. Many of her stories, to name a few, Luckily I Didn't Get The Beak, Honeybees provide an interesting interlude, Outdoor Exploration, and Shop Online; avoid problems (Opinion), were published in her local Press Journal/TCPalm.com. She is a professional artist who loves painting with acrylics and oils. She illustrated, What Mama Used to Say by Patricia and Greggory Pitts.

Connie graduated with high honors and received her A.S. degree in Graphic Design Technology. She fought Non-Hodgkin's Lymphoma Large B Cell cancer and won that battle. Connie has lived a life of sobriety for over 37 years. She shares her experience, strength, and hope with others and has found that doing so strengthens others and herself.

The Lakinshires and Gala's Conflicts is Connie's first fantasy novel (sprinkled with a bit of Science Fiction). Her upcoming book, Abstinence Therapy Remedy, is a sequel to her memoir, Be Careful Where You Fish, Walk, or Swim.

CPSIA information can be obtained
at www.ICGtesting.com
Printed in the USA
JSHW080450270623
43834JS00001B/1